THE
LIGHTHOUSE
Brides
COLLECTION

6 Romances Develop at
Historic Light Stations

THE

LIGHTHOUSE

Brides

COLLECTION

DiAnn Mills,
Andrea Boeshaar, Lynn A. Coleman,
Paige Winship Dooly, and Sally Laity

BARBOUR
PUBLISHING

Print ISBN 978-1-62416-250-3

eBook Editions:
Adobe Digital Edition (.epub) 978-1-62416-509-2
Kindle and MobiPocket Edition (.prc) 978-1-62416-508-5

Cover image © Rudy Balasko/Shutterstock

Published by Barbour Publishing, Inc., P.O. Box 719, Uhrichsville, Ohio 44683, www.barbourbooks.com

Our mission is to publish and distribute inspirational products offering exceptional value and biblical encouragement to the masses.

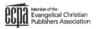 Member of the
Evangelical Christian
Publishers Association

Printed in Canada.

Contents

WHEN LOVE AWAITS

by Lynn A. Coleman

Dedication

To my oldest son, Jonathan, my gift from God.
May your course through life always be
fixed on the Light.

Let your light so shine before men,
that they may see your good works,
and glorify your Father which is in heaven.
MATTHEW 5:16

Chapter 1

Ocracoke, North Carolina, 1825

Sand particles bit into Fiona's cheeks. She forced herself to endure the pain, a sentry with a mission. The ever-graying horizon, swirling clouds, and lightning strikes could only mean one thing. . . "Hurricane's coming." Her words struggled to come out. A list, her father's training, surfaced in her mind. She ran back to the red brick lighthouse to begin her appointed task.

Battening down the storm shutters of the small house first, she then quickly assembled a basket of food and blankets to keep her through the night. The barrels of oil for the lamp were full and ready. She pulled out some wicks and wrapped them in an oilcloth. Dry wicks were essential during a storm, and if she read the clouds correctly, the small island of Ocracoke on the outer banks of North Carolina lay in the path of the hurricane. Her foul-weather gear, as well as her parents', hung on posts at ground level of the lighthouse. *"Be prepared,"* echoed through her mind, her father's words a sharp reminder of how fast a storm could come upon them.

"Oh, Lord, keep Father and Mother safe." They were gathering supplies from the mainland and due back tomorrow. Hurricane season tended to begin in late June. This storm, two weeks early, obviously didn't keep track of calendars—and Fiona was alone.

Fiona's confidence in her ability to handle the light at nineteen years of age wasn't the problem. Her concern was this island. So low to the ground, so flat, an overgrown sandbar had been her first impression after arriving the previous year. But last year they never encountered a hurricane—some minor squalls but nothing of a serious nature. How would the island fare? Would it be washed out to sea?

Fiona stopped in front of the mirror and stared at her windblown hair and reprimanded herself. "Lord, forgive me and my doubts. The island has been here since before the first settlers came from England. Surely it can withstand a severe blow. Give me peace and strength to maintain the light. Protect the sailors on the seas tonight. In Jesus' name, Amen."

She squared her shoulders, lifted her pack, and brought the supplies to the base of the lighthouse. Once inside, she climbed the circular stairs up to the first landing, then proceeded to the lantern housing. Fiona pulled out a cloth and wiped the soot off the parabolic reflector. The Argand lamp was a vast improvement over the Spider lamp they'd used at her father's previous station. This new lamp was smokeless, compared to the Spider that would send her out of the lantern housing with her eyes and nose burning from its acrid fumes.

She slipped off the cylinder glass chimney, trimmed the wick, and polished the glass clean before replacing it. Next she wiped the bull's-eye lens down.

Fiona stepped outside to work on the outer windows of the lantern housing. The wind whipped at her skirts as she scurried from windowpane to windowpane. Gray sky now enveloped the small island. She put down her cleaning rags and bucket and stepped back inside to fire up the lamps. Perhaps it was a bit early, but it would serve to warn both the local pilots, who sailed the vessels through the inlet to the mainland, and the fishermen. Although, she reckoned, the old salts were already well aware of the approaching storm.

With the lamps lit, she continued polishing the glass windows that housed the flame. Her father had left her in charge. The task of keeping the light, albeit a temporary one, hung on her shoulders. Her older siblings were grown and married with families of their own. Fiona intended to prove to her father, and to the world, that she could do this job as well as anyone.

Fiona liked the secluded life of a lighthouse keeper. Ocracoke seemed like a city to her with its couple hundred residents. Their last assignment had been a secluded island off the coast of Maine. No one lived on the island except for her family.

There they enjoyed peace and quiet, where a person could work from sunup to sundown and not have any worries. Oh, sure, there were times when the flour ran low, but fish and shellfish abounded. The wild berries from the island produced enough jams and jellies to keep her sweet tooth happy. Yes, she liked the simple life. The more people, the more bothersome life became.

Like the constant visiting of Mr. Ian Duncan. The man came by nearly every day, always talking with her father at great length. He wasn't even her father's age. His twenty-five years matched her older brother David's. Why he didn't stay in his own home every evening, Fiona would never understand. No, an isolated island where she could tend the light and keep men and ships alive called to her. Just as it had been for her father and brothers. Of course, a husband would be a nice companion someday, but she didn't see any prospects on the horizon worth filling that bill.

The neighing of some of the island's wild ponies brought Fiona to the present. They were beautiful creatures. No one seemed to know where they came from, but she loved watching them race down the shore at nightfall. One pony in particular she had a genuine fondness for, a chestnut with white boots in front and a white stripe that ran down his nose and pointed up to the top of his head. He would now take food from her hand. The next step would be in putting a bit and bridle over him. Fiona smiled. Perhaps this island did have its own charm, and perhaps she could get used to so many people.

Finished with the windows, she slipped back inside the lantern housing and down the circular staircase. She opened the door at the base of the lighthouse, only to find Ian Duncan huffing and puffing.

"Aye lass, ye lit the light? 'Tis goin' to be a bad one." He raked his hand through a full head of dark mahogany hair, settling it back in place.

"Appears to be quite a blow." She didn't have time for small talk, and patience was her father's gift, not hers.

"Would ye be needin' some help?"

"No, thank you. I've taken care of everything. Just have to wait it out now."

"I'd be happy to stay an' lend a hand. Yer father—"

Fiona cut him off. "I'm quite capable of tending the light. I've been doing it since I could walk."

Ian took a step back. "I'm sorry, Miss Stemple, I was simply offerin' a hand."

Fiona gave him a single nod and trekked toward the marsh. *Who does that man think he is, anyway? He spends nearly every night chewing Father's ear off, and he thinks he knows how to handle a light during a hurricane?* Did he think he needed to hang around because she was a woman, and no one expected a woman to be able to handle the duties of a lighthouse keeper? In either event, her words were spoken angrily, she realized, and she'd need to spend some time on her knees.

≈❧

Ian watched Fiona traipse down the small footpath to the shore, no doubt to check the skiff and make certain the life rings and ropes were in order. Her gentle frame did not blend with her not-so-gentle personality. "Fiona's fine on the eyes, Lord, but hard on the ears," he mumbled as he headed back to Pilot Town.

The one-room shack he'd rented from an old pilot fancied well to his purse, but he counted the days when he could purchase some land and build his own home. The weathered gray boards seemed to darken as the storm approached.

Seagulls hovered over the harbor. Many seemed to be flying toward the mainland. The old saying, *Seabirds hovering on land is a sign of bad weather,* rang in his mind. He'd seen the warnings all afternoon. The other shipbuilders couldn't stop talking about it. The last few hours had been spent battening down the hatches of the boatyard.

Ian shook his head and looked down at his hands. He was a builder, a craftsman, forced to live in this humble shanty. "Lord, I know there be a reason. But there are times a man needs to show the woman he cares for who he really be."

Ian's heart ached. Would Fiona ever see him as a man? Evening after evening he'd gone over to the Stemples' home, hoping, praying for a moment alone with Fiona. But she seemed to dislike him so. Finally he gave up trying to have some time with her, hoping she'd at least get used to his presence.

Nothing, not one glimmer of hope. Richard spoke so fondly of the lass, but after all these many months, could it be just a father's blindness to his own flesh and blood? Had Ian let his heart be swayed by a beautiful woman with golden hair the color of beach grass, with eyes so blue they sparkled like the sun dancing on a crystal lake? *Aye, the woman be beautiful, but her heart...*

Her heart be a stone.

Ian flopped on his single bunk bed. This shack would provide little shelter from a severe storm. He pulled out from under his bunk a cast-iron padlocked box. Inside were his personal papers and every cent he'd earned since he'd come to the small island. In reality he had enough for the land. He'd held off purchasing it, waiting on Fiona.

He slid the box back under his bunk and headed for O'Neal's house, where a man could buy a hot meal. The small chimney in the shack provided the heat for a man in the winter and he could cook some in there, but Ian missed his large clan from Scotland and all the more so at mealtime.

Ian pushed his chair back from the table, his belly full, and groaned, his head spinning from the talk of the men. Some of the old salts speculated a hurricane was brewing. Some talked about heading to the lighthouse if winds were too strong, because the shacks were unsafe. Word passed that everyone needed to get their gear and bunk up in some of the larger homes. Ian finished off his hot tea and returned to his shack. He packed his clothing in his duffel—his tools were at the shipyard—and pulled the cast-iron box out once again.

Fiona's brick house would endure the storm, but she'd be in the lighthouse. Perhaps she wouldn't mind him bedding down in her house. Then again, it would probably anger her more. He prayed her Christian charity would grace him and any others who'd happen upon the home as a safe haven. Richard had told many stories of sailors being rescued and how his family would put them up until they found passage on another vessel.

He wasn't a sailor, but he did build ships. Ian grinned. Which storm would be worse, the one raising her heels at sea or the beguiling figure that had turned a reasonable man's head since the moment he first laid eyes on her?

Ian cinched the strap of the duffel and fought the wind, heading into the direct assault of the approaching storm.

The front door of the lightkeeper's home was unlocked. Ian plopped his duffel and his strongbox in a corner near the fireplace. Wind and rain drummed the roof of the small home. He contemplated lighting a small fire but decided to wait until later. "Fiona must still be in the lighthouse." Ian drew in a deep breath through clenched teeth. "Better to confront her now than later."

"Fiona!" Ian yelled as he approached the lighthouse. The rain pelted his cheeks. Grains of sand and debris stung as they bit into his exposed skin.

"Fiona!" he hollered again.

Ian pounded on the door at the base of the lighthouse. Grasping the cast-iron latch, he paused momentarily between knocks. Should he just walk in? Would it invoke her wrath once again?

He opted to bang the door. It rattled in its doorjamb. "Fiona!" he bellowed. No response. Working at the top of the light, she'd never hear him over this storm. "Wrath be hanged," he muttered and pushed the door open.

"I'll be right down," Fiona called.

She'd obviously heard the door open. "Fiona, 'tis me, Ian Duncan." Before she could protest, he added, "I'd be indebted to ye if ye let me stay in yer home until the storm passes."

"Don't you have. . . ?" Fiona's eyebrows raised, and she amended her response. "Do you live in. . . ?"

"Yes, I have a small pilot's shack in Pilot Town. The lot of us is seekin' temporary shelter in the larger homes."

"I understand. You may stay."

"Thank ye, Fiona. I'd be honored to lend a hand, if I may. Seems only fittin' for a man to earn his keep."

Fiona's delicate shoulders relaxed. *Lord, she does have a tender side.*

"There's not much to be done at the moment. I need to watch the horizon. Other than that, I just have to keep the lens and reflector clean of soot and the flame fueled."

"Whatever ye need. I can cook up a pot of fish chowder. Can't cook much, but I know how to make a grand fish chowder," Ian offered.

"That would be wonderful. Thank you, Mr. Duncan. Do you suppose others might come from Pilot Town then?"

" 'Tis possible, depends on how bad the storm is."

"I'm fairly certain it's a hurricane and a large one. This is just the outer edge. The real force of the storm is hours away."

Ian sobered for a moment. Medium-sized trees swayed wildly from the constant battering of the wind. "Do ye have all the oil ye need?"

"I'm fine for the night, but I'll need more from the storeroom in the morning."

Ian nodded. He realized she expected this storm to last more than through the night, and she'd have to keep the light burning through the next day. She'd need rest. He'd need rest. Richard Stemple had shown him how to load the oil into the lanterns. He could help. But he saw in Fiona's rich blue eyes determination to prove her abilities.

"I'll fix a large pot of chowder." Ian tipped his hat and slipped out the strong oak door.

🐚

Fiona had never met a man who willingly would cook before. Of course, she hadn't met that many men. Well, that wasn't exactly true. Most of the people she'd had contact with over the years were men. Sea captains, sailors, and her brothers. As for cooking, she and mother shared that chore. She supposed sailors could cook, but the way they praised her mother's cooking, the cooks on board the ships couldn't be all that great.

Fiona crinkled her nose. Would Ian's cooking be the same? Something to fill the stomach, but not much pleasure in the experience of it going down? She didn't have time to consider the question. Fiona marched back up the circular stairway to the lantern housing and watched the horizon. "Dear Lord, I pray no ships will run aground." From the ever-darkening horizon and the growing intensity of the surf, Fiona knew the storm's potential impact. And alone with oars she'd never make it out far enough to rescue anyone. All indications were that her small craft would end up at the bottom of the ocean floor, never reaching her destination.

Chapter 2

The wind whistled through the doorway to the outside gallery around the lantern housing. Fiona rolled her shoulders and stretched her back. Hours had passed since Ian left for the house. The sun had set an hour or so ago, though no one could have seen it.

Thank the Lord, a few ships had made it safely into the creek, a small inlet of water where the pilots and fishermen tended to anchor their boats.

The storm whipped around the light in the gathering darkness as the beacon stood firm against the continuous bombardment. Fiona couldn't see anything beyond the windows except a sheet of black and an occasional streak of yellowish-white lightning.

She refilled the reservoir with whale oil and decided to check on her guest. Ian Duncan wasn't a bad man, he just. . . Fiona shook her head from side to side. He simply visited too often. Could she be jealous of all the time he spent with her father? She cherished the one-on-one time she and her father had setting up the light as dusk covered the earth. Ian's constant interruptions kept her away from the lighthouse. It didn't matter. Tonight, in her father's absence, the responsibility to see that the flame never went out rested on her shoulders, and on hers alone.

Fiona tied the oil-skinned coat about her waist then plunged into the elements. The wind howled against her ears. She pulled the thick wooden door of the lighthouse shut and found a rope tied from the house to the lighthouse. Fiona grasped it, grateful for Ian's thoughtfulness.

Hand over hand, she worked her way to the house. The wind pushed at her body, and she tightened her grip to press forward. The skirt of her dress whipped like an unfastened sail behind her. The rain drenched her face within seconds. At first it felt warm. Now the cold drops worked their way down her neck and dampened her collar.

"A few more feet," she pleaded with her body. She could make it; she just had to stay focused. She pressed on, her hands tired and cold, straining to keep a secure hold on the damp hemp rope.

The house proved to be a good blockade against the strong wind. Fiona eased her body up against it and squared her shoulders. Returning, she'd be going with the wind. The only problem would be not letting go of the rope, allowing the wind to slam her up against the lighthouse. This would be her one and only trip to the house until the storm passed, or until they were in the eye of the storm, she resolved. Ian Duncan would need to fend for himself. She didn't have the time, nor the strength, to wait on houseguests.

The warm, tranquil air of the kitchen greeted Fiona as an old hymn sang within her heart.

> *Jesus, Lover of my soul,*
> *Let me to Thy bosom fly.*
> *While the nearer waters roll,*
> *While the tempest still is high. . .*

The heavenly scent of fish chowder made her stomach gurgle.

"Fiona!" Ian graced the doorway of the kitchen from the living room. "I canna believe ye came with the winds blowin' so hard."

Fiona pursed her lips. In spite of herself, she loved the exotic sound of his thick Scottish brogue. *Guess I shouldn't have concerned myself about my guest.* "Thanks for the rope."

"Ye're welcome, lass." In two quick strides, he sidled up beside her, helping her remove the saturated oilskins. "Let me dry these by the fire for ye. The chowder's warm an' simmerin' on the stove. Grab a bowl an' join us." Ian marched out of the kitchen.

Us? Who else had sought shelter in her home?

Fiona ladled a bowl of the rich creamy chowder and ambled into the living area. Her eyes scanned the room where half a dozen men sat on various pieces of furniture. One young man with red hair and a scruffy beard removed himself and an empty bowl from the table.

"Here you go, miss." He smiled and bowed, appearing to be the perfect gentleman.

Somehow his lack of a few front teeth made her fight the amused expression that pleaded within her to form on her face.

"Thank you." Fiona placed her bowl of chowder on the table and sat in the warmed chair. Bowing her head, she offered a quick prayer of thanks to her heavenly Father for the warm food and asked for protection. She'd never been alone with half a dozen male strangers before. Her father, mother, and brothers had always been close by.

"Thank you for allowing us to hole up here during the storm," an older man, perhaps around fifty, spoke after she raised her head.

"You're welcome. I'll be staying in the lighthouse through the rest of the storm. Wind's too strong to make regular trips to the house."

"Jacques Peters, miss. Thank you for manning the light. Me and a couple of the boys here used it to get back to Ocracoke."

That sweet praise meant more to her than Mr. Jacques Peters could ever know. "You're welcome. Just doing my duty."

One of the others, a slim man who stood warming himself by the fire, agreed. "Never would have guessed a woman was caring for the light. But you did a right fine job, miss."

In spite of her resolve not to show pleasure in the praise, an unruly smirk curled her upper lip.

Ian spoke up. "Miss Stemple's been raised keepin' the lights. She'll do a right fine job. Richard, the lighthouse keeper, speaks very highly of his daughter."

"Where is your father, miss?" An older man with bushy gray eyebrows seated across from her asked.

"Gone to the mainland for supplies to prepare for hurricane season. Guess this one decided to come early." Fiona spooned another bite of Ian's wonderful fish chowder.

"I thought it was a hurricane, didn't I tell ya, boys?" Jacques commented. "Praise be, we made it back alive."

A round of mumbles and groans in agreement rumbled through the small room.

Fiona finished her chowder. Her silver spoon rang as it settled in the china bowl.

"May I refill yer bowl, miss?" Ian's calloused hand reached out. A hint of a smile edged his deep brown eyes.

"Wonderful chowder. Thank you, Mr. Duncan."

"Ye're welcome, lass. Now, will ye be wantin' some more?"

"Yes, thank you."

Ian winked, and Fiona felt her face flush. What silly nonsense was this?

≈

Ian held back a grin. *She blushed, Lord. Does she have some affection for me?* Or was she simply embarrassed by his forward gesture of winking at her? In either case, Ian clung to a glimmer of hope. He scooped up some chowder and poured it into her white china bowl. So fragile and delicate, but it truly did the job. Just like Fiona herself, he thought. She'd need this hot meal to keep her through the night, he reasoned and topped off the bowl with another pour from the ladle.

He returned to the room where Jacques had captivated Fiona by retelling the story of his arduous journey back to port. She sat on the edge of her seat, hardly noticing her replenished bowl.

"I swear, miss. Them waves were fifteen, twenty feet tall."

Fiona knitted her eyebrows. "How high is the island?"

Ian caught the concern in her question. "Jacques, thirty minutes ago ye told me the waves were ten feet."

Jacques replied with a sheepish grin.

Ian turned to Fiona. "My guess is he had eight- to ten-foot waves. Which isna abnormal for these shoals en stormy weather."

Fiona nodded and grabbed her spoon.

"Sorry, miss. Didn't mean to get you stirred up. The storm's a big one, that's for sure."

"Fishermen do tell fish stories," Fiona grinned.

Jacques feigned offense, slapping a hand to his chest. "Never more than a foot or two."

A roar of laughter broke the tension in the room. Ian relaxed. He could see she'd been wondering if the island would be hit with a huge tidal wave or a high tidal surge. No doubt some areas would experience flooding. The creek and most of Pilot Town would be under some water.

Fiona finished off her second bowl of chowder. "If you'll excuse me, gentlemen, I have to return to the lighthouse."

"I'll be saying a prayer for you," the red-bearded man said.

"Thank you. Pray for the sailors out at sea," Fiona asked, carrying her empty bowl to the sink.

Ian grabbed her oilskins that were drying by the fire and brought them to the kitchen.

"Fiona," he whispered. She jumped, unprepared for his presence. "Sorry."

"I'm sorry. My mind was elsewhere."

"Can I help?"

"I appreciate the offer, Mr. Duncan, but all is under control." Her stiff voice spoke volumes.

"Let me escort ye back to the lighthouse."

Her eyebrows raised, and she placed her hands on her hips.

"For my peace of mind. I know ye'd be fine, lass. 'Tis a proper thing for a man to do." He dared a second wink.

The gentle toss of her head from side to side said no, but the slight hint of a smile on her pale, rose-colored lips said she wouldn't turn him down.

"Thank ye, Miss Stemple." He thought of adding how her father would have his hide if he didn't assist the lass. She sought her father's approval, he knew instinctively, so he held his tongue.

The howling wind and the pelting rain made it impossible to have any conversation. Fiona hustled down to the lighthouse as if it were her sanctuary.

Sanctuary from what? Ian wondered. *Me? The storm?*

She opened the heavy oak door and slipped into the dimly lit base of the lighthouse. Ian wanted to follow, wanted to understand this woman, but now was not the time. She had work to do, and so did he. He fought the storm, ignored the biting rain, and inched his way back to the house. Once inside, he settled the men in for the night. He took care of the dirty dishes and placed a small pot on the back of the stove to soak some dry beans overnight.

❦

The oil lamp dimly burned next to him as he took a moment of solitude in Richard and Mary's bedroom. Silently he read the old Bible he found on the nightstand and prayed. Well into the night he fought the desire to be with Fiona in the lighthouse. She wouldn't welcome him. If he went, he'd be pressuring her. Pressure and being forced were things he'd fought since he was a teen. His father had always wanted him to become a farmer. He'd come to America to be his own man. Ian understood Fiona's independence, but he felt his spirit leading him to go to her.

Unable to rid himself of the feeling, he decided he couldn't make more of a fool of himself than he already had in the woman's eyes, so he turned down the lamp and went outside. The storm's winds had increased. In the glow of the light from the lighthouse he could see the trees bending. Tall branches that normally reached for the sky licked the ground.

"Dear God, please keep those out to sea safe an' anyone on this island from harm."

The howl of the wind roared past his ears. Salt and freshly churned soil assaulted his nose. The intensity of the storm bore down on the island. Ian grasped the rope with both hands. His feet nearly flew out from underneath him. Cautiously he eased himself into the full brunt of the elemental forces. A stray limb from a tree flew past mere inches from his face and eyes.

"Help me, Lord."

His hands slipped down the rope. Unsure his strength could match the intensity of this wind, he grasped the rope tighter. Ian considered himself a strong man; he fought to keep his ground. The short trip to the lighthouse from the house exhausted him. He pulled open the oak door and stepped inside.

"Hello?" Fiona called from above.

" 'Tis I, Ian."

"Ian Duncan, you're a foolish man."

He heard her approaching down the stairs.

"Aye." More foolish than she had ever known, he suspected.

"Thank you for coming."

Ian looked up. Her eyes were red and swollen. "Are ye all right, lass?"

"Aye," she smiled.

Ian's heart warmed in his chest. "Ye be talkin' like a Scotsman en no time."

Fiona laughed.

Ian shed his overcoat and hung it on the peg. "Why were ye cryin'?"

"Nothing really. Lonely is all."

"Aye, that's why the good Lord wouldna let me sleep. I'm here to keep ye company."

"I appreciate it. I can't sleep. The wind is frightening."

"'Tis worse outside." Ian gave her a smile of encouragement. "Ye be doin' a wonderful job. I havena seen the light dim once."

"These new lamps burn well. The reservoir is deeper; I can load more oil so they can burn longer."

"Yer father told me about those horrible Spider lamps."

"Those things were so smoky you'd have to leave the lantern housing just to get some clean air in your lungs," Fiona recalled.

"Are the lamps filled?" She needed rest, he noticed. Her shoulders drooped—not her normal posture.

"I just finished filling them when you came in."

"Then go to sleep. I'll keep watch. When the oil is low, I'll wake ye."

"I'm. . ."

"Doesna the holy Scriptures say that unless the Lord watches over the city the people labor in vain?"

"Yes, but. . ."

"Fiona, trust me. I will wake ye." Ian placed a hand on her shoulder. "Ye need the rest. Ye an' I both know this storm is still coming an' will be hours before it has passed."

She nodded her agreement and laid down on the small bunk under the stairs.

⁂

Fiona woke, struck by the silence. How long had she slept? "Ian?" she called out. No response. She sprang out of bed. Had something gone wrong? Had he abandoned his post? She shouldn't have let him convince her to rest. Fiona straightened her skirt and grabbed a bucket of oil to replenish the lamps.

Upon reaching the lantern, she saw Ian outside on the gallery holding the handrail and looking out to sea. Fiona checked the oil reservoir and it was nearly full. Ian must have. . .

She placed the bucket of oil on the floor and joined him on the gallery. "Ian?"

"Hi, remarkable, isna it?" His hand spanned the dark horizon. A few stars peeked out.

"We're in the eye," she stated.

"Aye, that we are, lass. Look around. The world be beaten an' blown by this here storm, an' right now, here in the middle, we're safe."

"But not for long." Fiona had often found storms exciting, yet she respected their fury.

"Aye, that be true. But I was ponderin' life, God, an' some of His words in Scripture."

"Which verse?"

"No particular verse at the moment. Just thoughts about how God keeps us safe if we walk en Him. I was thinkin', if we could stay in the center of the storm, we could travel with it an' never be harmed by it. And how, if we stay in the center of God's will, He'll be protectin' us from the storms of life that come crashin' down upon us."

Fiona gazed at the darkened horizon. Lightning danced around the eye on all sides. The power of God in nature always struck a chord of awe and wonder in her. Ian stepped up behind her and whispered in her ear. "Did ye sleep well, lass?"

"Yes, thank you."

He placed his hands gently on her shoulders and slowly kneaded them. An audible groan of pleasure escaped her lips. He turned her to face him. His rich chocolate eyes explored her face then locked on her own. Gently he removed a strand of her wayward curls and smoothed it back in place.

A trickle of excitement raced through her. She placed her hands on his chest. His heart pounded an intense message. Slowly she moved her hands up to his shoulders. Was he going to kiss her? Was she going to kiss him? A force more magnetic than the storm drew her closer toward him.

"Aye, Fiona, I feel it too."

Chapter 3

He kissed her forehead and pulled her deeper toward his chest. "Not yet, me darlin', not yet. "

Fiona didn't know whether to be furious or grateful for Ian's self-control and strength. Everything inside of her shouted the rightness of the moment. But what about her call to be a lighthouse keeper? Ian built ships. How could they have a life together?

"Don't think, me love, just enjoy the moment an' pray for God's wisdom an' peace."

Could he read her mind? Fiona closed her eyes and nestled her head into the crook of his neck. For such a strong man, he comforted with tenderness.

"As much as I love holdin' ye, me darlin', I'm afraid we need to get back inside."

What? Fiona pulled herself away from him. The storm. How could she have lost track of it? How could he remain so calm?

"Come, Fiona, come inside. We need to talk."

He reached for her hand and led her back inside the lantern house. They descended the stairs in silence. Down one level, then the second, and finally the circular stairway into the base. He turned up the wick of the oil lamp on the table and escorted her to the cot.

Unable to speak, to think, she followed his lead. He, on the other hand, stepped away and sat on the stairs.

"Fiona, I'm not a rich man, but I make an honest wage."

He's talking marriage, she thought to herself.

"I believe God ordains one special person in every man's life."

She couldn't argue with him there; she believed it too. But something wasn't right here. Granted, she felt comfort, warmth, perhaps even love in his arms, but marriage—after one brief embrace?

"I've prayed for months."

Months?

"I see it en yer eyes, me love. This is new to ye, perhaps a bit of a shock."

And how does he read my thoughts so well? And what on earth is wrong with me? Why can't I talk? Oh, Father, God, give me something to say.

"Please, Fiona, speak to me."

"I don't know what to say. Are you inclined to change your occupation?"

Ian rubbed his hands across his face then raked his fingers through his hair. "No, Fiona. I'm a shipbuilder. 'Tis what the Lord gifted me to do."

"And I'm a lighthouse keeper; it's what the Lord gifted me to do."

"I don't agree. He gifted yer father, an' ye've learned the job, an' ye do it well. But I believe there is more for ye to do with yer life than to tend the light."

"I'm responsible for saving lives. What can be more important than that?"

Ian stood up and walked farther away.

Fiona continued. "You heard the men in the house—they're grateful to me and for what I do. They would have been lost in this storm and possibly have lost their lives if it wasn't for me. I know God has called me to this."

"How do ye know, Fiona?" Ian's sharp words cut into her stream of thought.

She got up from the cot and walked over to him, placing her hand on his. "When I read His Word, verses about not hiding your light under a bushel and others like that just agree with my spirit. I see my call the same as I see my father's."

Ian turned and faced her. "I see it a different way." He caressed her cheek with his thumb. "I see it as for a season ye've been called to serve alongside yer father. But I believe God wants us together, as man an' wife. I know ye've never heard these words from me. Ye've never given me the chance to speak with ye. But I love ye. Aye, me love, I love ye, an' me love for ye is grand in me heart. I told the Lord I would wait for ye, an' I will wait. But pray, me darlin'. Pray like you've never done before.

Pray if yer duty in life might be shiftin'."

Tears burned Fiona's eyes. Drawn to a man for the first time in her life, she puzzled over the fact that he didn't share her dream, her call. This couldn't be right, and yet her body, her soul, hungered to be in his arms. To feel his breath on her neck. To kiss those tantalizing lips. *Oh, Lord, is this lust?*

His dark eyes scanned hers and softened. "No, me darlin', yer desires for me are the same as mine for ye. Pray, Fiona. I know I'm bein' bold, an' I know I should have waited to share my heart with ye. But holdin' ye in me arms on the gallery. . . Our love, 'tis too strong to deny it."

"I'm attracted to you; I can't deny it. But love? I can't be sure."

"All I ask is for ye to pray, Fiona." Ian pulled her fully into his embrace once again, kissed her forehead, and slowly lowered his warm soft lips down to her cheek. She'd never felt anything like this. Desire drove her to want more, to have his lips on hers, to run her fingers through his rich mahogany hair. To hold him. To squeeze him. And yet something stopped her. Good common sense, she hoped, because every ounce of it seemed to have left her body.

Ian pulled away. "I'll leave ye to yer thoughts, me love. I'm goin' to the house an' get some sleep. We'll talk some more tomorrow."

Fiona reached for his hand. He stopped. He didn't want to leave her. She'd slept four uninterrupted hours, and if his confused thoughts were equal to hers, she'd have no trouble staying awake.

He gently squeezed her hand. "Tomorrow, lass."

He pulled the door open and stepped out into the eye of the storm. The air was still, too still, he realized. Nothing moved. He left the rope and marched straight to the house. Inside he found his empty bedroll waiting for him.

Closing his eyes, he prayed, *Father, be with Fiona. Keep her safe. And if we're to be together, give her the same understandin' in the matter that Ye've given me. Amen.*

He set his heart's desires aside and drifted into a deep sleep.

❧

The crash of broken glass jarred Ian from his sleep. His eyes focused on the other men, who were grabbing an old wool blanket and covering the gaping hole.

"Winds blowin' the other way. Looks like we're on the back side of the storm," Fred stammered, brushing his unruly red hair from his face.

"The eye passed over awhile ago," Ian mumbled as he worked the sleep out of his neck and body.

"Depending on the size of this here hurricane, we might be seeing the end of her strength."

"Aye, but she's a bad one." Ian pulled his boots on and went to the kitchen to retrieve a broom.

After cleaning up the broken glass, he made pancakes for the men, topped with maple syrup.

"I went to the lighthouse during the storm last night," Ian said to no one in particular.

"What you do a fool thing like that for?" Henry, the oldest of the group, asked.

"Couldna sleep. Thought I'd check on the lady."

Rance's thin frame bopped up and down like a rowing oar. "Bet Miss Stemple wasn't pleased," he grinned.

Ian didn't want to go into his personal life with these men and fought the smile that threatened to take control of his lips as he remembered holding Fiona in his arms. Tactfully, he changed the subject. "I came back when the eye was over us. I noticed the chicken coop had been blown to bits."

"Me and my men can repair that after the storm. That's a small price to pay for a safe dry place," Jacques proposed.

"Thanks, I thought we could all lend a hand." Ian forked another stack of the sweet cakes.

Henry cleared his throat. "Iffen ya don't mind, I'd like to work on the coop. You younger ones can go chasing the chickens."

"I imagine more than the Stemples' chickens are loose after this blow." Mike stood up and brought his plate to the kitchen. "No doubt they'll be more than a few days cleaning up from this one."

A round of "no doubt" circled the room.

Henry sipped his coffee. "Fishing should be great. All that warm water being brought up from the Caribbean ought to bring us a good haul."

"If a man has a boat left to get back out there." Mike placed his hands on his hips. "Will you be busy repairing the ships?"

"Aye, canna see how that can be avoided. Unless the good Lord spared the boats." Ian finished off his pancakes and pulled a couple more from the stack.

"Won't most of the men try and repair their own?" Fred asked.

"Aye, depends on the damage. No tellin' if the warehouse is still standing. We might have to rebuild the shop before we can repair the ships." Ian enjoyed chatting with the fishermen. He'd seen them in passing from time to time but had never gotten to know them. Storms had a way of bringing folks together, of bringing the good out in them, Ian mused.

His stomach full and the conversation waning, he got up to clear the table and begin a pot of fresh stew. He decided on a change of menu and made a pot of vegetable stew with some dried beef thrown in.

"Smells great," Fred volunteered, coming into the kitchen.

"Thank ye." Ian stirred the soup and replaced the lid.

"Don't know how to say this, exactly." Fred shuffled his feet on the wooden floor. "Are you courting Miss Stemple?"

Ian smiled. "No, but I aim to."

"You won't be minding if I try and convince her I'm the better man, would you?" Fred winked.

Ian tossed his head. "I'd be mindin', but she's not bound to me. So I canna be tellin' ye to stay away." Although that was exactly what he wanted to say.

"Thought I'd let you know my intentions." Fred extended his hand. "May the best man win."

"Aye, but 'tisna about winnin'. 'Tis about the best one God fashioned for ye."

"She's pretty to look at. A man could do worse."

Ian couldn't believe Fred's attitude toward women, and particularly Fiona. If the younger man thought he'd win her heart with that attitude, a major shock was headed his way. Ian could see Fiona verbally going up one side and down the other, cutting poor Fred in two.

"Aye, a man could do worse," Ian agreed. Much worse, in his humble opinion. Fiona represented everything he'd ever wanted in a wife and more, oh, so much more. Loyal, hardworking, and content away from the bustle of the cities. Yes, Fiona Stemple's beauty paled in comparison to the true woman of character he'd fallen in love with.

Fred rejoined the others in the family area.

Ian paused. *Lord, Ye know me heart. Me relationship with Fiona is so fragile, I don't think I need the competition for her heart. Could Ye possibly turn Fred's affections toward another?*

A selfish prayer? Ian questioned then amended it. *Lord, If I'm not supposed to marry Fiona, give me the grace to accept another man in her life.*

≈§

Fiona scanned the horizon. The black thunderclouds lightened to gray. Lightning continued to dance all around her. She reflected on the awesome power of God as He stirred up the wind and rain. She loved watching the storms from the safety of the lighthouse, high enough so most debris didn't fly up to her observation windows. The lighthouse itself had a lightning rod so if lightning should strike it, the charge of energy would go harmlessly into the ground.

The dark sky appeared as night, yet daylight peeked through the edge of the horizon. The storm had raged all night, and if she read the sky correctly, the small island of Ocracoke would continue to be hit for several hours to come. The wind whistled through the glass door out to the observation galley, which rattled from the wind's constant ravaging.

But Fiona's mind kept going back to being in Ian's arms, to his tender lips upon her forehead and cheek. How could she respond so easily to his touch? And why would a man bring up marriage the first time they had any encounter at all?

Her senses protested. Life was supposed to be ordered. You court, you fall in love, then you marry. You don't simply fall instantly in love and marry, do you? *Goodness, Lord, this doesn't make sense. Haven't You called me to be a lighthouse keeper?*

Perhaps Ian would change his mind about his career choice. Fiona paced. No, Ian had emphatically let her know that would not be the case. Fiona paced some more. She peeked into the oil reservoir and checked its contents. "Half full," she noted.

She placed a hand over her stomach as a deep, rumbling, empty feeling over came her. *Must be hungry,* she thought. *On the other hand, I might just be torn with the confusion of these new emotions and desires for Ian. Of all people, Lord, why Ian? It's not that he's an unattractive man to look at, but. . .* Her thoughts trailed off as she worked her way down the various platforms to the lower level where the circular stair casing made its way to the base.

The strong winds prevented her from venturing back to the house. Fiona unwrapped the sandwich she had prepared the day before. Ian's hot fish chowder sounded really good at the moment. She chomped down on the cold ham sandwich. For the first time in her life she felt truly alone. Never before had it bothered her. She loved, relished, her privacy. The seclusion of her father's former assignment had been perfect. So, why now? Why during this storm did it bother her to be alone?

Fiona took another bite and chewed it slowly. "Stop fooling yourself. You know it's Ian. . .his arms. . .his words." She shivered as gooseflesh erupted on her arms. The dry morsel of sandwich caught in her throat. She swallowed and left the rest of her brunch on the cot. The strong wind wailed in its efforts to come in from under the door.

"Get to work." She reached for a bucket to fill with oil. "It's the only thing that will keep you sane."

Chapter 4

Sunlight pierced the shutters, beckoning the men to evacuate their sanctuary. Ian, first outside, hung onto the thin-framed screen door. "The storm is passin'," he called out to the men.

He fought the wind for control of the screen door, the intense winds turning it into a sail. "She's still blowin', but I see white clouds on the horizon."

"Praise be, we've lived through another." Henry's thick hand clapped Jacques's back.

"Aye, we can thank the good Lord for that and for the state putting up this here light. Can't imagine our getting back if it weren't here."

"Amen," the men agreed, acknowledging the uncertainty of their plight. Ian realized he didn't have the right to take Fiona away from her call. Was he so selfish as to want a woman who played such an important role in other people's lives? How could he have been so blind? Her value to the community left him little doubt. If she were his wife. . .

Ian's shoulders slumped. As much as he loved the lighthouse, his curiosity ended with Fiona. All these months he'd sought her affection, not her father's companionship. Granted, a friendship with Richard would be helpful if he ever entertained the thought of asking for her hand.

Ian's footsteps faltered. He had asked her. He stopped mid-stride on his way to the lighthouse. How could he face her?

No, he reasoned, she felt wonderful in his arms. A connection, bond, possibly something spiritual, flowed between them with the same ease of taking a single breath. *Father, lead me. I don't know what to do,* he prayed. Fighting the wind, he pressed on. Last night he'd walked with the wind;

today he forced his body forward one careful step at a time.

"Fiona," he called as he slipped into the protection of the lighthouse. He glanced back at the others still watching from the doorway.

"Fiona." He raised his voice. She didn't respond. Filling the reservoir perhaps? Even on the bluest of days, hearing someone enter the base was difficult.

"Ian," she replied. The sound of her footsteps on the stairs beckoned him. He climbed the first set of stairs to meet her on the first landing.

"Hi. The storm is almost passed."

Her smile upon seeing him caused his spirit to soar. Yes, he had been right. They were to be together as man and wife.

"Yes." She placed an empty bucket down on the floor. "We need to talk."

"Aye lass, we do." Ian tenderly grasped her hand. Her tiny hand shook in his. He grasped it tighter and pulled her close. "Shh, me love, it'll be all right."

"I'm so confused."

Ian didn't know what to say. He simply allowed his thumb to gently caress her hand. He wanted to show her tenderness, love, and affection. He wanted to be her helpmate in every decision she would make. But her future, their future, rested in her choices.

"How can I be so attracted to you and yet have avoided you at every possible moment?"

"Could it be that yer soul knew it was meant to be, yet ye have convinced yerself there is only one future for ye life?"

"I know I've been called to be a keeper of the light." Her eyes searched his face.

"Aye, but which light, me love?"

Fiona knitted her eyebrows. Ian clasped her other hand in his.

"The light of the Lord," he answered her unasked question.

She shook her head and removed her hands from his. Turning her back on him, she moved farther away.

Silently he stepped up behind her and placed his hands on her shoulders. "I will not force ye to leave yer call. I know with every ounce of me bein' we are meant to be together. Just pray, Fiona. Pray an' ask the Lord."

A tear fell down her lovely rose-colored cheek.

"I have been praying since you left." Fiona squared her shoulders. "I'll not be given to emotions, Mr. Duncan."

Hearing his formal name from her lips, Ian lifted his hands from her shoulders.

"Very well, Fiona. No emotions, no physical contact. I'll even stay away an' I'll wait upon ye." Ian stepped back. "An' Fiona, I will wait."

Ian slipped down the stairs. He thought he heard her cry. He paused to see if she'd call.

She didn't.

He left.

Walking back to the house with the wind on his back, he made it in record time. He turned and saw her looking out from the lantern housing. He waved, and she waved back. Ian smiled. "She will come around, Lord. I just know it in me bones."

Fiona's raised palm lay on the glass. She stared at her hand as if it belonged to someone else. She'd never before put handprints on the glass, knowing how much work it took to keep the windows clean. Since the age of three, she'd been cleaning lighthouse windows. Of course she was meant to be a lighthouse keeper! She had been trained. She enjoyed her solitude. She didn't need a man. . .

Perhaps that wasn't true. Mr. Ian Duncan had certainly wormed his way into her heart. How could one man's touch be so intoxicating?

If only Mother were here. She'd explain these feelings. But how could she tell her mother of her intimate moments with Ian—of his kisses. Fiona touched her cheek where his last cherished kiss had landed.

No. Emotions were foolishness. Didn't the Bible speak of the heart being full of folly? Besides, Ian said he wouldn't push, that he'd wait for her.

Whatever had happened between the two of them was probably due to the highly charged electricity in the air more than to actual love or compassion. Hadn't she avoided him? Didn't his very presence at the house day in and day out annoy her? How could she be so foolish?

No, she had a job to do, and she would do it to the fullest of her abilities. Tomorrow she would pen a letter to the treasury department and ask for a position to serve as a lighthouse keeper. At this point it didn't matter where, it just mattered that she get her life back on course. She wasn't about to run aground on Ocracoke.

⨳

By late afternoon the winds died down to faint whispers and gentle breezes. The ocean waves continued to churn. The surf, brown with bits of sand and tons of seaweed, hammered at the shore. The men who had stayed in her home had cleaned up the house, boarded up a broken window, and even repaired the chicken coop in some fashion. There weren't any chickens, but the birds would find their way home when they were hungry, Fiona thought, justifying her lack of desire to scurry around the woods chasing chickens. She needed rest. The sun would set in a few hours, and she would need to tend the light yet again. Her father and mother, no doubt, wouldn't arrive until tomorrow.

Fiona took advantage of her parents' room and slept on their soft feather mattress, a gift to her mother from her father shortly after they married—meant to make their lives a little less harsh. As a child she remembered saving the goose feathers to restuff the mattress from time to time.

She snuggled deeper into the pillow. She could smell her parents' scent. Since childhood, snuggling in her parents' bed, she recalled, was among her most cherished moments. When life got her down, she'd curl up with a book or her thoughts and surrender to the security of their warm, fluffy mattress.

How would she manage alone? But if Ian would become a lighthouse keeper, they could serve together. "Lord, please show Ian I am called to be a keeper of the light like my father. And give him the desire to serve with me. Amen."

Fiona's body shook from the lack of rest. Slowly her mind closed itself down, and sleep overcame her.

⨳

Last night, after the storm, had been the loneliest of Fiona's life. Never had she felt so out of sorts. No matter how much she prayed, paced, or cleaned to keep herself busy, it was not enough. Few boats made their way out, and several came in. She watched the pilots go out to the larger boats and bring them through the channel.

New sandbars had emerged from the storm. The inlet had shifting sands, and local pilots were necessary to navigate large vessels. Fiona had been told that the first settlers on the island were pilots and a few fisher-men. Now there were more fishermen than pilots, but most worked as both. Ian was one of the few shipbuilders, part of a small but steady island indus-try. This year she'd watched the launching of the *Lodge,* a thirty-nine-foot schooner that looked grand on the sea. Her sails filled and she rose up and down, sluicing through the water as if she were one with it.

Ian had been particularly proud that day. The yard used some of his techniques in building the ship. He'd come to America to fill the posi-tion, having corresponded with the owner. He loved his homeland, but opportunities for a man to work outside his clan were limited, and his family were farmers, not shipbuilders.

A knot tightened in her stomach. Ian's talent came from God. It wouldn't be right to ask a man to give up his God-given talent to work with her. Salt stung her eyes until she released the demanding tears.

"Evenin', lass." Ian's velvety voice cheered her soul.

"Ian?"

"Aye lass, I've brung ye..."

Fiona wiped her eyes and turned to face him. He dropped the chick-ens he'd been carrying and ran up beside her.

"Fiona, are ye all right?"

His eyes examined her from head to toe, looking for an injury of some sort.

"I'm fine. I just miss Mother and Father."

Ian nodded and stepped back.

"What brought you here tonight?"

Ian looked at his empty hands. The hens were wandering off as fast as their feet could carry them. He groaned and set off chasing them.

Fiona watched with delight this grown man slip and slide trying to capture a silly little bird. He leaped toward one and caught it, coming up completely covered in mud. Fiona burst out laughing.

"Ye could give a man a hand," he challenged.

"But it is far more pleasant to watch you scurry around in the mud," she teased.

"I'll be needin' to wash me clothes after this."

Fiona laughed. She didn't have the heart to tell him that he had mud splattered in his hair and that he'd be needing a good washing as well.

His eyebrows shot up. "Do tell, lass."

"You'll be needing a scrubbing yourself."

"Aye, I needed that before I came. But I found these chickens, an' I think they belong to ye."

"How can anyone tell one chicken from another? They all look the same."

"Aye, I suppose they do. Do ye know how many ye had before the storm?"

"Six. Father was going to pick up some chicks before the storm."

Ian carried the single chicken across the yard to the mended coop as Fiona followed. "The men said they'd come by an' fix yer chicken coop as good as new to thank ye for a safe place to stay durin' the storm. I'm afraid it will take them a few days. Jacques's boat was severely damaged. We've hauled it over to the shipyard, an' we're repairin' it."

"I'm sorry to hear that. Do you know of anyone else who suffered losses?"

"Aye, most of the pilots' shacks were toppled over. Some were broken beyond repair, though others are repairable."

"What about yours?" Fiona hoped Ian's home hadn't been destroyed. She wished no homes were destroyed.

"We righted it, an' I've repaired it so it won't leak. I'll be puttin' in a bunk bed for one of the men who lost his shack."

"That's very kind of you, Ian."

"Just the neighborly thing to do. What about ye? Did ye go to town?"

"No, I stayed here. Slept what I could yesterday in order to stay awake last night."

"Aye, that would be best." Ian looked around. He needed to do something with his hands or else he would break his vow and approach Fiona. When he'd seen she'd been crying he'd fought himself to remain in control, to keep a distance. Physical contact with this woman made his head and heart spin. He'd promised to keep his distance, and he'd broken that already by returning the chickens. Who knew whose chickens they were, and who'd care? But it seemed like a good excuse at the time.

Chickens! He had two when he arrived. Slowly he scanned the area. Where had the other run off to? Spotting it, he ran toward it, praying he wouldn't land in more mud. He could feel the mud from his earlier tumble caking on his face. He must look a terrible fright. His prey within inches, he swooped down and captured the foolish bird. "Gotcha."

Fiona applauded.

Ian grinned. "Don't think you'll be gettin' any eggs from these ladies tomorrow. I think they're a bit unsettled."

"Of course they'd be unsettled—to have a huge man like you plop down on them, and twice, the poor dears."

"Poor dears? Ye got to be kiddin'."

Fiona chuckled and turned toward the house.

Their time had ended. Now he needed to clean up and find a hot bath. A hot sponge bath was probably the best he could muster up.

"Ian, do you need a place to bathe?" Fiona whispered.

"Aye lass. That I do. Would ye be offerin'?"

"Aye, 'tis the least I can do." Fiona winked. "After all, you returned my chickens. You can bathe by the pump. I'll put on the hot water and return to the house to give you some privacy."

Ever-practical Fiona—a man couldn't help but love a woman like her. At least he couldn't. Ian fished the tub from the shed and rolled it to the pump. He had always wondered why they had a wall in front of the pump. Now he understood. Of course, it had come down during the storm. Ian didn't care much for the idea of Fiona being seen bathing. . . "I'll fix this right away."

He worked the pump handle up and down until his tub was two-thirds full. Then he looked around for tools and some wood to repair the wall. Seeing none, he decided to return tomorrow with a couple tall posts. The other boards from the fallen wall were fine. He looked up at the sky. Perhaps he had enough time to go to town and. . . No, that wouldn't work. Posts were in high demand. He'd need to repair these temporarily, then when a new shipment of lumber came in, he'd fix them permanently.

"Ian," Fiona called, "can you lend me a hand carrying the water?"

He ran to the back door. Fiona's hands were covered with padded mitts as she carried the bucket. Ian followed suit and lifted another bucket. Together they poured the hot water into the tub.

"I'll fix the wall so ye can bathe," he offered.

"Thank you. I'm in need of a good scrubbing."

Ian, for the life of him, couldn't see a speck of dirt on the woman, and her lilac-scented perfume hardly offended him. To the contrary, he found it intoxicating.

"I'll get some of Father's clothes and a clean towel for you." Fiona skirted her eyes away from him and scurried back to the house.

Ian unbuttoned his shirt and draped it over the pump. *I'll rinse me clothes in the bathwater after I'm done.* He thought of Richard Stemple's build, his waist, a bit broader than his own. Ian removed his leather belt and set it aside. Next came his mud-caked leather boots.

"Oh, my," Fiona gasped.

Chapter 5

Ian turned, his hands outstretched, and faced her. "What?" he asked, looking around the yard for any possible reason for her concern.

"You're naked!" Fiona couldn't stop staring at his broad shoulders and rounded biceps.

"I'm not naked," he protested. "Me pants are on." He marched over to the pump and grabbed his soiled shirt.

"I'm sorry, Ian. I've not seen a man in such a state for several years. It just. . .startled me."

"Aye lass. I understand, an' 'tis I that am sorry. I should have thought. Ye've been raised proper. I've been livin' with men in a common area an', well—propriety isna a concern. My apologies."

Fiona timidly stepped closer. He looked so adorable with the mud caked on his face, his brown eyes all the richer, and the small golden flecks seemed to stand out more.

He smiled.

She took another step. Memories of the other night, of the wonder and comfort of being in his arms, flooded her senses. Tentatively, she reached out her hand and touched his forearm.

"Fiona, don't. I–I. . ."

How it happened, she didn't know, but she found herself swallowed up in his embrace. "Oh, Ian, why does this have to be so difficult?"

"Because we're meant to be together, Fiona. Canna ye feel it?"

"Yes, but. . ."

"Shh, me love, don't think. Just relish the moment. We will be married one day, I know it," he whispered in her ear.

A few moments later, Ian released her and stepped back. "I'm sorry, I shouldna have done that. I told ye I'd wait, Fiona, an' I will wait. I'll wait until ye know what I've come to know."

"But. . .I'm so confused." Should she give up her dream just for the physical connection between them? Was this love or sinful desires stirring within her? In his arms all thoughts, questions, and worries slipped away. Apart from him, she didn't understand the attraction. Not to mention, he wasn't called to be a lighthouse keeper as she.

"Go en the house an' fix us some dinner, Fiona. I'll be en shortly."

Fiona turned and headed back to the house. Why did she follow his orders so easily? This didn't make sense. When her parents asked her to do something, she tended to do it without question, though she'd wonder why she had to at that very moment. But here Ian had her in his arms for a brief moment, and she obeyed his every command. She'd never given much mind to what anyone else ordered her to do. Even her brothers were furious with her on more than one occasion because she wouldn't do what they asked. The fact that they asked her to do dumb things might have had something to do with it. But here she was marching into the kitchen to fix a man his dinner. A man whom a few days ago she'd tried to avoid with a passion. Why was she obeying him?

As she rounded the corner of the house, she heard, "Fiona." Her father stood before her, rigid. Her mother seemed startled.

"Father, Mother, it's so good to see you." Fiona looked over her shoulder. Had they seen Ian and her in that embrace? The prickly feeling of heat blushed her cheeks.

Her mother placed her hand lovingly on her father's forearm. "Richard, I'll go inside with Fiona. You can speak with the young man in back."

Fiona groaned. "Father, Ian is taking a bath." Goodness, that didn't sound right. "He fell in the mud catching our chickens," she quickly amended.

Her father released a pent-up breath. "I have no doubt the man may be in need of a bath, but—"

"Richard, not now, let's give them a chance to speak."

He nodded and stomped into the house. Her mother put her arm around Fiona. "Come on, dear. Seems more than a hurricane has been happening here."

Ian had never felt better. Fiona's growing affection encouraged him. After his bath he put on her father's clothes and rinsed his own, then went straight to work on fixing the fence that would give Fiona privacy. He splinted the poles and wrapped the splints with some cable he found in the shed. It wouldn't hold through another storm, but it would stay put until the new lumber arrived. He rinsed and refilled the tub and the two buckets they had heated on the stove for hot water.

He whistled while carrying them to the house. He didn't knock but marched right in and placed the buckets on the stove. "Fiona," he called, "I've put the buckets on the stove." Ian walked into the living area where Richard and Mary sat.

"Welcome home. . ." His words trailed off. Tears stained Fiona's face. Richard looked like a man about to explode. How long had they been here? Did they. . . *Oh, no, Lord, this is all me fault,* he thought, suddenly aware of the embarrassment he'd put Fiona through.

"Richard, I, we. . ." What could he say?

"I'm not a man given to a temper, son. But what I saw in my own backyard has me hotter than the hottest day in August."

"Sir, I apologize. I wasna thinkin' when I took off me shirt to get ready for me bath." Why had he accepted Fiona's offer for a bath? *Because ye couldna pass up the opportunity to spend more time with her.*

"A bare-chested man? Fiona's seen that before with four older brothers. That isn't my concern. You had her in your arms, caressing her as—as lovers!" Richard fumed.

"Aye, I had her in me arms, an' I do love yer daughter. But we've shared no more than a few embraces. I've been wantin' to ask for Fiona's hand in marriage, properlike, but I've wanted to buy me own land an' build a house first."

"And just how long have you two been carrying on behind our backs?" Richard sent an accusing glance to his daughter.

"Only since the storm," Ian admitted. "I've had an interest in Fiona for a long time, but she's—"

"Father," Fiona snapped. "I've never been so insulted in all my life. To think my own father would think I'd do something so, so—"

"Richard, calm down," her mother interrupted. "Fiona, get control of yourself. Ian, take a seat." Mary stood up. "I see no point in getting everyone upset any further. Richard, we need to talk privately." She turned toward Ian and Fiona. "We'll be back in a moment."

With that, Mary ushered her husband to their room.

"Fiona, I'm so sorry," Ian whispered.

"It's my fault as much as yours. I shouldn't have reached out for you. We both know we are far too attracted to each other."

"Aye, but that isna a bad thing."

"I don't know, Ian. I really don't know. Just look at the pain it's caused my parents."

And what could he say? A proper gentleman wouldn't have put a woman in such a compromising position. Yet he had.

"Ian," she continued, "I'm so confused. In your arms I have no worries, no cares, and hardly any sense of what is right and wrong. I think it best that we don't see each other until I can sort these emotions out."

"I don't agree. I think we need to meet, to talk, to have the time for ye to develop an' understand these feelings."

Fresh tears flowed down Fiona's face. "No, Ian, I need time. . .time alone."

"All right." Ian got up and marched to the closed door of her parents' room. He tapped it lightly.

"Yes?" Mary called out.

"Richard, Mary, I'm leavin' now. Ye won't have any more concern regardin' me and me actions with Fiona. She's asked for time alone. If ye need me for anythin', ye know where to find me.

"Good-bye, Fiona. You know where to find me." Ian nodded, and with every bit of self-control he could muster, he walked quietly out of the house and down the hill. Once he turned toward Pilot Town, he let out a strangled groan, kicked a clump of dirt, and proceeded to give himself a thorough tongue-lashing. For months he'd exhibited all manner of self-control with Fiona, holding his feelings at bay. Yet today he couldn't help himself and had taken the woman into his arms. If he hadn't exercised some restraint he would have kissed her. And with the amount of passion he felt, it wouldn't have been a chaste kiss. He'd waited months to even approach her, so why did he have to have her now? Why the sudden urgency?

He reckoned some of it had to do with his Scottish blood and the passion with which his people did everything. *Aye, I be a passionate person, Lord. Father, forgive me for anythin' wrong I might have done. An' show me where I was wrong. Obviously, Richard feels I've scorned him, an' for that I'm sorry. Maybe Fiona is right, Lord. Maybe we do need time apart. But help me to give her the time an' space. The thought of not seein' her every day tears at me heart, Lord. Help her, Lord. Give her comfort; give her peace.*

Ian's temper waned as he prayed. He found himself outside his temporary home with Alden waiting for him on the steps. "Evenin'," Ian greeted his guest.

"Evening, Ian."

"Let's get buildin' that bunk for ye, Alden. The place is too small to have ye sleepin' on the floor."

Alden clapped his hands together and got up from his perch on the stairs. "You're the boss; just tell me what we need to do."

Grateful for the distraction, Ian went straight to work. His empty stomach grumbled, but the thought of food made his stomach tighten.

Within an hour they had the bunk built. They hung Alden's saturated mattress to dry. But at least he was off the ground and had a roof over his head.

"So you've set your mind on Fiona Stemple?" Alden asked, attempting some small talk.

"Aye."

"She's pleasant on the eyes, but I hear she can be hard on the ears."

Ian chuckled. "Aye."

Alden laughed. "Doesn't matter, huh?"

"Afraid not. She's won me heart, pure an' simple. Guess that's what they mean in those weddin' vows—for better an' for worse."

"Ouch! I think I'll stay single."

"I hear ye. But I'm countin' on more of the better and less of the worse." Ian brushed off the sawdust from Richard's borrowed pants. His own clothes still hung behind Fiona's house. How he could bring back Richard's clothes and gather his own without seeing Fiona, he didn't have a clue.

"Hungry?" Ian asked.

❧

Fiona couldn't believe the change in her father when he returned to the living area. He apologized for his temper and asked her to forgive him for not believing in her. She'd seen her mother do this on more than one occasion, but she didn't think she'd ever seen her father, a fairly even-tempered man, so angry. Her mother assured her it had more to do with her being a daughter and having grown up. As she lay on her cot in the family living area that night, she replayed the day over and over. The one event that really stood out was being in Ian's arms once again. Proper or not, she'd wanted to kiss him. If he had held her a moment more, she probably would have found her lips searching for his. She could no longer deny the attraction between her and Ian.

Her father tended the light that evening while Fiona slept soundly. She didn't hear him, not even once, coming and going during the night.

≈❧

"Good morning, dear," Mary said as Fiona walked into the kitchen. "Did you sleep well?"

"Very." The rich scent of bacon tickled her nose and made her all the more aware of her empty stomach.

"Would you like to talk about Ian?" Mary asked.

"Yes. I had so many questions I wanted to ask you, but now they seem unimportant."

"How so, dear?" Mary forked the sizzling bacon in the frying pan, turning over the strips as they browned.

"I can't justify a relationship with Ian and my calling to be a light-house keeper."

"Oh?"

"I know I'm meant to carry on the tradition of our family," Fiona explained.

"I see. And which tradition are we talking about?" Mary asked.

"Keeping the lights, you know, like Father."

"Hmm, and like his father before him?" Mary teased.

Fiona smiled ruefully, remembering that Grandpa was a farmer, not a lighthouse keeper. "But I'm good at it; I've saved lives," she protested.

"Seems to me you're trying to convince me that keeping the light is more important than another job. And yet my father and your father's father were men who worked the ground and produced food for others. Equally as important, wouldn't you say?"

"Yes, but—"

"Fiona, I'm not saying you should or shouldn't be a lighthouse keeper. What I am saying is that you've lived a very sheltered life. We were so isolated up in Maine. The only thing you've known of a man's occupation is a lighthouse keeper. Sure, you've seen some sea captains and fishermen, but you've never experienced the kind of work they do. Is it possible there is more for you in your life than simply being a keeper of the light?"

How could she argue with that? And was her mother saying she and Ian should develop a relationship?

"One of the reasons your father and I took this post was to expose you to other people, other ways of life. There have been no lack of men wanting to seek your hand. Your father's turned down quite a few offers since you turned sixteen."

"He has?"

"Why, of course, dear. You weren't ready."

"But. . .I don't understand."

"I know, Fiona. That's why we brought you here. In spite of what happened yesterday, your father and I both knew Ian was attracted to you. Your father just didn't expect to find you in his arms so quickly."

Fiona's checks flamed.

"Now, would you like to talk about that?" Mary placed the bacon on a rack for the grease to drip off the fried meat.

"I guess I don't want to discuss it yet."

"Very well. When you have a mind to ask, you'll ask me. In the meantime, set the table. Your father will have an incredible appetite this morning, and I want to be ready."

"Yes, ma'am."

Fiona went to work setting the table and then slipped into her parents' room to dress for the day. Her father had turned down suitors? They moved here for her? Yet she wanted to move back to Maine. There was simply too much information, too many new emotions. She needed some time to think and to pray.

Chapter 6

Fiona glanced at Ian's clothes still hanging on the line. Days had passed with no sign of him. She found herself no better off than when he'd left and told her he would wait. Her mother's conversation a few days ago hadn't helped any either. She respected her parents, but why did they feel she needed to be exposed to more people? Was there something wrong with her?

The thought had nagged her for days. The entire time they'd been living on Ocracoke, she'd been dying to return back home. Yet Maine was the very place her parents felt she needed to leave. It didn't make sense. Granted, her brothers had left the island for a time to continue their educations, but she had all the education she needed to run a lighthouse.

Prayers were useless. She tried and tried but found no relief. She had stopped praying for God to change Ian's career days ago. But could she really pray and expect God to show her if she was wrong? Who she was as a person, her life's career, was all based on the call to be a lighthouse keeper. Who was she if she wasn't that?

Fiona ironed and folded Ian's clothes. She needed to see him. He didn't have to stay away...completely. Determined to get her life back under control, she wrapped Ian's clothes in brown paper and marched to Pilot Town. She had no idea which shack he lived in, but as far as she knew, he was the only Scotsman on the island. He shouldn't be too hard to find.

"Excuse me, can you tell me which home is Mr. Ian Duncan's?" she asked a leathery-faced fisherman tending his net outside his small wooden abode.

"Over there, miss." He pointed behind him and to the left.

Fiona walked through the narrow path of chipped scallop shells to Ian's. A slightly older man than Ian, with a receding hairline, sat on the steps. As she approached, a wide semi-toothless grin greeted her. "Hello."

"Does Mr. Duncan live here?" She bit her lower lip for fear it would quiver. These were strange men, and she probably shouldn't be alone.

"Aye, miss. I'm afraid he isn't here."

"Oh." Fiona's hopes vanished. "Could you give him this?"

"Be my pleasure, miss. Who should I tell him this is from?" he asked as he grabbed the bundle from her hands.

"He'll know." Certain this must be the man Ian said would be staying with him for awhile, she nervously continued refusing to give him her name.

"Have a good day, sir."

"Thank you, Miss Stemple," he winked.

Fiona prayed the ground would open up and swallow her whole. He'd either guessed her name or knew her by sight. She didn't know, and she didn't care to stay there and discuss the matter. Uneasy with the feeling that everyone would know why she'd come, Fiona retreated. She nearly ran out of the small housing area and worked her way back up to the lighthouse. Of all the stupid things she could have done, she chided herself.

Instead of going home, she walked past the lighthouse and east toward the open woods and beach. She hadn't visited the ponies since before the hurricane. To sit and watch those graceful animals run, buck, and play would help her take her mind off herself and one Ian Duncan. "Oh, Lord, make it so. I can't take much more of this," she proclaimed to the waves and the wind.

She sat on the bluff, her bluff, her secret place. Finally alone, maybe she could think straight. She breathed deeper and more slowly. Yes, she needed solitude. Just what she'd asked Ian for. She watched the tall grass stalks dance and tease each other, the surf rise and fall as it crashed on the beach.

&

Alden greeted him, grinning like a Cheshire cat. Ian couldn't believe Fiona had come by. He grabbed Richard's clean clothes and went to her home. Mary greeted him warmly.

"Is Fiona here?" he asked.

"I'm afraid not, Ian. She left while Richard and I were in the lighthouse. Is something wrong?"

"No, she dropped me clothes off an' I wanted to thank her."

"You're welcome to stay and visit for awhile," Mary offered.

"Thank you, but I'm afraid I have some work to do before the sun goes down. Just tell her I came by."

"Ian, before you go, you should speak with Richard." Mary reached out and touched his shoulder. "I believe it would be wise."

"Aye, I think ye're right. Is he in the lighthouse?" Ian asked, looking over to the red brick tower.

"Yes."

"Thank ye, Mary, an' I do apologize for any grief I may have caused ye an' yer family."

"You're forgiven. Now go make your peace with Richard."

Ian nodded his agreement and walked toward the lighthouse. Today the sky was blue and the wind but a whisper. An invisible force—guilt? fear? confusion?—worked against his legs with more power than the mighty winds of the hurricane a few days before. Richard had become a friend, a man whom he respected. He had betrayed that trust by being so forward with Fiona. He understood that now. He still didn't believe it was wrong to hold the woman you loved, but he understood, in part, how it must have hurt Richard.

He took hold of the handle, turned the latch of the thick oak door, and called out. "Richard?"

"I'm up on the second level, Ian. Come and join me." His tone seemed friendly.

Ian took in a deep breath and took the steps two at a time. "Good evenin', sir." Ian held out his hand.

Richard grasped it firmly, giving it one quick shake. One of the things Ian found most curious were how soft the man's hands were, and yet they were as strong as any man's he'd known. He'd come to the conclusion that the older man having his hands in whale oil day in and day out probably accounted for the smoothness. So unlike his own calloused hands.

"I ordered a couple posts to replace the ones that hold up the wall near the pump." Ian flushed, remembering it was the very spot where he and Fiona had embraced each other.

"Thank you; I appreciate it. Ian, I was a bit hasty with my words the other day. I apologize." Richard shifted his gaze toward his feet.

"I understand, sir. I'm sorry to have offended ye. I appreciate our friendship, an' I don't want to lose that."

Richard's eyes met Ian's. "Understood." A simple reply from a straight-forward man.

Ian released a pent-up breath.

"So, you've asked Fiona to marry you?"

Ian felt the heat crawl up his neck and knew he was turning a bright shade of red. "Aye, we talked about it. I've not asked her formal-like. I'd be needin' yer permission before I do that."

"How would you provide for her?"

"I make a good wage craftin' boats. I've saved enough to purchase some land an' start to build a house on it."

Richard plopped his large hand on Ian's shoulder. "I'm impressed, son."

"Thank ye, sir. I'm plannin' to buy the land today."

"Are you aware of Fiona's desires to be a lighthouse keeper?" Richard resumed polishing the oil lamps that lit the stairways.

"Aye. We be findin' that a bit of a touchy subject."

Richard chuckled. Ian realized the man understood his daughter. "Do you love her?" Richard asked.

"With all me heart. But she isna ready yet." Ian sighed. "I believe the Lord has brought us together an' desires us to be husband an' wife. I've prayed long an' hard before I even approached her, but she needs time. An' I do, as well."

"And what kind of time do you need?" Richard asked, putting his cleaning rag down.

" 'Tis me Scottish blood, sir. In my country, when a man has these powerful. . ." Ian cleared his throat. "These emotions for the woman he loves, an' she for him, he takes her into the highlands an' makes her his wife."

Richard's eyes bulged and his face reddened.

Ian quickly added, "But I believe God wouldna be pleased for me to do as me ancestors would, that He wants me to get ahold of me emotions and be a stronger man for it."

"You're not in Scotland, and I wouldn't take too kindly if you ran off with my daughter." Richard's warning was clear.

Ian looked at his feet then raised his glance back to Richard's. "I understand, sir. An' I wouldna dishonor ye."

"I'll hold you to it. If Fiona wishes to marry you, you'll have my blessing."

"Thank ye, sir." Ian's heart soared.

"But I think it best that you and she always have someone close by until then."

Ian nodded. How could he object? He'd just confessed how passionate his people were, and he couldn't deny his own strong feelings for Fiona. "I'll respect yer wishes. But ye should know, I won't be around much. I've told Fiona I will wait for her. So she will decide when we will meet again. In the meantime, I'll be buildin' our house, but I'll ask ye not to tell her. It will be me weddin' present."

Richard smiled. "I understand."

"Thank ye, sir. She's a fine woman."

"With a bit of a strong will."

"Aye, but once tamed it will make her a stronger woman."

"Tamed, huh?" He winked. "You understand my daughter well. You'll have my blessings and my prayers." He chuckled.

Ian realized it would take a strong man with a gentle spirit to handle a woman like Fiona. He prayed God would keep him humble and give him the strength and grace for the blessing of such a wonderful gift as her. She could stand a man on his ear with her tongue, but he suspected she could strengthen a man with one word of encouragement that twenty years on his own would never have done.

"I best be goin'. I have some land to purchase." Ian grinned.

"Good night, son. Godspeed."

With a greater sense of urgency, Ian hustled down the stairs. One day Fiona Stemple would be his wife. He just prayed it wouldn't take her too long to decide.

☙

Fiona rose from her slumber to the sound of ponies baying. She'd fallen asleep on the dune. The chestnut with white boots glistened nearby in the setting sun. His dark brown eyes stared at Fiona. She grabbed some wild sea oats and waved them at him. He shook his head up and down and pranced his front legs.

"Come on, Boy," she called to the timid stallion.

He nodded his head and snorted, his nostrils flaring and his velvety lips fluttering with the escape of air from his lungs. With his right front hoof, he demanded that she advance.

Fiona walked over to the animal and held out the oats. He took them and chomped noisily. She stroked the white streak painting the front of his forehead to his muzzle, then across his cheek and around the under-side of his neck near his head—one of his sweet spots she'd discovered on previous encounters.

She had planned to bring a bit and bridle the next time she came, but today was an unplanned visit. "You're a handsome beast. I shall name you."

But what kind of a name would fit this animal? "With your dark coloring and firm muscles, you remind me of Ian. Have I told you about him? Well, if I had, you'd not have heard a kind word, I'm afraid." Fiona continued to stroke the horse.

"I'm glad you made it through the storm. It was that storm that forced me to see another side of Ian. He's a kind man. A bit demanding, but for some strange reason I don't mind doing what he asks."

The horse nuzzled his head on her shoulder.

"If I knew more of horses I'd try and mount you. But I've only ridden a time or two."

He pulled his head off her shoulder as if insulted.

"You were made to carry a man."

He wagged his head from side to side.

"Oh, you think not," she chuckled at the wise animal. "So, you think you're to be free to run and play?"

He bayed.

"Since you remind me of Ian, I'll call you Highland. He often talks about the strong rugged hills in the highlands of Scotland. Highland, it fits you."

The horse tilted his head to the left as if something had caught his attention. A shiver went down his fine chestnut coat. Fiona looked and saw nothing but knew animals could hear far more than she could. Highland backed slowly away.

"Go on, Boy, do what you must."

The horse trotted away.

For months she'd been getting familiar with Highland. For months she'd been blind to his similarities with Ian—the glorious dark coat and Ian's rich mahogany curls. Both had deep chocolate eyes and strong muscles. Of course, she hadn't felt Ian's strong muscles, or even been aware of them, until a few days ago. But as wonderful as it was to run her hand down Highland's neck, it did not compare to the feeling she had when she caressed Ian.

Stop it! she yelled to herself. *Thoughts like those will get you nowhere.*

Fiona stormed back to her home, no more the wiser and definitely not calmer.

Chapter 7

Days turned into weeks and weeks turned into months. No sign of Ian. Fiona's interest in staying up all night manning the light had waned tremendously. She found herself spending more and more time with Highland. She'd bridled him a few weeks back and ridden him bareback a few times. As much as she wanted to bring him home, she didn't have the heart to put him behind a pen.

Ian had moved from the shack but was still on the island, she'd been told. Fiona could never muster enough courage to go to the shipyard and find him. And no matter how many times she told herself he said he would wait for her, she still felt hurt and angry that he never came around.

One day began as it had the day before, and the same as the day before that, sitting at the breakfast table discussing the weather and the condition of the lighthouse with her parents.

"Father?"

"Yes, dear."

How could she ask him without sounding like a lovesick puppy? "Have you seen Mr. Duncan of late?"

"Why, yes, ran into him in town the other day. He's doing well." He forked another stack of pancakes onto his plate. "Why do you ask?"

"I was. . .concerned."

"Hmm."

"Perhaps you might look him up?" her mother suggested.

"He's moved. I don't. . ." She held her words. She'd just exposed herself and her previous attempt to see him.

"Richard, tell her," Fiona's mother encouraged.

"Tell me? Tell me what? He's all right, isn't he?" A sudden fear that he might have suffered an injury at work crept across her face.

Her father placed his hand upon hers. "He's fine, child. Do you love him?"

She couldn't deny it any longer. He'd been in her thoughts day and night since the hurricane. The summer had passed with no further storms. Autumn leaves now colored the island with streaks of gold, orange, and red. The entire summer she'd argued with her thoughts and emotions and fought with God about her call. Ian had been right. It was her father's call, not her own. But she found herself adrift, not knowing who or what she should be or do.

"Yes," she whispered.

"Then I suggest you find him and tell him how you feel," her father said, dabbing his mouth with his napkin.

"Do you know where he is?" Fiona asked.

"Working, I presume. But what you need to speak with Ian about would be better suited to a private conversation."

Mother's chair scuffed the floor as she got up and went beside her daughter. "Richard, give Ian an invitation for lunch."

Lunch—four more hours. They would be the longest four hours of her life.

Her father tossed his napkin down and rose from the table. "I think that is a grand idea, Mother." With that, he silently left the room, the screen door springing back and clapping the doorjamb behind him.

"Are you ready to talk about it?" Mother asked.

"I've prayed, Mother, all summer. I'm more confused than when Ian left. I do know that God wasn't calling me to be a lighthouse keeper, but I have no idea what I'm supposed to do. I love Ian. But is that enough? I just don't know."

"Come, sit on the sofa with me, dear." Her mother walked over to the sofa and waited patiently for Fiona to join her.

"Growing up on the farm, I always felt I would eventually marry a farmer, have a few children, watch them grow and marry, then be a grandmother one day. I'd either live on a neighboring farm or on the same farmstead as my parents and my father's parents before them. That is, until I met your father." Her mother's eyes twinkled with excitement.

"Your father, bless his heart, had no patience with the land. He yearned for the sea. And once he had visited the ocean, he knew that was the place for him. For years people made sport of his convictions. He didn't know exactly what he would do on the sea, but he knew it would be something.

"He was a striking young man—all the girls thought so at the time—but they all stayed away because of his crazy talk about working on the sea.

"Now, mind you, I didn't understand it either, but there was something about him, about his deep convictions, that drew me to him." Mary placed her hands on her lap. "I suppose you, being raised in our home and being our only daughter and thoroughly loving your father, caught that same excitement and desire to be on the sea."

"I always thought it was a higher call to do the work of a lighthouse keeper. The hours are so demanding, and many people's lives depend upon what you do."

"Certainly it is a high calling and holds a great responsibility, but it isn't your father's highest calling in life."

"I don't understand."

"Fiona, dear, your father loves his work; he's committed to it. But before his job are his children, and before his children is me. But even I take second place in his life, as he does in mine. The Lord and what He desires of us stands above all the rest."

"I've had it backward, haven't I?"

"Yes, dear. The job is a good one, and a noble one, but should always be after your relationship with the Lord. You've wanted your own way, and perhaps, being the baby and the only girl in the family, we've given into you a time or two when we shouldn't have. You do tend to have a stubborn streak." Mother winked.

Fiona chuckled.

"I'm glad you've at least sorted out your affections for Ian Duncan. Now, perhaps the two of you can explore whether the Lord wishes you to get together."

"Ian says He does."

Mary chuckled. "Maybe so, but I think that is something a man and a woman need to discuss and pray together about before one decides for the both of you."

Ian worked hard all morning. Richard's revelation that Fiona wished to see him made his spirit soar and his mind take flight. He'd missed more nails and pegs than a twelve-year-old apprentice on his first day. The noon hour couldn't come fast enough. When he mentioned to his boss he might be away for awhile during lunch, the man gave Ian the rest of the day off, claiming it cost him more money having him work.

Ian hadn't shared with him why he couldn't keep his mind on his work. Relishing the release from his employer's tasks, he headed back home, figuring he had a little time to do some painting on the place. He prayed Fiona would like the house. He'd given Richard a progress report a few days ago in town. Although nearly completed, he'd done little work in the past couple days. Richard had also informed Ian that Fiona never spoke of him. He also spoke of his growing concern over her daily wanderings from the house.

The sun shone brightly on the new house. The interior still needed finish work, but the exterior was completed. On more than one occasion, several of the pilots and fishermen who lived in Pilot Town and some of the men he worked with had come to lend a hand. When he first purchased the land, they helped him clear it in a day. Digging the foundation alone had put a few more muscles on his back. They returned to help raise the roof, and a few continued to come every once in awhile when they had nothing better to do.

All in all, Ian was pleased with the small, two-bedroom home. And he had the plans for building additions as their family grew.

He placed the paintbrush he'd been working with in the bucket and stood back from the front door. He'd painted it the same shade of blue as her eyes. He glanced up at the sky and the placement of the sun. He had just enough time to clean up and meet Fiona. "Oh, Lord, help me be a patient man. Don't let me overwhelm her as I did before," he prayed.

He washed the brush, himself as well, and put on some fresh clothes. He'd even considered wearing his kilt but decided against it. While custom dictated traditional clothing when a man went calling on a woman in Scotland, it hardly seemed appropriate on Ocracoke.

His heart raced as he approached the small brick house. He reached up and gently rapped on the door.

"Ian, I'm so glad you could come." Mary smiled and let him in.

Admittedly, he'd hoped Fiona would have greeted him. Mary closed the door, and he proceeded into the family living area.

His heart lurched in his chest. Fiona stood in the center of the room, her hair more golden, her blue eyes sparkling as brightly as the ocean in summer. "Fiona, me love, ye're beautiful."

A gentle blush rose on her cheeks.

"Hello, Ian. I've missed you."

"I've missed ye, too." His tongue barely obeyed his thoughts.

"Come, sit on the sofa for a moment." Fiona pointed to the far side of the room.

He reached out his hand and led her there. She sat down with the grace of a dove landing on a small bush. He sat beside her, afraid his legs would give out. How did her very presence drain him of his strength?

He caressed her fingers with his thumb, not having let go since escorting her over to the sofa.

"Ian, I've done what you asked, and I've prayed about my call."

Ian swallowed hard. Perhaps she'd still decided to remain as a lighthouse keeper.

"And you were right. I wasn't called to be a lighthouse keeper. It is my father's calling."

Ian could feel his grin widen.

"But..."

His grin slipped.

"My mother made me realize just this morning that I was putting the call, or rather my interpretation of the call, before God. I put so much emphasis on it I forgot about the One who called me."

Ian nodded. He understood putting God to the side and the need to put Him back in the center of his life. He'd done the same on more than one occasion.

"I guess what I'm saying is, I need to get right with the Lord before we can pursue a relationship."

His heart sank deep into his gut. He closed his eyes and held back the bile that rose in his stomach.

"Aye lass, I understand yer need to put God in His proper place. But..." Ian didn't think he could wait another three months or longer before she would consider a relationship with him.

"I'm sorry I've hurt you. I didn't mean to. I'm not saying this right."

"No, ye be sayin' it just fine. I do understand, an' I'd be lyin' if I said I wasna hopin' for more. I cana imagine not seein' ye again for so long."

"Oh, Ian. I want to see you. I need to see you. I've missed you terribly. I just know I need to put God first."

"Aye, me love. I think I can help ye with that."

"You can?"

"Aye, I believe I can." Ian reached out and touched her silky golden hair. Her eyes rapidly searched his own. "Yer hair is a wonder to me fingers. 'Tis silky an' sweet an' crowns ye with golden splendor. But as much as I love ye—an' Fiona, I do love ye—I don't have the patience to count each an' every strand upon your head."

"Of course not. No one can."

"Exactly. But our Father in heaven says He knows the exact number of hairs upon our heads. I could never love ye like He loves ye, cares for ye, an' will always be there for ye. I can promise to love ye the rest of me days, but I could never be there at every moment. Our heavenly Father can."

"I understand. But what does that have to do with me not putting Him first in my life?"

"I'm gettin' to that." Ian chuckled. "I trust ye repented when ye realized this was somethin' ye'd done?"

Fiona nodded.

"Then He is first in your life."

"But—"

"Me love, if the Lord has brought us together, He'll show ye. We can begin to spend time together, pray together, an' see if I be the one for ye."

He made sense. Maybe she didn't need to do this on her own. "I'd like that."

Ian flashed his wonderful smile once again. His hand had never left hers, and yet he held it with such tenderness and strength.

"So would I, lass." He winked. He looked behind them and then back to her. "Where are yer parents?"

"I don't know. But they can't be far." She truly hadn't seen them leave, but they were gone, perhaps sitting on the front steps, waiting for them to finish their private conversation.

"Ian, I've missed you. Where have you been?" she asked.

He grinned. "I bought some land an' am buildin' a house."

Their house? He had said he planned to do that months ago. Would he build it not knowing if she'd ever come around?

"Aye lass, 'tis me gift to me bride."

His bride! Her pulse raced with anticipation, but she still needed to discover who she was before she. . .

He interrupted her thoughts. "All in good time, me love. For now, let's get to know one another an' fill our bellies with that delicious fish chowder I smell."

The door creaked open, and her parents entered the room. "Can you return for dinner?" Fiona asked as he ushered her to the table.

"Aye, an' I can stay the afternoon. Me boss gave me the day off. He said somethin' about me mind not bein' on me work today. I canna imagine why, can ye?" He winked.

Fiona giggled.

Her mother interrupted. "Are you hungry, Ian?"

"Starvin'." His gaze lingered on Fiona, and she could feel the blush deepen on her cheeks.

Father cleared his throat. Ian's eyes traveled back to him. "Let's pray."

Chapter 8

Fiona didn't know when she'd spent a more pleasant afternoon. She and Ian talked about everything from lighthouses, to ships, to houses, to Highland, and the Lord. The strength of Ian's faith captivated her, and he gave her practical ideas of how to keep God first in her life. He'd confessed times in his past when he'd put something or someone ahead of God and how he'd always find himself in trouble. He had a way of showing her things that made sense.

That night, the house stood quiet as she lay on her bed, continuously replaying the conversations of the day. Her musings drifted off into the warmth of Ian's arms wrapped around her and his tender kiss upon her forehead.

With eager anticipation, she waited for Ian's return visit each day. The evenings they would spend together, talking, laughing, until Fiona realized her love for Ian had removed the doubt and confusion of the past three months. He had been right about her not being a lighthouse keeper. But could he be right about their being made for one another? She hoped so.

He had told her the general location of his land. Fiona trekked through the dew-laden grass, making her way to his home. She tapped the basket filled with fresh rolls and sweet jams she and her mother had made during the summer, her mind focused on other things.

Is it possible to love a man too much and lose sight of You, Lord? she prayed, hoping her love for Ian was God-breathed.

A small wooden house came into view. The bright blue door and trim made it stand out against the cleared land and cords of wood. Her heart beat faster. Ian had made this house with his own hands. Taking in a deep breath, she marched to the front door and knocked.

His heavy, approaching footfalls made her smile. Ian opened the door. "Fiona? What brings ye here?"

"You." She winked.

"Aye, me love, I've longed for ye to come to our home." He fanned his arm back. "Come in."

"I. . ." Was it wrong to enter a man's home? She thought she remembered hearing that somewhere. "I want to see the house, but. . ."

"Ah lass, ye're afraid of what others might say."

Fiona nodded her head.

"Do yer parents know ye've come?"

Fiona felt her cheeks heat. "No," she confessed.

"Then I'll come out an' sit on the front steps with ye."

"I've brought a small breakfast of some rolls and jams I've made."

Ian smiled. "Ye've made? For me?"

"Oh, Ian, I'm terribly afraid I've fallen too much in love with you. I think of you all the time and. . ." Fiona's hands trembled.

"Fallin' in love with me isna a bad thing." He took her hands into his own.

"But I need to put God first."

"Ahh. Tell me why ye think yer love for me is greater than yer love for our heavenly Father?"

Fiona explained that even while reading the Scriptures and praying thoughts of Ian came flooding into her mind.

"So, ye be thinkin' 'tis best for us not to see each other as often?"

Fiona nodded.

Ian released her hands and clasped his own, putting his elbows to his knees and leaning forward slightly.

"Fiona, when ye take care of the lighthouse all night, do ye have to stay alert an' constantly replenish the oil reservoirs?"

"Of course; you know that."

Ian grinned and took her hands again. "Well, that's the way 'tis with our relationship with God. We constantly need to pray an' read the Word. If we don't, we burn out."

"I know, Ian, and I have been praying, but you keep interrupting my prayers."

Ian chuckled. "An' ye think ye don't interrupt mine?"

"Really?"

"Absolutely, Love. But the same is true with us. To keep the flame of love burnin', ye need to tend it."

"How can I do both—keep the Lord's light burning and tend to our love?"

"By givin' our love over to God an' praisin' Him for the gift of it." He pushed back her hair. "Every time a thought or image of ye flashes before me mind, I praise God for ye. I ask Him to protect ye and keep ye safe. An' whatever else pops into me head."

"And God doesn't mind your interrupting your time with Him?"

"Of course not, Darlin', because I'm thankin' Him an' givin' Him credit for ye an' the gift of our love."

"Oh, Ian, I want what you say to be true."

"Trust me, Fiona."

Her hands trembled under his. He pulled her into his arms and wrapped them protectively around her.

⁊❀

Ian held on to Fiona with all his devotion. He couldn't imagine life without her. He couldn't lose her—not again. The summer had been horrible. If it hadn't been for the goal of building this house, he never would have made it and would have broken his vow to wait on her.

"Marry me, Fiona. Help me tend the light of our love an' fill this house with our children."

"Oh, Ian, yes." She reached up and caressed his face. Warmth, love, and fear mingled on her fingertips as they trailed his jaw and seared his lips. "Kiss me, Ian," she whispered.

"With pleasure, me love." Her tender lips, smooth as velvet, completed the noose around his heart. From the very moment he'd seen her, he'd fallen in love. And in a year's time she'd worked her magic, igniting love in his heart for her like no other. There'd be storms ahead, he chuckled to himself. Two strong-willed people were bound to have a blow or two. If they were ever-watchful, they could tend the light of their love for each other and their Creator, and be the stronger for it.

Ian pulled away before passions overtook common sense.

Fiona's eyes fluttered open. He watched those clear blue orbs slowly focus. "Oh, my," she whispered.

"Aye lass, an' the good Lord has so much more in store for us."

Fiona's eyes widened, and she pulled away. A gentle blush painted her cheeks and neck.

"I meant to say that I know the Lord has a grand adventure for us in our marriage, that together we will grow stronger in Him an' in raising our children. Ye're a fine woman, Fiona. . .one a man—this man—will be honored beyond words to have as his wife."

"What about Father? Do you think he'll approve?"

"Aye, I spoke with him a long time back. He said if ye loved me, we would have his blessin'."

Fiona smiled. "The day my parents invited you for lunch, that was his first question. 'Do you love him?' he asked. I responded yes. How could I deny it any longer? I tried the whole summer to bury our love. You came into my life like that hurricane, fast and furious."

"Ah, but unlike the hurricane, I plan on stayin' around for a very long time."

"I noticed." Fiona chuckled. "Do you suppose there's room for Highland here?"

"Of course. Are ye sure ye want to pen him in?"

"Hmm, I've corralled one Scotsman, maybe I don't need another." Fiona winked.

"Ye've corralled me, huh?"

"Let's compromise and agree we both got snared."

Ian knew this wouldn't be the last compromise they would have to agree upon. "Aye, 'tis a grand compromise. So when shall we wed?"

Fiona had come over to make peace with her soul and possibly arrange to see him less often. But she knew in her heart of hearts that only when she and Ian were married would she ever be completely calm.

"I suppose we ought to ask my parents."

"Yes, that would be the proper thing to do. Since ye an' I are to be married, is it all right for me to show ye the house now?"

"I'd be honored." Whatever her parents decided, it wouldn't be too long. Her brothers hadn't had long engagements.

They spent the next hour going from room to room, Ian telling her his plans and asking her what she would like. He'd built them a fine house. Through his eyes she could picture all his grand plans.

When they told her parents, a whirlwind of plans were launched. Ian needed a couple weeks to finish the master bedroom and kitchen. Her father offered to help. They settled on a month away for the wedding. Hurricane season would be past, and it would give her brothers time to come if they were able to leave their posts.

"Fiona, I need to get back to the house, but could I speak with ye before I leave?"

"Of course." Fiona followed Ian out the door after he said his farewells to her parents. "What's the matter?"

"Nothing is the matter, me love, relax." Ian pulled her against his chest.

She wound her hands up and around his neck. "I don't think I'll ever tire of being in your arms."

"Aye." Ian nuzzled his head into her neck.

"What did you want to talk about?" Fiona whispered.

Ian straightened and pulled back slightly. "Fiona, ye know I'm Scottish."

Fiona giggled. "Of course."

"Well, bein' Scottish an' from me clan, there is a formal attire for a man to wear when he's wed."

"The skirt?"

"Kilt, me love, 'tis called a kilt."

"You're going to wear a kilt? For our wedding?"

"Aye. But let me try an' make ye understand. The kilt is pleated, with a tartan design on the cloth. The plaid an' striped design varies from clan to clan. So when I wear the kilt, I'm payin' homage to me clan an' to me ancestors."

"Ian, if it means that much to you, I'd be honored to see you in your kilt."

"I do not wish to embarrass ye, but it does mean a lot to me."

Fiona smiled as an image developed in her mind of Ian standing in the front of the church in his kilt.

"What?" he asked.

"Oh, I just tried to picture you in your kilt," she teased.

Chapter 9

Fiona's stomach flip-flopped. Her legs trembled. She tightened her hold of her father's arm. The noonday sun shone brightly. The trees were colored with rich hues of amber and gold. The gentle flow of the church organ called people to their seats. The day had finally come. Fiona met it with excitement and nervous anticipation.

Her father stood proud in his dark black suit. Her mother beamed as her eyes misted with tears. Fiona's father placed a protective hand upon hers as they stood in the vestibule awaiting the moment they had prepared for. Her dress, aged with years, gave a pleasant ivory shading to its white satin. Her mother's gown. Fiona couldn't believe how well it fit. A few minor alterations and it slid on her body like a glove.

"You're as beautiful as your mother." Richard kissed her head. His strong arms firmly held her close. His soft hands caressed the top of her own. "He's a good man, Fiona."

"I know, Father. I'm truly blessed."

"And you're a fine woman. You'll be a good helpmate."

"Thank you."

Fiona waited for the music to shift. A sea of gasps and murmurs drifted through the open doors to the sanctuary. She smiled. Ian must have come out and stood proudly in the front of the small church.

Father chuckled under his breath.

The tempo of the music changed. A heavier tapping of the keys announced it was time.

Her father eased forward. "Ready?"

"Yes."

They reached the doorway. Fiona's eyes sought her love. He proudly stood in the front of the church. His eyes smiled. She glanced down to his dark shoes, then up the white knee socks which covered his muscular legs. His kilt, a delicate blend of plaids and stripes of mostly green and blue with a hint of red, hung on his hips and appeared very masculine. *Definitely masculine,* she mused.

The sporran hung in front, a decorative brown, oval-shaped leather, with a series of three feathers and a silver covering on top. *Goodness, he's handsome,* she thought. A white shirt with a tartan cloth draped over one shoulder finished off the Scottish outfit. He said he wore it for his clan, his heritage, but Fiona couldn't help but wonder if he wore it for her as well.

Her gaze stayed with his while her father led her to the front of the church. His rich mahogany hair crowned the wonderful gift the Lord gave her on this day. Her heart raced with excitement.

❦

Ian couldn't take his eyes off the vision of purity walking toward him, his bride, coming to join him at the altar. Today they would begin their journey as husband and wife.

He'd noticed she seemed pleased seeing him in his full Scottish attire. At the last moment he'd considered wearing the brown suit he'd purchased when he came to America. But his parents would never understand why he did not wear the customary costume of his people. It would be hard enough for them not to be at their son's wedding. But his letter should have reached them by now, so they knew he would be bringing home his bride for a short visit.

"Who gives this woman to be this man's bride?" asked the minister, dressed in a full black robe.

"I do on behalf of her mother and myself." Richard clasped Fiona's hand and brought it to Ian's.

Ian's pulse hammered. He focused on two things, Fiona and the pastor. Nothing else mattered.

He examined the delicate lace that lined her sleeves and bodice. She glowed with a radiant love for him and for her heavenly Father.

The service continued. He stumbled through. Her words were simple, so powerful, her commitment to him so undeniable.

"You may kiss the bride." The bearded smile of the pastor was only glimpsed. Instead, Ian focused on Fiona and her ruby red lips, relishing their sweetness.

The pounding in his ears stopped as he captured his bride and escorted her down the aisle.

"Fiona, ye're beautiful," Ian whispered as they entered the vestibule before the others.

"Thank you. You're rather handsome yourself. If I'd known how handsome you were in a kilt, I would have encouraged you to wear it ages ago."

Ian let out a deep barrel laugh. "Aye lass, 'tis a good thin' I waited then."

People soon gathered with hugs and handshakes, congratulating them. Fiona's brothers and several others teased Ian about his "skirt," but all in good humor.

"Fiona, I love ye with all me heart," Ian whispered and pressed a kiss gently upon her ear. She shivered from the nearness.

"I thanked the Lord so many times for you today, Ian, I've lost count." She placed her hand on his and he caressed it with his thumb.

"Aye, me love, I've been doin' the same."

"How long do we have to stay?" she asked.

"No longer than we must." Ian winked.

Their love for each other was a powerful force. God had done a wondrous thing in Fiona's heart. He'd used Ian, a man with a simple faith, to show her where she had been wrong in her life. To show her joy and love as God intended it for a man and a woman. And to show her the most important lesson of all. She was to be a light in much the same way as the reflector shields of the lighthouse lanterns, to show God's light, love, mercy, and peace, and that He was the only true shelter during the storms of life.

"What?" Ian asked.

"Oh, I was reflecting on God's patience with me—and yours." Fiona blushed.

"Aye lass, but when love waits, its union is sweeter an' brighter."

PHANTOM OF MY HEART

by DiAnn Mills

Chapter 1

Summer 1845
Massachusetts

Every heart tells a story, even the ones who've been wounded.
Lynette folded the letter and laid it on a small branch. She tucked a cluster of fresh daisies into the splintered limb and pushed it out to sea. With a smile, she blew a kiss to where her loved ones were cradled in the deep. The penned words were symbolic of her love, the mere act bringing her peace. She would not give in to despair. Her father had instilled courage in the midst of tragedy, and she refused to disappoint him.

The ocean waves of the Atlantic rolling against the shore lulled her, the gray waters offering life in one breath and death in the next. "Home," she whispered. How could she live her days as the sole inhabitant of the tiny two-acre island, but how could she ever leave?

The people on the mainland at Sippican Harbor searched for a lighthouse keeper. They needed a knowledgeable man to help those tossed by angry waves find their way safely ashore. But the stories of a female spirit haunting the tower and sightings of an apparition stopped any man from accepting the position. If she were assured of her skills to keep the lights burning, she'd take on the task herself. How admirable to be entrusted to such a noble cause. Surely not every man was afraid of that which was not real.

Whaley brushed against her skirts. "Yes, my prince. You're wanting to play, and I'm lost in my musings." She patted his huge head, and his sorrowful brown eyes searched her face. Many feared the beast of a dog, but he was more gentle than a kitten. And now he was her only companion.

Except for Amanda's phantom spirit.

Lynette looked behind her to the walkway leading to the stone cottage. The surroundings appeared foreign for want of love, but flowers were growing and soon the whole area would be immersed in beauty.

Whaley wagged his tail and barked. Oh, he was such a persistent friend.

She laughed. "Let's walk for awhile, then we'll play. Perhaps we'll have visitors by the evening." So many sought to see the female ghost of Bird Island Lighthouse who stood on the catwalk, casting her gaze to the sea. Yet how could Lynette ever be afraid of dear Amanda?

ॐ

McNair Hattchery had never believed in apparitions, and he refused to allow the threat of one to spoil an opportunity. He longed to experiment with whale oil that would not freeze and the countless other ideas that filled his journal about improving lighthouse conditions.

"I'm sincerely interested in accepting the position," McNair said to Jonathan Adams, the mayor.

Mayor Adams walked to the window of his office and looked out to the small island. "Splendid. You come to us with excellent credentials."

McNair joined him, immediately captivated by the lighthouse. An apparition was tomfoolery, no doubt the vision of an idle mind. What he needed was a place to work and forget the past. "I've committed my life to showing the sea-weary traveler to shore."

"A special calling, and this community is grateful." In the light, Mayor Adams's bald head gave him an ethereal glow.

"When can I take residence?"

"There's another problem." Mayor Adams scratched his whiskers. "The previous keeper had a family."

McNair nodded. "I understood all perished at sea. A dreadful accident."

"Yes, sir. But one of the daughters was not in the capsized boat. She lives in the cottage."

McNair paused while he considered the living conditions on Bird Island. How scandalous for a single woman to dwell on the island with him. "Surely she knows she must take residence here in town."

Mayor Adams smiled, but melancholy filled his face. "The young woman is a bit odd since the unfortunate incident. She refuses to leave and rarely talks to those who visit the island. I remember her once-lighthearted manner. Kind ways that befit her beauty. But the townspeople who once treasured her company have turned their backs on her." He sighed. "I'm concerned she might do away with herself."

Ah, he saw the mayor's gloom. "Does she have family here on the mainland? Or friends who would open their home to her?"

"None who are able, considering her delicate condition."

McNair frowned. "I see the problem. Her heart must be broken, possibly clinging to the hope her family will return."

"Her family passed on her eighteenth birthday."

"How did she learn about it?"

"When they didn't return, she rowed at night to inform me." Mayor Adams drew in a breath. "The next day the constable found the empty boat."

"How devastating."

"I remember her arrival that night all too clearly. She brought her beast of a dog with her. Guess that's all she had left."

McNair was not fond of animals, except horses. "Is the dog a tyrant?"

He chuckled. "His bark and size are enough to grind fear into any man's bones." The mayor's eyes watered. "I watched Lynette, Miss Brittmore, grow up into a fine young woman, and I am saddened at how this has affected her."

"How regrettable there's not a benevolent soul to help her."

Mayor Adams stiffened. "We desperately need a lighthouse keeper, but this situation makes it difficult."

McNair moistened his lips, an idea forming. "Is this not a Christian community?"

"A strong one, sir."

"Is there someone, perhaps an older woman or a couple, who could be a resident chaperone for the woman? How generous if a chaperone could provide solace in her time of grief. Then I could take residence in the home without damaging the woman's reputation. My nights would be in the lighthouse, and I'd sleep a good bit of the day."

Mayor Adams's eyes brightened. "Brilliant, Mr. Hattchery. I have a candidate in mind, but first I must consult with Miss Brittmore. She must be agreeable to the arrangement."

"Shall we visit her this day?"

"We can leave within the hour."

McNair shook the mayor's hand while warmth swirled in his belly. He had no time for a woman, especially one who was weak with grief. Neither did he want to cause her any more sorrow.

Chapter 2

Lynette laid an armful of wood beside the cookstove and noted the diminishing stack. The mainland folks were good about bringing firewood, even when she was too deep in her thoughts to thank them. They also brought drinking water. The house was stocked with provisions, and she had a cow and a few chickens. But eating alone was another matter.

"Whaley, I need to move past what happened and find a way to be myself again."

The animal perked his ears.

"Yes, you heard me. I'm not ready to leave here, and I must plan for the future. I will not disgrace what Mama and Papa taught me, to carry on despite misfortune." She sighed. From the concerned looks Uncle Jonathan had given her during his last visit, she suspected the rumors were true. . . . Her mind was not as it should be.

Lynette bent to the dog and lifted his mammoth face. "I'm not mad— do you understand me? I simply prefer your company to those who ask questions and insist upon a response."

She didn't expect an answer, which suited her just fine. Before the afternoon melted into sunset, she wanted to check on the lettuce, onions, and radishes pushing through the soil. The cow needed milking, and eggs had not been gathered. Later on, she'd force herself to eat dinner, and God willing, she'd keep it in her stomach instead of poured out on the ground as a bitter offering to her grief. Then she and Whaley would pick their way along the rocky shore, and perhaps the walk would tire her. Too many nights, sleep had evaded her. Such was her life. She'd gotten into a dull routine when her life used to be full. Very little about these long days and nights resembled the past.

Stepping into the warm sunlight, she shielded her eyes beneath her bonnet to catch a glimpse of the black-capped seabirds. She envied their freedom to fly wherever they chose. How they seemingly cared for each other. An idea sailed into her mind. She hurried back inside and retrieved a precious sheet of paper and pen and ink.

Again seated outside, Lynette noted Whaley looking at her curiously. She patted his side. "Not another letter so soon. I'm going to make a list of how I'm going to survive. What I must do now that I'm alone." She studied the seabirds again. "I am free. Free in the Lord to walk this earth as long as He sees fit."

She walked to the shore and found a smooth rock to sit on. Tucking her skirts beneath her, she dipped her pen into the inkwell.

By the grace of God, I will:
1. Be faithful to Scripture reading and prayers.
2. Eat regularly, although my stomach twists and turns.
    Mourning doesn't mean starving myself. My life is God's.

She stared across the rippling water, and for a moment she was mesmerized by the lifting waves. The sun sparkled like jewels, a sight she likened to heaven's portals. If anything good had come from two months of intense sorrow, it was her closeness to God. Before the accident, she'd simply gone through the motions of prayer and Scripture reading, a habit often filled with regret. But her relationship with God had changed, and now she found His presence comforting. Lynette smiled. She lifted her eyes to the billowy clouds. Mama and Papa were pleased.

Turning her attention to her task, she wrote number three:

3. Find a way to provide for myself. I am a fair cook, and I could make a living cooking for others.
4. Move to the mainland in four months. By then I'll be able to handle the loss and be myself again. If not, I shall perish or be locked away.

5. Continue to write letters to Amanda, Mama, and Papa, and send their missives off to sea. Sharing my thoughts is almost like they are here.

Realization swept over her like a sudden chill. She could never love again. The agony of losing what she treasured most had nearly taken her own life. At times she'd wanted to walk into the waters and join her family.

 But not with George.

6. Find a way to discover how my family died.

Lynette had only six things to accomplish before winter set in. Papa always said a plan bathed in prayer was blessed. But none of the items on her list considered a new lighthouse keeper, and the sailors desperately needed a beacon to guide them safely. Lynette swallowed hard. Whether a single man or a family moved to the island, she'd be forced to leave her home.

At one time she wanted to help George keep the lanterns burning, since Papa could no longer climb the tower to teach her. But her desire to learn was before he and Amanda were married, and her sister was concerned George might seek Lynette's affections. So Lynette abandoned the idea. Soon after George and Amanda had married, he changed from a gentleman to an evil-tempered brute.

For a moment, the memories of how he'd abused Amanda and then Papa and Mama made her physically ill. George's behavior toward Lynette was deplorable, too. . . . Had he really meant well the day he asked for her parents to join him and Amanda on a boat ride while Lynette prepared dinner for them? The truth lay at the bottom of the sea.

Oh, Amanda, I'm so sorry. Why didn't I seek out Constable Smythe instead of Uncle Jonathan? Is it really you the mainlanders see? Or is it the killer?

Whaley's roar of a bark snatched her attention. A small boat eased toward shore, the oars rhythmically pushing aside the waves. Ah, Uncle Jonathan was coming for a visit. She'd put on the kettle for tea and surprise him with her resolve. Perhaps a bit of conversation would show him that her health was mending.

Lynette drew in a breath. Someone joined him. Could it be a candidate for a lighthouse keeper? Selfishness rushed over her, although she despised her feelings.

Not yet. Please.

Chapter 3

McNair studied the small island that held the lighthouse. His chest swelled at the thought of being one of the chosen few guardians of the American shores. He longed to explore every inch of the stone structure.

"I see the excitement in your face," Mayor Adams said.

"'Tis true. I love the sea, but more so I embrace the calling of helping ships find their way."

"We're proud of our lighthouse. It's withstood many a perilous storm. Recent renovations have made it sturdy. However, the cistern needs repair. Until that's completed, I'll bring water from the mainland."

"My father was a seaman, lost in violent wind that capsized his ship."

"I'm sorry. Are you married? The life of a lighthouse keeper can be lonely."

McNair shook his head. "No wife for me. I'm married to the sea." He laughed at his own childish prose.

The Bird Island Lighthouse rose majestically as though challenging the fog, storm, or perilous waters. If only. . . He stood in the boat.

"Mr. Hattchery." The alarm in the mayor's voice caused McNair to chuckle.

"I'm aware of my size," McNair said. "I grew up on the coast of Maine, and I can do the minuet on your boat."

Mayor Adams coughed. "Please, sit, sir. I'm a poor swimmer."

"But I'm not. Do you want to see me?" He poised one foot over the boat.

"Sir!" The mayor's eyes widened, the oars stiff in his hands.

"What about diving for fish? I did that as a boy. Still do on occasion."

"If you lose your bearings and drown, I'd feel responsible."

McNair resumed his sitting position and laughed until his sides ached. Despite the situation awaiting him with Miss Brittmore, the thrill of attaining a dream had made him ridiculously happy. "I'm sorry, my good man, but I grew up with six sisters—three older and three younger. Teasing is how I survived."

The color in Mayor Adams's face slowly returned, and the oars dipped into the water. "I'm wondering how you and Lynette will get along."

"Why? I certainly wouldn't want my teasing to run her off." Well, maybe that wouldn't be a bad idea, since it had worked with some of his sisters.

"Quite the contrary." The mayor lifted his chin. "She has a propensity to be rather mischievous."

Interesting.

"I'm afraid her carefree ways were before the tragedy."

McNair watched the lighthouse and cottage grow larger. A slender woman waved.

"Praise God. Miss Lynette hasn't greeted me for weeks."

Was that a monster or a dog beside her? McNair sensed his stomach rising to his throat. The animal stood nearly as tall as she, and his barks sounded like a bear. Indeed an animal to be revered. McNair shivered and longed for Providence's care.

Miss Brittmore wore her hair down, flowing in walnut-colored waves. As the boat neared, her smile warmed him, both an agitation and a welcome.

A once-lighthearted woman with a beast of a dog? Certainly not what he'd anticipated for his new position. Not this creature who appeared part whimsical and part haunting. The young woman with pale skin and blue eyes that rivaled the ocean and sky rendered him speechless.

He refused to have his fate altered by a woman.

❧

Lynette's lips quivered, yet she envisioned her father encouraging her to be brave. Indeed, her heavenly Father promised His helping hand, and she gratefully clung to it.

"I can do this," she whispered to Whaley. When the dog rushed toward the boat, challenging the two men inside, she called him back. "Sit at my feet," she said. Whaley could be ferocious when he thought she was in danger.

"Good afternoon, Uncle Jonathan," she said. "What a pleasant surprise."

His smile spread over hollowed cheeks, and his kindly eyes twinkled. "Good afternoon to you. My, you are a feast for this man's eyes. I see my child is on her way to good health."

"I'm no longer a child, Uncle Jonathan." Lynette added affection to her childhood name for him, a dear friend of the family. "But I appreciate the concern you've shown during the past two months."

Mayor Adams took her hand in his. "I would have done even more if I had known how to put color into your face."

"I will keep the rosiness just for you. I promise." She turned to the man beside him, a robust fellow. "You've brought a guest."

Uncle Jonathan gestured to the man beside him. "Miss Lynette Brittmore, I'd like to introduce Mr. McNair Hattchery."

She gazed into eyes that were warm as maple syrup. He lifted his hat and revealed thick hair the same color. He trembled, which surprised her. Ah, Whaley had shaken him to the core.

"I'm pleased to meet you, Mr. Hattchery," she said. "I seldom bite, but sometimes my dog does." She took his damp hand and laughed, her first expression of happiness in weeks.

He held onto her hand a little longer than necessary. "That's excellent information, Miss Brittmore," he said. "Does your dog—"

"Whaley. I named him because of his size."

He released her hand. "It suits him. I was wondering if he climbs the lighthouse steps."

She patted Whaley's head. "He's quite agile, sir. He chased away the last gentleman who sought to be a lighthouse keeper. Is that your intention?" She purposely widened her eyes. He was easy to tease. What had gotten into her? Maybe she had gone mad. The lighthouse needed a proper keeper.

Mr. Hattchery swallowed hard. "I plan to accept Mayor Adams's generous offer."

Fire burned in the pit of her stomach. Her mirth and a glimpse of her old self faded. She swung her attention to Uncle Jonathan. He must have seen her panic, for he touched her arm.

"You don't have to move from the island," Uncle Jonathan said, his tone gentle. "Mr. Hattchery has a marvelous idea, and we want to share it with you."

Lynette shook off the trepidation. She'd listen and pray. "I have the kettle on for tea."

"Splendid." Uncle Jonathan held out his arm for her to link into his, and she allowed him to escort her.

Lynette would not let Mr. Hattchery see her upset when she'd been rude to him moments before. Obviously he'd made a decision that affected her future.

She didn't like him.

She didn't trust him.

Chapter 4

After enjoying a hot cup of tea and feeling thoroughly invigorated, McNair excused himself while Mayor Adams explained the proposed chaperone arrangement to Miss Brittmore. The mayor had an older woman in mind, a godly woman who was highly respected.

Surely Miss Brittmore would agree to the arrangement in order to keep her home. He was amazed she wanted to live alone when those her own age lived across the harbor. But grief could be a formidable enemy.

A young woman of Miss Brittmore's rare beauty would be a treasure to a man seeking a wife. Never had he seen eyes so blue that the sky had to take a step back. But marriage was not in his life plan. An impossibility. He needed to separate himself from her. She had a peculiar effect on him, probably compassion for her plight.

McNair stood outside the cottage in the afternoon warmth and gazed up at the thirty-one-foot tower. Excitement tickled his belly. With quick strides, he walked across the covered walkway to the lighthouse's entrance. Like a child at Christmas, he longed to see his own ship of sorts. He'd stay here this evening if propriety allowed, but he must be content in knowing Mayor Adams had his best interests and Miss Brittmore's at heart.

Inside the narrow circular stairwell, he climbed until he thought his breath might escape him. When he reached the top, he inspected the lantern, fueled by whale oil. It offered a light that focused on a mirror-like dish, sending a beam out to sea.

On the catwalk, the stunning sight confirmed the climb was worth the ache in his side. Nothing could be more exquisite than the blending of earth and heaven into one glorious view. He yearned for this postion and prayed the situation with Miss Brittmore proved satisfactory.

He took a downward glimpse at his middle, and embarrassment convicted him of his sad physical condition. How shameful that he'd allowed his personal appearance to hinder his calling. But that's what happened when a grown man lived with his mother. He'd studied during the day while his mother practiced her sole purpose in life—cooking for him day and night. And he'd begun to wear her calling.

With this climb, he'd soon be fit again—

A bark, more like a roar, startled him. McNair whirled to Whaley who loomed in the doorway. Perhaps the animal was the apparition.

"Hey, big fellow. I'm a friend." He hoped his words convinced the dog to leave him alone.

Whaley took a step closer, his growl more menacing than a thunderstorm.

McNair looked for something to defend himself. But nothing availed itself to him that wasn't intact. He'd been warned far too many times that an animal sensed a human's fear. Whaley voiced his displeasure again. The size of the dog's teeth would shake the devil.

Dare he swallow his pride and seek assistance?

"Help." His call seemed pitifully weak. Oh, that Miss Brittmore heard him before he became the creature's dinner. Although he'd just bemoaned his size, this was not how he envisioned reducing it.

He cleared his throat. "I'm in the tower with the dog, and he's not pleased." That had more of an authoritative ring to it.

He waited for the young woman or Mayor Adams to respond.

"Miss Brittmore, your dog needs attention. We're in the tower." He recalled her teasing and could only imagine what she'd say with his predicament. He'd taken great pleasure in tormenting his sisters, but he didn't enjoy being the recipient.

The dog stepped closer. What had he done to offend the beast? "Miss Brittmore? Mayor Adams?"

A steady clip on the steps indicated deliverance was at hand.

"Whaley?" Miss Brittmore said in the doorway of the tower. "Are you tormenting our guest?"

The dog didn't budge, but he no longer growled.

Her lithe frame gave her a fairy-like appeal. She glared at her beast. "Down," she said to the animal. "I'm ashamed of your behavior."

Without hesitation, Whaley descended the steps.

"Thank you." McNair tugged on his jacket. His pulse had yet to return to normal. "Your dog has taken a dislike to me."

She shook her head. "I'm sorry. It's not you. He's been protective since Papa gave him to me. More so since I've been alone."

"I see." Perhaps she'd discourage the dog to climb the tower's steps.

"I'll make sure he doesn't bother you in the future."

McNair's eyes brightened. Dare he believe? "You and Mayor Adams have come to an agreement?"

"We have." She lifted her chin. "He plans to talk to the potential chaperone before the day passes."

Relief calmed him. "I'm pleased."

She pressed her lips together. "I suggested that he row back to the mainland to tend to the arrangement. If you'd like to stay longer to acquaint yourself with the lighthouse, you can use my boat. You'll need it to bring your things upon your return."

"How kind of you." Yet he didn't think her hospitality was heartfelt.

"The dinner hour is approaching, and you're welcome to join me. A simple meal, if that is suitable. I'd planned to have eggs, cheese, and bread. Whaley will be subdued, I assure you." A mischievous sparkle touched her eyes. "Once he makes friends, you'll find him an enjoyable companion."

"Oh, I shall be much too busy to enjoy a pet."

She laughed. "Sir, pardon my glee at your expense. I can tell you're frightened of my sweet dog."

"Merely cautious."

"Let me make up for your discomfort. Will you join us this evening?"

How perfect. Maybe he'd misjudged her. Having dinner was more than he'd wished for. Without the dog. "I would be delighted, and I shall be gone by nightfall."

She tilted her head, a delightful pose and most fetching. "Have you been warned of the apparition?" she said.

"It's nonsense."

"Some of the mainlanders are convinced otherwise."

"And who do you believe it could be?"

"My older sister Amanda." She drew in a breath. "I think."

"Why so, instead of your parents?"

"Those who claim to have seen it believe my sister's spirit is grieving her life. I, on the other hand, believe her sorrow lies in her demise."

He hadn't heard that part of the story. "Surely her spirit is with God."

"She was Christian I assure you." What did her vagueness mean?

"Then you've noted the mysterious ghost?"

She smiled. "A troubled mind can have manifestations."

"What have you seen?" Curiosity prodded him. "Tell me, so I will understand."

"Mr. Hattchery, if you have a chance encounter, we can discuss what evil shrouds the island." With those words, she nodded her dismissal and left the tower.

Evil? Whatever did she mean? A nudging in his spirit left him flabbergasted. Had he been too eager to claim the title of lighthouse keeper?

Chapter 5

Lynette spooned eggs floating in butter, dotted with pepper and a pinch of salt, onto Mr. Hattchery's plate. She added thick slices of ham, tender potatoes, and buttered bread baked yesterday. Fresh blueberries and cream would top the meal. She wanted to show him hospitality by making the meal special.

Being alone with the new lighthouse keeper made her nervous, but Uncle Jonathan trusted him, said he had excellent credentials.

Mr. Hattchery sat opposite her at the table, the table that held many delightful memories of her family. She handed him his plate of food.

"Thank you for your graciousness," he said. "I'm most beholding."

"It's been a while since I prepared food for someone other than myself. It's not enjoyable to cook for one. But that will change with you and our chaperone living here." She took a deep breath, amazed she could hold an intelligent conversation without weeping or losing her thoughts.

"My mother is a fine cook." He gestured at his middle. "As you can see. I think a few weeks of climbing the tower will put me back to my former size." He smiled. "However, with meals as fine as this one, my plan may take longer."

She met his smile, and in the fading light, his kindly face calmed her. "Would you ask the Lord's blessing upon our meal and our time together?"

He did so and appeared at ease, even with Whaley on the floor near him. Mr. Hattchery stuck his fork into the potatoes. A few minutes later, he sighed. "Not since my mother have I tasted such an excellent meal."

"Good to know I haven't lost my gift for cooking."

They finished in silence, but she noted a few times he started to say something then obviously changed his mind. "I haven't teased you since our first moments when you arrived," she said.

"The incident in the tower provided you with much fodder. And Mayor Adams warned me of your wit."

She covered her mouth to stifle a laugh. "You were fast becoming a fixture with the lenses."

"Your rescue was rather humbling." He glanced at her, and reassurance from the Divine told her she had nothing to fear.

"In your defense, Whaley is a large dog."

"I appreciate your not revealing my embarrassment to the mayor."

She tilted her head. "Why do you want my lighthouse, or should I say this lighthouse?"

He dabbed his mouth with a napkin. "My father, gone now ten years, loved the sea and he passed that admiration on to me. Rather than be a seaman and break my mother's heart, I chose to be a lighthouse keeper."

"Even then, the sea can be dangerous. Papa spoke of a few poorly constructed lighthouses that fell prey to an angry sea."

"I agree." He leaned forward. "I want to make a difference, Miss Brittmore. I want to discover new and better methods for sailors to find the shore. One goal is to find whale oil that won't freeze in the winter."

"Admirable, sir."

He shrugged. "I'd like to see if the light can be brighter or seen farther away. I've followed the work of a Frenchman, a physicist by the name of Augustin Fresnel, who has developed glass prisms and lenses which would be valuable in showing sailors the hazards for their vessels."

"My father would have loved to hear about Mr. Fresnel's work," she said. "I pray you're successful in your endeavors."

He resumed eating. Oddly enough, Whaley moved to sit at his feet.

"Shall I have him removed?" she said. "He's already eaten, so I doubt if your leg would appeal to him."

He chuckled then slowly patted Whaley's head. "I think we're fine. Aren't we, sir? Has he always had a dislike for others?"

Lynette barely knew Mr. Hattchery, and explaining the nightmarish circumstances surrounding her family's disappearance was impossible. How could she tell him Whaley had warned her. . .warned them all by never making friends with George?

"Whaley is my dog, but he was also the family pet. However, he seems to have premonitions."

He studied the dog. "He does have an interesting face—when he isn't barking or growling. You think he knew your family's end was coming?"

Her heart ached. "Possibly so."

﹏

McNair pulled Miss Brittmore's boat close to the shore of the mainland and secured it. His thoughts stayed fixed on the enigma of a young woman. He'd left her behind on the island, but he felt as though she'd shared the boat with him. Miss Brittmore. . .strangely alluring, not as a man views a woman but as a man who's intrigued by a woman's mind.

Before night set, he'd visit with Mayor Adams and learn of the man's progress since the afternoon.

The mayor strode in front of his cottage smoking a pipe when McNair arrived. "I've been expecting you," he said. "And I have good news."

McNair shook his hand and followed Mayor Adams inside where he was introduced to his wife, Wilda, a straw-thin woman with a pursed mouth. "Would you like bread and tea?" she said.

"Only tea, thank you. Miss Brittmore prepared an excellent meal."

"I'm sure she did." The woman didn't smile.

"She's a quite capable cook," Mayor Adams said. "My wife and I have enjoyed many a fine meal on the island."

"Lest I remind you that was before the untimely deaths of her family," his wife said.

Once seated and sipping tea, McNair caught Mayor Adams's attention. "Your news? I'm most anxious."

"A woman from our church, a saintly widow by the name of Mrs. Creed, has consented to move to the island. She can do so tomorrow. The cottage's three bedrooms are small, but I believe the arrangement will work nicely."

"Mr. Hattchery, what of the apparition?" Wilda Adams said. "Are you not fearful?"

"Tsk." Mayor Adams frowned. "'Tis but a rumor. Miss Lynette has not spoken of it, and she would inform me."

"Husband," Mrs. Adams said. "Miss Lynette is a peculiar one, and

Mr. Hattchery needs to be aware of the repercussions of associating with her."

McNair raised a brow. "I found her congenial, and I enjoyed her wit."

"She's been called a witch."

"Wilda!" the mayor said. "I forbid such talk."

"Then why is her sister seen walking the shore? Miss Amanda must know the accident was due to foul play. Miss Lynette wanted her husband."

"Enough." Mayor Adams's voice was barely above a whisper. "I despise gossip, and the dear girl had nothing to do with the deaths of her family. Neither did she have any interest in George Zimmerman."

"You'd believe anything she said."

"I would, and I do." The mayor's voice rose. "Lynette walks the shore because of her grief. Not Amanda."

"Then we'll see how long Mr. Hattchery survives."

A knot formed in McNair's throat. He despised witnessing the couple's confrontation. "I appreciate your concern, ma'am. But I don't believe in anything I can't see or touch, except faith in our Lord. If I detect a problem, I'll act upon it."

Mrs. Adams huffed. "When you and Mrs. Creed no longer walk among the living, then you'll know my words were true."

He'd barely met Miss Brittmore, but he liked her mannerisms. He'd always prided himself as a good judge of character and had no reason to doubt his intuition now. For certain, one of his duties over the next several weeks was to restore the young woman's honor.

Too bad Whaley couldn't speak.

Chapter 6

Lynette watched Mrs. Creed embroider a tea cloth. The white-haired woman hunched over her work, rarely speaking. Her language was in her artful creations.

Three weeks had passed since the arrangement began, and it was working well with Mrs. Creed as a proper chaperone for her and Mr. Hattchery. He tended to the lighthouse while Mrs. Creed labored over her stitching. The older woman was good company, and when she did choose to converse, pure wisdom poured from her lips. The lines in her face reminded Lynette of victory over tragedy, and Mrs. Creed had lived through many tragedies. Her husband had died unexpectedly of a heart ailment, and her three sons had journeyed west, never to be heard from again.

This evening, darkness had settled on the tiny island and dinner long since cleared. McNair was in the tower with Whaley, and Mrs. Creed continued to stitch by candlelight. But Lynette paced the floor of the cottage.

"Do you need to talk, child?" Mrs. Creed set her work aside. "I'm here for you."

What a sweet woman. "I'm fine. Simply restless."

"Is Mr. Hattchery in your thoughts?" Even in the faint light, her eyes twinkled.

"Mercy, no." How odd. "Do you think I'm displeased with his presence here?"

"Quite the opposite."

Lynette frowned, not sure what Mrs. Creed meant. "I'm confused."

She sighed. "You will see soon enough."

Rather than question the woman further, Lynette gathered up her writing material. "I'm going for a walk."

"Ah, the physical exertion might help you sleep better."

"How did you know that I have problems sleeping?"

"I hear you pacing your room, and sometimes you leave the cottage. During those times I pray for your peace of mind."

Lynette hugged the frail woman. "You're a blessing. Thank you."

"Grief can be a friend or foe," she said.

"How so? Losing my family pains me. Sometimes I'm physically ill."

"Memories are healing. You remember the good times, cry, and sometimes laugh. But when you dwell on them and make yourself ill, then you're not honoring God."

Lynette startled. "How am I not honoring God?"

"When you fail to accept that God called your family home, then you're disrespectful of His sovereignty."

Lynette hadn't considered her grief as sinful, but perhaps she had been. "I'm trying to understand why they're gone."

"My child, God expects you to miss your family, and He knows you need to shed tears. But don't let their absence send you to an early grave. Dwell on those treasured moments and find the blessings of healing."

She didn't think she could try much harder. "I've been leaning on God since it happened." She took a deep breath. "But I will concentrate on my relationship with Him." She gave the woman a kiss on the cheek. Tonight's letter to her family would be a little different than she had originally intended. Not that she planned to write them forever, but until she came to terms with their deaths, it seemed like the right thing to do.

Outside, seated on her favorite rock and the lantern by her side, she began. . . .

Dear Papa, Mama, and Amanda,

I'm trying not to be angry with God for taking you away from me. Some days are easier than others, but I'm doing much better. I wanted you to know about the new people in my life. Mrs. Creed is staying here because Uncle Jonathan has hired a lighthouse keeper.

His name is Mr. Hattchery. He's a single man, and so Mrs. Creed is my chaperone. I'm enjoying her company, and her wisdom.

I'm cooking again, which I love. Mr. Hattchery loves to eat, and he's also fun to tease. I'm being respectful, and I do enjoy his company. Whaley has warmed up to him, and they've become friends.

I feel safe. God is with me.

Your loving daughter,
Lynette

McNair watched Miss Brittmore labor over something near the shore, either reading or writing. By the lantern light, her small frame gave her an angelic appeal. Oh, he'd compared her to many beautiful creatures.

She was such a kindly woman. . .gentle, a loving spirit, beautiful, kept his clothes clean and in good repair, and a grand cook. In fact he should tell her how much he appreciated her friendship and all she did for him. Since the moment they'd met, she'd not once spoken a harsh word.

He chuckled. She did have an impish glint in her eyes whenever she planned to tease him a bit. No harm done. He rather enjoyed it, and her wit kept him on his toes.

No signs of an apparition had appeared. Utter nonsense. Evil didn't exist on this small paradise.

McNair looked at Whaley, who'd become a good companion. "Come along, chap. Let's see what Miss Brittmore is doing. We won't take much of her time. Then back to work."

Good heavens. He was conversing with a dog.

The two made their way down the winding staircase with Whaley in the lead. How his life had changed, and he loved every minute of it. Dear Mrs. Creed and of course Lynette. Dare he refer to her by her given name in his thoughts?

In the darkness, all he could see was the young woman. . . . Had he gone daft, or was this stirring in his spirit the beginnings of something he'd never thought possible? He couldn't let his heart fall prey to the charms of an honorable young woman.

Lynette glanced over her shoulder. "Mr. Hattchery." She started to stand, but he stopped her.

"Please, you look so comfortable. May I join you for a moment?"

He saw the paper and inkwell. "Excuse me. I'm interrupting your correspondence."

"I'm finished." She patted a rock beside her. "I relish sitting here at the end of the day, listening to the waves slap against the shore."

"Like a lullaby." He took a place beside her and found her closeness unnerving. Grasping his senses, he pointed to her letter. "Would you like me to post this for you? I'm headed to the mainland in the morning."

"I think not. I have my own way of posting it."

Was a boat expected on the morrow?

She folded the letter into a child-size boat. "Sir, this is a missive to my parents and my sister. I write them on occasion to. . .tell them I miss them. It soothes me." She sighed. "But this letter tells them about Mrs. Creed and you. And that I'm doing better." She walked to the water's edge and sent the missive on its way. "I pray God tells them the contents."

How lonely her life must have been before he and Mrs. Creed arrived. "I'm sure it has helped to send your feelings to them."

She stared out across the dark waters. "Do you think I'm touched for doing so?"

"Absolutely not. I find your method of healing commendable." Perhaps he should consider it for his own grief.

"Some people on the mainland believe I've lost my sanity. Uncle Jonathan's wife included."

He reserved his thoughts of Wilda Adams. "Rubbish, Miss Brittmore. I don't listen to gossip. And you're certainly sane. Intelligent, too."

"Thank you."

"The reason I joined you was to express my appreciation for all you've done since my arrival."

"You and Mrs. Creed have given me purpose." Her gaze focused above him, and she touched her heart. "Mr. Hattchery, who is in the lighthouse?"

His attention flew to the tower. Standing on the walkway was a man holding a lantern, his frame silhouetted by the lighthouse's flame.

"I used to think it was Amanda," she whispered. "Whatever it is, 'tis evil. Don't you feel it?"

Indeed he did. He shivered from his head to his toes. "Shall I investigate with Whaley?"

"No, sir. I fear something might happen to you like Mama, Papa, and Amanda."

"What of your brother-in-law?"

"I fear he is who we see."

Chapter 7

Lynette studied the apparition, the familiar stance. . .the way he leaned onto his left hip, the tilt of his head. In the past, she hadn't seen the figure clearly enough to note if it were a man or a woman, wanting to believe Amanda had risen from the depths of the sea. Now she knew the ghost to be George. Only his sinister ways could produce the fear coursing through her soul. Only George, who'd once said he wished they all were dead, could manifest himself as Satan.

"I'm afraid," she said. "George is a killer. I feel it in my soul."

"Tell me about this fellow." Mr. Hattchery joined her at the water's edge. "No need to convince me of your fear. I see you're trembling."

Could she trust this man?

"I'm foremost your friend, Miss Brittmore. Aye, before being a lighthouse keeper." Sincerity breathed into his every word.

"When George first came to the lighthouse, he was charming. Polite. Uncle Jonathan said he had excellent recommendations, but no lighthouse experience. Papa's health had deteriorated, and he could no longer climb the tower steps, but he could teach. We were going to stay only until George had learned from Papa's years of tending lighthouses."

"But George was here two years."

Lynette nodded. "He said he didn't trust himself alone with the lighthouse, a statement I've often questioned because he grew to despise us. In the beginning, he favored me, but I wasn't interested." She remembered George's anger when she refused his advances. "Then he sought Amanda's affections. My sweet sister was smitten." She hesitated. How much dare she tell? Certainly not all. "He still wanted my affections while he courted her." She held her breath. . . . Oh the memories. "A short while later, he asked Papa for Amanda's hand. He also requested we stay on longer so he and Amanda could have family close by."

"The arrangement should have made him a happy man."

Lynette recalled the times he'd found her alone. . . . His hot breath tasting of spirits. "He changed, Mr. Hattchery. His temper worsened, like a demon possessed him. My dear sister suffered the most."

"You don't have to tell me more if it pains you."

"I need to tell someone. I confided in Uncle Jonathan's wife, but she turned against me. I think because George was kind to her." Lynette swiped at the wetness beneath her eyes. Enough tears had been shed for something that could not be changed. "He hit Amanda. Papa tried to talk to him, but to no avail. I went to Uncle Jonathan, and he spoke to George, too. But the abuse continued until the day of my birthday."

"What happened then?"

"George apologized for all he'd said and done. He wanted things to be different and for Papa to give him another chance. He asked to take my parents on the boat while I prepared dinner. He and Amanda had a surprise for them."

"I'm sorry." He pointed to the tower. "I'm going up there and facing whoever it is."

Lynette touched his arm. "Please. Don't. You could be hurt."

"I'm not a coward, Miss Brittmore."

"Take Whaley with you. George is afraid of him." She drew in a breath. "My dog can be fierce."

"Very well. Come along, Whaley," he said. "You and I have business with the man in our tower."

She tried to laugh, as though they discussed a game, but a knot in her stomach stopped her. "Is your rifle up there?"

"It is. But if he is a true apparition, a firearm would not protect me or rid this island of the evil."

"Then I'm going with you."

"I think not." His authoritative voice surprised her. "I protect sailors, and I protect you. Like Whaley."

"But I could talk to George. Perhaps convince him to leave."

"From what little I know of apparitions or your brother-in-law, there is no talking sense to either of them." He tipped his hat. "Perhaps you should see to Mrs. Creed and wait for us."

"Mr. Hattchery!"

He chuckled. "Oh, the lady is upset with me. For once I have the last laugh."

But she was not amused, not with her heart aching in fear. "Would you like the lantern?"

"No thank you. I like the element of surprise."

❧

McNair had voiced more courage than he truly felt. But Lynette's story of how the previous lighthouse keeper had treated her family made him furious. What kind of man threatened others who were powerless? The tremor in Lynette's words told him more had happened, but McNair would not pry. He could only imagine the depravity of the fellow.

Whoever or whatever walked the tower had no right to be there, and McNair intended to tell him so. Obviously a ghostly character wouldn't be mentioned in his next report. But apprehending a trespasser might be appropriate.

Upon reaching the lighthouse, he considered walking softly or stomping up the steps. Ah, he'd tread quietly to catch the man. But there was only one way down, no matter how McNair ascended.

Each winding set brought him and Whaley closer to the top. The rapid beat of his heart had nothing to do with the climb. Whaley brushed against his legs behind him. Surely if the animal sensed George was at the top, he'd bark.

As if the dog had read his mind, he bounded past McNair and on to the top. Whaley's deep-throated growl echoed in the tower. The ferocious dog could hold the man down while McNair secured rope to tie him. . . and demand an explanation before hauling him to Mayor Adams. As a hero, McNair would insist Wilda Adams apologize to Lynette.

McNair hurried after Whaley. Caution seized him. Had he given any thought to how he'd defend himself against a hostile intruder? What a fool. The man could use McNair's rifle against him.

Did guidelines exist on how to overcome an apparition?

The light from the lenses lit the doorway. McNair clung to the wall then peered around the opening. Whaley stood near the entrance to the outside walkway where the man had appeared. The animal no longer growled. Simply paced.

Where had the intruder gone? McNair had seen him holding a lantern and gazing out to the sea. He walked to the spot where the man had stood. Diving into the water below invited a sure death. Yet how had the man vanished?

He inhaled. . . . Nothing but the sea air filled his nostrils. His eyes had not deceived him—a man had stood here.

Bewilderment stomped across McNair's mind. If Lynette hadn't detected a splash, then indeed, the two had seen an apparition.

Chapter 8

Lynette held her breath while she waited for Mr. Hattchery to report on who was at the top of the lighthouse.

Oh, Lord, keep him safe.

The sound of Mr. Hattchery's footsteps, the rhythm she'd come to recognize, graced her ears. A few moments later, he leaned against the door frame. The lantern from inside the cottage touched upon his features, and they were pale.

"What did you find?" she said.

"Nothing." He met her gaze. "Did you hear someone dive?"

"No, sir."

"What are you two talking about?" Mrs. Creed said. "Surely you haven't seen the apparition."

"Mrs. Creed, I can't believe it myself." Mr. Hattchery straightened. "Miss Brittmore and I saw a man at the top of the tower with a lantern. When I investigated, he was gone."

Mrs. Creed lay her needlework in the basket at her feet. "We shall discuss this rationally, for those on the mainland will declare us daft or claim the island is of the devil."

"Yes, ma'am," he said. "I have never believed in such nonsense, and I will get to the end of the matter." He paced the cottage floor. "All those involved need the matter finished." He nodded at Lynette. "You, Miss Brittmore, deserve answers to your family's untimely deaths."

"I agree," she said, her whole body feeling the warmth of his friendship. "It has become my life's quest. But how?"

"Prayer," Mrs. Creed said. "I shall be the white-haired warrior to accomplish it."

Lynette studied the two good people coming to her aid. She'd done nothing to deserve their kindness, and yet they were reacting as though the problem was their own. "I've been seeking God on the matter since their disappearance, since I first saw the figure."

"In the same place?" he said.

"Once near the shore by the clump of trees. Other times along the rocky shore. But always at night."

McNair grabbed a chair. "If we are to conspire against this thing, then we must have rules. You two handle the prayer, and I will force the man's hand."

"How can you?" Lynette said, her ire rising that she'd be isolated from the task.

"By keeping a continuous vigil day and night. I don't require much sleep."

"Mr. Hattchery," Lynette began, "I insist upon helping. I vowed long before you set foot on this island to learn the truth."

"Prayer only or I will use force."

She laughed at how ludicrous he sounded. "How so? Tie me up? Who will cook for you? Wash your clothes? Maybe you need to find an apparition to take care of those things." She pointed a finger at his chest. "You need me, sir. But I don't need you."

His face reddened, and immediately she regretted her harsh words. But not enough to apologize.

"You have no idea how difficult I can be," Lynette said.

"I'm learning."

Mrs. Creed stood. "I believe the two of you have met your match. Both of you are stubborn as mules."

Lynette reached for her shawl. "I'm going for a walk."

"Not without me." He clenched his fist. "I have things to say, and you will listen."

"I won't be talking to you."

"For once, I'm a blessed man."

ᏋᏨ

McNair had been furious a few times with his six sisters, and he'd always known how to manage them by making them think his bidding was their idea. But Lynette Brittmore tested his patience.

"Since your apology has been chained and the key tossed into the sea, I shall do it for you." He laughed to keep the anger from his voice. "I'd like to get formalities out of the way so we can discuss George Zimmerman. 'Mr. Hattchery, I do apologize for my rudeness. I know you have my best interests at heart.'" He stole a glance, but she paid him no mind. "Thank you, Miss Brittmore. Your apology is accepted."

Still she said nothing. What a strong-willed woman.

"Seriously. This fellow sounds like a dangerous man. If he is the same one, then we should inform Mayor Adams. In fact, I shall do that very thing."

"No!"

"You are able to talk." He smiled. Now he could add one more reason he remained a single man.

"You are infuriating."

"And in this matter, I'm right."

"Don't flatter yourself. I will be involved."

He could work around this. "Very well. I'll watch for him at night while I tend to the lighthouse. You can do the same during the day."

"But he only appears at night."

"Then you and Mrs. Creed will be safe while I sleep."

"While you take the biggest risk." They walked to the shore. "We should work out an amiable solution," she said.

Finally the woman had reached her senses. "Excellent idea. And so far we have. I need to know everything you remember about George."

She folded her hands at her waist.

"Everything, Miss Brittmore, beginning with his physical stature."

She hesitated, no doubt seeking a rebuttal. "He's medium height, sandy-colored hair, and eyes so piercing blue that at times they looked black. I suppose his eyes should have been my first indication of his sinister mode. He's pleasing to look at. . .until you get to know him." She shuddered. "Hindsight is always better than foresight."

"I'm sorry to put you through this misery, but I have to know what manner of man I may be encountering."

"I understand. He always wears a crease in his brow. Peculiar for a younger man."

"What else?"

"His voice is very deep, as though he has a perpetual cold threatening to snatch away his voice." She sighed. "Everything must always be in order."

"I see," McNair said. "Then he's been in the lighthouse more than once. I left a mug of tea on the railing, and the next morning it was empty and on the step. I thought the matter had slipped my mind."

"When did this happen?"

"During the day while I slept," he said. "I'll leave something else out of place and trap him."

"No, I will. You must sleep during the day."

He swallowed his sarcasm. "Promise me if you see him, you'll wake me instantly."

"Only if I can put a bullet in him."

"Miss Brittmore, you surprise me."

"Or push him over the tower."

"Are you an executioner? Maybe I should fear crossing you."

She laughed. "We're even. And yes, I promise to seek your aid. If you're willing to help me, then I will try my best to behave."

McNair relaxed slightly. God should award him an extra jewel in his heavenly crown for dealing with this woman. "Anything else?"

"Thank you for believing me when no one else has. In the beginning, Uncle Jonathan thought George was a good man. I'm not sure what he thinks now. The gossip has turned away many of those I once called friend." She paused. "I apologize for my earlier outburst."

"You're welcome." How could one not trust her words? Her courage touched him more than he cared to admit.

They walked along the shore in silence. . .a comfortable companionship.

Another notion entered his mind. "If the lights ever go out in the lighthouse, I'll seek your help," he said.

"For what?"

"Why, Miss Brittmore. All I'd need to do is make you angry, for the fire in your eyes would light the way for miles."

"I shall get even again, Mr. Hattchery."

"I have no doubt."

Chapter 9

Two weeks later, Lynette prepared a hearty meal for Uncle Jonathan and his wife. Uncle Jonathan had informed McNair of the visit earlier in the week, stating his wife was concerned about Mr. Hattchery's welfare. That was a subtle warning for Lynette.

Knowing Uncle Jonathan's wife, she wanted to make sure Lynette had not disposed of him and Mrs. Creed. The thought would be humorous except Lynette knew Jonathan's wife wanted others to believe the worst about her.

Ever since she'd voiced her trepidations about George, Wilda Adams had been against her. At the funeral and twice when Lynette had rowed to the mainland for church, some of her parents' friends had kept their distance.

Today Lynette would win back the woman with kindness and hopefully reestablish the fondness they'd once held for each other. Mrs. Creed's influence had prompted charity and forgiveness instead of a sharp tongue. Beef stew simmered over the fireplace, biscuits would be baked just prior to their arrival, and a dried apple cobbler stayed warm on the hearth.

Now to figure out how to praise Uncle Jonathan's wife. The woman had developed such a surly temperament. Lynette had vowed to be more like the Lord, and this was still her resolve. She dragged a wooden spoon through the thick stew. At one time, before George, Uncle Jonathan's wife had been kind. Smiled more. Lynette and Amanda had adored her.

"I see the look on your face," Mr. Hattchery said, startling her reverie. "Are we excited about our visitors?"

"Most certainly. I've prepared their favorite foods." His stare felt most discerning. "What is bothering you, Mr. Hattchery?"

"Is there a way to mend this rift between you and Mrs. Adams? Or is that none of my business?"

Lynette glanced at Mrs. Creed, who appeared to be engrossed in her Bible, but Lynette doubted her ears were engaged in reading. "I plan to try."

"Wilda is filled with silly notions," Mrs. Creed said and closed her leather-bound Bible. "I nary believe a word of her gossip. Told her so, too." She lifted her frail shoulders. "Of late, I'm the target of her rumors, too. Last I heard, she claimed my mind was slipping."

"I'm so sorry," Lynette said. "But I'm grateful for your friendship. Today will be interesting."

"I doubt I'm one of her favorites either." Mr. Hattchery positioned his hat. "I defended you when she warned me about you."

Lynette lifted her shoulders and chased her sadness away. "Then I'll save the apple cobbler for a celebration when she leaves."

Mrs. Creed burst with a set of giggles as though she were a girl. "Why punish the good mayor?"

"True." Lynette pitied Uncle Jonathan. "I'll go back to my original resolve and kill her with kindness."

"We need to swallow our pride, ladies, for our visitors have arrived." Mr. Hattchery squinted, and Lynette followed his gaze.

Her laughter rang through the cottage. "She's brought Mary Elizabeth Sanders, a woman sorely in need of a husband."

"Does that mean she's hard on the eyes?" Mr. Hattchery said.

"She's kind and does much for the elderly," Lynette said.

"Which means she's plain," he said.

"You two remind me of children." Mrs. Creed rose to view the boat nearing the shore, but she didn't hide her laughter.

He offered Lynette his arm. "Shall we greet our guests?"

"And find our manners." How long had it been since Lynette had experienced a pleasant encounter with Uncle Jonathan's wife? She had no reason to believe it would happen today.

∽❧

McNair felt a peculiar sensation with Lynette's arm tucked into his. Her nearness sent his pulse racing. Strange. Frightening, too. Rather than dwell on what was happening to him, he focused on Mayor Adams and the two female companions with him.

"Good day." He nodded at the mayor and then his wife. "I see we have another guest. Whom do I owe the pleasure of meeting?"

Mayor Adams cleared his throat. "Miss Mary Elizabeth Sanders, I'd like to introduce you to Mr. McNair Hattchery."

The woman held out her hand. Mercy, she was worse than plain. The woman's nose resembled a pig. Perhaps an unfair assessment, but definitely true. She spoke a proper greeting.

"We thought you'd enjoy female companionship," Wilda Adams said.

What was Lynette, one of the birds here? And Mrs. Creed? Already his mood had soured.

"I have food ready," Lynette said with a smile he knew she didn't mean.

"I've looked forward to this time for the past week," Mayor Adams said. "Lynette, your cooking rivals anyone on the mainland."

"Mary Elizabeth is a fine cook." The mayor's wife sent a glare to her husband that reminded McNair of daggers. "However, we're not hungry, are we, Mary Elizabeth?"

"I adore Lynette's meals," the young woman said.

"Both of you shall partake," Mayor Adams said.

During the meal, Wilda Adams spoke endlessly about the finer points of Miss Sanders.

"Mary Elizabeth is an excellent seamstress."

"Mary Elizabeth plays the piano for our Sunday services. You must borrow Lynette's boat and join us for a service."

If he did choose to worship with them, he'd bring Lynette and Mrs. Creed.

"Mary Elizabeth also teaches school. The community is thrilled with our children's progress."

Was there anything Miss Sanders didn't do well?

At the close of the warm apple cobbler, McNair hoped the visitors would choose to leave. He enjoyed Mayor Adams's company, but his wife? He'd rather spend an hour adrift on the sea with sharks surrounding him. In fact, she and man-eating sharks had much in common.

Wilda Adams placed her napkin on the table. "Husband, I think it's time you spoke to Lynette privately."

Mayor Adams frowned. "I shall, and I'd like for Mr. Hattchery to join us."

His wife stiffened. "Why?"

He scooted back his chair. "My business, Wilda." He smiled. "I think it only appropriate for you and Miss Sanders to clean up from this fine meal while we're discussing an important matter."

"Miss Sanders is a guest," his wife said.

"Right you are. Then let her converse with Mrs. Creed while you tidy up things."

McNair did his best to conceal his mirth. Lynette coughed into her hand.

What did Mayor Adams need to discuss with Lynette?

Chapter 10

Lynette had no idea what Uncle Jonathan's wife wanted from her, but it couldn't be good. And why had Uncle Jonathan insisted upon Mr. Hattchery being present for the discussion?

Must be to save him from Mary Elizabeth's enticing charms. She scolded her own thoughts. It wasn't Mary Elizabeth's fault that she was plain. The woman had an endearing soul, and the whole community benefited from her many talents.

"Let's walk along the shore." Uncle Jonathan rubbed his face. Perspiration streamed onto his collar, and the temperatures were moderate. Not a good sign.

When beyond hearing distance of the cottage, Lynette could wait no longer. "What do you need to speak to me about?"

Uncle Jonathan shook his head. "It's not favorable news, my dear. I'd give anything not to be the bearer of this."

"Rather from you than anyone else."

His face softened. "Thank you, dear. I don't understand my wife. Wilda wasn't always this way." He exhaled. "She's instigated a rumor that has captured the attention of Constable Smythe."

"I'm confused. Why would Constable Smythe be interested in my doings? Is he upset about your bringing us water and provisions?"

He cleared his throat, a peculiar habit when he formed his words. "She believes you were the cause of all the deaths."

A chill raced up her arms. "Because of what George said to her?"

"And her fondness for his genteel ways."

Out of respect, she'd not ask more about his wife and George.

"Excuse me," Mr. Hattchery said. "What did George say to your wife?"

"Jealousy, sir. He insisted Lynette was distraught about his marriage to Amanda, and she planned to kill her family so the two could be together. He even said how and when."

Lynette gasped. "I wasn't aware. Now I see why she abhors me."

"I know, dear one," Uncle Jonathan said. "You are like my own daughter, one I never had. And I wanted to spare you the ugly rumors. George told Wilda you confided in him of a way to eliminate them on your birthday. You'd insist upon cooking a fine feast. Then poison them. You wanted George to place the bodies into the boat and puncture a hole before pushing it out to sea."

"What utter lies," Lynette whispered, her knees weak. "How did she explain George's disappearance?"

Uncle Jonathan moistened his lips. "George refused to go along with the plan, and you killed him, too."

Her stomach twisted. "Am I to be charged with murder?"

"I hope not. Constable Smythe is talking to others about your character. . .and George's."

"He was the more congenial." She shrugged. "Of course, you know his mannerisms. Why is this happening?"

"I have no idea. Wilda will not let the notion rest." Uncle Jonathan walked closer to the water, but she saw him swipe at a tear.

Instantly she was at his side and touched his back. "There's more, isn't there, Uncle."

He gave her a grim smile. "There is."

McNair joined them. "What is the rest of the news?" he said. "Surely it can't be any worse."

Uncle Jonathan focused on McNair. "It concerns you. My wife claims Mrs. Creed is too old to be a fit chaperone. The old woman is interested only in her stitchery and sleeping. Her mind drifts in and out of reality. My wife claims you and Lynette have ample opportunity to—"

"I've heard enough." McNair's voice thundered. "If you can't control Mrs. Adams, then I shall speak to her myself."

"Wait, sir." Uncle Jonathan's face flushed. "I've attempted to stop her meddling, but it continues."

"Has she spread this second lie among the community?" McNair's voice resembled Whaley's low growl.

"A petition has been circulated within the church. It's on my desk. I've refused to act on it, but she's encouraging others to pressure me."

For once Lynette was speechless. Why would God allow the tragedies to continue? And to think her new friends were involved.

"Then I shall inform her of what the Good Book says about lying."

❧

McNair heard Lynette calling after him, but fury stopped him from heeding her call. How could Wilda Adams be so vile? He'd known Lynette for only a short while, but one would be a fool not to see her good heart.

Murder?

Inappropriate behavior?

And what of Mrs. Creed?

How could an intelligent woman listen to George's lies?

Lynette tugged on his arm. "Please, Mr. Hattchery."

"McNair. The name is McNair. If we're being accused of such. . .well, we should be on a first-name basis."

"All right." Her tender voice brought him to a halt, and he refused to look into her blue eyes. "But think about your actions," she said. "Please, give me one minute of your time before you burst in there like. . .Whaley when he thinks I'm threatened."

"Glad to see I've now risen to the status of a dog." He remembered the times his temper had caused him regret. "What is it you'd have me say? My good name is at stake here, too."

"If you cross Uncle Jonathan's wife, she will use it against us. She'll interpret your righteous anger for a denial of the truth."

Her words made sense. Taking a few deep breaths, he regained his logic. "I see your point, but I will have a few—"

"Oh, Mr. Hattchery," the object of his fury called from the cottage doorway. "Mary Elizabeth has a song for you about the sea. I've heard it, and the words and tune are most enjoyable."

Lynette tilted her head. "How can you refuse the entertainment?"

"By stuffing cotton into my ears?"

"You'll need it. Singing isn't one of Mary Elizabeth's finer gifts."

"I have work to do in the lighthouse. Mrs. Adams would want me to earn my pay."

"Mercy. I'll send her and Mary Elizabeth up there to keep you company."

"You wouldn't do me such an injustice."

"Mind your tongue and act like Uncle Jonathan who didn't reveal a thing. We'll find a way to let the truth rise like rich cream."

He warmed with her words. "How can you be civil to her after all she's done?"

"I'm not sure. Mrs. Creed must be praying for both of us. I do know it's wrong to return evil for evil."

He'd once done that very thing, and his actions had nearly destroyed him and his family.

Chapter 11

Long after midnight, sleep still escaped Lynette. She stood in the doorway of the cottage and studied the flickering lights on the mainland. Before McNair had taken his post in the tower and Mrs. Creed had retired for the evening, the three had prayed together. In the morning they'd discuss the situation.

Dear Papa, I miss your wisdom. How wonderful if all of you would appear and put these rumors to rest. But Constable Smythe had found the empty boat. . .with a hole.

She touched her neck. The constable could use it as evidence against her. Murderers were hung. At least she'd be in heaven with her family. Could she take the punishment for a crime she didn't commit? Running held a glimmer of hope. Out West no one knew her, and she could begin again. Was living a lie worth freedom from a hangman's noose?

Yet her life had taken a better turn before today's news. Friends. . .how could she be so blessed? Papa would have enjoyed McNair. A tingling at the thought of using his given name spread through her, and it wasn't the first time she'd felt a stirring for him. If her feelings ever surfaced, Uncle Jonathan's wife would have plenty to tell others.

Leaving the island and talking to Constable Smythe might be the best solution. Then Mrs. Creed and McNair would be spared more injustice. What did she have to live for with everyone she touched falling into a sea of pain?

For a moment she allowed herself to dwell on McNair and a relationship growing between them. She adored his temperament and the way he challenged her thoughts. Maple-syrup eyes laced the sweetness she felt when he gazed her way. A life with him would never be dull. She'd seen his glances and knew what they meant.

"Dear, why not talk to Mr. Hattchery?" Mrs. Creed's voice calmed her worried thoughts. "His nighttime hours are lonely in the tower. And there's no point in both of you being robbed of sleep."

"He may enjoy the solitude."

"Or he may welcome the company." The woman touched Lynette's shoulder. "You don't know until you try."

"I'm uncertain of my role with him."

"You two are blind to what God is doing."

"What if he doesn't share in the same feelings?"

"He had them first."

Lynette smiled into the darkness. "I know little about Mr. Hattchery."

"There's always a beginning. Most men don't reveal much about themselves willingly, so we women need to ask questions."

Lynette listened to the waves' rhythm, God's comfort to a struggling soul. "I'll take him a cup of tea."

"And I'll continue in my role as a prayer warrior. My list gets longer as I breathe."

Lynette hugged the dear woman. "Thank you for being here."

"This is one test of faith I didn't wish for you. Wilda's lies have me baffled."

Lynette sensed the heaviness in her chest. "It will get worse, I fear. Much worse."

McNair questioned the footsteps approaching the top of his domain. Could it be George Zimmerman? Normally McNair took a break to walk off the sleepiness that occurred at this hour, giving the fellow a moment to invade the tower. But he soon recognized the lightness in step came from Lynette.

Whaley wagged his tail. "We welcome the company," he whispered to the animal. He'd grown fond of Lynette in a short time. Very fond.

As the footsteps grew closer, his pulse quickened. Where were these unexpected emotions leading him?

"A cup of tea for your evening?" she said in the doorway. Her dark hair hung about her shoulders, and he could envision her ocean-blue eyes.

"Splendid." How easy it was to smile into her angelic face.

"I couldn't sleep so I thought I'd help you keep watch for George."

He chuckled. "If he appears, we could subdue him together." Now why had he used the word together?

"You already know how I wish to deal with him." She handed him the tea.

"For shame." He lifted the steaming cup as a toast. "Thank you. It will keep me awake. Today was strenuous."

"Which is why I'm not sleeping." She touched a finger to her lips. "My heart goes out to Uncle Jonathan. He's torn, and I never wished misfortune to address him." She sighed. "But I'm not here to discuss today. I want to talk about you."

He raised a brow. Did she know? "What about? I'm a boring fellow."

"Since we're using our given names, then we should be more than mere acquaintances."

"Oh, I think we long since entered the world of friendship." He caught himself before saying more. "Carry on, and let me hear what's on your mind."

"You've stated your mother's a widow, and you have six sisters. Are they all married?"

"One is also a widow." He hesitated with a pang of regret for his sister. "And I have nineteen nieces and nephews."

"A large family. How nice. And where do they live?"

"In Maine, near my mother."

"I suppose you miss them?"

He took a sip of the tea. "It was time for me to leave. Living with Mother caused me to grow lazy." Answering personal questions was not his favorite pastime. "My turn. How long have you lived here?"

"Since I was eight and Amanda was nine. Mama schooled us, and Papa taught me about the lighthouse."

He startled. "You know how to operate the lenses?"

She nodded. "I wanted to ask Uncle Jonathan for your position, but grief paralyzed me. If you ever do need help—other than to use the fire in my eyes to light the way—I'm available."

How enchanting. "I'm surprised and pleased." How fetching she looked in a pale green frock that accented her creamy complexion. "Tell me why you're not married or being courted?"

In the light, she blushed, and he found the sight refreshing. "I was being courted, but after the tragedy, he chose to see someone else."

"The man was a fool."

She tilted her head. "Or possibly intelligent enough to see the road ahead would be rocky. . .with the suspicions. Do you think women are to keep the home tidy, cook, clean, keep children in tow, and not be studious?"

An unusual question, but he'd be honest. "From my experience, a woman who is devoted to house and children is separated from a man who would welcome stimulating conversation."

"My papa thought the same," she said. "What books shall we discuss? I have Plato, Shakespeare, and of course the Bible."

Would this woman ever cease to amaze him?

Chapter 12

Two days later, on Sunday morning, McNair announced he wanted to escort Lynette and Mrs. Creed to church. No point in hiding on the island while rumors simmered like hot tallow. "It's time we worshipped in church instead of here," he said. "After all, the mayor's wife invited us to hear Mary Elizabeth play for the service."

"She invited you, not me." Lynette clenched her fists.

"We're a threesome," he said. "I'd like for you ladies to consider the venture. None of us want to face God one day and be accused of not worshipping Him properly."

"We'd be brave souls to step into church," Mrs. Creed said. "And yet our appearance would show we're not cowards."

"Will you accompany us?" he said to Lynette.

"I haven't been to church since shortly after the funeral." She lifted her chin. "I can't hide forever."

In less than an hour, McNair rowed the three to shore. A gentle breeze cooled their faces from the warm day. He watched the tall steeple of the white church grow larger. It stood as an anchor to the community, the center of life. If he could convince Lynette and Mrs. Creed, they'd return each Sunday, establishing their credibility as Christians and showing God their devotion.

By the time they entered the church, bells were ringing and Mary Elizabeth was playing a prelude.

"Near the front," McNair said. He took each woman's arm and escorted them to a pew. "I won't let anyone tarnish either of your reputations." Mrs. Creed whispered her thanks, but Lynette trembled.

Maybe this wasn't such a good idea.

After a robust sermon based on purging the church of evildoers, McNair questioned the logic of exposing himself and the women to scrutiny.

We live a virtuous life on the island. It's not us who need to be cleansing our hearts.

The last amen spoken, McNair glanced at Mrs. Creed and Lynette. He'd ignored the people when they entered. Departing the church would be more uncomfortable than entering it.

"Dignity, ladies," he whispered.

In the rear stood Wilda Adams and three other women. All glared.

"The woman on the left who looks like she kissed a lemon is the reverend's wife," Mrs. Creed said. "Oh, watch me heap burning coals on her head." She broke away from McNair and strode toward the women.

"This should be interesting," Lynette said. "We may receive an ultimatum never to return."

McNair hoped not. If he were to live among these people, mutual respect needed to accompany both sides.

"How wonderful to see you, Sarah," Mrs. Creed said to the woman and took her hand. "I thought you'd come to see me on the island."

"I've been busy." Sarah pulled from the grasp.

"Isn't it time to make quilts for the needy? What of the orphans and widows? Do Lynette and I not qualify for Christian charity?" Mrs. Creed startled. "I declare, only one of you have visited us."

McNair held his breath. Lynette gripped his arm.

"Let me introduce you to our lighthouse keeper," Mrs. Creed said. "He's quite a savior, you know. When your loved ones are out to sea on a starless night, he will light the way."

She made the introductions, and the women responded. . .stiffly.

"We'd love to have you for tea," Lynette said. "It's quite peaceful on the island."

Wilda Adams lifted her nose. "We don't want to associate with those who romp with the devil."

McNair sensed the blood pouring into his brain. "Then why do these good women associate with you?" He nodded at the other three. "Have a pleasant afternoon."

He no longer cared if he offended the mayor's wife.

On the way out, the reverend did not offer to shake any of their hands. Nothing was said until they were midway across the water.

"I'm sorry," he said.

"There's nothing to apologize for," Lynette said. "I will not run. Those who oppose me without cause have no idea how hard I can fight. I'm ready, McNair. I will move to town until this is settled."

"I disagree," he said. "The three of us are in this war together."

≈❧

Less than a week later, Harley Smythe, the constable, rowed to Bird Island. Mrs. Creed saw him first, relaying the news to Lynette about the arrival.

"We expected it," Lynette said, although she'd hoped the constable would have disregarded the gossip. She patted Mrs. Creed's hand. "Never you mind. I'm sure he's here only to ask a few questions."

"I shall find Mr. Hattchery."

"He'll learn soon enough." She forced a smile. "Constable Smythe could be bringing good news."

"Have you ever known Harley Smythe to be a messenger of pleasant tidings?" Mrs. Creed's eyes moistened. "I'll put on water for tea."

From the cottage door, she watched McNair help Constable Smythe bring his boat onto the shore. They shook hands, and it occurred to her the two hadn't met.

She hesitated, evaluating the situation. Calmness settled on her, and she knew God would give her strength to withstand whatever the future held.

The two men talked on the way to the cottage, and she breathed relief. Perhaps her fears were not warranted.

Lynette stood in the doorway. "Greetings, Mr. Smythe. Mrs. Creed has just heated water for tea."

Mr. Smythe's solemn face should have frightened her, but she rejected any signs of intimidation. "This is not a social visit, Miss Brittmore. I have many questions for you."

Lynette gestured for him to sit. "Whatever you have to ask can be voiced over tea and in the company of my friends."

"I hope the inquisition will be short," Constable Smythe said. "Your father was a respected man in the community, and I trust he raised you to be the same."

"He instilled in me truth and the precepts of God." She seated herself across the table from him. McNair and Mrs. Creed joined them.

"As constable, I must establish the truth of what happened to the Brittmores and Mr. Zimmerman. Why weren't you with your family the day they disappeared?"

How many times had she gone over this story? She responded with the same details that she'd provided more than two months ago.

"Were you involved with your sister's husband?"

"No," she said and forced down her ire. "I detested him."

Mr. Smythe frowned. "Why?"

Lynette repeated what Mrs. Creed and McNair had heard before.

"Did you kill them?"

Lynette leaned in to him. "I'm not the person you are looking for. George Zimmerman is, and I believe he is alive."

"Where is he?"

She pressed her lips together. "Close by. Probably on the mainland."

"You tell me where to find him, and I'll discuss his involvement with the deaths of your family."

If necessary she would find the man.

"Do you understand you're under suspicion for murder?" Constable Smythe said.

"I do. God will render me innocent. Tell that to those who are spreading lies about me and my friends."

"I'm nearly finished with my investigation." Constable Smythe rose from his chair. "The evidence points to you. I suggest you find yourself an attorney."

Chapter 13

McNair wound around the staircase to the bottom of the lighthouse, his mind heavy with Constable Smythe's declaration. He didn't care a whit about his own reputation, but the thought of Mrs. Creed being slandered because of her good deed. . .and the false accusations against Lynette. . . .

What little he knew of the young woman told him of her perseverance. He also realized she'd do everything within her power to usher in her innocence. That's why she sat in her typical spot along the shore with a lantern beside her.

Light—they all needed a way to see through to the truth. His fears told him she was planning something dangerous. If this George fellow had killed her family, he'd not hesitate in ending her life, too. She'd be defenseless against a man who knew how to murder and get away with the crime.

The thought sickened him.

She turned to see him and shook her head. "McNair, I need time alone. I appreciate your friendship and advice, but this is my battle," she said. "Whaley must be sleeping, so we don't have a chaperone."

Even in her dire situation, she found humor. "Lynette, we must talk. You need an attorney." McNair heard the tenderness in his own words. Had he allowed himself to feel love? "I know what you're planning, and it won't work."

"So you can read my mind? Uncle Jonathan's wife would have a fine time with that confession. And I don't have the money to pay for legal representation."

He seated himself beside her. "I would consider it an honor to help you."

She stiffened. "No, and don't ask me again."

He'd secure her an attorney on his own. "You can't look for George on the mainland. He's the enemy, as well as the mayor's wife. He destroys the body while she strikes at the heart."

"Nicely said, McNair. But pretty words won't clear my name and bring justice to my family."

"That's why you need my help."

She inhaled deeply. "I must do this alone. He won't show his face to me on the island, but we know he comes here. It's the why that is bewildering."

He wanted to touch her, hold her, but his past wouldn't allow it. "Listen to me for a moment."

She shook her head. "I've made up my mind."

"Since my words won't dissuade you, I'll speak anyway. If you go to the mainland looking for a ghost, those who are against you will declare you insane. . .and guilty of murder."

"I have to find George."

"I understand. Let me be the one to search for him."

She tossed her attention his way. "Your name has been tainted, and those who could be your friends scorn you. Aren't you involved enough?"

He'd been involved since he'd set eyes on her. "No one will suspect me. I could seek out those who like to talk. Sift their words for the truth." When she didn't reject his logic, he continued. "I'll let Mayor Adams know what I'm doing. That will ease his mind. Then I'll talk to Constable Smythe and whoever else I can."

"How would you go about it?"

"I'll state my discontent with the situation. Reveal my desire to have the matter rectified, which is true. I won't lie, but I certainly won't give them my real reason for conducting the investigation."

She slowly nodded. "Are you thinking George will expose himself?"

"Yes. Maybe we can find out why he shows up here at night. If he wished you ill harm, I think he'd have acted by now. My one concern is him approaching you and Mrs. Creed in my absence."

"I agree." Lynette shook her head. "He had plenty of opportunity to do me harm before you arrived."

"What about the boat? Will you and Mrs. Creed be all right for a few days? I'll ask Mayor Adams to check on you."

"We'll be fine. There used to be two boats. . .before the accident."

"I'll take care of that problem when I'm on the island."

"Would you mind bringing water when you return?"

"Done. And if I'm successful, we'll have a celebration."

"It's hard to imagine George's arrest." She stared out to sea. "McNair, what does he want? I thought I understood what drove him to murder, but his actions of late make little sense."

"He's a clever man. To have disappeared and yet taunt you with his ghost-like appearances means he's confident." Not until this moment had McNair been so certain of George's ruse. His very soul wanted to prove Lynette right. "I want you to have peace about what happened to your family. And answers as to why he killed them."

"Thank you. You're a good friend, perhaps my best since Amanda died."

He wanted to be more if it were possible.

"What about your duties here?" she said.

He smiled. "You can manage the lighthouse. Your abilities are extraordinary. If I were lost at sea and knew you were in the tower, I'd feel safe."

Her typical sigh touched his ears, the sigh that said her heart was burdened.

"What harm can I do on the mainland?" he said.

"I fear you could be killed." She nibbled at her lip. "I don't want to lose you."

Oh, the words he wanted to hear but to which he couldn't respond. "I'll be careful." Dying for such a woman would be an honor, as though justifying what he could not change.

❧

Lynette leaned against the cottage door and watched the sun rise, its rays sparkling across the water. Hope. And she desperately needed a glimpse of something to believe in.

McNair. Who would have ever thought God would send such an unlikely man to help her? She'd tucked a note beneath the oars of the boat, a quote from Plato, one of Papa's favorites—"Courage is knowing what not to fear."

"My dear, did you not sleep last night?" Mrs. Creed's sweet voice broke her hours of introspection.

"I will tonight. Much to think about."

"How much did you give to God?"

Lynette pondered the question. "Some. I prayed for direction."

"Can't expect direction if you don't give Him the problem."

Lynette laughed. "One of the things I love about you is your wisdom."

"How often am I right?"

Lynette cringed. "The question is when are you wrong."

Mrs. Creed pointed to McNair rowing the boat across the harbor. "I see Mr. Hattchery has business on the mainland."

"Indeed he does. He'll be gone a few days."

The older woman coughed, a ragged sound that shook her body.

Chapter 14

McNair bit his tongue to keep from losing his temper with Wilda Adams.

"It's about time someone saw that Lynette Brittmore needs to be behind bars," the woman said.

"I want to learn what happened to her family." McNair chose his words carefully, not wanting to lie and not willing to condemn Lynette. "Something is not right on the island. That's why I'm here."

The woman's eyes widened. "Have you seen the apparition?"

McNair hesitated—purposely. "I have seen and heard things that demand an explanation." He toyed with the brim of his hat. "Thank you, ma'am. I appreciate the names of those who can tell me more about Miss Brittmore, her family, and her brother-in-law."

"Be glad you're still alive, young man."

Mayor Adams pounded his fist onto the kitchen table. "Wilda, must you always condemn and pass judgment?"

Mrs. Adams huffed from the room. The mayor said nothing, but the lines deepened around his eyes. That's when McNair departed. . .with a prayer for Mayor Adams and Wilda.

McNair wished his friend had an easier home life. He strode toward the parsonage with the realization of how long it had been since he'd earnestly sought God's help. Too much sadness when his nephew died, catapulting his worship into a meaningless habit. McNair had kept the rules of church and isolated God from his heart.

How could the death of good people ever be a part of God's plan? He longed to have the answer, but he longed more to feel the presence of God in his life.

Lord, forgive my shutting You out. From this moment forward, You hold the light that shows me the way.

He paused and stared out at the island. With God's help, he'd find justice for Lynette.

"Mr. Hattchery. May I have a word with you?"

McNair swung to face the mayor. The man was pale, obviously beaten by the fate of his circumstances.

"I have information," Mayor Adams said. "Both good and unfortunate." He gestured forward. "Let's walk so my wife will not question me later."

McNair obliged the man. After all, he didn't have to live with the woman. "We could venture on toward the parsonage."

The mayor nodded. "First of all, I apologize for my wife's actions. She wasn't always this cruel."

"You don't have to tell me this."

"But I do. You've heard me say very little when she's insulted Lynette and you. I'm sure you've questioned who's the head of my household."

"I have pondered the matter."

"And rightfully so. You see, we are childless—five infants who lived only a few hours after birth. Each time my Wilda's dreams for family were destroyed. Each time it was more difficult to bury our child."

They walked on past a general store and a bakery.

"The result is my wife has grown bitter. . .blames herself but takes it out on others. In the past, it was me. Before the deaths of the Brittmores, Wilda adored Amanda and Lynette, and they referred to us as aunt and uncle. I thought she'd found a substitute until George poisoned her mind about Lynette. Then when the Brittmores and George disappeared, she became increasingly difficult." A sob escaped Mayor Adams. "I have almost given up. Lynette is dear to me, and to have my wife turn her back on the girl when she needs comfort is most disturbing."

Now McNair understood. "I'm so sorry."

"Wilda was the most beautiful woman in the city, her heart and her features. But instead of allowing God to heal her sorrow, she's chosen to make others miserable."

McNair realized he could do the same if not for his faith in God.

"If I can do anything to help, please call upon me. At the very least, I can pray and listen."

"Thank you, Mr.—"

"McNair. We are friends."

"And my given name is Jonathan." The mayor pulled a handkerchief from inside his jacket and dabbed beneath his eyes. By then they were at the parsonage beside the church. "I have information about George and a word of caution. My wife has spoken with him."

McNair startled. "You're certain?"

"Most assuredly. I followed Wilda yesterday evening after she thought I was asleep. She met the scoundrel at the pier." Jonathan appeared to study the cross mounted on the church's steeple. "I wanted to believe my wife would never be unfaithful." Pain drew the man's features into a mass of devastation. "But her interest in George was confirmed." Jonathan held up his hand to silence McNair. "I'll confront her when this is over. George is using her to build a case against Lynette, but my poor wife is too infatuated to see what he's doing."

"They discussed Lynette?"

"He told Wilda that he'd been meeting with Lynette to persuade her into a confession. Supposedly Lynette wants to run away with George, but he wants his wife's murder settled."

"Then why doesn't he go to Constable Smythe?"

"My wife stated the same. But he claims Lynette will kill him. Already tried." Jonathan shook his head. "How could my wife believe such absurdity, especially from a younger man? McNair, I've loved her for years, but devotion obviously isn't enough."

"Do you have any idea how I can find George?" McNair said.

"That's why I'm here. He and Wilda plan to meet at the pier tomorrow evening at ten-thirty. She's supposed to tell Constable Smythe that Lynette is influencing you about her innocence." Jonathan blew out his disgust. "If George refuses to run away with Lynette, then she'll turn her affections to you."

McNair moaned. "I have to find George and get to the bottom of this."

"Even if you present him alive to Constable Smythe, will he believe your story or the one Wilda has spread over town?"

McNair would do anything to help Lynette escape the corruption, but everywhere he turned, a wall of lies stopped him.

"I see you care for her," Jonathan said. "Your secret's safe with me."

McNair glanced about as though someone might have overheard. "She's a courageous young woman."

"Always has been. I have three reasons for proving George guilty of murder," Jonathan said. "He's been successful in destroying the lives of beloved friends, turning my wife against me, and conspiring to bring false charges against Lynette."

"We'll work together. With God on our side, evil will not prevail," McNair said. "George thinks he's committed the perfect murder, and if we can't trap him in his lies, then Lynette will pay with her life."

Chapter 15

Lynette urged Mrs. Creed to drink a little tea that contained honey for her cough and feverfew to chase away the chills. Chicken broth simmered over the fire with basil. The dear woman had been too ill to read her Bible today, so Lynette chose Psalms to encourage her.

"You need to rest before you're up all night tending to the lighthouse," Mrs. Creed whispered, indicating her weakness and possibly a sore throat.

"I'm fine. You're my concern." Tonight would be long, and she'd check on Mrs. Creed at every given opportunity.

When would Uncle Jonathan check on them or McNair return? Mrs. Creed needed more care than Lynette could provide. The woman's chest rattled like a baby's toy. She'd suffered through the same chest ailment a year ago and had barely survived.

Mrs. Creed's age. . . . She held the title of the oldest woman in the community at eighty-four-years old. Was it selfish to want her to heal when she could walk the streets of heaven with no pain or sorrow?

A parchment-thin hand rested on Lynette's arm. "I need to say a few things in case the good Lord calls me home."

Tears brimmed in Lynette's eyes. "Please. Don't speak of it."

A smile danced on the older woman's lips. "But it would be grand to see all who've gone before me." She took a deep breath. "McNair. . .no man would go to this length to prove a woman's innocence unless love ruled his heart."

Lynette wanted to believe so, but the thought seemed incredible. "He hasn't said anything to indicate so."

"Yes he has. You haven't listened to his heart." She closed her eyes as though garnering strength. "I found something in your parents' bedroom that belongs to you."

Lynette hadn't gone through their belongings because it had been too painful. "What did you find?"

"Money, my child. Enough to take care of you for a long time. I found it by accident when making room for my clothes. It was wrapped in a baby's blanket in a drawer. I assumed you knew it was there. Yet when we questioned why George would dispose of your family, you never mentioned it."

Lynette had forgotten until now. . . . "Papa said his girls need not marry so someone would take care of them. I thought he meant we shouldn't marry the first man who asked. But he must have meant he'd provided for us. This explains so much."

"I should have told you when I made the discovery. Truthfully, I felt uncomfortable, as though I'd been snooping."

"I'd never think badly of you." Lynette walked to the window overlooking the harbor. "Amanda may have told George about the money but not where it is." She whirled to face Mrs. Creed. "That's what he's after." Her mind raced. "He wanted me to stay here that day, to cook for everyone." She'd not mention what else George wanted from her. "He must think I know where the money is hidden. That's why he hasn't killed me."

"By making your family's deaths look like you were the one responsible, he could force you to give it to him."

And pressure her to be with him. "Then why hasn't he? Why didn't he search for it the Sunday we went to church?"

Mrs. Creed raised a finger. "I think he did. When we returned, my things were in disarray. I should have told you or Mr. Hattchery, but we had so much on our minds."

"If I'm arrested, you'd no longer be needed here. And George would have access to the house." She shook her head. "Then McNair would be in danger."

"We must believe God will fight for us."

Lynette hugged her. "Thank you. I hope Uncle Jonathan or McNair return soon. You need a doctor's care, and we need protection from George."

"Is the rifle loaded?"

"Yes, and I know how to use it."

❧

"Wouldn't you like to learn what happened to the Brittmores?" McNair said to Constable Smythe.

The man scowled. "That's my job, but what you're proposing is preposterous. Upstanding citizens have testified to Miss Brittmore's motive to eliminate her family."

McNair assumed convincing Constable Smythe would be difficult, but he came armed with his best resolve. "Mayor Adams could come with us."

Constable Smythe stepped back as though slapped. "Are you saying the mayor has proof of his wife's infidelity?"

"He's the one who told me." McNair leaned in closer. "Sir, we all want the same thing—this mystery solved."

Constable Smythe rubbed the back of his neck. "All right. Meet me here at ten-fifteen. But leave Mayor Adams out of it. If indeed your reporting is accurate, the mayor doesn't need to view his wife's behavior."

At the arranged meeting time, McNair arrived at the constable's office. Jonathan had insisted upon accompanying them. Perhaps he hoped his wife had been a victim and not part of a horrible crime. The three men silently made their way to the pier. The smell of fish wafted through the air while a faint breeze cooled the evening. McNair could only pray George would reveal a portion of the truth, enough to convince Constable Smythe to doubt the gossip.

At the pier, two people stood in the shadows, the same place where Jonathan had seen Wilda and George the previous night.

Stealing through the night, George's words grew more distinguishable, his voice low and raspy as Lynette had described.

"My darling, Lynette means nothing to me. Only you. Did you visit the constable?"

"I did," Wilda said. "I assured him Lynette had planned the demise of her family and admitted the crime to me." Her last words were spoken victoriously.

"Did he ask why?"

"Yes, and I told him she was upset because you'd left her. Remember, Lynette and Amanda were once close to me. He believed every word."

"Thank you. Soon he'll make the arrest, and we can be together."

"Oh, George, I can hardly wait." Wilda's words churned McNair's stomach. "I'll go wherever you wish."

"Has Lynette told Jonathan the whereabouts of her father's money?" McNair perked his attention.

"I don't think so. This evening I prepared his favorite meal and asked him how Lynette planned to support herself. He had no idea."

"We need that money, Wilda. Is it possible you could befriend Lynette?"

"I despise being around her, but for you I'll do my best."

George drew Wilda to him. "That's all we need to leave this town."

Constable Smythe walked toward the couple. "George Zimmerman, Wilda Adams, stop where you are. Both of you are wanted for questioning in the deaths of the Brittmore family."

George ran toward the water's edge.

"Stop!" Constable Smythe hurried after him.

Wilda screamed.

McNair faced her, shoving his anger to a place where it wouldn't surface. "How could you do this to Jonathan?" he said evenly. "And what about the young woman you betrayed for the likes of a murderer?"

She lifted her chin. "George is innocent of any crimes. He loves me."

McNair pointed to the ocean. "If he loves you so much, then why is he rowing out to sea and not here declaring his innocence?"

Wilda touched her heart. "He's afraid of Lynette and Jonathan."

"Since when did love mean abandoning someone when they need you? You're here facing arrest while he's free."

"You have no idea what you're talking about."

But he did. "Love doesn't mean murder."

Chapter 16

Lynette blinked at the sand-like tears stinging in her eyes. She'd been up and down the lighthouse steps all night with Mrs. Creed. Fever raged, and Lynette feared the worse. The time was shortly after midnight. How long could this night be?

Prayers stayed on her lips—for the woman to regain her health, for McNair and his mission, and for George to be found. She now understood why her family had been killed and why she was being blamed. But without proof, she'd be tried for murder.

McNair. Indeed she missed him. The sight of him stayed fixed in her mind—warm brown eyes and thick dark hair. She treasured the lingering look that left her wondering what was in his heart.

For the first time, love had stepped into her life. But she could do nothing about her tender feelings unless McNair broached the matter. She'd not risk having her feelings rejected.

Glancing at the sleeping woman, she hurried to the lighthouse. Once everything was in order, she considered George again. How had he gained entrance to the lighthouse? The walls were thick, and the winding staircase narrow. Could there be. . . . She studied every inch of the circular wall, running her fingers across the rough surface.

She pressed on the stones until an indentation the height of a man confirmed her suspicions. A doorway opened and revealed a hidden stairwell. Surely Papa had not known about this. Grabbing the lantern, she followed the steps to the ground where the doorway exited on the opposite side of the exposed stairway. Brush hid the stones that moved wide enough for one to steal in or out.

Satisfied she'd put together how George had maneuvered his charade as an apparition, she checked on Mrs. Creed before ascending the main stairway to the top.

In the tower, Lynette saw George, his back to her. He stared out to sea in the stance she well remembered. He swung around, and she knew he'd been expecting her.

"Why now?" she said. "You've had so many opportunities to approach me when I was alone."

"I had to make sure you hadn't lost your mind." George sneered, the same contemptible look he'd given all of them.

"What do you want?"

He stepped closer. "Many things, my dear. The money your father left you is a good beginning."

She forced down the rising fear. "I have no idea what you're talking about."

"I take what I want. You should realize my determination by now."

"Like the murder of my family?"

He smiled wryly. "You're getting smarter. Do you want to know how I eliminated them?"

"No."

He laughed, and the insane sound sent chills up her spine. "You'll hear anyway," George said. "Your father was first. The sniveling man had crossed me too many times. His demands. His threats. I tossed him over the boat and hit him in the head with an oar."

"Please." Her stomach twisted.

"Then your mother joined him in the same way. Dear Amanda was hysterical. She slapped me. Tried to take the oar, as if she were any match for me. I used my knife to silence her. Getting rid of your sister was my biggest treat."

"She was carrying your child."

"What I wanted was you and the money. Their deaths are your fault."

Why hadn't they seen his madness? "My sister loved you."

"To her demise." He took another step toward her. "You want my life, the excitement, the challenge?"

"I'd rather be dead." And she meant it.

"Do you prefer the new lighthouse keeper?" He reached to grab her, but she moved around the lenses.

Lynette lifted her chin. "Mr. Hattchery understands the meaning of integrity."

"He's deceived you, my dear. I have a tidbit of information about him. Wilda Adams so graciously keeps me informed of all her husband's business. It seems Mr. Hattchery delayed in rescuing a nephew, and the poor lad drowned. What do you think of your hero now?"

"You expect me to believe you?"

"It doesn't matter." He pointed to the catwalk. "Are you going to join me out there willingly, or will there be a struggle?"

"There will be a fight."

George laughed. "My stubborn Lynette, I have your death all worked out. You could not bear the guilt for what you'd done to your family and jumped into the ocean."

Lynette thought about the rifle. Even if she could escape him and claim it, George could overpower her and hurt Mrs. Creed. "There is no money."

"Then your lighthouse keeper will find your body floating in the water."

"He'll know better." She heard footsteps.

"Lynette," McNair called. "Are you there?"

"George has me," she said.

McNair's steps came faster. Whaley growled. Oh, her protectors.

George grabbed her waist and dragged her to the catwalk. She stared at the hidden stairwell that George had used.

"You could escape and leave us be," she said.

"Not until I have what I want. I'm not afraid of your lighthouse keeper." He clasped his hand over her mouth.

She sunk her teeth into his hand. He cursed, and she tried to wiggle free as Whaley and McNair emerged from the staircase. Whaley leaped at George, knocking her and her assailant to the floor. McNair pulled her from harm and stood over George where Whaley had him pinned.

"You, sir, will meet justice for your murderous actions," McNair said. "Wilda Adams has confessed to everything." Lynette handed him rope, and he flipped George to his stomach. "Keep him down, Whaley, while I bind his hands." Once finished he glanced at Lynette. "Did he harm you?

Because if he did, I'll end his life myself."

She trembled even though the danger had ceased. "He admitted to murdering my family."

"And I'd do it again," George said. "They deserved it for making my life miserable." He spit at McNair. "Lynette knows of how you let the boy suffer and die."

Lynette's gaze flew to McNair. His face twisted into grief. "'Tis true."

Chapter 17

McNair and Lynette watched the evening sky of yellow and orange fade into dark blue. Two days had passed since Constable Smythe had arrested George for the murder of the Brittmores. Wilda Adams had been arrested, too, and Jonathan was heartbroken. He'd sent to Boston for a lawyer, but the woman claimed she was as guilty as George. Although McNair had coerced George to believe Wilda had confessed her part, in truth she'd stayed loyal to her lover.

Mrs. Creed had rallied with the aid of the mainland's doctor. McNair didn't want to think of Lynette having to deal with one more death. Yet he faced an even more difficult challenge—telling Lynette how his nephew had died.

"I need to tell you what happened before I took this position," McNair said. "George spoke the truth about my nephew. The boy drowned, and it was my fault."

She crossed her arms over her chest. "Did you try to save him?"

He nodded, the memories as vivid as the afternoon of the drowning. "But I was too late. My hesitation contributed to his death."

She turned to him, touching his arm. "Simply tell me what plagues you."

"Robbie was eleven, a mischievous boy. Loved life. Loved to play pranks on others." An image of the sandy-haired boy flashed through his mind. . .and the despair of his mother who'd already lost her husband. "Since his father died, Robbie had developed a need for others to give him attention. Many times he cried for help when nothing threatened him. That's what happened in the river. I thought he was teasing, and I wanted to teach him a lesson."

"The hesitation."

"Yes. When he cried for help the second time, I dove into the river. The last thing he shouted was about a cramp in his side. I pulled him from the water, but I'd let him drown."

"McNair, you can't blame yourself for his death."

"Why?" He heard the bitterness in his voice.

"It was an accident."

"My sister blamed me."

"Grief can cause one to blame anything or anyone." She fought for obvious control. "I blamed God for the deaths of my family, for allowing George to end their lives. Mrs. Creed helped me to see things in a different perspective."

"How?"

"She said our lives are in God's hands. We may not understand the why of an untimely death, but it's all part of His plan, a perfect plan even if we don't agree. Perhaps the reason for my family's deaths won't be clear until eternity, but I have to trust God knows best."

"That doesn't justify my actions with Robbie." He removed her hand from his arm, and he despised himself for it. "Lynette, I'm not a good man for you."

She gasped. "Don't I have a say in the matter?"

"I can't say what's in my heart. My deeds stop me."

"I don't care what you've done."

He stood. "I'm going back to the lighthouse. We have nothing because I have nothing to give."

"Your heart, McNair, is all I want."

He stared at the harbor. "We don't have a future. I'll be resigning my position here." He walked away. The past tortured him, and a future without her left him numb. How could a man love and fear love at the same time? At times he thought he might suffocate without her presence. Such a man he was—a coward and yet he'd die to protect her.

꧁꧂

Lynette had taken a bold stand and spoken her heart, and McNair had turned away. She'd allowed herself to believe the two of them could have a life together. But she obviously meant nothing to him. How foolish she felt. Picking up a handful of sand, she let it fall through her fingers. Lost. . .so much had been lost.

She'd titled him noble, giving, a man much like Papa. McNair had helped her bring George to justice and settled what happened to her family. He'd saved her life and risked his own. But he was leaving.

Brushing the sand from her hands, she resolved not to be selfish. She'd leave in the morning. Those who looked to the lighthouse for guidance needed McNair more than she did. God had brought her through the grief of losing her parents, and He'd carry her through the loss of love.

Lynette thought of her list of accomplishments before leaving the island. Not all had been fulfilled, but she could move on. With her inheritance, she'd open a boardinghouse and a fine eatery.

"A plan," she whispered and begged her tears to dry.

Inside her room, she packed some of her belongings, and the rest she'd send for later. Mrs. Creed was well enough to make the short trip.

As though the older woman knew of Lynette's despair, she appeared in the doorway. Frail and in a white gown, she seemed to know Lynette needed her.

"Tell me what troubles you," Mrs. Creed said.

"If I don't leave, McNair will resign."

"Oh, my dear girl. Why?"

"He doesn't share in my feelings."

"Hogwash."

Any other time, Lynette would have laughed. "He said we don't have a future."

"He's a blind fool. I know what I see."

"Maybe we wanted something to be so and didn't see the truth."

"We'll weather this together, my child. My home has plenty of room for the both of us."

A thickening in Lynette's throat stopped her from accepting the invitation. Instead she nodded her appreciation. "Is God testing me to see how much I can take? I forgave George and Aunt Wilda. I understand what revenge and regret can do to a person's soul."

"God has this matter resolved. Whatever He has for you is far better than anything we could hope for."

Mrs. Creed's wisdom fell like shells in scrambled eggs. The familiar loneliness that had stalked her since she realized George's madness had seized her again. Lynette knew she should be filled with gratitude for all God had done on her behalf, but her heart ached for a man who'd rejected her.

"Maybe he needs time to figure out what he wants," Mrs. Creed said. "Men are creatures who don't make decisions lightly."

"And what am I to do in the meantime?"

"Wait. Pray. Go on with your life until God shows you a different path."

Chapter 18

Two weeks later, McNair still fought the heaviness weighing on him. Lynette was gone, but what did he expect? What happened to Robbie stood in the way of their happiness. How could any woman respect a man who'd hesitated before trying to save a drowning boy?

Jonathan had taken Lynette and Mrs. Creed to the mainland. Mrs. Creed had hugged McNair good-bye but Lynette had kept her distance, her way of not causing either of them any more discomfort. If he left Bird Island, where would he go? Certainly not home where those whom he loved blamed him for a child's death. He'd thought the lighthouse position would help him forget. Then he met Lynette, and everything he'd wanted in life had rushed over him.

She'd left a poem for him, and he read it every day. He pulled it from his pocket and reread the memorized lines.

Oh fickle heart how easily you were deceived,
  The lies have left me alone and bereaved.
Shall I ever see the truth your lips failed to tell,
  Or will I want for you until my last breath fails?

On the kitchen table he'd found a slip of paper with only two lines.

Sail away, dear heart, to where the sea meets the sky,
  And maybe then I can say my tender good-byes.

McNair descended the tower with Whaley at his side. She'd left the dog for him, and the animal's presence helped keep her memory alive. Entering the cottage, he smelled the loneliness. The days of Lynette's smile and all she had to give were gone.

With the kettle on the fire for tea, he roamed outside. A boat rowed his way. Probably Jonathan. The poor man needed someone to talk to as much as McNair needed a listening ear. Wilda had chosen to remain in jail near George, although Jonathan visited her daily. He'd tried to resign his position as mayor, but the town claimed they needed him.

Whaley barked. A woman sat in the boat with Jonathan. Yet it wasn't his Lynette. Curiosity overcame him, and he made his way to the shore.

Rachel. . . What business did his sister have with him? Clenching his fist, the memories of Robbie's accident tormented him. The words she'd flung in sorrow and hatred.

Lynette would tell him to trust God.

Rachel waved, and he returned the gesture. McNair's pulse sped away. What did this mean? Jonathan helped her from the boat, and she ran to McNair. Rachel's smile met him. The anger had disappeared. When she reached to hug him, tears filled her eyes, and he held her close.

"I've missed you," Rachel said, her small frame reaching up on tiptoe.

"And I you," he said.

"I've come a long way to talk to you, brother." Her soft voice calmed him for whatever she had to say.

"I'm going to take a walk," Jonathan said. "Let you two talk privately."

McNair nodded, wishing his friend would stay. "What is it, Rachel? Are there problems at home? Is Mother in good health? Our sisters?"

"Everyone is in good health. They wish you well, hoping you can plan a trip home soon."

"I don't understand the meaning of this."

She took his hand, the way she used to do when they were children. "I'm here because I need to ask your forgiveness."

McNair stepped back. "Why? You've done nothing."

She blinked. "Yes, brother. I blamed you for Robbie's death when you did all you could to save him."

He started to speak, but she touched a finger to his lips.

"One hour before the accident, I asked you to help me stop him from shouting danger when nothing was wrong. He needed to work through missing his father, but not by lying and worrying others with his constant need for attention."

McNair hadn't thought about their conversation since before the drowning. "But that's no excuse."

"I. . .I would have done the same. I'd have let him drown, thinking he was only wanting someone to notice him. No one is to blame. It was an accident."

McNair drew his sister into an embrace, the sister who'd been closest to him, the sister he'd protected and treasured. He'd never been one to shed tears, but these were a blend of sadness and joy.

"I told Mother I wouldn't return without your forgiveness," she said.

"And you have it."

Rachel lifted her chin, the stubborn stance he remembered from their childhood days. "One more thing. Mr. Adams tells me you've met a young woman of whom you're quite fond."

He frowned. "I sent her away."

"So I heard." She wagged a gloved finger at him. "Don't let happiness escape you because of your pride. Go to her. Make things right."

He ran his fingers through his hair. "I doubt if she'll speak to me after the way I treated her."

"Try, brother. For me." She batted those huge brown eyes, just like she'd done when she was a girl.

"All right."

"Today?"

"You and I need to spend time together."

"We have. I'm going home so I can report to the family that you're well. Write me tonight and mother also. Tell us all about this young woman who's snatched your heart."

McNair glanced at the harbor and the houses dotted on the mainland. Fishing boats bobbed in the water. "Today I'll talk to Lynette, and tonight I'll write no matter what she says." He smiled. "She's beautiful. . . inside and out."

"Good!"

"I have water on for tea. A few minutes with your favorite brother?"

She laughed, and he heard the girl in her. "You're my only brother."

An hour later, he hugged Rachel good-bye and shook hands with Jonathan. God was good, sending him what he needed at just the right time.

He walked back to the cottage and tidied up. Hidden in a drawer was his mother's wedding ring. If only Lynette would believe his words of love.

At the shore, he bid Whaley to wait for him. "I'll return before dusk," he told the dog. "Wish me luck." McNair chuckled at talking to the animal. Maybe he was really talking to God.

Chapter 19

Lynette watched the chicken turn in the fireplace, its juices spitting into the fire and the aroma filling Mrs. Creed's home. While the woman slept, Lynette kneaded bread to rise. She recalled how McNair had said the smells of her cooking would call a wayward sailor to shore long before the lighthouse. Memories of loved ones always soothed her. Her last letter to her family had been sent the day she left the island. Mama, Papa, and Amanda lived inside her. . .just like McNair.

A knock at the door captured her attention. Probably Uncle Jonathan needed to see a kind face. The past few weeks had been horrible for him, and she wanted to be a listening ear.

She opened the door to McNair, standing with his hat in hand. Startled, she hoped he couldn't see how his presence affected her.

"Do you have time to speak with me?" he said.

"Yes. . .please come in." She gestured for him to sit at the table while bidding her body to cease trembling.

"How is Mrs. Creed?"

"Doing well. And you?"

"Better now." He told her about his sister's visit, but he seemed extremely nervous, shuffling his hat from hand to hand.

"Thank you for telling me." The brother-sister reunion helped fill the void in her.

"There's more." He took a deep breath. "Can I have a glass of water?"

"Surely." Lynette gasped. Where were her manners?

Once he took a long drink, he stared at her. "My sister heard about you from Jonathan."

How curious.

"I told her how I'd turned you away. How I felt I could never be the man you deserved." He took another drink of water while her heart might just burst from her chest. "I'm here because I want to make things right between us. Your poems have touched me so." He pulled them from his pocket. . .wrinkled and obviously well read.

"What is it, McNair?" She smiled. "How can I help you?"

He took her hand. "I love you, Lynette. Can you forgive me for hurting you?"

The world seemed to stop. "Of course." The words were spoken, but she didn't know how they'd come.

"And if I've not destroyed your feelings for me, would you consider being a lighthouse keeper's wife?"

She giggled. "Only if the lighthouse keeper is you."

"Oh, it is." He squeezed her hand then reached into his pocket. "This was my mother's ring. I'd be honored if you'd consider it your own."

"So you're asking me to marry you?"

"I am."

"And you can take my teasing, my cooking, Whaley, and my love for a lifetime?"

McNair took both of her hands and drew her close. He kissed her tenderly as though she were fragile as porcelain. "Does that answer your question? I'm yours, Lynette, and I will spend the rest of my life proving how much I love you."

A BEACON IN THE STORM

by Andrea Boeshaar

Dedication

Brightly beams our Father's mercy
From His lighthouse evermore,
But to us He gives the keeping
Of the lights along the shore.
Let the lower lights be burning!
Send a gleam across the wave!
Some poor fainting, struggling seaman
You may rescue, you may save.

"Let the Lower Lights Be Burning"
by PHILIP P. BLISS, 1838–1876

Chapter 1

November, 1868

The frigid north wind slapped at Captain Cade Danfield's numb face while the icy waters of Lake Michigan tossed his three-masted schooner, *Kismet,* as though it were a child's bath toy. The pelting sleet had taken up a collection on his bushy, blond mustache, and Cade tasted blood from his cracked lips.

"Cap'n! This is some kind of storm," Hosea Benkins, the first mate, hollered over the din of the gale. "Came out of nowhere."

Cade nodded a reply. However, truth be known, he had weathered worse squalls off the eastern shores during the war. From '62 to '64, he had manned a federal gunboat and patrolled the rough, uncertain waters of the Atlantic.

The war. The awful, bloody Civil War.

As always, its memories were suffused with images of his beloved wife, Isabelle. Would she be alive today if he had been home to care for her instead of out at sea? He'd never even gotten the chance to say good-bye. . . .

"Papa?"

Cade swung around in horror at the sound of his daughter Jenny's voice. "What are you doing out here?" he asked more gruffly than intended. "Get down below where it's safe!"

"But Papa," the ten-year-old argued as she clung to the handrail near the wheelhouse, "people are vomiting because of the roll of the water, and it's a ghastly sight, and everyone is so frightened. I tried to tell them that my father is the captain of this ship and he has a good mind for what he's doing, but they won't listen."

Cade almost grinned. Almost. In another place, at another time, he

149

would have found his daughter's courage amusing. From the determined set of her slender chin to the adventurous twinkle in her blue eyes, it was obvious that Jennifer Leigh Danfield wasn't scared a wit of this tempest. What's more, she was as sure-footed as the best sailor on board. And why not? Cade had taken her with him everywhere for the past four and a half years. He scarcely let the golden-haired girl out of his sight for fear the Almighty would take her too—like Isabelle. But if God didn't snatch his precious Jenny from him, this storm might well take her life.

"Back to your cabin, and that's an order!"

She pouted but acquiesced. "Yes, Papa."

Cade stared hard into the blinding wind to be certain the little imp made it safely into the hull. He sighed with relief when the last of her yellow oil slicker disappeared below.

His first mate's chortles reached Cade's ears as another gust cuffed his face. "What are you laughing at, Benk?" he growled, more at the inclement weather than at his longtime friend.

"Your little princess, that's what. Are you raising a seafarer or a daughter?" The man chuckled again.

Cade shot him a dubious glance. Benkins was aware of Cade's plans to sell the *Kismet* and put the maritime life behind him forever. Hadn't he secured a position at Milwaukee's Grain Exchange? Hadn't he bought a house for the two of them on Newberry Boulevard? It was all for Jenny's sake. Cade knew she needed proper schooling and training in the fine arts of becoming a lady. He knew his Jenny needed so many things he couldn't provide as a single father, and it caused him many a sleepless night. But one thing he had settled in his heart for sure: His shipping days were over. This was his last voyage.

He only hoped they would make it to shore alive.

Suddenly the wind blasted its fury down upon the schooner again, and a sickening, splintering of wood shook Cade from his reverie.

"It's the main topmast, Captain!" the lookout bellowed from the bow. They watched it topple into the seething lake like a dead tree limb.

"We can sail without it," he assured his crew. He had been forced to navigate ships in worse conditions.

The wind howled, and the ship pitched violently. Cade's frozen hands refused to hang onto the wheel another moment, and he was thrown backward. Benkins took his place in an instant while Cade fought for a handhold, lest he get hurled into the angry waves. The biblical story of Jonah flittered through his mind. Was he, Cade Danfield, like that prophet of old, running from God?

He knew the answer: He most certainly was!

❧

"Mother, please sip just a bit of this hot tea," Amanda urged, putting the spoon to the dying woman's lips. "Please."

"The light," Evelyn Lewis rasped, "I must tend the light."

"No, Mother. It's well past dawn and the storm has blown over. I cared for the light all night long. I didn't let it go out. And now," Amanda said, setting the teacup on the tray beside her mother's bed, "I've covered the Fresnel lens so it will not magnify the sun's rays and start the lighthouse on fire."

"Did you clean the lens first, child? You must clean the lens—"

"Yes, Mother. The windows and lenses are spotless. Everything is fine. Now, won't you please eat a tiny bite of this poached egg?"

Evelyn gestured with her hand in a feeble protest.

Amanda sighed with frustration and growing concern. Perhaps she should call for Dr. Edwards again. *No*, she decided, *it wouldn't do any good*. Dr. Edwards had said Mother was dying and suggested Amanda begin "making arrangements."

Gazing down at the woman's pasty complexion, Amanda knew what the doctor said was true. Each breath her mother took seemed labored. Her limp, brown, gray-streaked hair was parted in the middle, shrouding the sides of her gaunt face.

"Oh, Mother, please don't die," she whispered in desperation.

The sick woman's eyes fluttered open, and she smiled weakly. "Death is inevitable, child, and I long to be in the arms of my Savior."

But what about me? Amanda wanted to shout.

As if guessing her thoughts, her mother reached out a cold, thin hand. Amanda grasped it at once. "You're nineteen years old," the woman whispered. "You're smart and strong. You will find your way in this world without me."

"But Mr. Sloan—"

"Let him take over the lighthouse."

151

"No!"

Amanda watched as her mother's lips trembled in sallow amusement. "The North Point Light is not ours. I was fortunate to get the commission. But when I'm gone, you must give it up."

"This is my home," Amanda protested, "and I won't give it up without a fight."

"God has another home for you somewhere. Go to Chicago and live with your older brother and his family."

Amanda swept her gaze heavenward. The idea seemed absurd. Her brother, David, was twenty years older than she, and Amanda scarcely knew him, his wife, and their daughters. She only saw them once, maybe twice, a year, and she hadn't found any reason to take up written correspondence, although they seemed like decent, Christian people.

"David will take care of you," her mother murmured.

"He's got four girls of his own. I'll only be a burden."

"A blessed burden."

"A burden nevertheless."

Her mother looked pained at the retort, so Amanda quickly changed her tone. "Oh, you're right, of course. I'll be just fine. But please, will you eat some breakfast before you rest?"

The woman moaned and closed her eyes. "I cannot eat a bite."

Nibbling her lower lip in consternation, Amanda decided not to push the issue. She kissed her mother's tissue paper-thin cheek and collected the bedside tray before leaving the room. She felt exhausted from tending the beacon all night, yet it was a job she knew well and one she'd lived with for the past thirteen years.

She scarcely remembered her father, who had died when she was five. A year later, her mother had been commissioned to be the keeper of the North Point Light—Milwaukee's first lighthouse. It was a life Amanda had grown to love. How was she ever going to give it up? But she would have to leave the stout, octagonally-shaped lighthouse and its neighboring white clapboard home if her mother died—and all because of that blackheart, John Sloan.

Entering the spacious kitchen, she set the tray on the counter, stoked the fire in the stove, then peered out the long window. The sun glistened on the new-fallen snow, and just beyond the bluffs, Lake Michigan's white-capped waves rolled toward the shore. During the storm the night before, Amanda had prayed for the safety of any ships on the water as she kept the beacon burning bright.

A hearty knock startled Amanda from her musings. Collecting her wits, she pulled the apron off of her calico dress, patted the loose knot of light brown hair at the back of her head, and went to answer the call. When she pulled open the front door, she found Will Trekman standing on the covered porch, wearing a broad smile.

"Good morning, Miss Lewis," he began. His brown eyes sparkled with interest the way they always did when he came to visit. But Amanda found it odd that he could never seem to work up the gumption to ask to court her. She didn't force the matter, either, since she wasn't all that taken with Will. But he was nice, if not downright entertaining.

She gave him a polite nod. "Mr. Trekman."

"Quite a storm we had last night. I suppose it kept you and your mother busy."

"Yes, sir, it did." Amanda refrained from telling Will that her mother lay deathly ill. No one knew, save Dr. Edwards, but of course, Reverend Reed would be added to the list soon enough, and then all of Milwaukee City would learn the news.

Amanda cringed inwardly.

"You're cold," Will noticed.

"Oh, where are my manners? Please, come inside. I'm terribly sorry."

His grin broadened. "Aw, nothing to be sorry 'bout, Miss Lewis. Fact is, I'm not making a social call. . . although, well, you know I wouldn't mind it being such." Will's face flamed with the admission, and Amanda couldn't hide a little smile.

He took off his cap, exposing shaggy, blond curls. "Mr. Harringer sent me today," Will informed her. "Seems the hotels in town are all full with that convention here for the next few days, and there's some folks he'd like to find rooms for. Since you and your mother have been known to take in boarders, Mr. Harringer wondered if you might consider the undertaking once more."

Amanda opened her mouth to refuse but then thought better of it. She'd have to explain to Will about her mother's diminishing health, and inevitably John Sloan would hear the news. The wicked man would be upon her doorstep in no time, demanding the details and ordering her to pack her bags. Well, Sloan had another thing coming. Amanda wasn't going to give into his whims so easily. He might associate with important people in the city, but Amanda knew her job, and she would prove herself competent and get the commission to stay on at the lighthouse one way or another.

She cleared her throat. "How many people did you say?"

"Three. A ship's captain, his daughter, and their family friend, another man."

"Three, you say?"

"Yes. And the little girl, bless her heart, said she would love to meet you. She credits you and your mother with saving her life. Apparently, she was on a schooner with her father and his crew during last night's storm. The vessel is badly damaged, but it made it to shore intact, thanks to your keeping the light."

Amanda could scarcely decline the request now. "Yes, of course. We'll take them in. Poor child, she must have been scared out of her mind."

Will looked doubtful. "I don't think so. She's a spirited little thing. Reminds me of you." He caught himself. "Oh! I didn't mean that as an insult, Miss Lewis. Please forgive me. I just meant. . .well, I admire your tenacity greatly, and—"

"It's quite all right," Amanda replied, smiling. "I'm sure your intentions were above reproach."

"Thank you." He bowed slightly but still seemed flustered as she showed him to the door.

"I'll expect three guests shortly, then."

"Thank you. And Mr. Harringer said he'll see to it you're well paid. He and the captain have important business."

Amanda nodded, thinking the extra money would pay for Dr. Edwards's visits and perhaps fund her mother's funeral also. She pushed the dark notion aside. *No! This can't be happening. Not my mother. Please, God, no!*

"Miss Lewis?"

She shook herself mentally. "I'm sorry. Did you say something?"

"Just farewell and—" Will cleared his throat. "I wondered if I might call on you again sometime soon."

"Of course. That would be lovely."

He gave her a pleased grin before striding purposely for his horse.

Amanda closed the front door and leaned her back against it, feeling like she might collapse from the weight of her burdens. She quickly reminded herself that God wouldn't give her more than she could bear. He would help her through this wretched time.

Now, if only she could remember that Bible truth.

Gathering her skirts, she headed upstairs to prepare the bedrooms for the imminent lodgers.

Chapter 2

Cade hadn't known what exactly to expect when Samuel Harringer's steward announced that he, Jenny, and Benkins would be staying with two female lighthouse keepers, but he certainly didn't envision the likes of Miss Amanda Lewis. When Will Trekman had mentioned "the Widow Lewis and her daughter," Cade imagined an old woman and a tall, skinny spinster with a jutting chin and a wart at the end of her pointed nose. Instead he'd been introduced to a comely young lady with light brown hair, freckles, and sparkling hazel eyes.

"I hope you'll find these rooms comfortable," she said as they stood in the wide, upstairs hallway.

"They're plenty comfortable," Cade replied. "We're indebted to your kindness, Miss Lewis."

She blushed prettily, and Cade couldn't help a grin.

"If you'll pardon me," Benkins cut in, "I'm going to snooze the afternoon away." He yawned audibly as if to prove his point. "I have to lie down before I fall down."

"Please, Mr. Benkins, by all means get your much-needed rest." She turned to Cade. "And you, too, Captain. . .and Jenny." She smiled at his daughter, who gazed back in respectful fascination. "I'll have you know I prayed for your ship last night while I kept the beacon burning."

"But how'd you know it was us?" Jenny asked.

"I didn't. I simply prayed for any ships out on the lake, lost in the storm."

"That was us, all right," the girl declared. "Except, we weren't lost. My father knew where we were and what he was doing the whole time, didn't you, Papa?"

Cade sent his daughter an affectionate wink since he didn't have the heart to tell her he'd been thrown off course by the storm. He might have sailed into the steep bluffs and missed the harbor entirely had it not been for the North Point Light guiding the *Kismet* to safety.

He looked at Amanda Lewis and gave her a mannerly grin. "Thank you for your prayers. The Almighty answered them." Cade wondered for the umpteenth time why his prayers for his beloved wife hadn't been heard years ago. He had begged and pleaded with God to spare her life, but to no avail.

And he hadn't prayed since.

"Forgive me for noticing," the young mistress of the lighthouse said, "but you do look weary, Captain."

Cade shook off the past. "Yes, I am. Actually, we're all quite exhausted after last night. I hope you won't think us rude if we sleep for a few hours."

She smiled. "I must confess I am as fatigued as you. I can only thank the Lord my guests want to nap. . .so I can too!"

They shared a brief, polite laugh.

"I shall be downstairs if you need anything."

"Thank you, Miss Lewis."

Cade observed Jenny staring after the young woman with an expression of awe on her face. Then she turned her blue-eyed gaze on him. "Papa, can I explore the lighthouse? I'm not tired."

"Yes, you are. You're overtired. That's why you don't feel sleepy."

"But—"

"No arguments, my dear. You will rest this afternoon even if you don't actually sleep."

Jenny pouted but obeyed and whirled into her ascribed bedroom. Cade followed to be sure she did his bidding.

"Papa, just look at all these doll babies on the shelves. Aren't they beautiful?"

"Yes, they are." A stab of guilt cut to his heart. Jenny should have dolls in colorful lacy clothes too, but instead Cade had forced her into a sailor's lifestyle. "When we move into our own house, I'll see that you have every doll you ever wanted," he promised her.

"And a pretty quilt like this one, Papa?" The girl ran her hand over the blue-and-white patchwork piece on the bed.

"Just like it."

Jenny glanced at him as a little frown began to mar her brow. "I think I'm going to miss the *Kismet*," she said.

Cade chuckled. "You'll miss her for a week, princess. But soon you'll meet so many new friends, you'll become a regular landlubber. Why, you might rue the day your father ever whisked you off on a sailing ship."

"I'll never 'rue' it," she stated doggedly. "Whatever *that* means."

After a good-natured laugh, Cade said, "It means you'll be sorry, but I hope you never are."

"I won't be sorry," Jenny vowed earnestly. "I have loved our years on the *Kismet,* but I'll love our new life just as much."

How Cade wished her declaration would continue to ring true in the weeks, months, and years to come.

"I wonder if this is Miss Lewis's room and she's letting me borrow it," Jenny murmured, letting her gaze roam over all four corners of the light blue walls.

"Could be."

"But where will she sleep if I'm in her bedroom?" Jenny wondered.

"That's Miss Lewis's business. She and her mother are our hostesses, and we ought not question their decisions. Now lie down and get some shut-eye."

"Aye, Captain," his daughter said with a mock salute.

Cade shook his head as she giggled and bounced back onto the bed. "Benk has influenced you, I see. Well, no matter. Soon you will have socially upstanding playmates and you'll forget all about that pirate."

"I heard that, Cap'n," his friend called from the next room.

Chuckling, Cade crossed the room and kissed Jenny's forehead. Then he made his way to his designated chamber, stretched out on the soft mattress, and promptly fell asleep.

❧

Amanda stoked the fire in the cast-iron cookstove near the enclosed porch. Her mother lay pallid on the daybed close by. During the summer months, the porch was open to the cool lake breezes, but in the wintertime, sturdy glass panes were tapped into the window frames so the room could be enjoyed all year round. It was Mother's favorite, so when she'd taken ill, Amanda immediately had set up a sickroom on the sunporch. However, it hadn't seemed to provide any measure of a cure. Then again, the doctor had said there wasn't a remedy for consumption. Gazing at her mother's ashen face, Amanda knew it wouldn't be long now.

Her mother's eyelids fluttered open and she stared back at Amanda. Her gaze was amazingly crystal-clear for a dying woman.

"Do we have company?" she asked in a brittle voice.

"Yes, Mother. A widowed skipper, his young daughter, and their friend, Mr. Hosea Benkins, are staying with us for a short while. They had nowhere to go, and I feared if I didn't take them in, news would spread of your illness." Amanda blew out an annoyed breath. "And the last thing I feel like doing is answering to that high-handed John Sloan and his indolent son."

"Mmm. . .a widowed skipper, you say?"

"Yes, his name is Captain Danfield."

"Captain. . .I dreamed about him."

Amanda shook her head and sat down. She raised her mother's listless hand and held it between both of hers. "You probably just heard Will Trekman making the usual introductions."

"Yes, I thought I heard Will. He's such a nice young man. But, no. . . this dream was different. It was unlike any I have ever had." After several labored breaths, she said, "Tell me what he looks like, this captain."

"Well, he's—"

"Handsome? Is he handsome?"

Amanda laughed softly, remembering the captain's dark blond hair, blue eyes, and bushy mustache that twitched whenever he smiled, as though he were trying to conceal the gesture. "Yes, Mother, he's handsome. I imagine he'll have a string of ladies at his doorstep by the end of the week."

"Mmm. . ."

A fanciful expression clouded her mother's blue-green eyes, and Amanda wondered if she envisioned herself young again. Perhaps she would have enjoyed being swept off her feet by the charming Cade Danfield, except he looked too young for her mother. Amanda guessed he was in his early thirties.

"The Lord has promised me He will take care of you," Mother suddenly rasped. "Now, I'm assuring you. Don't be sad when I leave this world,

Amanda. Don't cry for me. I'll be in a better place, and you'll be taken care of by your heavenly Father, who loves you more than I ever could."

She closed her eyes, looking so very tired.

"Wait, Mother," Amanda pleaded, "please don't leave just yet."

"You. . .you have been a. . .a good daughter," she managed to whisper before lapsing into a deep sleep.

Chapter 3

I'm telling you, that little lighthouse keeper is hiding something, Cap'n."

Cade sat back on the settee near the fire and watched his friend pace the parlor rug. He wondered if there were any truth to Benk's suspicions.

"Didn't you notice her brooding expression at the dinner table?" he asked. "And didn't you see how skittish she was when Jenny wandered into the kitchen and happened near the back porch door?" Benk shook his dark brown head. "I'd wager Amanda Lewis is hiding a man in there."

Cade threw his head back and hooted. "Not likely."

Benk raised a thick brow. "Oh?"

"She's not the type," he said, still chuckling. He'd seen the young lady's innocent blush at least twice since they'd first met that afternoon. However, he did have to agree about the somber countenance; obviously something troubled Amanda Lewis to the point of distraction.

"All right, then I'll bet she's involved in something illegal."

Benkins scrunched his face into a frown. For all his twenty-eight years, the man looked twice his age. But Cade knew a harsh upbringing, flagrant lifestyle, and military duty were to blame. Still, he marveled at the fact that Hosea Benkins had been gloriously born again some six years ago. They'd been on the Atlantic, patrolling the North Carolina coast. The sea had rippled like black velvet as their gunner sliced through the water. That very night Cade had led Benk to a saving knowledge of Jesus Christ.

It was the year before Isabelle died.

"And where's her mother?" Benk railed on, drawing Cade from his reverie. "Miss Lewis told us the woman had errands but changed her story not an hour later and said her mother was visiting a sick friend. Bah! I don't believe it."

"Amanda Lewis is not a good liar, is she?"

"The worst."

Cade grinned at the retort. Sure, he had picked up on the variance in explanations, but he figured it wasn't any of his business to challenge the young lady.

Exhaling a long breath, he sat forward and lifted his cup and saucer off the polished table. He sipped his coffee thoughtfully.

"You know, Cap'n, I heard it said lighthouse keepers are sometimes the worst of pirates. The rumor goes they loot disabled ships that run ashore. Could be the Lewis women are hiding booty right under our noses."

Cade raised a brow. "I think you possess an overactive imagination, my friend."

"Is that right? Well, let me remind you that your daughter is up in the lighthouse with our little buccaneer as we speak."

Cade narrowed his gaze, and then Benkins nodded emphatically.

"All right," he said in vexed agreement. He set down his coffee cup. "I'll supervise Jenny's lighthouse tour if it'll make you feel any better."

"Good. While you're gone, I aim to have a look-see in the back porch."

"It's none of our business what's out on that porch. We're guests here, remember?"

"I ain't plannin' on doin' no harm, Cap'n." Benkins's features were masked by a virtuous expression.

Cade snorted. The wag. Benk could get him to laugh during the worst of times.

"Oh, very well," Cade said in parting. "Just mind your manners."

"Of course, sir."

He shook his head over his friend's intentions while making his way to the lighthouse.

As Cade crossed the dusky, moonlit yard, he felt the snow crunching beneath his feet and heard the roar of the waves pounding against the shoreline below. Immediately, he took note of the bluff just beyond the lighthouse, which was located some one hundred feet from the house. To his dismay, he realized if the incline became just slick enough, Amanda Lewis might find herself sliding off the cliff and into the frigid waters of Lake Michigan.

She and her mother need to hire a man to build some sort of safety fence, he concluded, wondering why no one had thought of the danger till now.

Reaching the lighthouse, he climbed the stairs. The structure wasn't terribly tall—Cade guessed some thirty feet high—and it had been manufactured in cast iron or steel, which made for icy walls along the winding stairwell. Nearing the top, he could hear Amanda speaking to Jenny about her work.

"The lantern must be lit every night by the time the sun sets, and I have to be sure it doesn't go out all night long."

"You stay up all night?" Jenny made it sound more like a privilege than a chore.

"Well, my mother. . ." Amanda cleared her throat. "My mother and I have always taken turns."

"I see. Well, on our ship, *Kismet,* I sometimes stayed up all night. But mostly Papa made me turn in before ten o'clock." She paused. "I wonder what my bedtime will be now that we're not going to live onboard anymore."

Cade grinned as he eavesdropped.

"Miss Amanda?"

"Yes?"

"Wherever did you get all those dolls? And is that your bedroom I'm sleeping in?"

"Yes, it's my room, and I received my doll collection from my older brother, David. Each Christmas, he buys me another one." Cade heard the smile in her voice. "David says, as a baby, I looked like a doll to him. I believe he still thinks of me as a child, even though I'm nineteen years old."

"Practically an old maid!"

Cade winced. Obviously he and Jenny needed to discuss primary social graces. . .and soon. But much to his relief, Amanda's light laughter echoed down from the lamp room.

Nineteen years old, he thought. She was thirteen years younger than he, closer to Jenny's age than his own—and hardly an "old maid."

With a lull in the conversation, Cade decided it might be an opportune time to make his presence known.

"Hello?" he called.

"Papa? Is that you?"

" 'Tis I," he answered in feigned formality, climbing the last few steps.

"It's very bright up here," Jenny informed him.

"Yes, it is." Squinting, he gave the device a quick inspection. "Fresnel lens, isn't that correct?"

"Yes, Captain. Fourth order." Amanda smiled, looking impressed by his wee bit of lighthouse knowledge.

"Miss Amanda says she has to trim the lantern's wicks every four hours during the night," Jenny explained. "It's in the rules for lighthouse keepers."

"And a good thing it is for us lake-faring sailors."

"But, Papa, we're not sailors anymore, remember?"

"How could I forget?" Cade replied, grinning at his daughter.

"I think my work is done up here for the time being," Amanda announced. "Shall we walk back down?"

"Certainly. Come along, Jenny."

"Yes, Papa." The girl paused. "Know what Miss Amanda said? She said she has to brave the catwalk that goes all around the lamp room to clean the outside of the windows. She's not afraid of heights or anything. Just like me."

"Is that so?" He tried not to envision the young lady out there on a windy day. Then again, he didn't have to; she painted a verbal picture for him.

"One time I was frightened," Amanda admitted, "when a bird flew into one of the panes and broke the window. It was during a fierce storm, and I had to go out on the catwalk and hold the tarp in place while Mother tried to secure it on the inside."

Cade berated himself. And he'd been worrying about her sliding off the edge of the bluffs? Blown from the catwalk seemed like the real threat.

"You sound like a courageous woman, Miss Lewis," he managed.

"I have to be, I suppose."

Cade purposely continued descending the wooden staircase at a snail's pace, hoping Benk had finished his snooping. Next, he entered the house noisily, complimenting Miss Lewis on a fine supper of homemade turkey soup, bread, and leftover Thanksgiving Day pumpkin pie.

"It really wasn't much, Captain, I assure you. But I'm glad you enjoyed the meal." She paused in the kitchen. "Um. . .if you'll excuse me, I need to take care of something." Her somewhat nervous glance included himself and Jenny. "Please make yourselves comfortable in the parlor, and I'll join you there shortly."

Cade nodded politely before escorting his daughter into the other room. Much to his relief, Benk stood by the hearth, one arm dangling from the mantel while he gazed pensively into the flickering flames.

"Jenny, run along and get ready for bed."

"But Papa, Miss Amanda promised to tie up my hair in rags so it'll be curly tomorrow."

"Then more's the reason you should change into your nightclothes."

Jenny gave an aggravated huff but stomped up the steps in a semblance of obedience.

"I'm definitely going to have a talk with that girl," he muttered in her wake. He glanced at Benk before striding purposefully toward him. "What did you discover?"

Benk's expression looked grim. "Miss Amanda does indeed have a dark secret, Cap'n."

"Oh? And what might that be?"

"There's a dying woman in that enclosed porch. Her grandmother, or mother, perhaps."

Cade lifted his chin and inhaled slowly, thoughtfully, wondering what all this meant. "Why would she keep such a secret—unless the woman had contracted some sort of plague or other terrible disease? But if the patient were contagious, why would Miss Lewis have consented to take us in?"

"Money? She needs the money."

"Maybe." Cade shrugged. "Well, no matter. I must investigate, seeing as I can hardly risk our lives for a few nights' lodging fees."

"I agree."

After pursing his lips in contemplation, Cade glanced at his friend once more. "Did the dying woman see you?"

"No, she's too far gone to see anyone. Might well be dead by mornin'."

The news disturbed Cade greatly, and it was all he could do to keep from hurling one question after another at Amanda the moment she stepped into the parlor.

"Miss Lewis," he began carefully, "my friend Mr. Benkins happened onto the porch adjacent to the kitchen while we were in the lighthouse." He watched the young lady pale slightly, but she maintained her ever-proper expression. "I wondered," Cade continued, "if you would explain to us about the invalid out there. We're a bit worried over our own health at the moment."

"The invalid, Captain, is my mother. . .and she's not contagious," Amanda replied in a sturdy tone as she seated herself. "Mother is dying of consumption. Yes, I lied to you earlier. But it's imperative no one find out about her illness until. . ." Her countenance suddenly fell, and Cade actually felt sorry for her. "Until she dies. Then I'll be unable to keep the truth hidden any longer."

Lowering himself into a well-worn upholstered armchair across from the settee on which Amanda sat, Cade relaxed slightly. "So money is not the issue?"

"No, Captain, although I will admit to owing on some medical bills."

"Hmm. . ."

Amanda glanced at him, then at Benk, then back to Cade once more. "Please don't say anything to anyone. Please?"

"I beg your pardon, miss," Benkins said, "but my guess is by tomorrow morning you'll be forced to contact the funeral director, your pastor, and anyone else involved with such sorrowful preparations."

She bit her lower lip as if to keep it from trembling. She regarded Benk curiously, no doubt wondering over his frankness.

"We're war veterans, miss Lewis," Cade explained. "Need I say more?"

She shook her light brown head.

"May I inquire over your mother's spiritual condition, miss?" Benkins asked haltingly.

"Spiritual?" Amanda smiled ever so slightly. "Oh, she has a great faith and loves the Lord. God is my consolation in all this. Mother's suffering will be over soon, and she will be with Him in heaven."

"Glory be!" Benk fairly shouted. "Well, I feel better. How 'bout you, Cap'n?"

"There is no glory in death," he replied sullenly, recalling his dear wife's graveside service. He'd missed the actual funeral since it had taken him so long to return home from the East Coast.

He forced his thoughts back to the issue at hand. "Tell me, Miss Lewis, what tragedy will befall you once word gets out about your mother's death? Why the secrecy?" Cade hadn't meant to sound so cynical, but he couldn't seem to help it.

Amanda answered forthrightly. "There's a prominent man in Milwaukee by the name of John Sloan, and for the past few years, his son, Leonard, has coveted my mother's commission as keeper of the North Point Light. Together the Sloans have made our lives miserable with their subtle threats and general antagonism. Furthermore, Mr. John Sloan is a good friend of our lighthouse's district superintendent. In essence, Captain, when my mother dies, I will be forced from my home."

The reality of her plight settled on him, and Cade blinked in understanding. "A most unfortunate circumstance, to be sure." He hoped his tone sounded kinder.

"Well," Amanda said, rising slowly from the settee, "I don't intend to leave without a fight. I know this job better than Len Sloan, and I expect to prove myself and retain my mother's commission!"

With thumb and forefinger, Cade rubbed his mustache along the exterior of his mouth in an effort to keep his mirth in check. But when Benkins cast him an incredulous glare, the grin escaped.

"More power to you, Miss Lewis," Cade replied at last. "I wish you all the best."

"Really?"

Cade nodded.

"In that case, would you be willing to write a letter of recommendation for me—one I could hand to the superintendent?" She tipped her head in a businesslike manner. "You told me you were thankful for the beacon in the storm last night. Would you care to document your gratitude on my behalf?"

From the corner of his eye, Cade could see Benk's shoulders shaking in silent amusement. His friend had most likely dubbed Amanda Lewis an imp among imps. However, Cade had to acknowledge the swell of respect he felt for the young lighthouse mistress. She possessed an uncommon inner strength mixed with a good dose of gumption. Not only had she tended the light all by herself for who knew how long, but she'd cared for her dying mother while tolerating three inquisitive, if not altogether nosy, boarders!

"Miss Lewis," Cade began warmly, "I would be honored to write a recommendation. . .or anything else which might help secure your position."

An invisible weight seemed to lift from her capable shoulders. "Thank you, Captain Danfield. Thank you ever so much."

For the first time all day, Cade saw Amanda Lewis's smile reach her golden-flecked hazel eyes.

Chapter 4

Three days later, Cade stood in the receiving line after Evelyn Lewis's funeral, waiting to extend his condolences to the young lighthouse mistress, her brother, and his family. As it happened, hotel accommodations had opened up the day before just as Amanda's relatives arrived from Chicago. Cade, Jenny, and Benk moved out, while David Lewis's clan moved in.

Their paths did cross long enough, however, for all of them to share the noon meal, and from what Cade observed, Amanda was going to have to fight more than the Sloans for her station at the North Point Light. She would have to contend with her brother also. The man had determined his "baby sister" would return to Chicago with him and his family. Nonetheless, they seemed like decent, Christian people who genuinely cared for Amanda's welfare. Her fate could be much worse.

The line inched forward, and Cade watched Amanda graciously receive the sympathies of a teary-eyed, older woman. He decided the young lady was handling her mother's death quite well, all things considered.

The line moved again, and Cade saw a balding gentleman in a dark suit extend his right hand to Amanda. When she blatantly refused it, Cade raised curious brows. He noticed the obstinate jut of her chin, and her hazel eyes were suddenly the color of icy Lake Michigan. To Cade's surprise, she stared the well-dressed gentleman down until he looked away, seemingly abashed.

Instantly, Cade knew the identity of the man. His next words confirmed Cade's thoughts.

"I'm John Sloan," the man said to David Lewis, thrusting his rejected hand at Amanda's brother. "I've known your mother for years. I'm ever so sorry for your loss."

"Nice to meet you, Mr. Sloan. Thank you for coming," David replied politely. Then he whispered something to Amanda, and by the chagrined look on her face, Cade could only guess her brother was telling her to behave.

He grinned, rubbing his mustache self-consciously.

"Plucky little thing, ain't she?" Benk muttered from behind him.

Cade couldn't help chuckling. He turned. "Must you make jokes at a funeral?" he asked in a hushed tone. His words were directed more at himself than at anyone else. He shouldn't have laughed at his friend's quip, but he'd been thinking along those same lines.

"Ain't no joke, Cap'n," Benkins replied, his brown eyes twinkling. "You saw it same as me."

Cade swung back around. He saw it all right.

A few more steps, and Cade stood in front of Amanda. In actuality, she was not the "little thing" as Benk had described but stood only four inches shorter than his six feet.

Cade offered his hand, and she placed her gloved one in his. "Please accept my deepest sympathies, Miss Lewis," he said, all amusement aside. "Jenny sends her regards as well, but under the circumstances, I didn't feel comfortable bringing her along. I allowed her to stay with the Harringers this afternoon."

"Of course." Amanda smiled slightly. "And thank you, Captain Danfield. Thank you for everything."

He grinned sheepishly. "You're most welcome, but it's I who owe you a word of thanks for tending the light so faithfully and taking us in."

Benk nudged him with his elbow. "You're holdin' up the line, Cap'n," he murmured.

Releasing Amanda's hand, Cade gave her a single nod and moved on to David Lewis. He was a quick-gestured man who seemed a trifle impatient, especially when it came to ladies' sensibilities. Then again, he most likely had his fair share to reckon with, seeing as his family consisted only of women.

"Nice to have met you, Captain," David said. "Perhaps our paths will cross again."

"Yes, perhaps they will." Cade had to fight the urge to glance at Amanda. What was the matter with him, anyway? It must be the solemn atmosphere in this dimly lit church that wreaked havoc with his emotions.

Moving down the line, Cade offered words of consolation to David's wife, Martha, a handsome woman with a regal constitution. Next came her four daughters, whom Cade guessed to be only slightly younger than Amanda. They seemed well mannered enough, and the youngest looked about Jenny's age.

Cade waited for Benkins at the end of the queue, and together they strode toward the door of the little church. Passing through the vestibule, Cade heard someone hail him. Turning on his heel, he spotted John Sloan, who stood with a small group of men and was waving Cade over.

" 'Scuse me for a minute, will you, Benk?"

"Sure. I'll wait outside."

Cade approached the small group of men.

"Captain Danfield, isn't it?"

Giving the elder Sloan's hand a shake, he nodded. "That's right."

"My name's John Sloan," he stated unnecessarily, "and this is my son, Len."

Cade nodded a greeting at the doughy-looking man with hair combed to one side in greasy strands. He appeared to be somewhere in his late twenties. Then the older Sloan introduced him to three other men.

"I understand you're working for Sam Harringer at the Grain Exchange," Sloan remarked.

"Right again."

"Well," he said, puffing out his chest, "if you don't like it there, come see me. I own the iron mill in Bay View."

"Is that so?"

Sloan nodded. "We're doing most of our exports by railroad, but I might be able to find work for a shrewd skipper."

Cade was tempted to explain his resolution to give up sailing but decided to save his breath. He had a feeling words were wasted on John Sloan. With him, money talked. He'd met enough John Sloans in his life to know the type.

But if that were true, Cade had to wonder why the man would desire the lighthouse position for his son. Everyone knew it was hard work and paid next to nothing. He glanced at Len and couldn't imagine the portly man running up and down the lighthouse stairs. He'd die of heart failure within a week.

Cade's suspicions blossomed and grew. Suddenly he remembered Benk's talk of lighthouse pirates who looted crippled vessels. Could it be the Sloans were desiring the lighthouse keeper's position as a means to conduct unscrupulous business transactions?

No. Cade quickly set the idea aside, considering it ludicrous.

"Mr. Sloan," Cade replied carefully, "thank you for your kind offer. It's always nice to have options."

"That it is. That it is."

With a parting nod, Cade left the small assembly and stepped out into the blinding sunshine. The air was crisp but quite tolerable for a November day.

"I've been meaning to tell you," Benk began as they started off for the hotel, "I got me a commission on a schooner leaving day after tomorrow."

The news sounded bittersweet to Cade, and yet he knew his friend had no intentions of giving up the seafaring life just because he had. "This will be your first voyage without me in many years. But I wish you the best."

"I know. . .and I'll miss ya, that's the truth. But a man's got to work, or he doesn't eat."

Cade gave him a friendly clap on the back. "The next time you're in Milwaukee I'll be settled in that little white house with the green shutters that I purchased for Jenny and me."

Benk grinned. "All's you need is a plucky little wife to complete the picture, eh, Cap'n?"

Cade grinned sardonically. "Have someone particular in mind?"

"Oh, no, no. . .why I wouldn't ever tell you your business."

"Of course not." Cade had to chuckle at the irony. Benk had a flair for butting into Cade's affairs, although he didn't mind it. Where would he be today if it hadn't been for his good friend's advice?

But as they continued their walk to the hotel, he mulled over Benk's reference to the plucky Miss Amanda Lewis. His longtime first mate was terribly misguided, suggesting that they'd make a good match. Admittedly, Cade was quite taken with her, but he felt as though he would be robbing the cradle if he pursued her. On the other hand, she hardly resembled a child. He figured she'd done plenty of growing up in the past few months, what with her mother so ill. Furthermore, he admired her spunk and courage. Life certainly wouldn't be dull in her company, and Jenny thought highly of her.

He shook himself mentally. What was he thinking?

After a few moments of silently berating himself, Cade pushed the irrational notion as far from his mind as possible.

"David, please be reasonable," Amanda begged her older brother. "I can hardly pack up this entire household in a day. Why not allow me to fulfill Mother's commission until the end of the year? That's when the superintendent of the district will have to make out his annual report and name the new lighthouse keeper."

"And I suppose you think it should be you."

"I'd like it to be me, yes."

Her brother, brown-haired and hazel-eyed, snorted disdainfully. "My dear, that was more work than two women could handle, let alone one."

"I am very capable of keeping this light," Amanda said through a clenched jaw.

To her amazement, her brother's features softened. "I don't doubt for a moment you can handle the job." He strode forward and took both her hands in his. "But where our mother, widowed with a young child thirteen years ago, felt she didn't have any choice as to her vocation, you do, Amanda. I would like to see you marry well and live comfortably instead of staying awake all hours of the night to keep that wretched beacon burning."

"But—"

"But nothing. My mind is made up. And since Mother appointed me your guardian until you take a husband, you will do as I say. You are coming to live with us in Chicago, and that's the end of this discussion."

"David," his wife, Martha, said in a diplomatic tone, "I'm sure Amanda has no qualms about living with us, but I do think she's right. We'll never get this house packed in the next day or two. I believe it would be wise to let Amanda stay in Milwaukee for the next month and tie up any loose ends. We can return at Christmastime and help her move."

"A month?"

"A few short weeks, dear," Martha replied. She caught Amanda's gaze and sent her an affectionate wink.

"Oh, I suppose a few weeks wouldn't hurt anything."

Amanda gave her brother a grateful smile. It bought her some time—time to write the superintendent and request to continue her mother's commission.

However, David's next warning gave her pause.

"But if I even suspect you're applying for the lighthouse tender position, I'll be on the next train, and you, Amanda, will be very sorry."

She raised a stubborn chin at the challenge. "I'm a grown woman, and Mother never intended for me to have a guardian at nineteen years old. She drew up her will long ago. So what can you do to me?"

"I'll take you over my knee, that's what I can do."

Amanda inhaled sharply. "You wouldn't dare."

"Wouldn't I?"

Her eyes locked with his, so similar in shape and color, and Amanda knew she'd met her match in her older brother.

"I'm not a child," she asserted but with a meeker tone.

"Then stop acting like one. Put away your childish dreams, Amanda. You cannot keep the North Point Light all by yourself. Your future is in Chicago with Martha, the girls, and me."

Chapter 5

David and his family returned to Chicago, and for the entire week afterward, Amanda could do no more than tend the light, eat, and sleep. In a word, she felt depressed. She missed her mother, and she felt so alone in the large house despite all her women friends who visited regularly and brought food, hugs, prayers, and sympathetic words.

Several men from church stopped by and offered to help Amanda with minor repairs, Will Trekman being the most enthusiastic of the lot. But when he showed up bright and early on Saturday morning with a wagon-load of wooden splats, Amanda had to wonder what he had in mind. She peered down at him from the lighthouse tower where she'd been cleaning the lens and surrounding windowpanes. As she watched him unload the wood, she set down her cloth and descended the spiral staircase, deciding to investigate.

"Good morning, Mr. Trekman," she called, stepping out of the lighthouse.

"A good morning it is, too," Will replied. He grinned at her. "The snow has melted and the sun is shining. . .it feels like a spring day. Wouldn't it be nice if it were the end of winter?"

Amanda chuckled. "Winter has only begun."

"I know, I know. . .wishful thinking on my part."

"So tell me, what are you doing with all this wood?"

Will looked confused. "It's for your fence."

"Fence? What fence?"

"The one Captain Danfield hired me to build."

Amanda's brows shot up in surprise. "He hired you to build a fence?"

"Yes. It's to run along the property line here, parallel to the bluff." Will pointed down the side of the yard in illustration.

Nibbling her lower lip, Amanda wondered if in all her grief she'd missed something. Had Captain Danfield mentioned a fence? She searched her memory but couldn't recall such a conversation.

"Wait," she told Will, "I think there must be some mistake. I never ordered a fence, and why should Captain Danfield hire you to build it?"

"I don't know. He asked me to do the job, paid me, so here I am." He frowned. "I thought you had worked out some sort of arrangement."

Amanda shook her head and released a long, slow breath. "No, I didn't. And I suppose I should seek him out and ask him about it."

"Would you like me to go instead?" Will offered.

"No. Actually, the walk to the hotel will do me good."

Will frowned. "The captain isn't staying at the hotel anymore. Why, he lives about half a mile away on Newberry Boulevard. Sold his schooner and bought a house."

"Hmm. . .I didn't know that. Well, if you'll tell me where it is, I could use the walk. I haven't really been out in awhile, and it's such a lovely day."

"Of course. The fresh air will do you good. But perhaps I should escort you."

"That's not necessary. Since the war, women have had to see them-selves everywhere around town. I will be fine."

Somewhat reluctantly, Will gave her the captain's new address.

"Thank you, Mr. Trekman, and please go inside and make yourself at home. There's coffee on the stove."

"I appreciate it," he replied with a nod. His brown eyes shone with earnestness. "But, um. . .don't you think it's high time you called me Will. . . Amanda?"

The question took her aback. Will was certainly overcoming his shyness!

After a moment's deliberation, Amanda agreed to the use of their first names. She'd known the young man for a year. He'd moved to Milwaukee from a tiny lumber town in northern Wisconsin and worked hard, hop-ing to make something of himself.

She lifted her hand in a parting wave. "I won't be gone long."

He looked so pleased when she took off on her stroll that Amanda felt somewhat giddy. Will Trekman was probably the sweetest man she'd ever met, and slowly an idea began to form. What if Will would agree to marry her? Surely she could easily renew her mother's lighthouse post under those circumstances. The superintendent wouldn't have any qualms then, and David wouldn't be able to bat an eyelash at her, let alone switch her.

Marriage to Will. That really wouldn't be so bad. He was almost charming when he put his mind to it. He enjoyed the lighthouse work, and he was diligent, strong, and a Christian man. He seemed romantically interested in her, so how could she go about eliciting a proposal from him. . .and soon? If it took Will a full year to ask to call her by her given name, it would most likely take him another five years to work up the courage to ask for her hand in marriage. What was a girl to do?

Amanda reached the captain's residence and knocked on the heavy wooden front door. It had been painted the same grass green as the shutters and trim of the white-sided saltbox. She pulled her dark blue woolen wrap tighter around her shoulders and suddenly felt self-conscious about her appearance. Having been up all night tending the light, she figured she looked disheveled at best. Smoothing her hair back, she wished she had taken the time to repin it.

The door opened, and a stout little woman with wiry gray hair and jowls like a bulldog stepped forward. "May I help you, miss?"

"Yes. I would like to speak with Captain Danfield, please."

The door opened wider and the woman beckoned Amanda into the foyer. "Your name?"

"Amanda Lewis."

The woman nodded politely. "Please wait here, and let me see if the captain is available."

As Amanda patiently awaited a reply, she glanced around the spacious front hall. Obviously the captain was still getting settled as there wasn't a stick of furniture in sight and the walls were devoid of any framed art.

"Miss Lewis, what a pleasant surprise."

Amanda fairly jumped as the captain's voice echoed from the back of the house. She smiled as he neared, noticing the contrast between his crisp white shirt and black trousers. Standing just inches away, he held out his right hand. She placed hers in his palm, and he bowed over it gallantly. Amanda felt her cheeks warm pink at the gesture.

"What can I do for you?" the captain asked, his mustache twitching with the hidden grin beneath it.

Amanda collected her suddenly scattered wits. "I, um, came to inquire over the fence you hired Will Trekman to build."

"Yes?"

"Yes." She paused. When no explanation was forthcoming, she said, "I wondered, Captain, why you felt I needed a fence and. . .well, why you didn't mention anything to me about it?"

"You didn't receive my note?"

"Your note?" Amanda immediately felt foolish. Cards and letters had been pouring in for days, but she hadn't read a single one.

"I sent the missive earlier in the week."

"Forgive me. I'm behind in reading my mail."

"Understandable. You've had quite a shock." Once more he held out his hand. "Allow me to take your wrap, and then won't you come in and sit down? I'm afraid the only chairs I've acquired thus far are in the dining area, but the room is very comfortable. We can discuss this matter further in there."

Amanda handed over her cloak in silent agreement and followed Cade through the empty parlor and into the formal dining room. A cherrywood table and matching chairs elegantly occupied the floor space, and in the corner, the hearth glowed with dwindling early morning embers.

"Please, sit down, Miss Lewis. May I have Mrs. Parson pour you some coffee or tea?"

"No, thank you." Amanda took a seat and watched as Cade claimed a chair. By the look of the newspapers tossed askew on the polished tabletop, she deduced she'd interrupted his morning reading. "Is Mrs. Parson your housekeeper?" she asked.

"Yes, and I feel fortunate to have employed her."

"And you're adjusting to your new position at the Grain Exchange?"

"Very much so."

"Good."

Once more, Cade's mustache wiggled with amusement, and Amanda wondered what he found so funny. Perhaps her hair stuck out every which way. Self-consciously, she patted the loose knot in the back of her head.

"This is a lovely home," she ventured.

"Thank you. But it will look more presentable once I buy some furnishings." He sighed as though he regarded decorating a burdensome chore. "All in due time."

"Yes." She cleared her throat. "And Jenny is well, I hope?"

"Quite well. She started school and has already made friends. In fact she's dressing for a birthday party this afternoon."

"I'm happy for her."

"And how are you faring, Miss Lewis?"

"Oh, I can't complain. The Lord has been looking out for me, just as Mother said He would, but it's still hard. I. . .miss her."

"Of course you do." Amanda saw Cade's blue-eyed gaze harden. "Death is never easily overcome. Weeping doesn't endure for just a night, and joy doesn't always come in the morning."

"You're speaking from experience, aren't you?"

He nodded ever so slightly.

"Your wife?"

"Yes."

"Was it recent, Captain?"

"Five years ago."

"And you still miss her terribly?" Amanda's heart ached for the poor man. No wonder he hid his smiles beneath his bushy, blond mustache.

"I think I would have gotten over Isabelle's death by now had I been able to say my good-byes. But I was on the Atlantic, manning a gunner, when I finally got the telegram. By the time I arrived home, she was. . . gone."

Amanda felt her eyes fill with tears, but she successfully blinked them back.

Or so she thought.

"I'm sorry, Miss Lewis. I don't know why I'm telling you all this. You don't need my burdens heaped on your own."

"No need to apologize, Captain," she replied in a strangled voice. "I know so many people who have lost loved ones in the war. And now hearing about your wife. . .well, you've helped me to see how very fortunate I really am. I said good-bye to Mother, and I know she's in heaven with the Savior."

"You're very fortunate." Cade lifted his coffee cup to his lips and took a long drink.

"Was your wife a believer?"

"Yes, she was." He set the cup back in its saucer.

"We can rejoice in that much anyway."

"Yes," he said once more, but his tone sounded doubtful.

The atmosphere between them had suddenly become strained.

"There, now, about this fence business," Cade began in a matter-of-fact tone. He sat back in his chair. "In my letter to you, I expressed concern over the close proximity of the walkway to the lighthouse and the bluff. I offered to have a fence erected as a token of my appreciation for your work, and I promised to inform the superintendent of the improvements in my recommendation."

"Improvements?" Amanda waved away the notion. "The superintendent is one of John Sloan's colleagues, and he won't care about enrichments to the property, especially if they're laid out for my benefit. Why, he would probably think it a convenience if the north wind blew me over the ledge one day."

"More's the reason I would feel better with something of a barricade there to halt a downward fall."

Amanda felt an uneasiness fill her chest. She hadn't expected the captain to agree with her. Regardless, she refused to let him know he had spooked her.

"Very well, Captain. I'll accept your kind offer of a fence in my yard. Thank you."

She stood.

He followed suit.

"I should be going. I left Will at the house. I'm sure he would like to begin his building."

"Indeed."

The captain showed her to the door, helping her with her cloak before she stepped into the cool November sunshine.

"Thank you again, Captain."

"My pleasure."

Amanda gave him a hesitant little smile. But then she had a thought.

"With regards to your wife," she began carefully, "I don't know if we can really communicate with those loved ones who have gone on to glory before us, but I imagine the Lord Jesus could give them a message. Why not say good-bye to your wife now? Ask God to tell her good-bye for you, and perhaps in return He'll give you His peace that passes all understanding." After a moment, Amanda shrugged, seeing Cade's stony expression. "I have probably spoken out of turn, and I apologize. Please give my love to Jenny."

On that final note of farewell, she ran down the stony walkway, wondering if Captain Cade Danfield would ever speak to her again.

Chapter 6

By early afternoon the following day, Sunday, Amanda experienced loneliness in a way she never thought possible. She had to mind the lighthouse grounds with no one to cover her for even an hour so she could attend church services. In the past, she and her mother had taken turns. Moreover, she and her mother had shared the responsibility for keeping the beacon burning all night long. Now it fell solely upon Amanda's shoulders—a position she sought and would fight for if necessary. Nonetheless, she was beginning to realize the great isolation that accompanied the job, and she would have to get used to it, especially with winter coming.

Lord, I need a husband, she prayed silently while settling into the daybed on the sunporch. She needed a nap. In just a few short hours, she'd have to tend the light again. During the winter months, the sun set at about four-thirty, and dawn didn't streak the eastern sky until approximately six o'clock. Sometimes even later, if fog or a storm loomed on the horizon.

Amanda closed her eyes, feeling the distant November sunshine warm her face. This room made her think of her beloved mother, and lying in the same place she'd lain days before her death somehow comforted Amanda, enveloping her with a love that transcended human logic.

Lord, please tell Mother I miss her, but let her know I'll be all right. With Your help, I will be just fine. . . .

Exhaustion overtook her, and Amanda fell into a deep sleep.

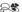

Some time later, Amanda awakened to the sound of knocking at the front door. Rising, she sleepily walked through the house, rubbing her tired eyes. When she reached the front foyer, she peered through the sheer, curtain-covered window and gasped upon seeing John Sloan's balding, spindly head.

"What does *he* want?" she muttered, her hand on the knob. After another peek through the window, Amanda realized two other men stood on the porch beside Mr. Sloan, one of them being his pudgy son, Leonard.

She knew what they wanted, all right. They wanted her lighthouse! Well, they weren't going to get it.

Amanda gave the door a tug and glared at her uninvited guests.

"Good day, Miss Lewis," Sloan began, seemingly oblivious to her outward hostility. "I'd like to present Mr. Kirkaby, an acquaintance of mine, and of course you know my son, Len."

Amanda gave them each a disinterested glance. "State your business, Mr. Sloan. I'm a busy woman."

He laughed cynically. "Oh, Miss Lewis—" He chuckled again. "You're busy? By your rumpled appearance, I'd say you were sleeping on the job."

She offered him a tight, little grin. "That only goes to show your ignorance of what is required to tend a lighthouse." She glanced at Leonard's doughy face before looking back at his father. "It's all-night work and sometimes all morning as well. Excuse me, Mr. Sloan, but even the keeper of the light has got to sleep sometime."

He shrugged. "No matter. We're here today because my friend, my son, and I wish to tour the grounds."

Amanda looked down to hide the flash of anger in her eyes. "I'm afraid now is not convenient. You'll have to come back another time." *When I've got Will here to protect me,* she added silently.

"Need I remind you the lighthouse is open to the public?" Len Sloan asked. His words sounded as though he spoke with a mouthful of marbles. "We have every right to our inspection."

"No, I needn't be reminded of the fact; however, polite society makes appointments."

After a final glower, she closed the door soundly. Whirling around, she leaned back against it and closed her eyes. Her heart pounded with such anxiety, she could hear the blood coursing through her veins like a veritable drum in her ears. She immediately realized her vulnerability as a

THE LIGHTHOUSE BRIDES COLLECTION

lone female in the large house. There was no stopping the Sloans, or anyone else for that matter, should they decide to. . .dispose of her. She swallowed hard. Not even Captain Danfield's fence would be able to save her.

"But my God can," she reminded herself. "My God is more powerful than the Sloans and stronger than any wooden reinforcement."

Amanda strode to the kitchen and looked out the side window. She frowned, noticing the Sloans and Mr. Kirkaby, whoever he might be, were taking their own tour in spite of her. Len pointed to the house, then out across Lake Michigan, and all the while it seemed to Amanda as though the three men were conspiring about some diabolical plan. What it was, Amanda could only guess. But the more contact she had with Len, the more she realized he was slow and thick-tongued. No doubt he did his father's iron business little good. Perhaps that's why the elder Sloan wanted the lighthouse position for him, although Amanda questioned whether Leonard could take proper care of the place. On the other hand, he definitely had an advantage over her, being a man.

"It's so unfair," she groused, arms akimbo. All the while, she kept her gaze on the Sloans and Kirkaby. She watched them cautiously until they finally took their leave.

⁊ॐ

"Good afternoon, Miss Lewis. What a surprise."

Amanda turned from the counter at the general store to see Cade Danfield. She smiled, nodding politely. "Captain."

"And how are you faring this brisk December day?" he asked. His hair, the color of wet sand, had been cropped short and his mustache neatly trimmed. He no longer bore the appearance of a rugged sea captain, but that of an enterprising businessman.

Amanda felt pleased he would stop to say hello since she had all but insulted the man the last time they spoke. All in all, he seemed to have forgiven her for her outspokenness.

"I'm doing well, Captain. And you?"

"Just fine."

Amanda gathered her armload of parcels and thanked the storekeeper.

"Here, allow me to help you with that," Cade said.

"Why, thank you. My wagon is right out front."

He easily carried the bundles to the rig and set them in the back.

"How's Jenny?" Amanda inquired. She'd been wondering about the girl for several days.

"She's doing splendidly. . .for the most part."

Amanda detected the hesitancy in Cade's voice. "Is there something wrong?"

"Well, only that Jenny is having problems with her arithmetic."

Amanda smiled. "Mathematics was my favorite subject. Just don't ask me to spell."

"Hmm. . .well, I can spell and I excel in mathematics, but don't ask me to teach a ten-year-old!" He shook his head, looking frustrated.

Amanda's heart went out to him. It couldn't be easy for a man to raise a daughter single-handedly.

"I guess I had better be on my way," she stated at last. "Thank you again for your help."

"Miss Lewis," he said, his mustache twitching over a grin that caused his blue eyes to sparkle, "it's quite a pleasure to see you again."

"Likewise," she replied as he assisted her up into the wagon. "Good day, Captain."

Slapping the reins against her horse's backside, Amanda headed for home, where Will had stopped by to help with a few chores during his noon break. She wished he were as captivating as the captain, but he was just hardworking Will Trekman. . .who seemed blissfully unaware of her need for a husband and equally as blind to her hints along those lines.

I'll have to be more persuasive, Amanda thought, her wagon rattling over the rutted streets. *The only question is. . .how?*

Chapter 7

Two weeks before Christmas, Amanda found herself tutoring Jenny Danfield. The same day Amanda had seen the captain in town, he had sent a message to her, asking if she would be interested in giving his daughter extra instruction in mathematics. Amanda accepted the challenge, although it really wasn't one at all. Jenny was bright and caught on quickly, and she provided companionship in those late afternoon hours when the winter skies turned gray and the house turned cold.

Jenny liked helping Amanda with the lighthouse duties, and occasionally they shared supper together if the captain worked late. Sometimes Will joined them at the table, although he wasn't any closer to discovering Amanda's wily plan to get him to the marriage altar.

"Are you sweet on Mr. Will?" Jenny asked one night as she and Amanda enjoyed a game of chess while awaiting the captain.

"Sweet on him?" Amanda chuckled lightly. "No, I can't say that I am."

"You act like it."

"Act is a good word, and unfortunately, theatrics are not my calling." Amanda forced a smile toward Jenny's puzzled countenance. The girl's bright blond hair had been plaited neatly on either side of her head, Mrs. Parsons's handiwork, no doubt. "Women are often forced to play a role out of necessity," Amanda added, but despite the vague explanation, Jenny did not look satisfied. "Oh, someday when you're older you'll understand."

"That's what Papa always tells me," the girl replied before moving her chess piece.

Amanda claimed it at once. "You're not concentrating."

"I guess I don't feel much like playing chess after all," Jenny stated with a pout. But then her face split into a wide grin. "How 'bout blackjack instead? Benk taught me lots of card games."

"A lady does not play blackjack," Amanda replied tutorially.

Jenny expelled a disappointed sigh. "It's boring being a lady."

"Yes, well, it's our lot in life, so we need to make the best of it."

"How do we do that?"

Amanda glanced up from the game board. "Good question, and I'm in the throes of discovering the answer. When I do, I'll be sure to let you know."

"All right." Jenny yawned. "I'm tired. Can I lie down while we wait for Papa?"

"Of course. I'll open the porch door, and soon it'll be quite toasty out there. You can rest on the daybed." Amanda laughed softly. "My mother used to call it a fainting couch."

Jenny followed her through the kitchen. "Do you miss your mother?"

"Yes. I think I'll always miss her, but I don't feel quite so sad anymore."

"I hardly remember my mother," Jenny murmured.

Amanda's heart ached for the child.

"Miss Amanda?"

"Yes?"

"May I hold one of your doll babies while I rest?"

She smiled. How could she refuse?

"Yes, you may," Amanda replied. "Go on upstairs and pick the one you want."

While Jenny happily ran to the second-floor bedroom, Amanda stoked the woodstove in the kitchen. When the girl returned, Amanda tucked her and the doll, whom Amanda had long ago named Abigail, snugly into the daybed, using one of the quilts her mother had sewn. Stepping back a ways, Amanda decided Jenny and Abigail made a precious sight. She smiled as she left the porch and began cleaning in the kitchen.

Shortly thereafter, Cade appeared at the door.

"Come in, Captain," Amanda beckoned. "I'll rouse Jenny from her nap."

"She's sleeping? Am I that late? It's not yet nine o'clock."

Amanda grinned. "Scholastics make a girl tired."

"Ah. . ." He nodded in understanding.

"Have you eaten? Are you hungry? I've got plenty of food," she offered.

"Food, you say?"

"Yes. Turkey stew with dumplings. Mother used to rave about my dumplings."

"You've successfully convinced me into trying a portion," Cade said, removing his woolen cloak. "The truth is, I'm famished."

Amanda immediately set to her task, noting that the captain seemed more than comfortable seated in the kitchen, watching her.

"I made quite a bit of stew tonight," Amanda explained, "because I thought Will Trekman might stop over for supper."

"I'm afraid Will was as busy as I today. . .and tonight."

"Well, that explains it. Will's not one to miss a meal."

Captain Danfield chuckled, and Amanda thought he looked less brooding and more contented of late. She figured his life on dry land must agree with him.

It wasn't long before she set a plate of steaming stew in front of Cade. "Smells delicious."

"Thank you, Captain. And now if you'll excuse me, I need to tend the lighthouse, but I shouldn't be gone too long."

"By all means. Don't let me get in the way of your duties."

After giving him a look of gratitude, she spun on her heel and stepped into the mudroom, where she donned her winter wrapper. Then she headed for the lighthouse.

Cade watched her go before praying over his meal. Praying. He smiled. It felt good to commune with the Almighty again.

When plucky Amanda Lewis had suggested he say good-bye to Isabelle using the Savior as a conduit, Cade had deemed the idea one of the most absurd he'd heard. But that night, in the quiet darkness of his bedchamber, he'd prayed those very words. He'd said his good-byes. And he trusted Jesus Christ to relay the message. Somehow, in the deepest recesses of his soul, Cade knew the Lord had agreed to his request. Christ did not have to; He was God. And the notion that the Almighty would stoop to do Cade's bidding, let alone die for his sin, caused him, a confident seafaring man, to feel ashamed for all the years he'd scorned and neglected his God. Even now, as he gazed at his plate of turkey stew, his eyes grew misty.

Thank You, Lord. Thank You. . . It was all the response Cade could think up. There weren't enough words in all the history of human language to begin to express what the Savior had done for his wounded spirit. Jesus had indeed lifted the load Cade had been bearing for so many years.

He finished eating, deciding the stew tasted exceptionally good. He wouldn't have minded another two or three platefuls. Carrying his dishes into the kitchen, he set them on the battered, wooden service counter and patted his stomach. He'd been eating much too well lately. That, combined with the lack of exercise he was accustomed to on board the *Kismet,* Cade realized, was making his clothes a wee bit tight.

Last year at this time, he, Jenny, Benk, and the rest of his crew were in the Gulf of Mexico. He loved sailing, the wind, and the water, but, oddly, he didn't miss it overmuch. His position at the Grain Exchange proved to be the challenge he had anticipated, and it kept his finances in the black.

Cade walked out onto the porch and checked on Jenny. She slept peacefully with her arm wrapped around one of Amanda's dolls. The scene tugged at his heart, and he felt like the luckiest man alive. He had a sweet daughter, a nice home, a good job. . .

He heard the door open and close, signaling his hostess's return from her lighthouse chores. He met her in the kitchen.

"The wind is kicking up," she said, with rosy cheeks. "I think we may see some snow by morning."

Cade grinned at her prediction, thinking she was probably right.

"I'm going to make some coffee. I'm chilled to the bone, and my night is just beginning. Would you care for a cup, Captain?"

"I would indeed," he replied. "What can I do to help you?"

Amanda turned from the counter, her brow furrowed slightly. "Would you mind terribly stoking the fire in the parlor? I forgot about it, and this house can get terribly drafty."

Cade bowed slightly. "I'd be happy to."

He strode to the parlor and, taking hold of the poker, kindled the flames, then added another log from the pile beside the hearth. With the task completed, he straightened and surveyed the tidy room, noticing the chessboard set up on a small table near the fireplace.

"Are you a chess player, Captain?" Amanda's voice came from behind him.

He turned. "I enjoy the game, yes." He grinned. "Were you and Jenny playing earlier?"

"Yes, but I'm sad to say she lost interest."

"Hmm. . .yes, and I see she wasn't playing up to her usual standard, either," he remarked, inspecting the board and the missing ivory pieces. He looked back at Amanda. "Shall we finish the game? I'll sit in for Jenny."

Amanda smiled. "I'd like that, although I do hope you're a worthy opponent."

Cade's brows shot up at the tart comment. But as he took a seat at the table, he thought he shouldn't be surprised. "I shall try to challenge your wits, Miss Lewis." He had little doubt that he could make quick work of this game.

"Good. I need my wits challenged," she stated candidly. "I'm not used to being alone so much. My mother was my best friend, and we did so many fun things together. But she never could beat me at chess."

Cade grinned wryly. "I rarely lose."

Amanda met his stare with a competitive little smile curving her lips. "As I recall, it was Jenny's move."

Cade examined the board then moved a pawn. "You said you're alone too much of the time? Does that mean Jenny is not a bother?"

"She's not a bother at all. I enjoy having her around." Amanda slid one of her pawns forward.

"She has a mathematics test tomorrow."

"We studied tonight, and I believe she's ready for it."

"Excellent." Cade moved one of his knights and captured a pawn.

Amanda frowned. However, she quickly recovered and pushed another pawn forward.

"Jenny mentioned Will Trekman is here frequently for supper. She wondered if you were. . .how did she term it? Sweet on him?"

Amanda grinned. "Jenny asked me about Will tonight, and I informed her that I am not sweet on him."

Cade moved out his other knight.

"But, Captain, if you must know, I am trying to do everything in my power to get Will to propose marriage. I need a husband."

Cade's eyes widened as she glided one of her rooks forward.

"I didn't tell Jenny that, of course."

"You need a husband?" Leaning back in the black leather chair, Cade folded his arms across his chest. "May I be so bold as to ask why?"

"Because if I were married," Amanda explained, "my request to obtain my mother's commission would be more credible to the superintendent." She gave him a look as if to say he should have figured that much out on his own. "Why else would I need a husband?"

Cade chuckled inwardly, stroking his mustache with his thumb and forefinger. "I see. And is young Mr. Trekman aware of all this?" He stretched out a hand and moved his knight again, claiming another of Amanda's pawns.

She navigated her bishop accordingly and captured his knight.

Cade narrowed his gaze at her, and she laughed softly.

"To answer your question, Captain, no, Will does not know I need a husband, nor is he aware that he is my targeted intended. But I believe he's interested in me."

"You don't love him?"

"No, but I'm sure I'll learn. Will is very kind, gentle, thoughtful, and he's a hard worker. Besides, marriages of convenience occur all the time."

"Quite true, except for one thing."

Amanda tilted her head curiously. "What's that?"

"The groom is usually aware of the, um, arrangement."

Cade watched in amusement as Amanda's cheeks reddened with chagrin. "My suggestion," he stated, nudging his rook across the board, "is that you discuss this matter with Mr. Trekman."

"How could I possibly do that?"

He shrugged. "The same way you discussed it with me."

"But you're different," Amanda argued, taking his rook, much to Cade's annoyance. "You're not the one I'm trying to snag, so I needn't impress you."

For some odd reason, her candid remark irritated him more than if she had put him in check. "It's a good thing you don't want to marry me," Cade muttered, scanning the chessboard, "because I wouldn't tolerate even half of your shenanigans."

He chanced a peek at her, thinking he would find her scowling at him, but instead she was smiling broadly.

"What's so funny?"

"Oh, nothing." She stood, her hazel eyes twinkling as they reflected the soft firelight. "But I think our coffee is done. I'll go fetch us each a cup." She started for the kitchen, then called over her shoulder, "And don't cheat while I'm away."

Cade brought his chin back sharply. "I never cheat, Amanda Lewis. I'm a man of integrity."

"Glad to hear it, seeing as you're about to lose our chess game."

He watched her go with a longing to take the sassy young woman over his knee. But then he forced himself to concentrate on the board. Sure enough. The little minx had somehow put his king in check. But after a few moments of study, Cade knew how he'd get out of it easily enough.

Amanda returned with the coffee, sipped from her cup, and waited for Cade to move his chess piece.

He deliberately bided his time, then maneuvered his king into safety.

Amanda promptly apprehended his queen. "Check."

Cade sat back, studying the board. He took a long drink of his steaming brew while analyzing the different strategies open to him.

Inevitably, he took to studying Amanda Lewis. She looked hard-pressed to contain her mirth.

"Will Trekman is not the man for you," Cade finally said with an edgy tone. "He's much too agreeable. You would run him over and live to become one of those bossy women who make my ears ring at church socials."

"I will not succumb to your insults, Captain," Amanda stated aloofly. "You're just angry because I'm winning." She gave him an impertinent smile. "Would you like more coffee?"

He had to clench his jaw in an effort to keep from grinning, but he didn't quite pull it off.

"Take your time," she quipped. "I have all night."

That did it. Cade dropped his head back and laughed loudly. "I like you, Amanda," he said at last. "May I call you Amanda?"

She nodded, albeit hesitantly.

"It's a very special woman who can keep a man on his toes."

"I will not succumb to your charm either. Now stop dallying and make your move."

He smirked. The chit. She'd successfully managed to jumble his faculties so he could scarcely think a coherent thought.

"Heaven help the man who charms you, Amanda," Cade teased, deploying his king over one square.

Her eyes twinkled mischievously as she boldly met his gaze. Then without so much as glancing at the board, she took her next and final turn.

"Checkmate, Captain."

Chapter 8

I would like to purchase a dress that's guaranteed to catch a man's eye—and his heart."

"Honey, if I could create such a dress, I'd be the richest woman in town." Chuckling, Lila Zenkowski placed her wide hands on her hips and tilted her graying head. "Any particular man you've got in mind?"

"Well, yes. . ." Amanda smiled shyly, uncertain if she should divulge Will Trekman's name. But since he had invited her to the ever-popular Christmas concert at the Shubert Theatre, Amanda decided she should have a new, store-bought gown—one that might extract a marriage proposal from Will. After all, her time was running out. David and his family would arrive at the end of next week to help her pack. . .unless she somehow secured the lighthouse position.

"Hmm. . ." The Polish dressmaker gave Amanda's tall frame a thorough scrutiny. "Let's see what we can do."

She began pulling dress after dress off the racks. Amanda deliberated over each one until she saw a deep green velvet gown that struck her fancy. She tried it on, admiring the way it made her look older than her nineteen years but despairing over the neckline.

"Can a Christian lady wear something so. . . risqué?"

"Risqué? What?" The stout dressmaker appeared shocked. "This is not risqué, my dear Miss Lewis."

"It's not?" Amanda examined her reflection in the framed looking glass. The dress was exquisite. The neckline, bordered with emerald satin, hung off her shoulders before giving way to velvet sleeves that came to her elbows. The fitted velvet bodice softly flowed into a full velvet skirt. True, her creamy-white shoulders were exposed, but nothing more.

"You'll be the belle of the ball. A tuck here, a tuck there, and it will be perfect," Mrs. Zenkowski said through the stickpins she expertly held between her lips.

"Think so?"

"Why, if that man of yours doesn't propose to you in this dress, he ain't fit to be called a husband."

Amanda worked her lower lip between her teeth as she deliberated. "All right, I'll take it," she declared at last.

The woman marked the alterations accordingly. "Do I hear wedding bells?" she asked with a grin.

"I hope so." Amanda strolled to the front door after paying for her new gown. She had somehow lived frugally over the last month and those funds, combined with the money David had left her, more than paid for the dress.

"Please keep me up-to-date on your love interest," the dressmaker urged. "In the meantime, I shall see your lovely dress is delivered later this afternoon."

Smiling with delight, Amanda left the dress shop and headed for home.

❧

The night of the concert arrived, and with it came a light powdering of snow. Amanda smoothed down the soft skirt of her dress, then patted her light brown ringlets nervously as she waited for Will. She had spent all afternoon primping and curling her hair, and she prayed she hadn't overdone it.

A knock on the door signaled Will's arrival. Amanda pulled on the knob and greeted him with a smile. "Good evening."

Will gaped while his brown eyes roved over her bare shoulders before he blinked and looked back into her face. "A–Amanda. . ."

She inwardly congratulated herself on a job well done. Will appeared positively enthralled.

"Do I look all right?" she hedged.

"Um. . .well. . .um. . .yes."

"I hope you like the dress."

Will swallowed convulsively, and Amanda had to swing around in an effort to hide her smile. She covered the action by grabbing her woolen wrapper off the peg and handing it to Will.

He seemed lost as to what to do next.

"Assist me with my cloak?" she prompted.

"Oh. . .y–yes, of course. . ."

With the task completed, Will stared down into her eyes wordlessly while Amanda carefully set her bonnet on top of her head, tying it under her chin.

"Shall we go?"

He nodded.

Amanda fairly propelled him to the awaiting hired hackney.

For the duration of the carriage ride, Will remained silent. Amanda did her best to engage him in polite conversation, but he appeared uncomfortable. Did he appreciate her taste in evening wear, or was he bothered by seeing her in something other than her daytime work dresses? Suddenly Amanda felt unsure of herself.

The driver pulled to a halt on North Milwaukee Street in front of the theatre, and Will nearly forgot to help Amanda alight from the buggy. They walked into the building and checked their overcoats before strolling into the lobby. Amanda felt grateful to happen upon some acquaintances from school, and she politely introduced them to Will, who still hadn't found his tongue. After Amanda and her friends' cordial exchange, she and Will moved on.

"Well, well, look who's here, Jenny."

There was no mistaking Cade Danfield's booming voice, and turning slightly, Amanda watched him approach. His daughter walked beside him, lovely in her pristine white dress with a red satin sash around her trim waist. And the captain himself looked dapper in his black trousers, multicolored woven vest, and black frock coat.

"Hello, Captain."

"Miss Lewis." He gallantly bowed over her gloved hand. "You look especially lovely this evening. I believe green is your color."

Amanda smiled, feeling her cheeks warm with a blush. "Thank you." She chanced a peek at Will, wishing he could be even half as charming as the captain.

"Hello, Miss Amanda," Jenny said, smiling up at her.

"Good evening, dear heart."

"Papa and I came to hear the concert."

"So I see."

The girl looked at Will, then at her father, and finally back at Amanda. Confusion crossed her features, and Amanda could practically hear the question going through the child's mind. *If you're not sweet on him, why are you all dressed up and accompanying him to the Christmas concert?* But, of course, the captain knew the answer to that one.

Amanda directed her attention to Cade and found him regarding her intently. He recovered in a heartbeat and turned to Will.

"Mr. Trekman," he said, sticking out his right hand, "it's always a pleasure to see you."

"Thank you, sir."

Several uncomfortable moments passed.

"Well, I believe the concert is about to begin," Cade announced, and Amanda found her hand being looped around his elbow. "Come along, Jenny. Mr. Trekman, let's find some seats, shall we?"

"Yes. . .sir. . . ," came the halting reply.

Amanda glanced over her shoulder and viewed Will's baffled countenance as he trailed them. She tried to disengage her hand, but Cade held it firmly in place. Jenny slipped her free hand into Amanda's other one. She smiled at the darling girl but frowned at the child's father.

"What do you think you're doing?" she hissed.

Cade didn't reply, instead lifting his clean-shaven chin and acting as though everything was as right as a December snowstorm.

They reached a row of six seats, and Cade deftly ushered Jenny in first, then Amanda, before he boldly took the wooden seat beside hers, leaving poor Will on the end with two seats left vacant next to him. Amanda felt the fury heating her face.

"I can tell you think this is most amusing, Cade Danfield," she whispered. "I can see the smile beneath your mustache. However, there is nothing funny about this situation."

"I am doing you a favor," he whispered back. He sat so closely, Amanda could feel his spicy breath on her nose. "Now, relax and enjoy the concert."

She wanted to scream. Of all the nerve! His name should be Cad, not Cade!

"What song do you think the orchestra will play first, Miss Amanda?" Jenny asked.

"I. . .I don't know, honey," Amanda said, trying desperately to calm her stormy emotions.

Cade moved his arm, and it overlapped hers. Amanda discreetly pulled away. *Incorrigible man!* Next she heard him engaging Will in talk of work at the Grain Exchange. The lout! She'd spent good money on a dress that would go unnoticed the rest of night. Perhaps Mrs. Zenkowski would allow her to return it.

The ornately decorated wall sconces were dimmed, and the orchestra began to play a set of lively Christmas favorites. At one point, the audience stood and everyone joined in singing "O Come, All Ye Faithful." Listening to Cade's deep but slightly off-pitch baritone voice somehow melted Amanda's wrath. By intermission, she felt content to stand in the lobby and converse with Cade, Will, and a host of others while Jenny met up with a few of her new friends. After a time, Will excused himself to fetch several glasses of punch.

"I take it you haven't discussed your, um, plans with Mr. Trekman yet."

Amanda gazed at Cade skeptically. "I was hoping for a chance to speak with him tonight."

"Yes, I thought as much." It seemed Cade was seasoned at holding a private discussion in a public place. No one could read his lips since they were covered by his bushy mustache, and as he continued to hold Amanda's elbow and speak softly into her ear, not another soul heard him.

But they saw him. Amanda felt sure of it. She blushed profusely and hoped he knew what he was doing. By this time tomorrow, half of Milwaukee City would have them labeled a couple.

"Have you prayed about a match between you and Will?" Cade asked.

She looked up at him, surprised by the light of sincerity in his blue eyes. "I told God I needed a husband."

"Mmm. . .and are you sure this is the Almighty's plan for your life, or are you running ahead of Him?"

"I. . .I want to keep my home." She clenched her jaw to keep her chin from quivering.

"Home is where your heart is, Amanda. Haven't you ever heard that expression before? The *Kismet* was my home for years. She was a faithful vessel and I'll miss her. But my home is now on Newberry Boulevard. Jenny is there and my heart. . .well," he chuckled lightly, "let's just say my heart is at least in the same city."

He gave her a long look and squeezed her elbow just as Will returned with the punch. Amanda thought she must have missed something. Cade's heart was at least in the same city? Did he mean as opposed to being out on the water? At sea? She shrugged inwardly.

At last it came time to reclaim their seats, and the good captain was just as clever as before in situating himself beside Amanda. However, this time Jenny sat to his right and to Amanda's immediate left was Will. She felt as though she ought to say something to him, but no words took shape in her mind.

Once the lights were turned down low and the orchestra began to play again, Amanda timidly considered the two men on either side of her. She had to confess to admiring Cade's commanding presence. Will, on the other hand, was obviously the passive sort. He hadn't even voiced a complaint about the captain inserting himself into their evening plans— and he should have. Were their roles reversed, Cade Danfield wouldn't have stood such nonsense for a moment.

Suddenly Amanda recalled the captain's comment about bossy women. Would she really become one of them if she married Will? As if in reply, the remembrance of how she had initiated things earlier that evening frittered through her mind. She hadn't exactly been bossy, but she'd had to fairly lead the young man along.

She realized in that moment Cade's assessment had been correct. Will Trekman wasn't the man for her, and a position as keeper of the North Point Light was not worth the misery they would likely suffer as husband and wife.

Her gaze finally shifted to the captain. She found him watching her, and Amanda offered him a tiny smile. She saw his mustache twitch before he turned his attention back to the orchestra.

The concert ended, and Amanda found herself feeling quite subdued. Her well-laid plans had disintegrated before her very eyes. She followed Will out to the lobby with Cade's hand around her elbow while Jenny babbled happily beside her about the Christmas concert.

Will fetched their winter coats, and he handed Amanda hers.

"It makes no sense for both of us to hire a hack," Cade said, taking it upon himself to assist her with her cloak. "Let's ride home together."

Amanda smiled at Jenny, unwilling to involve herself in this particular decision. But, as she expected, Will complied without comment.

Inside the carriage, Amanda settled in beside Jenny while the captain and Will sat across from them. She listened as father and daughter discussed the concert at great length, although from time to time, Amanda briefly glanced at Will. If he felt disappointed with the night's outcome, he didn't look it. In a word, he seemed confused.

And so was she.

The carriage halted in front of the boardinghouse where Will currently resided. Amanda was only half surprised by their first stop. After an all-encompassing "good night," Will hopped out, closed the buggy's door behind him, and sauntered off. The carriage lurched forward.

"So, Amanda, did you have an enjoyable evening?" Cade asked in a tone that bordered on mockery.

"I. . .I'm not sure," she hedged.

He chuckled lightly.

"Didn't you adore the symphony tonight?" Jenny asked.

"Well, yes, but. . ."

She eyed the captain in suspicious wonder, trying to make out his features amidst the nighttime shadows. She could tell he stared back at her. What was he thinking?

"I had a splendid time tonight," he announced at last. He sounded sincere.

Next to her, Jenny sidled up and rested her head against Amanda's shoulder. "I did too, Papa, but now I'm sleepy."

"Well, don't doze off just yet. We have to see Miss Amanda safely back home."

Jenny yawned. "I'll do my best to stay awake."

Cade chuckled, and Amanda had to stifle a yawn of her own. She'd have to brew a pot of coffee to keep herself awake through the night.

At last they reached the lighthouse, and Cade stepped out from the carriage before helping Amanda alight.

"You stay put, Jenny," he instructed. "I'll only be a few minutes."

Amanda's heart did an unusual flip.

"Yes, Papa. Good night, Miss Amanda."

"Sweet dreams, and I'll see you tomorrow after school."

Jenny nodded vigorously before Cade closed the carriage door and escorted Amanda to the side entrance.

"I suppose I should apologize for my boorish behavior tonight," the captain began as they stood on the porch.

"I'm sure Will Trekman would appreciate it," she replied tartly.

Amanda saw him smile beneath the sliver of moonlight peeking out from under the overcast sky. "Are you saying you don't require an apology from me, or does it mean you won't forgive me?"

This time, she had to grin. "Nothing to forgive, Captain, although I must admit to feeling perturbed at the onset of this evening. But I soon realized what you said is true. Will is not the man for me, and I have no business trying to dupe him into marriage." Feeling abashed, Amanda looked down at the snow-dusted porch floor.

Cade cupped her chin, forcing her to meet his gaze. "I don't think you would have duped Will into anything, Amanda. He might be somewhat timid and naive, but he knows his own mind. On the other hand, I'm very glad to hear you've decided against marrying him in order to secure your position here."

"You are?"

"Yes. I am." Releasing her chin, Cade lifted her hand and pressed a kiss on her gloved fingers. "Good night, my dearest Amanda."

She swallowed hard. "Good night."

She watched him take his leave before entering the house. For some odd reason, she felt a bit giddy. If only Mother were here to advise her. Was the captain romantically interested in her? It seemed so, but why hadn't he stated his intentions? Had he been merely looking out for her welfare tonight as an older brother might guard his little sister? His actions certainly weren't those of a sibling.

Amanda sighed as she mounted the steps to her bedroom. She pushed her tumultuous thoughts of Cade Danfield aside. For now she needed to change her clothes and tend the light. It still burned as brightly as when she'd left for the concert, but the lamp was sure to require a spot cleaning and wick trimming, not to mention a good dose of oil.

But try as she might, she couldn't seem to rid her memory of a pair of startling blue eyes above a twitching, blond mustache.

Chapter 9

Amanda glanced at the letter in her hand once more. It stated that she had been granted a hearing. The superintendent of the Great Lakes district agreed to hear her arguments as to why she felt she qualified to take over her mother's commission as keeper of the North Point Light.

She swallowed hard. David would be furious if he found out. Still, she knew in her heart that she had to try for the position. But she still felt incredibly anxious over this meeting. She wished she had someone to accompany her, and there was only one man she could think of asking. He would be objective, had a good business sense about him, wouldn't treat her like a child, and wasn't intimidated by the Sloans.

Captain Danfield.

However, after last night's concert and with her own befuddled sensibilities, Amanda felt almost too timid to make the appeal.

A knock sounded at the door, and Jenny looked up from the book she'd been reading. "Is it Papa?"

Amanda stood, smoothed the skirt of her simple brown wool dress, and glanced out the window. "Yes. He's early tonight."

"Oh, good!" the child cried, jumping up from the settee. "I can't wait to tell him my score on my arithmetic exam."

Smiling, Amanda followed Jenny to the entryway, where they bid the captain welcome. Then as Jenny returned to the parlor to gather her belongings, Amanda decided to broach the subject of her impending hearing.

"I, um, received this today," she said, handing Cade the letter.

After giving her a curious frown, he read it over. "Hmm. . .day after tomorrow."

"Yes, and I wondered if I might ask you a favor. But let me preface it by saying, I understand you're a busy man and can't be bothered with trivial matters. . ."

Cade lifted an inquiring brow. "What do you need, Amanda? You know I'll help you if I can." His voice sounded so kind and gentle that it somehow spurred her on.

"I wondered if you might attend the hearing with me. I'm. . .well, I hate to admit it, but I'm more than a little apprehensive about the whole thing."

"Quite understandable, and I'm happy to escort you to the meeting. I'll even act as your advisor if you'd like."

Amanda tried to appear grateful rather than surprised, but by the way Cade chuckled, she knew she hadn't fooled him.

"Thank you, Captain," she managed.

He inclined his head slightly in reply. "And now I have a question for you."

"Yes?" She wished her heart wouldn't beat so fiercely whenever the captain gave her such an intent look.

"I wondered if you might dine with Jenny and me tonight in our home."

"Tonight?" Amanda didn't think she was dressed for such an occasion. It would take her hours to get ready.

"It's very informal," he said, as if sensing the reason behind her hesitation. "Just the three of us. . .and Mrs. Parsons, my housekeeper, of course. She's agreed to cook for us."

"Well. . ."

"It will all be quite proper, I assure you."

Amanda grinned. "In that case, Captain, I accept your invitation." Then more seriously she added, "But I need to tend the light before I go."

"Fine. Jenny and I can wait in the parlor for you," he said, just as his daughter reappeared, looking set to leave. Cade explained their delay, while Amanda pulled on her cloak and headed for the tower.

Up in the lamp room, she performed her regular routine of cleaning the lens and surrounding glass panes. Next she trimmed the lamps' wicks.

All the while she wondered over the captain's invitation. She wished once again her mother were alive to tell her what it all meant. Was Cade Danfield kindly repaying her for tutoring Jenny, or was there more? She couldn't be sure.

Amanda released a long, frustrated sigh and descended the winding stairwell. Men were extremely difficult to understand. But at least the captain had agreed to accompany her to the hearing. She felt as though a weight had been lifted from her shoulders.

Reentering the parlor, she found him and Jenny waiting. Within the next few minutes, they were riding off in his buggy, heading for his house on Newberry Boulevard.

Dinner proved a delicious medley of meat and potatoes, and the mealtime conversation started Amanda in on a fit of laughter as Cade and Jenny reminisced about their seafaring escapades.

"Are you going to miss your shipping business and life on the water?"

"Oh, a little bit," the captain replied. "But eventually I hope to purchase a small pleasure schooner."

"This time I'll be the first mate, right, Papa?" Jenny asked.

"We'll have to see about that," he replied with an amused grin.

Amanda and Jenny traded baffled frowns.

"Well, now, my dear, it's your bedtime," Cade said, giving Jenny a kiss on the forehead as the three of them stood in the nearly vacant parlor. Only a multicolored Oriental rug and a single burgundy-upholstered settee had been placed in the room.

"But, Papa. . ." Jenny argued.

He bent over and whispered in the child's ear. Jenny's eyes grew wide as dessert plates. She glanced at Amanda, then back at her father.

"Now, git," he commanded, inclining his head toward the stairway.

"Yes, sir," Jenny replied, smiling broadly.

The girl ran upstairs, and Amanda wondered over the scene. She glanced at Cade, who sat down on the settee just as Mrs. Parsons carried in a large tray complete with a porcelain coffeepot and two matching cups, a sugar bowl, and creamer.

"I'll have to set this on the dining room table, sir, seeing as the rest of your furniture hasn't arrived yet."

"That's fine. Thank you."

The portly woman nodded, set down the coffee service, then exited through the dining room.

Amanda glanced at Cade. "Allow me to pour."

"If you insist."

She did. Serving up their coffee gave her something to do besides standing there feeling ridiculous. She remembered Cade liked his brew straight-up black, while she preferred two lumps of sugar and a good helping of cream. Cup and saucer in each hand, Amanda returned to the parlor. She handed the captain his coffee.

"When is the rest of your furniture due to arrive?" Amanda asked.

Cade's mustache twitched, and his eyes twinkled in amusement. "Whenever I purchase it, but don't breathe a word of that to Mrs. Parsons. She has been fairly browbeating me into buying items for the house, but I can't seem to make up my mind." He sipped from his porcelain cup. "This room, for instance. . .what would you do with it?"

"Me?" Amanda shook her head. "I'm sure I wouldn't know."

"Come now. You have an opinion on everything else."

She smiled and shrugged her shoulders. "Yes, I suppose I do. All right. For starters, these mustard-yellow walls are the wrong color for this dark woodwork. It's. . .depressing in here. It needs some cheer. How about papering the walls with a rose-colored pattern?"

"I knew you had a comment inside you somewhere." He chuckled.

"And you need a piano in that corner," she said, pointing across the way.

Cade raised a brow. "A piano? Whatever for?"

"Jenny should have lessons. That's all part of becoming a lady."

"Hmm. . .yes, I suppose you're right." With a pensive expression, he took another sip of coffee. Then he peered at her from over the rim. "Amanda, sit down, will you? Relax. I won't bite. I promise."

She inhaled sharply at the remark but acquiesced and carefully took the only place in the room—that on the settee beside him.

"Tell me about the Sloans and what we're up against at this hearing."

"Where should I begin?"

"For starters, I'd like to know why you think Sloan wants the commission for lighthouse keeper so badly."

"Personal vendetta."

Cade raised a skeptical brow.

"It has to be," Amanda insisted. "It started right after the war. Mr. Sloan and his son, Leonard, began harassing Mother and me then, and it's lasted for over three years."

"What sparked the harassment?"

"I–I haven't a clue," Amanda replied honestly.

Cade shook his blond head. "No. My hunch is it's not personal. Sloan wants something only that position carries with it. Access to the lighthouse or to the house itself." He paused, and a teasing gleam entered his blue eyes. "Benk thought there might be buried treasure on the property."

Amanda laughed, feeling some of her tension slowly ebb. "Hardly, Captain."

"I do have a first name, you know."

Amanda swallowed hard and gazed into her coffee cup. "Yes. . ." It was all she could think to say at the moment. *He wants me to refer to him by his first name!*

"All right, in regard to the Sloans. . ."

Back and forth they went, trying to unearth the mystery of why John Sloan would want the lighthouse position for his son. Amanda voiced her ideas—Len was too inept for his father's rapidly growing iron mill empire, although he seemed even more inadequate for the lighthouse duties.

"But I can't imagine why the Sloans are interested in keeping the light in the first place," Amanda said. "They are both railroad enthusiasts. They have no interest in shipping at all. Why, I heard Martin Moore say the Sloans predicted railroads would overtake the shipping industry in the next two years. They have staked a lot of money on that claim, as well."

"Who is Martin Moore?"

Amanda felt herself redden. "He owns a tavern in town," she said in a hushed little voice. "I happened to be in line behind him at the general store and heard him talking."

"Why are you whispering?" Cade asked, looking thoroughly amused.

Amanda blushed even brighter, realizing how silly she must seem. However, she didn't want anyone to think she kept company with a barkeep!

Cade laughed. "You are delightful."

Amanda brought her chin back sharply. "I am?"

"Yes, you are," he said with another light chuckle.

Oh, dear, he must be interested in me, she thought. *Am I interested in him?* She nibbled her lower lip in consternation.

"Well, I may have figured out the Sloans' little scheme," Cade said. "If they take over the lighthouse, they could find some inane reason to close it down. Without the North Point Light, Milwaukee's shipping industry would be forced to decrease, while the Sloans could make sure the city's railroad enterprise increased."

Amanda shook her head. "That's too simple an explanation. The Sloans have worked far too hard at trying to oust Mother and me."

"Ah, but my dear, you have no idea how important your job really is to captains and crews. The North Point Light hails ships coming into Milwaukee and guides them safely into harbor. Without it, ships would be forced to sail south to Racine or farther to Chicago. In either case, the railroad would be strategic in bringing goods in and out of Milwaukee.

"But the Sloans' plan will never work," he continued. "Alexander Mitchell runs the Marine Bank, and while he's a known investor in the iron mill, he has a penchant for the grain trade. Nearly fifteen million bushels of wheat were brought through Milwaukee's port this year. Because of Mitchell's financial backing, shipping in this city will never die…unless, of course, Lake Michigan dries up."

Smiling at the pun, Amanda mulled over his explanation. She couldn't quite believe it, but in some ways it made perfect sense. In essence, she was an innocent bystander, caught in the war between the railroads and waterways.

Cade rose and poured them each more coffee. Then he reclaimed his place beside her. "Here's what I want you to do at the hearing, Amanda," he began. "First of all, no tears. Understand? This is business."

She nodded.

"Next, I want you to document every incident of persecution you and your mother suffered at the hand of the Sloans."

Again, she nodded, making mental notes.

By the end of the evening, Amanda felt immensely fortunate to have Cade Danfield on her side.

"How will I ever thank you?" she asked after he saw her safely home.

She watched him grin beneath the moonlight. "Not to worry. I'll think of something."

⁂

"What is taking so long?"

"Patience, Amanda," Cade whispered back to her as they sat in the lobby of the Cross Keys Hotel. He gave her gloved hand a reassuring pat. "These things take time."

After a brief nod in reply, she glanced across the way at John and Leonard Sloan. They seemed quite confident about the outcome of the meeting, and Amanda had a feeling they had a right to be. If only the superintendent would hurry and meet them, they would all hear his verdict. They had been waiting nearly an hour.

Amanda lowered her gaze and stared at the brown tweed traveling suit Cade had insisted upon purchasing for her. She had tried to refuse it but lost the debate when the good captain pulled Mrs. Zenkowski into it. Of course, the seamstress immediately assumed he was the man whom Amanda had set out to impress, and the woman deemed her green velvet creation a success, much to Amanda's chagrin and Cade's utter amusement.

"Captain Danfield," John Sloan said from his chair several feet away, "I must say I was surprised to find you accompanying Miss Lewis to the hearing this morning."

"Oh? And why's that?"

Amanda admired Cade's casual bearing as he replied to Sloan.

"Well, I. . .I guess I didn't realize you knew each other." He gave Amanda a curious glance before looking back at the captain. "I mean, you did just arrive in town a month ago. . . ."

Amanda felt herself begin to seethe, even though she wasn't exactly sure she'd been insulted. But Sloan's tone of voice implied something wrong was going on. Why, Cade ought to give the man a piece of his mind.

Much to her surprise, he simply sat beside her calmly and uncon- cerned. He did not give Sloan a tongue-lashing, nor did he offer an explanation as to why he came with Amanda. Across the way, John Sloan shifted uncomfortably, and she wanted to applaud. So that was the way to deal with louts like him!

She looked over at Cade, who caught her eye and sent back a

confidential wink. Amanda decided then and there she liked this man. She liked him a whole lot. In fact, she—

Amanda tore her gaze from his and halted her thoughts, shocked by the direction they'd taken. Had she really fallen in love with Cade Danfield?

The superintendent strode into the lobby just then, and Amanda cast her musings aside. She, Cade, and the Sloans stood.

"Gentlemen, Miss Lewis." He bowed slightly in greeting. "I have deliberated over all the information, and in spite of the fact Mrs. Lewis and her daughter have done an adequate job over the years, I've decided to commission Leonard Sloan as keeper of the North Point Light, effective January 1." The superintendent stuck out his right hand and grinned. "Congratulations, Mr. Sloan."

"Thank you," he replied, his thick lips curved in a dopey smile.

Amanda felt Cade's hand at her elbow, but he needn't have been concerned for her emotional well-being. She had known all along this would likely be the outcome. Still, a lump of disappointment swelled in her throat. She swallowed it as the Sloans approached her.

"Miss Lewis, you must be so disconcerted at the moment," the elder Sloan said mockingly.

"Hardly. I prayed about it and believe this is God's will." She lifted her chin and squared her shoulders, holding her hand out to Len. "Congratulations."

He took it, thanked her, and held onto it longer than Amanda cared for. She fairly pulled her fingers from his fleshy grasp.

"Well, I guess this just proves it's still a man's world, eh, Miss Lewis?"

"Yes, you're quite right, and frankly, you men can have it."

She heard Cade chuckle then felt his hold on her elbow tighten. "We should be on our way, Amanda."

"Yes, of course." She turned to the superintendent, thanking him for his time, then allowed Cade to escort her out of the hotel lobby.

Once outside, the air was brisk, the sky a dismal gray, and Amanda thought the weather suited her mood just right. Cade waved down a hackney and assisted her inside.

"I must return to work," he stated apologetically.

"I understand. I'm ever so grateful you were able to attend the hearing with me."

His mustache trembled with a hidden grin, but in his eyes she saw a look of concern. She willed her chin not to quiver. There would be plenty of time to cry her heart out when she arrived back home.

Home. It wasn't hers anymore.

"You were very brave, Amanda, and I'm proud of you," Cade said, giving her hand an affectionate squeeze.

She pushed out a little smile. "At least I won't have to contend with my brother's wrath."

"Indeed." Reaching into the inside pocket of his wool jacket, Cade pulled out a colorfully wrapped, long, narrow box. "I have a present for you."

"Captain, you shouldn't have." Seeing his frown, she corrected herself. "I mean. . .Cade."

"That's better, and I'll buy you a gift anytime I please."

His eyes shone with amusement, and Amanda shook her head at him.

"But this one, I would prefer you opened in private. When you get back to the lighthouse."

"All right." Puzzled, she took the proffered box. "Thank you."

"You're very welcome."

With that, Cade closed the door to the carriage and a moment later, she was on her way.

Curious, Amanda decided she couldn't wait until she got home to open Cade's gift. She tore at the paper only to discover a gray velvet box beneath. She had a hunch it contained jewelry, and with delight and trepidation she opened it. A sliver bracelet gleamed before her eyes. On it hung a tiny lighthouse charm with a diamond lamp. Amanda sucked in a quick breath. She'd never possessed such a treasure!

Lifting the bracelet, she saw a penned note underneath. Unfolding it, she read:

My Dearest Amanda,

Please accept this gift as a small token of my appreciation for a job well done as keeper of Milwaukee's light. I write this not only as a ship's captain, but as your friend and admirer.

Truly,
Cade Danfield

"My admirer?" Amanda fretted over her lower lip. What did he mean? He admired her skills at tending the North Point Light? Well, of course that was it. What else could he possibly admire?

She fingered the lovely bracelet and suddenly hoped their relationship blossomed into something more than a unique friendship. Paradoxically, she didn't think her heart could stand another disappointment.

Chapter 10

L ook what just arrived!" David said, walking into the parlor where Amanda, her sister-in-law, and four nieces were packing. He waved an envelope in the air. "It's an invitation to an exclusive Christmas party this Saturday evening at the Newhall House." He frowned slightly. "Amanda, isn't the Newhall House that elegant hotel on the corner of Michigan Street and Broadway?"

"It's the very one," she replied, wrapping some glassware in old linens. She tried to calm the rapid thumping of her heart. "Who is the invitation from?"

"Captain Danfield."

Amanda had assumed so, and lately she found her insides doing the strangest things at the mere thought of the man.

"It appears we're all invited. It's addressed to Miss Amanda Lewis, Mr. David Lewis, and family." He grinned, looking pleased. "What a splendid surprise. I must have impressed the captain somehow at Mother's funeral."

Amanda gaped at her brother but quickly recovered.

"I hear Danfield is extremely successful in the grain trading business," David added.

"Yes, he is," Amanda told him, earning a quizzical glance from her sister-in-law.

She didn't say anything more.

"David dear," Martha began, "the girls and I are going to need new dresses if we're to attend such a dignified party."

He sighed wearily. "Yes, I suppose you will, and they'll likely cost me a fortune." He turned to Amanda. "My guess is you'll require something suitable to wear as well."

She suddenly felt like Cinderella. "Well, I—"

"Of course she needs a new gown," Martha cut in. "We will *all* have new gowns. Surely there's a dress shop here in Milwaukee that can accommodate us. After all, Saturday is only four days away."

"Yes, there is. It's Lila's Dress Shoppe on Grand Avenue." Amanda decided Mrs. Zenkowski was sure to adore her for bringing in all this business of late.

Suddenly Amanda's nieces couldn't contain their excitement, and the four began chattering about what color gown they wanted and how they would curl their hair.

It was a conversation that lasted throughout the day and occupied their minds while they packed crates. But despite her own excitement, Amanda said nothing about her relationship with the captain. Simply put, she didn't know what to say.

∾⧵

The very next morning, a large package arrived for her. Much to Amanda's embarrassment, she was forced to open it in front of her curious family members. Lifting the box top, she gasped, seeing the tawny silk gown with its collar of French lace. She held it up and watched the golden skirt sail to the floor in ruffled tiers. Martha and the girls swarmed over the fashionable dress.

"I'm sure it cost plenty!" her sister-in-law exclaimed upon closer inspection. "Who's it from?"

"That's what I would like to know," David said, looking stern.

Amanda didn't have to look at the enclosed card to know who had sent this magnificent gift, but she wasn't sure how to explain it to her brother. Cade hadn't come out and stated his intentions, although the light in his blue eyes the last time she'd seen him all but gave his feelings away. However, knowing her brother, if Amanda divulged the truth, he would likely accuse her of making a pest of herself. He would never believe a man like Cade Danfield would be romantically interested in his troublesome little sister— especially since Amanda could scarcely believe it herself.

David grabbed the card from her fingers and then read it aloud. "With love, WCD." He frowned. "Who is WCD?"

Amanda swallowed. *With love?*

"I want answers this minute."

"David darling, calm down. Amanda will tell us." Martha smiled. "Won't you, dear?"

She nodded, having just created a most convenient reply. "WCD," she began, "is a friend from church." It wasn't a complete falsehood. She, Cade, and Jenny had worshiped together last Sunday. That very afternoon, she'd learned the *W* at the beginning of Cade's initials stood for Woodrow, a name he detested. Thus, he preferred to be addressed by his middle name, which was actually his mother's maiden name. . .Cade.

"A friend from church, of course," Martha crooned, except Amanda could tell by her expression that she didn't entirely accept the explanation.

"Obviously, a wealthy friend," David said with a frown. "Amanda, I do hope you haven't made yourself a charity case. That would be most humiliating for me. I am perfectly capable of providing for my family, of which you are a part! Mother, bless her soul, refused my offer of financial support. But you, young lady, do not have that option."

Amanda smiled impishly. "For your information, brother dear, I have no plans to turn away your money. If you give it to me, I'll gladly take it."

After giving her husband a devoted smile, Martha laughed softly.

Saturday evening arrived and the Lewis women were dressed in all their finery. They resembled a veritable rainbow of silks and satins. David said he felt like the luckiest man alive to escort such lovely ladies to a most sophisticated event.

They arrived at prestigious Newhall House, and after they were formally announced, Cade appeared at once to greet them. Amanda thought he looked especially dashing in his deep brown trousers and frock coat, amber-colored vest, and crisp, white shirt, complete with mahogany-brown bow tie.

"Amanda," he said, lifting her gloved hand and bringing it to his lips, "I'm so pleased you could come."

She smiled a reply, uncertain if she could trust her voice.

"And Mr. and Mrs. Lewis," he said with a polite nod. To the girls, he bowed gallantly. "Ladies."

"Captain." David cast Amanda a curious look. "Thank you for inviting us."

"Indeed, it's my pleasure." He placed Amanda's hand around his elbow. "Allow me to show you to our table."

As she walked alongside Cade and across the marbled floor, Amanda could practically feel her brother's and sister-in-law's stares boring into her back. Perhaps she'd erred in keeping her relationship with Cade from them—but what exactly was there to tell? Rapid heartbeats, inklings, and three expensive gifts were hardly the equivalent of a marriage proposal.

Cade seated them, making certain he introduced Jenny. Then he excused himself to greet one other guest who had just been announced, and Amanda thought she heard the name Hosea Benkins.

"Amanda," her sister-in-law began softly, "is there something you wish to tell David and me?"

They were seated to her left, and Amanda gave them each a guilty look. "I–I'm not sure," she hedged.

David frowned. "You're not sure?"

"It seems all so complicated. I think Cade might be interested in me, but—"

"You *think?*" Martha smiled warmly. "Sweetness, I haven't been here five minutes, and I *know* he's interested. Why, this is most exciting."

Amanda released a breath of relief. Hearing another person say what she'd hoped and prayed in the past few days somehow made it real.

"Is he the one who sent you the dress?" her sister-in-law asked.

Amanda nodded. "And he gave me this bracelet," she added, holding out her wrist.

"Look at this, David. How generous of the captain."

"How long have you been calling Danfield by his first name?" David wanted to know.

"No more than a week."

Amanda decided her brother seemed perplexed, if not mildly annoyed, and she wondered if his tender ego hadn't suffered a bit of a blow.

"I'm sure Cade realized I come from good stock after he met you," Amanda said. More than once, she had noted Martha's diplomacy and figured she'd try her hand at it.

It worked. David suddenly lifted his chin and beamed. "Good stock... I should say so!"

Martha patted Amanda's knee approvingly.

Cade returned with Hosea Benkins, and not long afterward dinner was served. A string quartet played Christmas music in the far corner of the room, and then a highly regarded soprano sang several numbers, which caused Mr. Benkins to make the most amusing remarks. It was all their table could do to keep from laughing aloud.

"Must you embarrass me at every social function?" Amanda overheard Cade ask his friend.

"Cap'n, you know I hate these hoity-toity events."

Cade sighed, then zeroed in on the two youngest girls' conversation. Jenny and Amanda's niece Charlotte had suddenly become the best of friends. Rightly so, since they were close in age.

After dinner, guests strolled around the vast ballroom, mingling and admiring the expensive paintings and sculptures. Cade and David soon disappeared, and Martha said she thought the captain was asking for Amanda's hand in marriage. Amanda felt so nervous, she could barely pray.

The two men reappeared just in time to say good-bye to Benkins, who declared it was high time to take his leave, and it seemed he couldn't get to the door fast enough.

When the dancing began, Martha insisted the Lewis family needed to go, stating she didn't think it proper for Christians to carry on in such a manner. David agreed.

Amanda felt a tad disappointed. She relished the idea of lingering in Cade's embrace as they waltzed around the polished floor, and she feared once she left, a host of other women would find him a most eligible partner. But to her infinite relief, Cade said he and Jenny were leaving also.

Nothing, however, was said about her brother's and Cade's mysterious after-dinner conversation, however. And for two days following the party, as they finished packing up the house, Amanda nearly went mad trying to figure out men's minds.

Finally she mustered the courage to bring up the subject to her brother—after all, they were scheduled to leave for Chicago the next day. David had informed Leonard Sloan that he could take possession of the lighthouse earlier than originally planned since Martha wanted to spend Christmas Day at their home in Illinois. Meanwhile, Amanda hadn't seen or heard from Cade.

"Do you love him?" her brother asked bluntly.

"I. . ." Amanda paused, searching her heart for the umpteenth time. She knew it would break into a million pieces if she had to say good-bye to Cade—or worse, if she never saw him again. "Yes, I believe I do."

"I see." David's head bobbed, and he seemed at a loss for words.

"I was under the impression that you and Cade had discussed this subject the night of the Christmas party."

Her brother hesitated briefly. "Yes, we did."

Amanda felt hopeful again. "And? What did he say?"

"He asked me not to repeat our conversation, and I gave my word."

"What does that mean? Did I misunderstand the captain's attentions?"

"No, I don't believe you did, but I'm not at liberty to comment further. I'm sorry."

Fat, sorrowful tears suddenly obscured Amanda's vision, but she quickly blinked them back. "He thinks I'm too young for him, is that it? Well, he's wrong."

"Amanda, I gave my word. . . ."

"Or did you discourage him, David?"

He brought his chin back abruptly at the accusation. "I did no such thing. In fact, I can't wait to marry you off, you little scamp!"

Amanda glowered at her brother before whirling around and exiting the now-empty parlor. A lot of good their discussion did; she felt more confused than ever!

The next morning, Amanda stood in the lamp room, staring out across the vastness of Lake Michigan. Gray and wispy-white flurries swirled the sky in the frosty December air. Tomorrow was Christmas Eve, and she would be living in Chicago. While she had every reason to feel excited about the new life which lay before her, Amanda mourned everything she'd lost. Her mother, her home. . .the man she loved. Except the latter she couldn't truly count as a loss; how did one lose something one never had? Besides, Cade might try to contact her in Chicago. Amanda hoped he would, anyway.

Hanky in hand, she dabbed her eyes just as footfalls echoed up the lighthouse staircase. She figured David had come to fetch her. Their train would be leaving soon, and if her older brother saw her misty eyes and tear-streaked face, he would be sorely disappointed.

Taking several deep breaths, Amanda smoothed out the brown tweed traveling suit Cade had bought her. She hadn't wanted to wear it, since the memories attached to the skirt and matching jacket were not exactly pleasant, but Martha had insisted. Her sister-in-law rarely put her foot down, so Amanda decided the fight wasn't worth it and complied with the request.

Turning from the floor-to-ceiling windows, Amanda walked to the doorway to meet her brother. Suddenly Cade stepped into view.

He's come to say good-bye, she thought as her heart dropped into the pit of her stomach.

She took a step back. "Don't say it. I don't want to hear it," she warned. The last thing she wanted to do was cry her eyes out in front of Cade.

He raised his brows in surprise. "It's a pleasure to see you again too, Amanda," he quipped.

She ignored the sarcasm and returned her gaze to the frothy lake one hundred feet below.

"Would you mind telling me what exactly it is you don't want to hear?"

She grimaced, sensing she wouldn't escape a tearful scene no matter how hard she tried. Well, so be it.

"I don't want you to say good-bye," she said, her eyes filling. "But, if you must, you may write to me in Chicago. Now, if you'll excuse me, I have a train to catch."

Cade fairly took up the entire doorway, and he didn't budge an inch.

"Kindly step aside and spare me a shred of dignity."

"Amanda. . ."

His soft voice was her undoing. Tears spilled from her eyes.

"Amanda," he said once more, this time taking her into his arms, "I have no intention of saying good-bye to you. There, there, now, don't cry."

With her nose in his shirt, she tried to swallow her sobs.

"Oh, my dearest, I'm so sorry. I never meant to hurt you. I wanted to surprise you." He gently pushed her from him and gazed tenderly into her face. "I love you, Amanda."

She sniffed. "I love you, too."

Cade grinned so broadly even his mustache couldn't conceal it. "I've longed to hear you speak those words— ever since the night of the Christmas concert." He leaned forward and placed a light kiss on her mouth. His bushy mustache tickled her nose. Then, grabbing hold of her hand, Cade led her from the lamp room and down the steps. "But you're right. We have to hurry. You do have a train to catch...and so do I."

"What are you talking about?"

"You shall soon see."

Amanda's mind whirred with questions until they entered the house and Cade escorted her on to the sunporch. There she was met by her family members, Jenny, Hosea Benkins, and Reverend and Mrs. Reed. The room, itself, had been decorated with white ribbons and bows. Amanda stared in shock.

"I'll have you know," Martha began, "I told the captain, here, along with my good husband, that you would much prefer a formal wedding in a church, with a beautiful gown and friends in attendance."

"We'll have a reception as soon as we return from our honeymoon," Cade promised.

Amanda shook her head, feeling dazed. "Wedding? Just one moment..." She looked at Cade. "Aren't you supposed to get down on one knee and *ask* me to marry you?"

Benk snorted with amusement as he helped Cade into his handsomely cut frock coat.

"And give you the chance to turn me down? Never."

She narrowed her gaze at him, while Cade's blue eyes twinkled with merriment.

"Better get on with it, Cap'n," Benk said, loud enough for all to hear. "I think her senses are returning."

"They're returning, all right," Amanda replied with an indignant toss of her head. She looped her arm around Cade's. "But I'll repay you for your trickery by forcing you to live the rest of your life with me."

"A fate worse than death, I'm sure," David said with a chuckle. "Although, Captain, if you're expert enough to handle a crew of seamen, I imagine you'll tame my sassy little sister in no time."

She tossed her brother an exasperated glare.

The reverend smiled and with a bony finger pushed his spectacles up to the bridge of his nose. "I have known Amanda since she was a tot, and it's hard to believe she's grown into such a lovely young woman." He gazed at her in a proud, fatherly manner.

Amanda felt herself blush.

"And after speaking at great length with Captain Danfield, I feel the two of you will make a good match." He looked at Cade before his aging eyes rested upon Amanda once more.

"Evelyn would be so pleased," Mrs. Reed added softly.

Amanda agreed and swallowed a fresh onset of tears. Suddenly she recalled her mother's dream. It was as if she had known this day would come. How fitting, Amanda decided, that she and Cade would be married in this very room. After today, it would no longer hold sad memories of her mother's death but joyous ones of marrying the man she loved.

"Shall we begin?" the minister asked.

Cade looked at her, questions in his eyes.

Amanda smiled her consent.

Within no time, it seemed, the vows were spoken. To have and to hold, to love, honor, and cherish. . .

Reverend Reed cleared his throat. "And now, by the authority vested in me by God and the state of Wisconsin, I pronounce you man and wife. You may kiss your bride, Captain."

But he and Amanda were a step ahead of the pastor. She was enveloped in Cade's strong arms, and he was already kissing her soundly.

Finally he released her. Congratulatory cheers broke out around them.

Jenny slipped her small hand into Amanda's. "I'm glad you're my new mama." She glanced at her father. "We're going to be a happy family, aren't we?"

"We most certainly are." Cade gave his daughter an affectionate wink, then gazed adoringly into Amanda's eyes.

Elation swelled within her, and Amanda couldn't help but marvel at God's handiwork.

True, she would sadly relinquish her life here at the lighthouse, but the Lord had given her a new beacon to keep burning brightly. . .

That of the fire in her husband's heart.

SAFE HARBOR

by Paige Winship Dooly

Dedication

For Troy. . .Thanks for being so great about climbing lighthouses,
driving through swamps, diverting along forgotten coasts on our trips,
and exploring mysterious southern locales with me while
in search of the perfect setting for each of my stories.
I look forward to many more years of epic adventures with you!
You're the best!

Chapter 1

St. Marks Lighthouse
Forgotten Coast, Florida—1883

I'm gonna find you, Keera, and when I do, it's off to bed with ya!" Regan tried to sound stern as she called out to her young daughter, but she couldn't help but laugh at the stubborn child's bedtime antics. The sea breeze tussled Regan's hair and blew a few strands into her eyes as she searched the ship's shadowy deck for signs of Keera's movement. She pushed the strands back with her forearm. "It'll be dawn before ya know it, wee one, and a bit of shut-eye before the day begins would be much appreciated by your mother."

"I'm right here, Mama." The giggle in four-year-old Keera's voice carried across the expansive deck like wind chimes, and Regan tried to follow the sound.

She ducked down, her slippered feet light as she moved quietly around the boxes and barrels. She used a tall stack of crates to hide her approach.

The skirt of Keera's pink gown, highlighted by a soft shaft of moonlight, peeked out from between two barrels as Regan rounded a corner. Before she could reach her daughter, she plowed headfirst into a large immovable object.

Firm hands steadied her. "I'm sorry, lass. I didn't mean to collide with you."

Stars circled Regan's head from the impact as she tried to focus on the grandfatherly sailor standing in front of her.

"It's okay, Joseph. It's entirely my fault. I'm sure you didn't expect anyone to be up and about at this hour." She closed her eyes to ward off the dizziness.

His booming laugh startled her, and her eyes flew open.

"Oh, nothing surprises me when it comes to you two lasses. I guess the little one's havin' trouble sleepin' again?"

Regan held her spinning head as she squinted up to look into the kind face of the friendly giant. "Aye. She still has her days and nights mixed up from the journey across the ocean. And she hates our tiny cabin down below."

"Maybe I can help." Joseph reached around Regan and scooped Keera up into his strong arms. "Follow me."

Regan followed as he led the way to the handrail at the side of the ship.

"Throwing her overboard won't fix the issue, Joseph," Regan teased.

Keera squealed and tightened her arms around Joseph's thick neck.

"Don't worry little one. I'd never throw a beautiful princess into the sea—only ruffians have to go overboard." He looked at Regan in the light of the full moon and winked. "I was thinkin' maybe she'd relax better if she could sleep beneath the stars."

"It's worth a try." Regan stepped over to the rail and yawned as she stared dubiously at the lifeboat that pressed close against the side of the huge vessel. "I can't blame her for not wanting to sleep below deck. The whole experience is strange to her with all the people jostling around down there. She doesn't know a one of them, and they get angry if she's restless and gets loud." She tugged one of her daughter's curls. "Which, as you've seen, is pretty much always."

"The seafarers can be difficult, I'll give you that. It's hard to keep a good disposition when livin' in such close quarters for days on end."

"Aye." Regan shuddered. "Then there are the ones who appear to be sick. I do my best to keep our distance, but it feels so much better for our constitutions up here on deck where we have fresh air and space." She spun around with her hands held high. "I have a hard time sleepin' myself when I'm down there. Our room is suffocatin' and claustrophobic."

Joseph's deep laugh rumbled. "It's obvious who she gets her high spirits from."

Regan dropped her hands with a smile. "Guilty as charged."

He set Keera down at Regan's side. "Stay here with your mama. I'll be right back. Can you be patient for me while I get you a surprise?"

"Aye!" Keera bounced. "I love surprises!"

Joseph slipped away, only to return a few minutes later with a stack of clean blankets and a fat bundle. "The rowboat is snug against the side of the ship. You don't have to worry about it slipping and cutting loose. I'll just settle these blankets like so"—he leaned over the side and wrestled the heavy wool into place—"and that'll give you a perfect place to slumber." He turned to Keera. "Now little missy, I want you to curl up on this blanket and count the stars for me. Can you do that?"

"I can try." Keera scrunched up her face. "I can only count to five."

"Five, eh? That's wonderful! When you reach five, start all over until you've counted them all."

"Aye, I can do that." Keera grinned, her blue eyes twinkling in the moonlight.

Regan frowned. "It's a wonderful idea, Joseph, and I appreciate it so much, but I can't have Keera so close to the water. What if I fall asleep and she doesn't? She could go over the side."

"It wouldn't be easy with the angle of the boat, but I had an idea to cover that, too."

Regan sent him a skeptical look and watched him while she busied her hands in an attempt to smooth Keera's unruly auburn curls into a semblance of order. Keera giggled and ducked her head to avoid her mother's ministrations.

Joseph opened the bundle that he'd dropped at his feet and held up a length of soft rope.

"I'll lash you both to the lifeboat. If she tugs at the ropes, it'll wake you. Sounds harsh, but it won't be. It's for her safety. We do it all the time when working the deck in rough seas."

"Can't be any worse than tryin' to sleep below deck. I can't count the amount of times she's bumped her head on the side of the ship when the ship rolls. I've considered tyin' her to me many a time, especially during each of the tongue lashin's I've received from the others she awakens with her wails. The walls are thin, and we've offended many a passenger. It hasn't been a pleasant journey in that sense."

"I know, miss. And I hope the difficult journey pays off for ya both when ya reach your destination."

Regan sucked in a breath of salty air as she turned slightly away from him to stare out over the moonlit ocean. She blinked back the rare feeling of unexpected tears. She felt helpless in the face of her future—as helpless as she did when it came to controlling their lives aboard this huge, unfamiliar ship. Lack of control wasn't something she was used to. She was used to being in control. She turned back to face her friend. "Thanks, Joseph. You've been nothing but kind. I hope you realize how much that means to us. We appreciate it more than words can say."

"Nonsense. You're the one who's done me the favor." Joseph studied her with concern. "I miss my wife, daughters, and grandchildren back home. I know my wife would appreciate knowin' my time away wasn't wasted and that I was watching out for someone else's daughter and grandchild in this situation. She's a good woman—I know you two would be great friends if you were ever to meet."

Regan forced a watery smile. "Aye. I'm sure we would be, too. I hope to meet her someday. I want to thank her for sharing you with us. And your daughters. . . I'm sure they miss you dearly. I know my father will thank you for watching over us if he ever gets the chance."

Joseph studied her for a moment more before he masked his concern and busied himself with showing her how to lash the ropes securely to the lifeboat. He'd already made it clear he didn't take well to the notion of a young widow traveling alone with such a young child.

Regan followed suit and tried to put his mind at ease. No need to go into detail with him over their uncertain future in America. "This looks wonderful. Only a few more days and we'll reach our destination. I just might be able to keep my sanity now." Regan lifted Keera into the lifeboat and settled her onto the blankets. Her daughter's eyes drifted shut even as she struggled to keep them open. "And what a perfect distraction to have her count the stars."

"I'll count 'em tomorrow, Mama," Keera mumbled, her words heavy with sleep.

"Your sanity is certainly a good thing to keep, Miss Regan. You're going to do fine, no matter your situation. I'll get your things and bring them up here come mornin'. I'll also alert the captain to your new accommodations so he'll not be startled if he finds you here. We'll be watchin' over ya so you can sleep."

"How can we ever thank you?"

"You can continue to take good care of the wee one. The two of you have made the trip less lonely for me. I'm gettin' too old to be away from my loved ones like this."

"Glad we could help." Regan slipped gracefully over the rail and slid down into the lifeboat. She settled beside her daughter and wrapped the rope around them both. The water lapped against the hull below them, the sound reassuring after their weeks of being cooped up in the dark, dank cabin below deck.

Keera's cool, soft hand reached over to cup Regan's warm cheek. Regan turned her head and kissed her daughter's tiny palm before closing her eyes, glad to finally have the chance to rest.

≈❧

Ian Morgan took a long sip of coffee as he leaned against the base of his lighthouse and looked out over the aquamarine waters of the Florida Gulf Coast. He contemplated his early morning prayer as he took in the beauty around him.

Granny made it clear that she thought it unnecessary for him to pray for extra provisions for her and his son, Johnny—insisting Ian provided everything the three of them could possibly need. But his son was withdrawn, and Ian wanted to do something to pull him out of his musings. Granny worked way too hard while making do with their meager supplies. They needed a diversion, something to liven things up around the lighthouse. Granny and Johnny did without far too often, and Ian didn't feel it was out of line to ask God to provide a few extra extravagances for them just this once.

"Thinking about your boat won't make it magically appear," Granny sing-songed, her words alerting Ian to her presence moments before she walked up beside him. He pulled away from the wall as the tiny woman hugged him with a strong arm. Her rolled-up dress sleeves hugged tan forearms, the color of her skin accentuating the fact that Granny spent her days hard at work in the hot Southern sun.

Johnny walked past them and slowly made his way to the water. Ian grimaced. Most boys his age would careen toward the shore oblivious to any hazards that might await. Not many five-year-olds would walk to the shore with such serious consideration. He shook off the thought and turned to his grandmother.

"Maybe I was thinking more along the lines of setting you to sail,

Granny. Perhaps I was contemplating sending you off to see the world in a fine boat made of the most up-to-date materials."

"Nonsense." Granny smiled up at him. "You know good and well that I don't have any aspirations to see anything beyond this beautiful view." She motioned toward the shoreline.

And what an amazing view it was. Small, random waves rode the top of the otherwise mirror-smooth water to lap gently at the shore. A pelican floated on the water's surface, his reflection blurred as he waited for an unsuspecting fish to swim within range so he could scoop it up with his long bill. Seagulls flew overhead, crying out as they dipped and swayed in the slight salt-scented breeze.

Granny squeezed his arm. "Besides, the small boat you prayed for wouldn't stand up against the ocean's strong pull."

"So now you admit I'm not too frivolous to wish for such a small vessel?" he teased. "You know I just want something that will get us around a bit easier, take some of the burden off you when we travel around the bayou."

"There's nothing wrong with my legs, Ian. I can walk anywhere you can."

"That is true. But the trip to town is a long one. A boat would make the trip easier." And an easier trip would mean more trips to town, allowing his lonely grandmother more visits with the friends she'd left behind when she moved out to the lighthouse to help with Johnny.

"I'm fine without my friends. I have you and Johnny to care for, and I can't imagine spending my life any other way. As a matter of fact, I was lonelier when I lived in town than I am now. I love it out here."

For a moment Ian wondered if he'd spoken his words out loud.

Granny laughed. "I see it in your eyes. You worry about me. Johnny's silence keeps you worried enough. You don't need to take on additional burdens. I'm perfectly content and happy." She rubbed his arm. "And Johnny will come out of his shell soon enough. You just wait and see. He had a hard blow—losing his mama at such a young age. He's resilient. He'll come through in time."

"It's been two years, Gran. How much longer do you think it'll take? He was barely toddling around when we lost her."

"You know he lost her long before she died, Ian."

"That's true. She hated it out here. That's why I worry about you. This isn't a place for a woman."

"It's a wonderful place for anyone." Granny's eyes widened. "How can you even say such a thing? Have I seemed unhappy or lonely even one day since I came out here? It's a gorgeous place to raise a child, to live as a family. I can't imagine living anywhere else."

Ian studied her. "Are you sure? Do you mean it?"

"I wouldn't have said it if I didn't. Since when have I ever told an untruth?"

He puffed out a breath. "Never that I know of."

She stood quietly beside him for a moment, but he knew the conversation wasn't over.

Granny turned from the water to study him. "The only thing I can see that might be missing around here is a wife for you—a mama for the young one."

"We're doing just fine, Granny. I don't need another wife."

"Johnny misses having a mother around."

"He has you. We've been through this, Gran. You saw Maggie. She couldn't cope with being so far away from town. She gave in to her illness—she even seemed to welcome death as an escape from her misery out here. Why would any other woman want to stay if this solitary life couldn't even satisfy Johnny's own mother?"

"Maggie wasn't well, even before you moved her out here. We just discussed that. She changed after she had Johnny. She never wanted to hold him—she cried all the time. I don't know what was wrong, but something snapped way back then. I hoped the change of scenery and the quiet life on the coast would pull her out of wherever she'd gone in her mind, but obviously the move didn't help."

"How can a mother not love her own child, Gran? I never understood that." Ian studied Johnny as he walked toward the cove. "He's such a great boy."

"He is a wonderful child, and I think Maggie loved him as best she could. She cared for the both of you in her own way. It just wasn't enough to keep her here."

Ian shrugged. "All I know is the last thing I need is a woman showing up to complicate things. I'm perfectly happy with you, Johnny, and the lighthouse. Nothing beyond that needs to change."

"Sometimes when we pray, unexpected things happen." Granny smiled a mysterious smile and motioned for Johnny to move away from the water's edge. Johnny turned back and fell into step beside her. They headed for the cottage, and Ian was left with his coffee.

Chapter 2

Regan startled as her lifeboat slammed hard against the sturdy side of the ship. Up until now, she'd never felt the small craft separate from the larger vessel. The mighty ship rose and fell roughly against the unseen ocean below them, making it obvious that a strong storm had moved in while they slept. Rain pelted against the tarp she'd stretched across the lifeboat.

Not sure what to do, Regan reached over to feel for her daughter. Relief coursed through her when her hand connected with Keera's soft skin. Surprisingly, despite the storm, her young daughter still slumbered away with the deep sleep of an exhausted child.

The past few days had passed unremarkably, a good thing in Regan's estimation, but a mixed undercurrent of both anticipation and dread hummed through her as they approached their final destination. The lifeboat arrangement had proved to be worth its weight in gold in keeping Regan's sanity while they'd traveled, but their time aboard the Ocean Queen was quickly coming to an end. And though she had little freedom from the mundane routines aboard ship, the end of the journey meant the end of the brief independence she'd enjoyed while she and her daughter had traveled.

Another huge bump had the lifeboat again swinging out and back. Regan thought she might be better off securing her daughter aboard the larger ship for the duration of the storm. But the jerky movement of the smaller vessel had her wondering if they'd fall into the sea if she tried to make it aboard ship. The crew most likely battled the elements, and it wouldn't do to bother the hardworking men with a request to help her and Keera aboard.

Besides, Joseph had assured her the lifeboat was secure and that there was no way the small vessel would break free of its moorings. Another huge swell caused the ship to rise and then rapidly drop. Regan's stomach lurched and she pushed up on her elbows. Regardless of Joseph's assurances, the abrupt bumps and bangs had her wondering if the storm might change their current situation.

The ship rose higher and higher on a wave and this time, when it slammed down, it listed alarmingly to the side. Keera woke with a scream, and Regan reached for her, talking in soothing tones even as she feared they were going to be dumped overboard into the churning ocean below.

"Lighten the load, lighten the load!" a terrified voice screamed from above. "She's struck a sandbar and we're going over if we don't do something quick."

Other voices joined in, the chaos nearly drowning out Keera's terrified cries. "Mama? I don't want to go in the water. I want to go below deck!"

"We're safer here, wee one. It'll be okay." Even as Regan consoled her daughter, she worked her foot under the bench of the lifeboat and hooked her bootless toe around the wood support, hoping to find a way to keep them aboard if the ship continued to tilt.

The larger boat would surely crush them if they tipped onto the sandbar, a thought Regan quickly pushed to the back of her mind. For the time being, the listing had stalled, and Regan could hear the splashes of large barrels and crates as they were thrown overboard into the raging seas.

Progress was made and the boat moved into a more normal position.

"See, love, the boat is rightin' itself. The crew is hard at work to get us off this sandbar, and we're gonna be just fine. As soon as we're free, we'll be movin' along toward Pensacola, and to Uncle Stewart's fine home."

If only my uncle and aunt were expecting us.

But she couldn't dwell on that at the moment. She had a daughter to console.

A large bundle slid against her shoulder. "Look, Keera, the supplies Joseph snuck over for us are trying to escape! They're tapping me on the shoulder."

Keera giggled. "Supplies can't move on their own, Mama. And I can't see anything, anyway. It's too dark under this tarp."

"Oh, silly me! Of course they can't. The tipping of the ship must be making them slip."

The lifeboat once again jolted sharply against the hull and Regan sucked in her breath.

"I don't like when it does that, Mama."

"I don't like it either, love, but it's a good thing. It means the boat is tilting back in the direction it needs to be so we can get back on course."

Except the rain pelting against the tarp, silence ensued.

Regan breathed a sigh of relief. "I think that's it, Keera. See? That wasn't so bad after all."

Suddenly they were free-falling through the air, the lifeboat dropping from beneath them.

Regan's scream drowned out Keera's cry of terror.

They hit the water hard, the lifeboat still beneath them. Regan's head slammed against the hard wood. She struggled to stay awake. Thank heavens they'd been tied in. Only a thin sliver of light passed through a crack where the tarp's heavy edge had pulled away from the boat. Violent rains continued to pound against the thick canvas.

Unconsciousness pressed in, but Keera's terrified sobs filled the air, forcing Regan to hold off the enticing darkness.

"I'm here, Keera," she mumbled, her words slurred. "It's gonna be all right."

But was it? She had no idea what had just happened. She clawed at the tarp, suddenly feeling claustrophobic with it blocking her view.

The material piled into the boat beside her and she struggled to see through the rain and darkness that surrounded them.

Keera pressed against her. "The ship's gone."

Regan's heart sank. "It can't be, hon. It's dark. I'm sure the boat is close by."

But it wasn't. The waves were still higher than normal; even this close to shore they hid the ship from view. The small boat was too light to settle on the sandbar as the heavier vessel had, and moved closer and closer to shore.

Panic coursed through Regan as she struggled to sit up. She searched the open sea for any sign of life.

"Lord, please help us find a safe harbor nearby. And thank You for keepin' us safe thus far."

Helpless to do anything, she sat with her hands folded on her lap. Once again she missed having a husband at her side—someone who was there to help make difficult decisions and to watch over them.

Dear Lord, I know You love us as much and more than any husband or father possibly could. Please help us safely find our way through this dark night. Keep us safe and calm.

Another wave of dizziness rolled through her and interrupted her prayer. She didn't dare settle on the boat's bench, fearful she'd topple them into the dark, churning water.

"What's next, Mama?"

"We wait. And we pray." The darkness pressed in again, and Regan felt the sticky wetness of blood at the back of her head. She fought to control her consciousness. What would Keera do if Regan passed out? What if she panicked? "God will show His plan to us as soon as He's ready, but for now we need to remain calm."

"Even when we're alone in the dark?"

"When we're alone in the dark is His favorite time to work His plans, Keera. He has our full attention right now, doesn't He?"

"I suppose He does." Relief laced Keera's words.

"Why don't you go back to sleep for a bit. I promise I'll wake you if I see anything exciting."

Keera yawned. "Yes, Mama."

"I might even catch a bit of shut-eye myself since nothin' is going on." Regan hoped her daughter bought in to her story, but didn't have time to check as she crumpled onto the bottom of the boat.

"What on earth?" Ian stared hard at the water from the upper window of the lighthouse and rubbed his eyes. Sure enough, the water teemed with bobbing brown barrels.

Johnny's voice carried from far below and echoed up the stairs. "Papa! Papa! Come quick! Your rowboat is here, and so are the supplies you prayed for! Hurry, Pa! Hurry! You have to see!"

Ian hurried down the lighthouse stairs as fast as he safely could. It wasn't as much what his son had said as the fact that he'd said so much! His foot treads echoed on the metal and then wooden steps as he made his way round and round the interior walls of the beacon. His prayer had been answered? He hadn't heard so much life in Johnny's voice since before Johnny's mother had died.

Ian burst through the outer door. "Where are you, son?"

"We're over here by the cove," Granny answered. "He's right, Ian. God has answered your prayers in a mighty way."

"I reckon He did." Ian skidded to a stop at her side. A weather-beaten lifeboat bobbed in the middle of the cove. He grinned. "A boat, too, huh? Johnny—we have ourselves a boat!"

"Go get it, Pa, before it drifts back out to sea."

Johnny was right—the boat was slowly but surely drifting back out with the tide.

Ian waded into the warm water. The boat moved farther away.

"It's getting away, Pa!"

"I see, son. Calm down, and let me get out there."

"He'll get it," Granny reassured. "You just wait and see."

Ian stretched his arm out and his fingertips brushed the wooden side. He leaned forward to peer inside. "It's full of tarps, but they're heavy."

"Why is there so much stuff in the water, Pa? Where did it all come from?"

"A ship must have been grounded during the storm this morning."

"What storm?"

Granny exchanged a raised eyebrow with Ian.

Ian didn't even try to contain his laugh. "You slept through a big storm, son." He solidified his grip and tugged the boat toward shore.

Johnny surveyed the horizon. "Where's the ship now?"

"Once they lighten the load, they move on. The weight of all the provisions weighs them down, and they get stuck in the shallower waters. They threw this stuff overboard so they could go on their way."

"So I guess they got stuck because of your prayer, huh, Pa?"

Ian cringed. "I certainly hope not."

"But you got a boat and supplies just like you wanted."

"Not necessarily. We don't know what the barrels hold."

"But we'll know soon, right? We get to open them?"

Ian didn't answer. He stood thigh-deep in the water a few yards off-shore and reached for the rumpled tarp. He gathered it up, while trying to keep it out of the water, and turned to toss it on shore.

A shrill scream rent the air around them. Ian whipped around as fast as he could in the thigh-deep water and assumed a defensive position, his arms stretched out before him. Perplexed, he stared at the tiny, wild-haired imp that had risen to her knees and had quieted momentarily as she sucked in air for her next scream. Her little chest rose and fell with terror, but the subsequent scream never came.

The hot sun on her face had her squinting against its glare, but even so the brilliant hue of her blue eyes stood out as she matched Ian's gaze with curious intensity. As she considered him, her breaths evened out and his presence seemed to have a calming effect on her.

She glanced over at Granny and Johnny, and back at Ian again. Her eyes went from his outstretched arms to his position in the water and a slight smile shaped her lips. Suddenly, her face transformed into a full-blown smile and the most contagious giggle bubbled out of her.

Johnny's line of questioning had ended with the scream, but when Ian turned to glance over his shoulder at his son, he saw interest chase away the fear. Johnny's lip turned up when he saw the amusement in his father's eye, and soon his giggles joined the little girl's. Granny motioned for Ian to bring the child to her, but though her lips also tipped with delight at the child's musical laughter, her eyes were full of questions and concern.

Ian waded over to the boat, which had drifted a few feet away, and reached his arms for the child. "It's okay. I won't hurt you. Let me carry you to shore. My granny over there will take care of you, and she'll find you something to eat. How's that sound?"

The child didn't reach for him but she didn't cower away, either. Instead, she stared at the bottom of the boat. "Mama won't talk to me, but iff'n she did, she wouldna want me to be goin' with strangers."

She had a delightful accent.

Her words registered, and with a sinking heart Ian leaned over to glance into the vessel. A petite woman lay motionless on the bottom of the boat. He couldn't tell if she was dead or alive, but he did know her daughter was watching his every move. Granny's voice cut through his indecision.

"Hurry, Ian, let's get them on dry land."

Ian glanced over at her. Granny's eyes continued to ask questions Ian couldn't answer. From his vantage point, he couldn't tell if the woman had survived whatever ordeal they'd gone through.

Ian already had the boat in hand and was dragging it closer to shore. He pulled it up as far as he could and swung the little girl onto the sand. Her dress was damp and her hair hung in tangled knots. "Tend to her, Granny, and I'll follow behind with her mother."

"I'm not leavin' my mama." Her statement wasn't said with rebellion, but rather stated as a fact.

"Papa, why's she talking like that? Her words sound funny."

Granny shushed Johnny with a squeeze to his shoulder.

"I'm guessing she's traveled over from Europe, is that right, honey?" He squatted down to the small girl's level. "Were you on a big boat before getting into this one?"

"Aye. We were on a great ship. I'm from Ireland, which makes me Irish. It's what gives me my fiery hair and temper. At least that's what Mama says." She turned to look at her mother, but the woman hadn't moved since they'd found her.

"Well, your mother will be worried if she wakes up and sees you standing here in a wet dress with your hair all awry. Why don't you go with my son, Johnny, and with Granny, and let her fix you up while I bring your mama to the house. See?" He motioned to the building nestled against the base of the lighthouse. "They'll take you right over there, and I'll bring your mama to join you as soon as I get her out of the boat."

"Come, love, your mama's in good hands. Let Ian take care of her while I find you some dry clothes." Granny reached out a hand. "What's your name, darlin'?"

"Keera." She took the offered hand and left Ian to his work.

Johnny lingered behind.

Keera looked at him from over her shoulder. "Isn't the laddie comin' with us?"

"He'll be along momentarily. Johnny, catch up as soon as you're finished talking to your father."

"Did you pray this into happening, too, Pa?"

Keera stopped in her tracks and turned to look at Ian with wide eyes.

Ian sighed. "No, son. My prayers had nothing to do with this woman and child being lost at sea." At least he hoped that was true.

Granny snagged Johnny's hand and led him off with Keera, while

Ian turned back to tend to the woman in the boat. Her chest moved. She breathed with the slightest motion, but at least she was alive. He released the breath he didn't realize he'd been holding.

"Ma'am?"

No response. He wished Granny had stayed close.

He reached in to touch her shoulder. "Ma'am, can you hear me? You've washed ashore during a storm. Your daughter is in good hands with my granny, but they want me to bring you to them."

She didn't move a muscle. Her light, steady breaths continued without change.

He squatted next to the boat, taking note of the water that had sloshed in to fill the bottom, the soaked tarps that had been pushed to the rear of the vessel to make a bed for Keera, and the ropes that must have held them in place during the storm. He had no idea how Keera had worked her way loose, but he was glad she hadn't fallen overboard before reaching shallow waters.

The woman's face was porcelain white—whether from inheritance or illness he didn't know—but it wouldn't be fair for long if he continued to linger in the hot summer sun. Her beautiful features were delicate like her daughter's.

He'd prayed for supplies and a boat. He'd received the items—and a woman and child to boot. He couldn't help but recall his grandmother's mention of wanting a wife for him.

He ignored the crazy thought and focused his attention on figuring out a plan. He considered his options on moving her. If she'd been injured, the last thing he wanted to do was cause her more pain or further the damage.

He snagged the tarp that he'd tossed to shore—it appeared to be the driest—and placed it on the sand next to the lifeboat. Gingerly, he lifted their guest from the hard wood of the vessel and gently placed her on the softer, sand-cradled tarp.

A soft moan drifted from her lips. So she was injured. His hand felt sticky with blood. He identified the source of the wound—a gash on the back of her head—by looking at the watery bloodstain on the boat's floor. He gently rolled her to her side and examined the small gash. The blood had dried for the most part, but the water that she'd rested in at the bottom of the boat had kept it from drying completely.

He needed to get her to Granny.

"I don't know if you can hear me, but I'm going to lift you and take you to our house. We need to get you out of the hot sun, and my granny can care for you there. Your daughter is waiting there, too, while playing with my son."

When she gave no sign of hearing him, he lifted her into his arms.

Chapter 3

Soft noises invaded Regan's consciousness but none were familiar. She struggled to open her eyes, needing to survey her surroundings, but her eyelids refused to cooperate.

Where am I?

After a few moments of wasted time trying to figure out her surroundings by sound, she remembered the storm at sea and the lifeboat dropping down from the ship and falling into the out-of-control waves far below. The memories crashed back as harshly as the angry waters had slammed against her lifeboat. Keera.

"Keera!" Regan pushed up onto her elbows. "Keera?"

She forced her eyes open, but the light coming in from a nearby window flooded her vision, making her squint. Her head pounded from the effort. She tried to get her bearings, but the settee she rested on was just as unfamiliar as the sounds.

She swung her legs over the edge of the couch, crying out when a sharp pain sliced through her temple. She pushed through the pain. "Keera! Where are you?"

Nausea, summoned by her swirling head, caused her stomach to churn. She gulped, trying to hold back the bile that rose in the back of her throat, and fought to keep her panic at bay.

If something had happened to her daughter, she didn't know what she'd do.

How did I end up in this strange place?

Footfalls sounded against a hardwood floor and a shadowy figure approached as a gentle hand stayed her shoulder. "Whoa there, you shouldn't be trying to get up."

Regan didn't have the energy to fight.

"Keera's fine. Rest a moment, and I'll fill you in."

The gentle authority of the male voice soothed her.

The man fluffed her pillows, and she leaned back against them.

"My daughter—Keera—she's. . ."

"She's fine."

The man had a kind voice, but between the sunlight coming in from a nearby window and the throbbing pain that pulsed against the back of her eyes, she couldn't see him. She raised a hand against her forehead in an effort to shield the glare.

It helped a bit. The handsome man smiled, his dark eyes warm and friendly. Long dark hair curled slightly where it dusted his collar.

"You and your daughter washed ashore this morning in a small lifeboat. Do you remember how you got there?"

"I do. There was a storm and our ship ran aground on a sandbar. Keera and I were in a lifeboat and with all the chaos, someone accidentally released it. Please. Where is my daughter? I really need to see her."

"Keera's right outside, playing with my son, under my granny's watchful eye. She's perfectly safe."

"Can you call her in please?" She closed her eyes. The pain in her head intensified from the strain.

Regan heard the floor creak and the door opened, letting in more rays of sunshine. "Granny, she's awake and asking for Keera."

Keera's squeal was music to Regan's ears. The little girl ran through the doorway and threw herself on top of Regan's chest. "I missed you, Mama. You wouldn't talk to me in the boat."

"I would have talked to you if I'd been awake, wee one. I hit my head on the bottom of the boat when we were released from the ship and it made me sleep."

Regan's eyes finally adjusted to the bright light. She hugged her daughter tight as she took in her surroundings. She appeared to be in the main living area of a house. A fire burned in the hearth across the room, and a table with four chairs nestled in front of it. The man she'd been talking with stood to the side of the fireplace with his hand on the shoulder of a young boy who waited beside him. The man reached up to muss the boy's hair with affection.

His son.

She could see the resemblance.

An older woman made her way through the door. Her mouth formed into a radiant smile as soon as her alert brown eyes—eyes that were very similar to the man's—met Regan's. "How wonderful to see that you're awake, dear. You gave us quite a scare."

"Aye. I guess I did. I'm sorry for that."

"No worries. Keera's had a great time playing with Ian's boy, Johnny. Ian showed her around the lighthouse grounds, but he said she had to wait for you to give your approval before she could go up to see the light."

"Lighthouse?" Regan had trouble keeping up.

The man stepped forward. He really did look to be as kind as he sounded. "I'm the lightkeeper, Ian Morgan. Keera made it clear she wanted to climb to the top, but we told her she had to wait for your approval. She wasn't very happy with us."

Regan laughed. "I can imagine. Patience isn't her best virtue. And I'm Regan. Regan Stewart."

"Regan Stewart, I'm glad to meet you." The man's twinkling eyes put her at ease. "Spunk isn't a bad trait to have. It'll carry Keera far. She sure adjusted well to all that the day has brought her."

Regan smiled down at her daughter still nestled against her and wound her finger through one of Keera's curls. "Aye, she adapts well. She's had to. She's been through a lot."

"And so have you." The older woman pushed forward and surveyed Regan. "Keera, why don't you go help Johnny set the table for dinner while I check on your mother."

Ian moved away. "I'll go tend to the light."

Keera pushed off Regan's stomach and jumped to her feet. "Can we go? You said we could ask when she's awake! She's awake now!"

Ian's eyes twinkled. "You're a persistent one. I did say that, but Granny has asked you and Johnny to set the table. Why don't you help with that, and we'll go up in the lighthouse tomorrow. That way, if your mama feels up to it, she can go with us."

Keera's shoulders sagged and she sighed. "Aye. I'll help set the table."

She dragged her feet with exaggerated drama as she slowly walked to the table.

Regan rolled her eyes, and Ian grinned. He made his escape and pulled the door shut behind him.

The older woman pulled a chair beside the couch and sat down. "My given name is Matilda, but you can call me Granny. If you don't like Granny, call me Tildy. But I likely won't answer. I've been Granny for such a long time I've mostly forgotten to answer to anything else." She glanced over at the kids. "Keera has made herself at home. We hope you'll do the same. I have to say, you've raised a delightful child."

"Thank you. She's spirited, as I'm sure you've discovered."

"She does keep a person hopping. And what about you? Appears to me mama has as much fortitude as daughter."

"Thank you. I'd like to think so." Regan laughed, then moaned as the throbbing in her head increased. She cupped her hands around her temples. "Ouch." She waited a moment for the pain to pass. "I like to keep a positive attitude as much as possible." She raised her voice a notch. "Nothin' much comes of sulkin'."

She sent a pointed look at Keera who still dragged her feet while setting the table.

Keera giggled and her entire countenance changed. Soon she and Johnny were working together to get the chore done.

"You seem to have come through the storm pretty well, Regan. One good bump to the back of the head, but otherwise you're fine. You had a small gash back there that I cleaned, so you'll want to take it easy for a day or two. I got you out of your wet clothes after Ian brought your things up from the boat. You were able to help a bit when I assisted you into the pink dress. Your valise came through pretty unscathed. A bit wet on the bottom, but I laid it and your boots out in the sun to dry. Do you remember anything about this morning?"

"No, ma'am. I'm sorry, I don't remember anything after the lifeboat left the ship and crashed into the sea."

"I can't imagine. What a horrifying experience!" Granny sympathized. "I'm so glad you made it safely to shore."

"Me too." Regan shuddered as repercussions of what could have been flashed through her mind.

Ian walked through the door, and Regan heard seagulls call in the distance. Nearby waves crashed against the shore. Regan could feel a different type of wave, one curling with nostalgia and homesickness, crash over her at the familiar sounds. She pushed back unexpected tears. She'd come too far to break down now.

"Dinner smells wonderful, Gran." Ian glanced over at Regan. "Do you think you can eat?"

Thankful for the diversion, she nodded. "Aye. I hope so. The aromas are settin' my mouth to waterin'."

"Stay put." Gran hurried to her feet. "Let me fetch you a bowl, and you can eat it right where you are."

"No please." Regan sat up again, this time taking it slow so she could get her bearings. "I'd rather eat at the table with you if you don't mind. I've had enough of lazing around."

"You've hardly lazed around." Ian laughed. "You've been unconscious the better part of the day and who knows how long through the night."

Regan ignored him and lowered her feet to the floor.

"But if you're going to ignore me and my brilliant words of advice, at least let me assist you to the table."

"I'd be obliged." Regan smiled up at him and let him take her arm. She eased to her feet and, while a bit wobbly, her head didn't swoon from the effort.

Ian held her right arm firmly with his while wrapping his left around her back to support her other arm. His strong grip and muscular chest made her feel safe in a way she hadn't since her husband had passed away. While she should have felt uncomfortable while being held so closely in a stranger's arms, instead she felt secure and protected.

Regan stumbled once on her journey across the room, but Ian held tight, not seeming to mind that she leaned fully against him.

Keera giggled and slipped into a chair opposite the fire.

Johnny stood at her side. "Papa, Keera's taken my spot."

Ian stopped at the table. "Here we go, Regan. If you'll take this closest chair, I'll pull another one up for Johnny."

Granny kept busy with placing a variety of food on the table. A platter of hot, flaky rolls and a saucer with creamy butter joined a large pot of hearty beef stew. "I thought the rainy day made a good excuse for a hearty meal, but wouldn't you know the sun decided to come out and warm the day up."

"We don't mind, do we?" Ian pulled up a chair for Johnny and then sat opposite Regan at the far end of the table. Johnny took the seat between Ian and Keera, and Granny had a side to herself with her back to the fire.

Ian, Granny, and Johnny reached to join hands. Regan motioned for Keera to join in. It was with great relief that she nestled her daughter's hand into hers. Granny squeezed Regan's other hand and gave her a warm smile.

Ian cleared his throat. "Dear Lord, we thank You for this meal we're about to eat. Thank You for bringing Keera and Regan safely through the storm and for bringing them to us. Amen."

Gran gave a final squeeze before letting go and reaching for the rolls.

Ian began serving up bowls of stew. "What brings you to America, Regan?"

"Keera and I are—" No matter how she said it, she'd sound pathetic. A grown woman going to live with her uncle and aunt. What would Ian and Granny think if they knew her own father hadn't wanted her? These people, whom she'd only just met, made her feel more loved than her own father had when he'd decided to send them away. "—heading for my uncle and aunt's home in Pensacola for a visit."

"How wonderful," Granny gushed. "Did your husband stay behind?"

"I lost my husband two years ago."

Sympathy filled Granny's eyes. "Ian lost his wife around the same time."

"He isn't really lost," Keera interjected. "He died when I was but a wee tot."

"I see," Ian said. "I'm sorry to hear that."

"We've done all right for ourselves," Regan hurried to say. She hated the sympathy that often came with the announcement. But at least she'd avoided the uncomfortable fact that her own father had sent them away. "We've done just fine on our own."

"Aye, we have." Keera nodded and spoke around a mouthful of food. "We moved in with Pappy, but he married Mama's best friend and said we needed to come live with our uncle and aunt. Mama said on the boat that she was glad because livin' with them was—what did you call it,

Mama? The most awkward thing ever?"

"Until now," Regan mumbled.

Ian choked on his food but had the decency to try to hide his smile behind his napkin. He failed miserably. His dark eyes flashed with mirth.

Regan stared him down. "You might as well give up the fight. Your eyes gave you away."

"Sorry." His full grin as he scooped his spoon into his bowl and looked up at her was anything but sorry, but it was also contagious and she found herself smiling back.

Regan's heart skipped a beat. He had a boyish charm about him that warmed her spirit.

"So I suppose we need to send a letter to your family so they don't worry."

"Aye. Please do. Though to be honest, I'm not even sure they know we're coming. My father sent a note, but I doubt it had time to arrive ahead of us. He barely penned it before we started across the ocean. Oh— and I'd like to send a note to the ship's captain. I'm sure they're horribly worried as to what happened to us. One of the crew members took a grandfatherly interest in us, and I'm sure he's mighty worried. He's the one that came up with the idea for settlin' us into the lifeboat. I'm sure he's sick that we're missing."

"We'll write them after dinner. The supply ship will be by in a few days and we can send the notes upriver with them." He wiped his mouth with his napkin and settled back in his chair. Broad shoulders tapered to a slim waist, and he folded his hands over a flat stomach. He looked very handsome in the firelight.

"Thank you." Regan corralled her eyes, trying not to stare. "If they have room, do you think they'd give Keera and I passage into town or to Pensacola?"

Granny looked over at Ian. "I don't know, dear. I think it's best if you stay here until you've fully recovered."

"I'm feeling much better already."

"And you look better, too. You have some color back in your cheeks. But still, the journey to Pensacola won't be an easy one. You might have to book passage on another ship to get there. We'll have to check into it, but for now, you're welcome to stay here as long as necessary."

Regan dropped her eyes and studied the table. She hadn't thought anything would be as bad as being dependent on an aunt and uncle she'd never met, but now she was dependent on total strangers.

Lord, I don't understand. Why did You bring us here? You know I've been struggling with being a burden on family. Now I'm a burden on strangers. Please help me find a way to stand on my own two feet.

She glanced up, and found Ian studying her with concern. "Are you feeling ill? I can help you back to the settee if you'd like. You shouldn't overdo."

"I haven't. Actually, I'd like to go outside and see the lighthouse after the table is cleared. Of course, I'll help with the dishes before we go out."

She started to stand and swooned. "Or maybe I'll just sit here in my chair a wee bit longer."

"Ian, help Regan out to the porch and settle her in a chair. The fresh air will do her a world of good. She'll enjoy the view out there as the sun sets. Stay with her in case she needs help back inside."

"Yes, ma'am." Ian winked at Regan, and her heart fluttered.

The head injury was muddling her mind.

"Johnny, Keera, why don't you bring me the dishes, and if you're very careful, I'll let you help me wash them."

"Can I, Mama? Please?"

"Aye, but of course. But you be very careful and you listen to what Granny says, okay?"

"Yes, Mama."

Keera bubbled with anticipation.

Ian helped Regan to her feet. With Ian's assistance, she headed for the door with as much enthusiasm as her daughter had for the dishes.

Once outside she took in her surroundings. A long porch ran the length of the house. Ian led Regan to a rocking chair on the end closest to the beach, but Regan couldn't make herself sit down.

Her eyes were drawn to the beautiful landscape spread out before her. Emerald green water lapped at the powder white shore. Hues of mint and aqua and turquoise water melted into the horizon. Seagulls dipped toward the water in search of a late-evening snack. And as the sun dipped down to join the water at the horizon, layers of pink, peach, and lavender lined the sky.

"Oh, Ian." Her voice cracked with emotion.

≈≤

Ian's heart sank. Though he barely knew her, for some reason he'd hoped that Regan would love the place as much as he did. Her opinion of their seaside home really mattered to him. But he shouldn't have expected her to like the desolate landscape any more than his deceased wife had.

He looked down at her as tears filled her eyes. "It's all right, Regan. We can go back inside if you'd rather."

"No! I—I love it out here! I've never seen anything so beautiful in my life. It almost takes one's breath away."

Relief coursed through him. His chest warmed with pride. "It certainly does."

He watched as Regan stepped up to the rail. The tears overflowed as she looked up toward the lighthouse. "It's just like home."

"Pardon?" Ian didn't follow.

"My father is a lightkeeper in Ireland. Who'd have thought we'd shipwreck and come ashore in a place all the way across the world, yet one so much like home? That can only be of God."

Ian smiled. "He does ordain beautiful things to come from hard situations."

She stood silent as the sun dipped farther into the Gulf of Mexico.

Ian respected her need for quiet.

A few minutes later, though she stared toward the sun that turned the sky a deep fiery orange and pink, she spoke again. "I'm sorry we've invaded your life this way."

"Don't be sorry. I'm not."

He heard a small intake of breath as she turned slightly to look up at him. "But we've turned everything upside down. I'm sure you have better things to do than sit out here with me."

"Not really. I sit out here every evening. Granny shoos me out the door the minute dinner is over. It gets lonely at times. Trust me, I welcome your company."

"Oh." She appeared to flush but the pink hues from the sunset made it hard to be sure. She looked back over at the lighthouse. "Can we go up?"

"Not tonight. It wouldn't be safe for you. But we'll see what the morning brings. If you feel up to it, I'll take you to the top."

"Thank you." Her green eyes crinkled with her smile.

Ian studied her. Her reddish-brown hair blew freely in the breeze. Her delicate, porcelain-like complexion glowed in the dusky reflection. Yet even with her daintiness, Ian knew she had a hearty constitution to have made it through so many tough situations.

She sighed. "The sunset would be even more spectacular from atop the lighthouse, but the view is breathtaking enough from here."

"It certainly is." He didn't take his eyes off her when he stated the words, but her eyes were focused on the horizon, and fortunately for him, she didn't notice the view to which he referred.

Chapter 4

Regan woke from a deep sleep to find the bed moving beneath her. For a moment she thought they were back at sea, but when she opened her eyes, Keera lay nose to nose with her, wiggling with anticipation, wanting to get an early start on their day. The dim light filtering through their window attested to the early hour and proved that the sun was barely peeking over the horizon. Granny still slept in the bed across the room.

"Child," she whispered, "what are you doing awake? We have at least another hour of sleep time left to us, if not more."

"Mr. Ian said we could go up in the lighthouse first thing in the morning," Keera whispered back. "I want to go say hello to Pappy."

Regan drew in a breath. "Oh, don't you know, darlin'—we're far from Pappy's lighthouse."

Keera's face crumpled.

Regan knew that Keera was prepping for a full-blown gale—one that would equal the power of the storm they'd arrived in—if she didn't divert her fast.

"Come, Keera." Regan clambered out of bed and dressed as quickly as she could, then hurried to dress Keera in the pre-dawn light. "We'll go outside and explore, and we'll talk about Pappy there."

Keera nodded and continued to sniffle but, thankfully, didn't release the wails that usually followed in such a situation. Regan didn't want to wake the slumbering family that had been so kind to her and would do most anything to avoid Keera throwing a tantrum.

The night before, Granny had moved Johnny into Ian's sleeping quarters, one room to the south, in order to make room for Regan and Keera. Ian had showed Regan the cottage's layout before everyone went to bed.

The lighthouse stood on the most southern end of the building, with the tower room connecting the lighthouse to the keeper's house. A door from the tower room connected to Ian's room—a spartan area that held a bed, a chest of drawers, and a small desk. Ian's room led into Granny's room, a space she shared with Johnny. Or at least she had shared it with him before Regan and Keera showed up to displace him. Granny had given up her double bed and had insisted her tiny frame would do fine in Johnny's smaller bed so mother and daughter could share the double.

At the farthest end to the north, Granny's room opened into the hearth room, where Regan now headed. She hoped she could be quiet enough to prevent waking any of the others. These strangers had reached out to Keera and her beyond what Regan could ever have imagined, to the point of taking them into their home and giving up beds for them. Regan didn't want to inconvenience them further.

Regan tiptoed to the door, pulled it open ever so slowly, and tugged Keera into the hearth room. As quietly as possible, which wasn't easy with the swollen doors in the seaside humidity, she closed the door behind them. She hesitated at the stove, wanting to light it for Granny, but the strange contraption didn't resemble the one she'd had back home in Ireland, and she decided against it. It would be better to err with caution and not burn down the keeper's house her first morning there.

She tiptoed into the entry formed by the four-foot-thick walls on either side and reached for the door. "Please don't squeak," she whispered.

Keera looked at her with confusion. "It's a door, Mama. It can't hear you."

Regan smiled and pulled the latch. The door squeaked slightly, and Regan hurried through.

Keera shook her head. "If it did hear you, it surely didn't listen very well."

"I agree," Regan whispered with a smile. "And I commend you for keepin' your voice low, wee one."

She put a finger to her lips and they headed down the steps. Freedom from the need to be quiet was mere moments away. As soon as they reached the water's edge, Keera could talk as loudly as she pleased. And Regan would explain how far they were away from Keera's beloved Pappy.

"You two are up bright and early this morning."

Regan shrieked while Keera clambered against Regan's skirts with a yell of terror. Regan pulled her close as she spun around.

Ian lounged on the far end of the porch. "I didn't mean to scare you."

With a hand on her pounding heart, Regan searched for her voice. After a few moments, she found it. "I was so focused on getting out the door without waking anyone, I didn't even think about anyone already being out here."

"I couldn't sleep."

"So I see." Regan took a few deep breaths, trying to steady her heart. She tugged Keera back up the steps. "And with those shrieks we probably undid all our good intentions of getting out of the house undetected."

"Granny and Johnny sleep like logs." Ian smiled. "And with the thick walls, I doubt they even heard you."

"I'm sorry. We've displaced everyone."

He chuckled. "It seems like the two of you are far more displaced than any of us are."

"Aye, 'tis true, but that doesn't mean we have to disrupt your nighttime routines."

"You haven't. I always tend to rise early. I like to sit out here in the early morning hours while the water is calm. If we go to the other side of the house, we can watch the sun rise up over the horizon."

Regan surveyed the serene view. "It is pretty."

When Regan had exited the house, Ian had been resting in a rocking chair with his feet propped on the rail. Now he contemplated them before standing. "I have an idea, but I guess it's up to Keera if we follow through."

Keera bounced at Regan's side. "What is it?"

"Your mama wanted to go up in the lighthouse and watch the sunset last night, but I didn't think it was a good idea with her head hurting. If it's okay with your mama—and if she feels up to it—and if we hurry, we can go up now and get there in time to see the sunrise."

"That's a lot of 'ands.'" Keera giggled. She spun around and grabbed her mother's hands. "Please, Mama? Say yes!"

"I'd love to."

She grabbed Keera's hand and started for the steps. Ian came up behind them and snatched Keera off her feet and swung the squealing girl up onto his shoulders. Regan laughed as he started toward the lighthouse's outer door at a run.

Breathless, whether from her days at sea or because of her injury, she followed him at a more sedate pace into the base of the tower.

"Wooden stairs. Interesting."

"Your father's lighthouse didn't have these?"

"No, his stairs were iron from bottom to top." Regan's voice echoed in the round room.

"The walls are thick here, too," Keera observed. "Why are the house walls so thick, Mr. Ian? They aren't like that in Ireland."

"They built the walls thick to protect the house during storms. There was a particularly big storm back in 1843 that flooded the house and lifted off the roof. When it was rebuilt, they wanted the structure to be as sturdy as possible, so they built it like the base of the lighthouse which has withstood many a storm. In the war it even withstood attempts to blow it up with very little damage."

"I'm glad they built it better." Keera smiled up at him.

Regan could tell the little girl was already as smitten with the man as Regan was intrigued.

"Me too." Ian started climbing with Keera still on his shoulders. "Sit tight, little one. I don't want you tripping on your skirts so I'll carry you."

"Pappy let me climb the stairs on my own."

"Oh he did, did he?"

Regan laughed. "Yes, but he followed you each step of the way and at such a sedate pace that we would surely end up watching the sunset later this evening instead of the sunrise right now if we did let you do your own climbing."

"Is that so?" Ian's teasing words carried over Keera's giggles. "Well, little one, I plan to get up to the tower room this morning, not at dusk. You'll have other chances to walk up on your own, but for now enjoy the journey to the top."

"Yes, sir."

Regan watched as Ian circled out of sight.

Enjoy the journey. His words, abandoned after being uttered, echoed throughout the tower, but as they did so, they freed something deep inside of Regan. She'd been so focused on the end result of reaching Pensacola, that she hadn't taken the time to enjoy the journey in getting there. Right then and there she resolved to follow Ian's wise advice and enjoy what God brought her as each moment came.

The painted wood was cool under Regan's bare feet as she began to climb. She'd only planned a quick walk along the beach when they'd struck off to explore. She hadn't expected to run into Ian so hadn't taken the time to pull on her boots. With a sigh she lifted her hem, ignored propriety, and followed them up the stairs.

Ian stopped in the watch room and waited for Regan to catch up with them. One look at Regan's face as she came into view had him swinging Keera down from his shoulders and settling her against the wall. "Stay right here and don't move until I tell you. Understand?"

"Yes, sir." Keera nodded, worry etching her features at his serious tone of voice.

He hurried to Regan's side and caught her as she fell. She collapsed into his arms. Keera's scream turned into sobs as she called out for her mama.

"It's all right, Keera," Ian shushed as he settled Regan beside her. "She'll be fine. I think we moved too fast after your mama's head injury, and she fainted. Climbing all those stairs must have made her dizzy."

He chastised himself under his breath.

"Maybe you shoulda carried her up the stairs," Keera said, her arms wrapped tight around her knees. "I told ya I coulda walked up by myself."

"That you did." He tweaked her nose while trying to hide his concern. "But you just watch and see. . .your mama will be fine."

He hoped his words were true. This hadn't been one of his better ideas. If Regan didn't wake soon, he'd have to carry her back down. With Keera along, the trip would be complicated. Granny would come looking for them eventually, but then Johnny would be in the mix.

He should have made Regan rest at least another day. But she delighted in the most basic things, and for some reason the idea of watching the sunrise with her overrode all common sense.

Regan moaned, quieting the thoughts cascading through Ian's mind.

She pushed her hair away from her face, her eyes huge and alarmed. "What happened?"

"You fainted. I never should have allowed you to come up here. It's too soon."

To Ian's surprise Regan's mouth quirked into a slight smile. She sat a bit straighter and laughed softly. "You obviously don't know me well enough yet to know that I rarely allow others to dictate what I'm allowed to do or not do."

"Oh." Speechless, Ian didn't know what else to say.

"Though I have to admit, in this case it appears you'd have been right on it being too early, even if I'd defied your orders."

"I don't tend toward giving orders." It was Ian's turn to smile. "The mandate to remain on the porch would have been offered as a mere suggestion."

"I see." Regan studied him as color came back into her cheeks. She shrugged. "A suggestion I'd have surely disregarded in my hurry to see the sunrise."

Three sets of eyes lifted to the lantern room above them. The light was growing stronger.

"Then let's not waste the effort we made to get here." Ian stood and lifted Keera, positioning her on the fourth iron step in front of him. He reached a hand to Regan and helped her to her feet. "Here's your chance, Keera, to climb to the top on your own. There are thirteen iron steps from here to the top, and I've put you on step number four. How many stairs does that leave you to climb?"

"I can only count to five," Keera sing-songed, her words laced with annoyance.

"You'll count to five and then to four before you reach the top. Hold on tight because these steps are steep and narrow, almost like a ladder."

"Her skirt will trip her up." Regan pointed out.

Ian glanced at Keera's feet. Though her skirt didn't brush the ground, it would still catch under her feet when she climbed. He reached around Regan, gathered Keera's skirt in his hand, and held it for her. Keera would need both hands on the steps and rail.

Regan smiled at him before lifting her own hem and starting to climb. Ian had to stay close behind her in order to hold Keera's hem. It made for a close ascent for all of them, but if Regan had another dizzy spell, or worse, if she fainted again, he'd be ready to catch her.

Keera scrambled lightly to the top. Ian and Regan joined her just in time to step out the door and see the early morning colors splash across the water as the sun lifted above the horizon. Ian lifted Keera onto his hip and pulled Regan close to his side.

"It's a long drop down if you topple over the rail," he whispered. He felt a shiver run through Regan, but couldn't tell if it was from his touch or fear from the thought of falling to the ground. Either way, she pressed a little closer, and he couldn't contain his grin.

"Beautiful!" Regan whispered. "This is even better than the sunset we watched last night, and that was as pretty a sunset as I've ever seen."

"It is pretty, Mama! Much prettier than the sunrises in Ireland, don'tcha think?"

"That's because our sunrises there happened over land. It's truly magical seeing the sun rise from over the water."

"Aye, it is magical."

Ian pointed to the east. "The lighthouse sits on a peninsula. The way the shoreline tapers to the south allows us to see both sunrises over the water to the east and sunsets over the water to the west. We're at a point between the Gulf of Mexico and the St. Mark's River. It's great during times like this but doesn't offer much protection from nature and, as you saw, makes for a rough ride during storms."

Keera lost interest in the sunrise and wandered around the rail, looking at the view. Ian kept a tight hold on Regan and followed.

"Mr. Ian, look! I see more crates and barrels in the water."

"I'll have to gather them up."

"And I see Johnny and Granny! Can I go down and play?"

Ian exchanged an amused look with Regan. "That was fast."

Regan shrugged. "Actually for Keera, this is pretty good. Her attention doesn't hold long for much of anything."

Ian motioned for Keera to come, and she hurried to his side. "I need to help your mama down the stairs. I'm going to put you on my back and your Mama is going to follow right behind us."

Regan nodded in agreement, and he lifted Keera onto his back.

"Regan, if you feel woozy at all, sit down immediately and let me know."

"Aye, I will. But I'm feeling much better now."

He started down and they progressed at a sedate pace. Every so often Ian asked how Regan was doing. He could tell she was getting exasperated with his questions, but he didn't intend to let her faint again on his watch.

Chapter 5

Papa, can we open the barrels now? You said we'd open them soon, and it's been more than a week."

Regan smiled as she watched the exchange. She'd grown to love watching the interaction between father and son over the ten days they'd been here.

The day couldn't be prettier. Endless blue skies met the multi-shaded water at the horizon, and gentle waves lapped against the shore. The early morning sun hadn't yet lifted high enough overhead to fully heat the air and chase them inside the cooler interior of the house.

"We can't open them yet, son. I want to wait until we hear back from the ship. They might want to send someone to pick them up. The goods belong to someone else."

"But, Pa! You prayed them here for us!"

Ian glanced over at Regan for help.

She shrugged. "I, for one, surely didn't pray for the ship to go aground. Look where that landed us!"

He tipped his head, his teasing eyes filled with challenge. "Exactly where did it leave you, Regan? Has your visit been completely unpleasant?"

"What?" She took a step backward. "I'm not sure I know what you mean." Guilt deepened her brogue. She knew exactly to what he referred. They'd spent the better part of the past week and a half walking the beaches while in deep conversation, sitting on the porch for long talks as the sun set, and working together on the lighthouse. She'd never felt such a deep repartee with her distant and older husband.

Ian leaned in. Regan's heart raced. He reached for a loose strand of hair that curled beside her cheek and twirled it with his finger, much as she played with Keera's wayward curls. His finger grazed her cheek. "Is it really that much of a hardship for you to be stranded here with us?"

Regan felt a flush of color creep up her face. Ian knew as well as she did that there was a pull between them. "I think you know it isn't a hardship at all. But still, being at the mercy of strangers. . ."

"You're living in our home like family. We're hardly strangers. Not anymore. Strangely, you never did seem to be a stranger to me."

"I agree. But you have to admit we're only living with you because you feel obliged to us! You didn't exactly have a choice in the matter."

"I will admit no such thing and I had every choice in the matter," he argued. "I could have packed you in the wagon and hauled you both out of here. I could have pushed your little boat back out to sea and you'd have never been the wiser that we even existed."

Regan's laugh escaped her. "You would do nothing of the sort, even if you wanted to. You have too kind of a heart."

"Oh, yes, that dratted kind heart of mine. Gets me in trouble every time! Just look—it has me bringing home every stray that crosses my path."

Regan lifted a brow and looked around them. "Not only do we seem to be the only strays in the area, but we seem to be the only people here in general."

"To quote a good friend of mine, ' 'tis true.'"

Johnny tugged Ian's shirt. "Papa! Stop talking to her so you can answer my question."

Laughter shone from Ian's eyes. "And to think he wouldn't talk more than a couple of words for the better part of the past two years. You and Keera show up and look what you've done for my son." He looked at Johnny with fondness. "I can't thank you enough."

"I think Keera is to be commended for that. She seems to have an effect on him."

"I agree. But you have an equal effect on me." His brown eyes twinkled as she again blushed to her roots. "But we'll finish this discussion later. For now, Johnny has a question waiting to be answered."

Ian lowered himself to Johnny's level. "I didn't pray for the ship to run into a bad situation, Johnny. I would never want someone else's bad fortune to gain things for us. I prayed God would bless us, and He did. I asked for some extra provisions for you and Granny—he brought Keera and Regan into our lives. God doesn't necessarily answer our prayers the way we want Him to. But Regan has been great company for Granny and for me, and Keera has been a wonderful friend for you. That's even better than anything I could have hoped for when I uttered my prayer that day."

A shrill whistle sounded offshore, interrupting their conversation.

Ian stood. "Looks like we have company."

A riverboat pulled alongside the pier. Regan shaded her eyes and watched it dock.

A familiar man stood at the rail. "Ahoy there!"

"Joseph!" Keera's scream of joy radiated across the yard. She zigzagged past the haphazard row of barrels standing along the shoreline and headed for the kind sailor who'd helped them during their journey. Joseph jumped onto the dock and swooped Keera up into his arms.

Ian glanced over at Regan, his expression questioning. He took in the huge smile that stretched across her face.

"It's Joseph, Ian! He's come for us."

His eyes searched hers, as if wanting to peer deep inside to read her inner thoughts.

"Joseph was the sailor we talked about—the grandfatherly one who helped us through the voyage when things grew hard."

A muscle ticked in Ian's jaw. "How kind of him—I'll go make his acquaintance."

He stalked off.

Regan, confused by his sudden distance, followed along.

Joseph carried Keera the length of the dock and met them on shore.

"Regan. You're safe." Tears filled the friendly giant's eyes. "That night, when I realized your lifeboat had gone missing—I've never felt anything like it in my life. The crew had to hold me back to keep me from jumping in. I didn't want to leave the waters without locating the two of you. When your note reached the captain, well, it was the happiest day I've had in a long, long time."

"I'm sorry you had to wait that long to find out. We're fine, Joseph. As I said in the missive, a small bump to the head and a slight gash and otherwise I did amazingly well. And Keera here had nothing bad to show for the adventure."

"Not counting the fact that her ropes had come undone and she could have fallen overboard at any time. And Regan here, she's suffered a few dizzy spells, one which almost sent her tumbling down the lighthouse stairs a week or so ago." Ian's words rang with accusations, as if Joseph himself were responsible for her decision to climb the stairs too soon.

"Ian." Regan placed a hand on his arm. "We're fine. Keera didn't go overboard, and I didn't fall. You were there to rescue us both when we needed you."

"Thank you for that." Joseph stuck his hand out, and Ian stared at it.

Ian opened his mouth to speak then apparently thought better of whatever he was about to say. He closed his eyes for a moment then opened them again. "I'm sorry. I don't know what's gotten into me." He shook Joseph's hand. "Ian Morgan. I've grown quite fond of these two rather quickly, as you apparently did on the ship. The thought of what could have happened to them makes me weak in the knees."

"Aye, I fully understand." Joseph continued to cradle Keera in his arms while giving Ian an appraising glance.

Granny called out and motioned them to the house.

Ian's manners had returned. "Would the crew like to come up? I'm sure Granny's made refreshments for everyone."

"No, they told me to do what I needed to do. They have ship responsibilities to take care of and, if you don't mind, they'll gather the barrels and load them onto the vessel."

"That'll be fine. I'm sure Granny will want to bring them a tray of goodies, too. Come along to the house."

Joseph stopped to look over the line of barrels. "You've gathered quite a few."

"I've tried. They drifted in throughout the week in batches."

They settled on the front porch where Granny had laid out tea and cookies. "The crew has things to do, Granny, but Joseph here said he'd join us."

"Pleased to meet you, Joseph. I'll take a platter down for the crew. Y'all enjoy."

Joseph thanked her and pulled a letter from his pocket. "I have a note from your aunt. She asked me to give it to you. She met us at the ship when we docked, and I had to tell her you'd gone overboard. She'd just received your father's note earlier that morning."

"Oh no! I'd hoped if she did get the original note, she'd just think we were late and wouldn't know what really happened until she read my note from here."

"Aye, I'm sorry it happened that way, too. She was completely grief-stricken, but as soon as we got word that you were safe I hurried to her home. She'd received her letter from you the same day and quickly penned this one for you when she found out we were heading over to collect the missing barrels."

Regan hurried to open the note. Maybe this would be the confirmation she needed that they were indeed wanted by her aunt and uncle—instead of being an unwanted burden. Her father had married her off as soon as he'd been able. Though Regan's husband had been kind, he wasn't the man she'd have picked had she had any say in the matter. When her husband died and she and Keera had moved back home, her father had seemed annoyed. She soon found out he'd been courting her best friend, and they had immediate plans to marry. Then Regan had been pawned off on her unknown relatives under her dad's guise that she "see the world while she had a chance."

She prayed that with her aunt and uncle, she and Keera would finally have the home Regan desired, a place with family where she'd be wanted. The fact that her aunt had grieved when they'd gone missing gave her hope. She quickly glanced down at the white paper and scanned the page. Her heart fell.

Ian was quick to notice her despair. "Regan, what is it?"

"My aunt and uncle apparently live in a small house, and my cousin and her family have just moved in with them." She paused and willed her voice to remain steady. "They don't have a place for us at this time, but my aunt said if we can wait a few more weeks she's sure they can figure something out for us."

She couldn't raise her eyes from the paper. If she did and either Joseph or Ian gave a sign of sympathy, she'd surely fall apart.

Joseph worried his hat in his hands. "I'll be headin' back home to Ireland in a few days. If you'd like, I can take you back with me. I'm sure the missus would love to have young'uns around again. She misses our girls now that they're all married and busy with lives of their own."

Regan couldn't help but smile at his kind offer. "Aye, I'm sure she does, Joseph. But I can't be a burden on you any more than I want to be on anyone else. I'll find a way to provide for Keera and myself."

"This is nonsense." Ian's exasperation carried through his words. "You'll not worry yourself about such things, Regan! You know you're welcome to stay here indefinitely. Granny loves your company—she was so lonely before you arrived and now she has someone to bake with and to talk to. We just talked about the way Johnny is thriving with Keera's company. And then there's me. . . ."

His voice tapered off when he looked over at Joseph.

"Spit it out, boy! The words aren't going to come out on their own."

Ian looked back at Regan. "I've enjoyed your companionship, too. The days are long out here and it's been refreshing to have someone around to talk to, especially since you understand my calling."

"So it's settled." Joseph's grin split his face from edge to edge. "You'll stay here at least until your aunt makes other arrangements."

"I don't. . ."

"You don't appear to have any other choice, love." Joseph stood. "Let's take us a little walk."

"Aye. A walk will clear my head."

Joseph reached for her hand but she didn't miss the wink he sent Ian's way.

Ian nodded. "I want you to stay, Regan. You carry more than your own weight here. You aren't a burden or a charity case." He headed for the lighthouse.

Joseph led her to the beach. "I know I don't know you very well. Maybe not even as well as that man we just left. But for whatever reason I've felt responsible for the two of you ever since I saw you on the ship."

Regan nodded. She knew he'd taken a special interest in them. She figured God had set Joseph in their path to be their protector while on the ship.

"Your aunt and uncle seem like good enough people, but they do have a small house, and it's close to the heart of town. I saw Keera on the ship. She needs lots of fresh air and open spaces. There aren't any places for Keera to play at your aunt's house. And to make matters worse, your aunt's rooms are filled with collectibles. Porcelain, glass, you name it."

Regan shuddered. What a horrible surrounding for her rambunctious child.

"I'm going to get personal here. What are the chances that you could make a life here at the lighthouse for Keera? The Morgans seem like wonderful people."

"I've barely just met them. . .how would I know?"

"Oh, I think you know." This time his wink was directed at her. "I think you owe it to yourself and to Keera to stick around and find out what lies in store for you here. God doesn't make mistakes, and I feel in my heart He brought you here for a reason. Meanwhile, your aunt said she'll ask around and see if anyone needs a caretaker or a maid that would be willing to let you bring Keera along."

"I see." Neither one of them would do well being cooped up in a stuffy house in town. They'd been spoiled by the vastness of space here on the coast. And Regan was able to help Granny or Ian while Keera ran free. What would Keera do in town while Regan was caring for an employer?

"Your aunt seems like a good person, Regan. But they're in a hard place right now."

"My father never should have sent us away."

"Aye, I agree with you there. I'm not in his shoes, but I'd never do what he did if one of my girls needed us."

"I know. You're a good man, Joseph." She stopped and grasped his hand. "And I appreciate all that you've done for us."

"Aye, it was nothing." He waved her off and headed for the boat. "Tell Ian I'm leaving one barrel here courtesy of the captain. I have no idea what he put in it, but he said to tell Ian thanks for all he's done."

"I'll tell him."

Granny, circled by men from the boat, waved them over. "I saved two more cookies for you, Joseph. You have a safe trip home and enjoy that family of yours. Regan's told me all about you."

He took the cookies she offered and motioned toward the barrel that the crew had unloaded. Regan nodded. Keera ran over for one last hug.

"Oh—one more thing," Joseph called. "The captain said to keep the boat. It'll be more trouble than it's worth to try to get back to the ship."

Regan grinned. Even with the barrels going back, God had still blessed Ian.

Chapter 6

Two more weeks passed. Ian came down from the tower and couldn't locate anyone. Regan and Keera had already become such fixtures around the place he couldn't imagine life without them. He headed for the house.

"Granny? Where's Regan and the children?"

Gran called back from the far end of the house. Ah yes, laundry day. "I shooed them out of here. She said she's taking them wading."

"That's odd. I looked up and down the coast and didn't see them."

"I think she said they were going inland, to explore. She wanted to take them north of here. I told them about the little creek that runs over there."

"The creek? The one that leads to the pond?"

"I'm not sure." Granny walked through the door with an armload of bedding. "She just mentioned that they wanted an adventure and asked if there was any clear water to wade in. I mentioned the creek, but didn't tell them which way to go."

Ian hurried over to take the laundry from her. He held the door open and followed her down the stairs.

Granny wiped her forehead. "Whew, thanks. It's really warming up today."

Ian set the laundry on the ground and took Granny by the shoulders. "Gran—you warned Regan about the alligators at the pond, didn't you?"

Granny's forehead wrinkled. "I don't think so, but surely it's come up by now in one of your many conversations? I'm sure she'll know to watch for them."

"I'm not sure she will. She won't expect them to be there, and since she's always stayed near the gulf, I never thought to warn her."

Ian took off running. He didn't know where to look. If they went west toward the pond, they could be in trouble. Even if they went the other way, several of the large creek's smaller branches led toward bayous and marsh grasses where gators liked to hide.

He made a quick decision and headed toward the lighthouse, taking the stairs two at a time. His legs burned as he reached the top and skidded out to the landing. He hurried to the rail, hating the wasted time it took to climb to the top, but he hoped in the long run the vantage point of the far-reaching view would save him time searching.

Sure enough, he saw the lavender of Regan's dress and the pink of Keera's on the path leading toward the creek. Johnny tagged along behind them. The gators didn't seem to congregate there for the most part, but if the trio headed left at the creek where it joined with the pond, they had a greater chance of disturbing one of the giant creatures.

"Regan!" He cupped his hands around his mouth. The wind carried his voice away.

He flew down the stairs, risking life and limb with the quick pace, but he needed to get to his family. He hadn't even kissed Regan yet, but he planned to remedy that situation as soon as he had her safely in his arms. He couldn't imagine anything that would make him decide otherwise.

The heavy lighthouse door impeded his progress, but he finally fumbled it open and tore through it. The blast of hot morning air after the cool interior of the stone walls hit him full in the face but he kept running. He had to get to them before it was too late.

❧

"What do we plan to do at the creek today, wee ones?" Regan asked, her mind, for the moment, more focused on the cloying heat than the children's answer. She still hadn't acclimated to the incessant heat in this lower hemisphere. She waved a large palm frond at her face, but had a sinking feeling that the effort produced more discomfort than it fixed.

Keera answered by stripping off her dress and running into the cool waters of the creek. She danced in her pantaloons, oblivious to any proprieties she might be breaking with the endeavor. Johnny giggled and followed suit, stripping down to the basics. They danced in the waters with the carefree abandon of young children.

Regan found herself smiling as she watched. Johnny had lost the distant look he'd worn when she'd arrived. To her he looked like a normal carefree child, enjoying a romp in the water. They hadn't been to this part of the coast before and Regan soaked in the beauty.

Occasional splashes of water thrown her way kept Regan cool, as did the shade of the leaves from the nearby magnolia she'd settled under. The bank of the creek was sandy and offered a welcome reprieve from the day's heat and chores. The scent of jasmine drifted around her.

She'd offered Granny the chance to come with the children, but Granny had insisted on doing the laundry while Regan took a well-deserved break. Regan acquiesced. She had finally mastered the stove and now delighted in showing off her cooking skills with Irish delicacies. Granny, Johnny, and Ian seemed to enjoy them. In return, Granny insisted on doing some of the more mundane tasks about the lighthouse. The balance worked well. But that didn't mean Regan didn't feel guilty sitting in the cool shade watching the frolicking kids with amusement while Granny worked in the heat doing laundry.

"We're only going to stay here long enough to cool off, and then we'll go back to help Granny finish up around the house."

The children chorused their displeasure.

Keera waded over to plop down beside Regan, her wet skin drenching Regan in the most delightful way. "Ack, that water feels so good I should grab your hand and run into the creek alongside you, wee one!"

"Do it, Mama! You never have any fun anymore. In Ireland you were full of spunk and vigor. Pappy always said."

"Aye. That he did. But a person has to grow up sometime and my time has come."

Keera tipped her head in confusion. "You look the same to me."

"Yes, but just like we had to leave the lighthouse to come here, I have to leave my childish ways and act like an adult."

Keera sighed. "Then I don't much look forward to growing up."

Regan laughed. "You'll like the idea more as you go. It's okay to keep some of the ways of the young."

A look of challenge passed across Keera's smiling face. "Then show me by going into the creek."

"Well, it does look inviting." Regan stared at the water, tempted. "And in this heat my dress would surely dry before we got back to the house...."

"Do it, Mama!"

"Please, Mama?" Johnny had come to stand in front of her, his huge eyes imploring in his small face. Her heart melted at his choice of words. She'd love to have the chance to be his mama.

"Maybe just this once." She stood to her feet, grabbed both children by their hands, and with squeals of laughter they ran down the slight incline. They entered the water with a large splash. Regan's laughter echoed over the young ones. When was the last time she'd had so much fun? She'd laughed quite a bit on the ship, but that was while watching Keera's antics, not while joining in.

She bent down and used her hands to drench the kids with water. Their soggy clothes hung on their tiny frames. They squealed and giggled as she chased them around in circles. Keera tripped on a rock and went down. Johnny tripped over her and tumbled head over heels, landing on his seat in the shallow stream. After a moment of introspection to make sure he was okay, his infectious giggle had them all three laughing once again.

Regan took advantage of the moment and surveyed their surroundings while standing in the water. The shallow creek ran over a sandy bottom that was littered with small round pebbles. A tiny current tugged at her skirts and ankles, but not with enough force to move her.

"It's beautiful here, Mama."

"Aye, Keera, it is."

"It's prettier than Pappy's lighthouse."

"You think so?" Surprise trilled through Regan. "It doesn't have Ireland's rolling green hills."

"No, but it has prettier water and the sandy beach."

"True." Regan hadn't really thought about it, but Keera was right. Ireland had rockier beaches, at least in their area.

"And it's warmer here, Mama."

"Much warmer, that's for sure." Regan laughed. "So much warmer I'm not sure that's a bonus point in Florida's favor."

"But it is! We can swim longer here. It was always cold in the water in Ireland."

"You have a point." Regan slowly made her way back to shore. Regan, without a doubt, wanted to stay. But she wanted to be sure Keera liked it before moving forward with that idea. "What about all the strange creatures and the trees and bushes—we have our very own jungle here."

"I love the jungle, Mama!" Keera followed at Regan's heels. "It's so pretty and there are birds I've never seen and lots of bugs."

Regan shuddered. She'd found a few too many bugs on their various expeditions, and even a few in the house. This, in her opinion, wasn't a benefit to living here.

Johnny giggled. "You don't like the bugs."

"No, I don't." She reached out to tickle him as he settled against her side. "I don't like the bugs at all."

Keera grew contemplative. "There aren't many shops."

"No shops," Regan agreed.

"The city is good because it has lots of places to go and see and enough shops to fill an entire street."

"Aye."

Keera had fallen back into one of their favorite games that they'd played when trying to survive city life. Regan had missed the solitary life of being a lightkeeper's daughter and had often told Keera stories of living by the sea. Her arranged marriage had taken her inland and even Keera missed the brief moments of freedom she'd found while visiting her grandfather. They'd taken to listing all the good things about city life when trying not to think about the bad.

"In the city, you can have anything you want on a moment's whim."

"Really?" Johnny asked. "I'd like to go to town. I don't get to go very often. Papa hates it there. He prefers the quiet of the lighthouse."

❧

Ian had heard screams and had pushed himself to run harder. In his panic over their safety it had taken him a few moments after his arrival to realize they were safe. He'd only heard the tail end of the conversation as he'd approached, but he'd certainly heard enough. So Regan wanted to go back to the city.

"Back to the lighthouse—all of you." Fear over what he'd imagined when he'd heard their screams, and disappointment at the conversation he'd overheard, made his words sound harsh.

Regan and Keera shrieked as he stalked up on them. He hadn't meant to sound so gruff, but at the moment his heart was breaking. And now they had Johnny longing for town!

"Papa!" Johnny, only weeks earlier so sullen and quiet, ignored his grumpy mood and jumped to his feet with a smile. "Come into the water with us! Regan did. It's cool and fun, and she made us laugh."

"I'm not coming into the water." Ian glared past Regan, surveying the shores. "There are alligators nearby. You shouldn't have gone in. You know better, Johnny."

Huge tears filled Johnny's eyes and flooded over onto his thin cheeks. "I–I'm sorry, Papa. I—I didn't think."

Ian felt worse. His cutting words had Johnny back to his insecure self. Ian wanted to punch something.

Regan and Keera had scrambled up the slight incline at Ian's mention of alligators, but now Regan was staring at him with questioning eyes. "We weren't in imminent danger, Ian. I did check the shore, and although I certainly didn't expect to encounter a gator, I gave the area a good once-over before allowing the children to jump in. I know snakes or any of the other wildlife that reside here could have been a problem. I made sure the children were safe."

Her musical Irish brogue deepened when she was stressed and now the lilting words practically rolled off her tongue. The hurt in her emerald eyes almost undid him. "Have we offended you somehow?"

You've broken my heart with your words of longing for the city.

Ian refused to voice that as the reason he was upset. Obviously, Regan missed the city and would continue on to her uncle and aunt's at the first opportunity. He'd been a fool to hope that she'd fall in love with the lighthouse—enough so that she wouldn't ever want to leave—in such a short time.

When he didn't answer, Regan ushered the children toward the path. "Come along, wee ones. We have chores to do at the house."

He heard the tremble in her words.

The somber group trailed back up the path and entered the clearing. Granny stood a few yards in front of them, working on the last load of laundry. She shaded her eyes as they approached.

"Ah, you found them, safe and sound. I was hoping you'd join them for a while, Ian."

Ian ignored her and stomped past.

"Ian?"

He rounded the lighthouse and hoped she'd let him be.

Granny left her laundry and followed him around the lighthouse.

"I'm sorry, but I don't want company right now, Gran."

"What on earth happened? I haven't seen you this upset since right before Maggie ran off and died. Was there a gator? Did it give you a scare? They're all safe, Ian."

"It wasn't a gator that gave me a scare, Granny. It was the words I overheard as I approached them at the creek."

"Whatever could sweet Regan say that would put you in such a mood?"

His words were raspy with emotion, even to his own ears. "She talked about city life to the kids, Granny. She was talking about how much she liked living there. Even Johnny chimed in on how he wanted to go."

He scrubbed a hand down his face in frustration. "I was hoping she'd fall in love with the area, Granny. And that she would fall in love with us. With me." There, he'd said it. "I wanted them to stay."

Granny walked over to place a hand on his arm. "I think you heard wrong, son. Regan loves it here. She's told me as much. And I'm pretty sure she loves you, too. I've seen it in her eyes and on her face when she looks at you. She watches for you and her emotions betray her thoughts."

Her words gave him pause, but he quickly dashed them away. "I heard exactly what she said, Granny! I didn't misunderstand. She and Keera were saying how nice it was having all the shops available there, and Johnny jumped right in. It's bad enough if they don't want to stay, but to skew Johnny's insight, too? It's too much. I was gruff with them. Now she's going to hate me."

"I'm sure they'll understand. And you were already upset about the possibility of alligators when you went after them. I'm sure her words just intensified the stress of the situation."

"What am I going to do, Granny? I feel like I'm losing Maggie all over again, only this time it hurts a lot worse. What does that say about me? I knew Maggie for years, and I've only known Regan for a few weeks."

"The heart knows, Ian. You hurt worse now because you knew how

Maggie was, and you knew you'd already lost her. Regan isn't Maggie, Ian. She loves it here. She's told me so many a time. You need to talk to her. Ask her how she feels. What do you have to lose?"

"Her, Granny." Ian refused to look at his grandmother as he fisted his hands and looked out at the water. "I could lose her."

"Then go fight for the woman you love, son. If you let her get on a boat and sail away, you'll have only yourself to blame. You'll never forgive yourself. And consider Johnny—if you can't do this for yourself—then do it for him. No matter how well we prepare him, he's going to be hurt if they leave."

"He can't handle much more hurt, Granny."

"That's what I'm afraid of. He's resilient, and I think he'll be fine, but we don't want to find out the hard way. And he's not the only one I'm worried about." She eyed him. "So listen to my sage advice and go have a talk with Regan."

Ian knew he didn't have a choice. He couldn't let Regan leave without telling her how much she meant to him. If she didn't feel the same way, he'd never see her again. So what did he have to lose?

Chapter 7

I t's time to open the barrel."

Ian's abrupt announcement had the children running. They'd begged him for weeks to open the lone barrel the ship's captain had sent—but Ian had wanted to wait until the right time.

Now, afraid Regan would leave before they had a chance to explore the contents, he rolled the barrel to rest at the base of the porch where all could see the contents.

Granny raised her eyebrows in question, but he avoided a response. He'd left her with the impression that he was on his way to talk to Regan. If Regan was into worldly goods he'd show her that anything she needed could be provided at the lighthouse, too. Maybe not as readily, but God always provided what they needed when they needed it.

He and Regan had talked often during their walks about God and His provision. This side of her surprised him. He wouldn't have pictured her a city girl, not from anything he'd seen during their time together.

He glanced up to where Regan stood on the step, hip braced against the rail, arms crossed at her midsection. She stared out over the water, her expression contemplative.

Ian forced his gaze away and pried the lid from the barrel. He scooped some packing material out of the way and pulled out a brief note.

"It says that we can do what we please with whatever we find in here—if we want to put some things away for the future to feel free."

"That's considerate of him." Regan stood a little straighter as Ian reached back into the container.

He pulled out three small dresses.

"Yellow and lavender and pink!" Keera squealed. "All for me? They're too small for you or Granny, Mama."

"Aye, it looks like the captain sent all three for you. What a thoughtful and extravagant thing for him to do."

"I guess he figured he owed you as much after dunking you both in the gulf," Granny quipped.

Ian held them out, and Keera snatched them from him, hugging them to her chest. "Thank you, Ian!"

Next were shirts and pants in matching hues for Johnny.

"Looks like brother and sister clothes to me," Granny stated. "You two can match next time we go into town."

Ian tried to control his grimace. Why'd she have to paint such a picture of family after the conversation they'd just had? If Regan was pining for the city, she might not stick around long enough to take a family-style jaunt into town.

Granny wasn't making this easy, and he had a feeling her effort was purposeful.

Johnny and Keera crowded closer, trying to see what was next.

"Food."

Both said the word at the exact same time, disappointment dripping from their tongues. Sacks of flour, sugar, and other staple items stacked up one by one.

"Food isn't a bad thing, wee ones," Regan explained. "We need to be grateful and to give thanks for everything God—and in this case the captain—gives to us. God is providing the basics, and we mustn't take that for granted."

"I'm sorry, Mama," Keera said.

"Sorry, Papa," Johnny echoed. "You prayed for provisions and God answered."

"That's right, son." Ian kept digging. "I know it seems boring, but look here—the captain sent some treats that we don't get very often."

"Candy!" Keera handed her dresses off to Regan and ran over to bounce at Ian's side, cupping her hands in anticipation.

Johnny looked undecided, then, with a shy smile, handed his clothes to Regan, too. She folded them over her arm as she had Keera's, and Ian couldn't help but envision her doing such a thing as Johnny's mother. She looked so natural taking his possessions and adding them to Keera's, as if she'd been doing so Johnny's whole life. Ian longed for the image to be true. He wanted that for his son. . .for himself.

Shaking himself from his reverie, he dug deeper. "Fabric for Granny and Regan."

Several folds of brightly colored fabrics and ribbon, threads and trim were added to the growing pile in Regan's arms.

"Beautiful." Granny caressed the notions. "We can make some beautiful skirts and dresses from the yardage."

"Aye, we can." Regan's voice held awe. "The captain was very good to us."

Granny touched her arm. "Your misfortune brought good things to all of us, Regan."

Regan blushed. "I'm glad you think so." She glanced over at Ian and when their eyes met her smile slipped. She looked away.

Ian turned back to the barrel. "Sturdy work pants and a couple of shirts for me. Those'll come in handy."

"They're nice," Regan responded. "The colors are good for you."

"Thanks." *Will you be around long enough to see me wear them?*

He didn't know why he suddenly felt her departure was imminent, but he wanted to make sure his feelings were known so she could weigh them in to any decision she made about leaving. If she truly missed the city, he figured she'd find a way to get there sooner rather than later.

Ian motioned Granny and Regan closer. "A few of these things at the bottom look like they might be good Christmas gifts. That must be what the captain referred to with his note."

The women peeked over the rim.

A rag doll for Keera, and a wooden train for Johnny. Warm slippers and sleep shirts in five different sizes, one for each of them.

"The kids would love waking up on Christmas morning to see that each of us received new sleeping clothes." Regan's delight showed on her features.

The response confused him. She didn't appear to be in any hurry to leave. He felt a tiny ray of hope that Granny was right, and that what he'd overheard hadn't been heard in full context.

"I agree," Granny added. "We'll slip them into the attic when the kids aren't looking."

"Aye, sounds like a wonderful plan."

"What else do we have, son?"

Ian dug deep into the barrel. "A new clock for the house. Socks for each of us. A few trinkets to decorate with. Spices for the kitchen. . ."

He leaned in and lifted the final object from the bottom. "And a family Bible."

"It's beautiful," Regan whispered. She reached out to touch the black leather of the huge book. "I've never seen a Bible as big as this."

"It's nice." Ian turned the first few pages. "Look. It has space to record weddings and births."

"What a wonderful way to document family history."

"I agree."

Silence was his response. He glanced up and looked around.

Keera and Johnny had lost interest in the barrel after the candy was unveiled. They sat together on the bottom step, sucking their peppermint sticks and giggling in quiet conversation.

Ian's heart lurched. He wanted them to grow up together. They seemed as perfect a fit of brother and sister as he felt he and Regan were as a couple. He wanted to write all four of their names in the family Bible, along with Granny's.

He didn't want to see Johnny's heart broken any more than his own. Johnny had never connected as strongly with the kids in town as he had with Keera. Losing the little girl's company would tear the boy apart.

He felt Regan's eyes studying him as they stood there in silence. In the moments he'd been watching the children, Granny had slipped away, leaving him alone with Regan. He continued to watch the kids.

"They have a special bond."

"Aye, they do."

It was now or never. "I've felt a bond between us, too."

"Aye, so have I." She watched him with her vivid green eyes.

"But the tug of the city pulls harder?"

Confusion clouded Regan's features. "I don't understand."

"I overheard you and Keera at the creek. You talked about town and all the things you could get on a whim. You seemed to miss it."

"It's true. You can walk down the road and most everything you could possibly need is there."

"I guess I see it as sort of being like this barrel." Ian waved a hand at the vessel in front of him like it was evil. "Candy, food, spices, clothes, fabric. The barrel is nothing more than a jaunt into town bundled up in a nice wooden package."

"I don't understand, Ian. You seemed angry at the creek and you seem angry now, but I have no idea who or what it is that you're angry at."

"I can't compete with the city, Regan. My life is here at the lighthouse."

Lord, please help me to understand what Ian is saying. Help me bridge the chasm he's placed between us.

"Why would you need to compete with the city?"

"Your heart seems to long for the life you've left." Ian slid his hands into his pockets, his dark features daring her to deny it. "I know you miss the city, so I have to assume it'll be a matter of time before you head to your aunt and uncle's."

"You think we want to leave?" She looked incredulous. A smile tugged at her lips. "You couldn't be more wrong, dear Ian."

He's upset because he thinks we want to leave! The realization thrilled her to the core.

Bravely, she stepped closer to him. "Keera and I would play a little game when we lived in the city. We tried to convince ourselves that the city held promise the lighthouse didn't. Of course, deep down the longing to return to my father's land never left me, but it seemed to help Keera tolerate life in town. So while we can get most everything we want in town, it isn't where I want to live."

"Most everything?" Ian now stared at her in confusion. "What can't you get?"

"You."

"Oh."

She stood directly in front of him. Her voice dropped to a whisper. "If you think I want to leave here, you're sorely mistaken."

She glanced over at the kids, but they weren't paying them any attention. Granny was nowhere to be found.

"You want to stay?" Ian's face transformed. His brown eyes closed with relief. The lines of stress on his face melted into dimples, and a warm smile bloomed where the lines of stress had been. He opened his eyes and searched her face. "Let me get this straight. You want to stay here?"

"Aye, I want to stay, but only if you want me to."

"Regan, I've wanted you to stay since you first washed up on shore."

She reached out to stroke a strand of his curly brown hair. She pushed it into place. Just like the man it adorned, it had a mind of its own.

He wants us to stay!

She couldn't believe her good fortune. God had brought them here, to this desolate place, and in doing so had blessed both families beyond belief. Her loss of independence had blossomed into a blessing beyond anything she could ever have wished for on her own.

"You really want us to stay?"

"Ah, Regan." He took her hand and held it against his heart. He stepped closer and put his forehead against hers. She stepped into his embrace. "I would love for you to stay."

"I'm sorry you misunderstood what Keera and I were talking about, Ian. The fact is, my heart is happiest when it's by the sea. The only benefit of living with my aunt and uncle would have been the fact that the gulf was within walking distance. Or at least that's what my father told me."

"You can't get closer to the beach than this." Ian swung Regan around and faced her toward the water. He stood behind her and pulled her against his chest. He wrapped his arms around her and she clung to them for dear life. Together, they watched the surf crash against the shore. "Would you be happy here?"

"Aye, that goes without saying! I love everything about this place." She couldn't resist sending him a teasing smile over her shoulder. "The lighthouse, Granny, the beach, Johnny, the sunsets. . ."

"Ah, so it seems you love everything about the place except me."

"Not everything but you, Ian." She turned and wrapped her arms around his neck. "I'm just saving the best for last—you."

"So you could see yourself marrying me and settling down?"

"If that's a proposal, then yes."

"It's a sloppy one, but yes. I'll give you a proper proposal soon. Can you live with that?"

"Aye!" Regan whispered. She'd found her safe harbor.

"Then I only have one more thing to say." Ian bent and pressed his lips to hers, his kiss filled with promise. "Welcome home, Regan."

WHISPERS
ACROSS THE BLUE

by DiAnn Mills

Dedication

To Tony and Cathy Barrett, who bless my life
with love and encouragement.

Trust in him at all times; ye people,
pour out your heart before him:
God is our refuge for us.
Psalm 62:8

Chapter 1

1875, Bolivar Point, Galveston, Texas

T his will be my last voyage, I promise," Captain Mason Channing said. He cupped Jule's chin with his hand, and she met his dark blue gaze—the same color as an angry sea. "I will return two months before our wedding, plenty of time to begin work with my father."

Jule's heart plummeted with Mason's words. "But you said you were finished with a sea captain's life, ready to enter your father's import/export business."

"I know," he whispered, and lines furrowed his brow. "Do you think I want to be separated from you for two months?" He paused and glanced out at the calm, glass-like waters. "I would gladly honor my word, except Father is insistent I take a cargo of cotton and rice to New York. I no sooner dock than I pick up a load of grain and set sail to Liverpool, where I will exchange the goods for tea and head back to New York. There, I take on coal before sailing home." He raked four fingers through his sandy-colored hair. "This is difficult for me too, Jule. When I told you I planned to trade a ship's anchor for two feet planted on dry ground, I meant it."

Shivers raced up and down her arms as she recalled the repeated nightmares of Mason lost at sea.

"You are remembering your bad dreams," he said, his voice soft and tender. "I can see it in your eyes."

He drew her close to him, and she gladly embraced his wide, strong shoulders. The muscles beneath her fingertips felt hard and strong from the years of hoisting sails and working side by side with his crew. She felt protected and loved, yet frightened.

"I cannot but worry about you," she said. "I want to be your wife and live out my days loving the ocean, not despising it because it took you away from me."

Mason grazed her forehead with a kiss and lightly trailed more down the side of her face, across her cheeks to her lips. She felt the fiery intensity of his emotions deepen, and she gladly returned the same depth of fervency. Silently, Jule begged for his kiss to last forever. In the same breath, she knew and understood the dangers of surrendering to passion and ignoring God's plan for a man and a woman. She mustered the strength to pull herself from him and saw his eyes moisten. Her captain, her handsome, beloved captain. Whoever thought the day he sailed to Bolivar Point and met Jule that their relationship would blossom into love?

She touched her fingertips to his lips and swallowed any semblance of tears. "When must you set sail?" she asked.

"In three weeks."

She stepped back to view Mason completely, to burn his image into her mind forever. Dressed fashionably, he wore a chocolate brown, tailed jacket and trousers over a double-breasted brown and dotted cream vest. At the neck of a crisp white shirt, he had tied a blue silk scarf. But beneath the finery dwelled a rugged, strong man who carried himself with the confidence of his hope in God. How proud she felt of him choosing her among the many belles of Galveston—she, Jule Portier, a shy, timid young woman who never dreamed the most eligible bachelor in southern Texas would set his sights on her.

"Say something," he urged with a chuckle. "You look a thousand miles away."

Jule felt her cheeks flush, and she glanced down at the white sand at her feet then up into his face again. "I am so blessed to have you," she whispered. "I can't stop you from taking this voyage—"

"The last voyage," he interrupted.

She smiled and brushed back a lock of hair that the wind had coaxed from beneath her bonnet. "Please take care of yourself. I love you too much to have you taken from me before our wedding."

He returned her smile and squeezed her hands lightly. "Again, I promise. Now," he reached for her waist and lifted her high into the air, "no more talk of such gloom. We have dinner at my parents' house this evening, and I want to show you how far the construction has come on our home."

Jule listened to Mason talk eagerly about the building of their house. He had called it home, but she couldn't bring herself to think of it as anything but a massive structure. She had spent the last ten years of her life in the two-story clapboard home beside the lighthouse on Bolivar Point. They lived simply—her parents, a younger brother, Joshua, and Jule—on her father's meager income as a lighthouse attendant. All the wealth associated with Mason's family made her feel uncomfortable, and she fretted constantly about committing social blunders. Now the house. . . Perhaps once it reached completion, and she and Mason were married, she could refer to it as home. Meanwhile, she must continue to feign enthusiasm for his parents' current project.

Captain Thomas Channing, one of the most affluent men on Galveston Island, had retired some years ago as a sea captain to start his own import/export business. With his never-satisfied ambition, he had accumulated more money than most folks deemed proper. Esther Channing, his wife, had no problem spending it. The house for Mason and Jule came as a desire for both parents to give their only son and his bride-to-be a lavish gift. Esther chose the house's design and planned to supervise the interior design. Thomas relinquished a large percentage of his business to Mason. Knowing the reputed volatile temperament of her future father-in-law, Jule guessed Mr. Channing had demanded Mason sail to insure his cargo arrived at the designated ports in the minimum amount of time.

Jule shuddered, recalling the stories often told in public gatherings about Mason. Young Captain Channing possessed a reputation for taking risks and riding out storms in open defiance of the sea's wrath. As did all clipper captains, Mason viewed wind as speed, and speed as time and money. Some said Mason needed a dose of good sense. Others claimed his father drove him to make foolish decisions in the name of money. Thomas Channing had a hold on Mason—almost like a hand around his throat—constantly reminding him of the wealth to come only if he measured up to his father's expectations. And that is what scared Jule the most: Mason's consuming desire to please his father.

Once, she asked him why he took so many chances and dared the sea to engulf him and his faithful crew. His reply had alarmed her.

"Because, sometimes when the captain is being so overpowering, I forget my real trust is in God. Unfortunately, I fear my father more than our Maker," he'd answered gravely, avoiding her eyes. "It's not his money or station in life; I care naught for those things." He shook his head as though denying his inner turmoil. "I have never earned real approval from the captain. . . and it pushes me to do everything over and beyond his expectations."

At the time, Jule wondered where she fit into Mason's life. Certainly other women were more comely, talented, and well-positioned socially. Inwardly, she wondered if his choice of her involved a slender thread of rebellion.

"You are the one treasure that no one can take from me, except God," he'd added. "For my father, I risk my life. For you, I would gladly step into the threshold of death."

"Why me?" she'd asked, taken back by her own boldness.

Jule would never forget his response, the shimmer of love in his stormy blue eyes and a strange, faraway glint of something she had yet to claim.

"You are my joy and my blessing. In you I see all I want to be—gentle, kind, faithful to God, selfless, and with a hidden strength that draws me like the allure of a huge wave. I can confide in you as my friend, tell you anything, and not risk ridicule." He smiled. "It does not matter who I am or what is associated with my name; you love me. Jule, you are beauty in its richest form." Then Mason had removed his derby hat, bent on one knee, and proposed marriage.

Now, as he grasped her hand firmly, she realized her place belonged beside him for as long as God allowed.

"Shall we walk along the shoreline?" Mason asked. "We have nearly an hour before leaving."

"Of course." Jule linked her arm into his, and they strode across the sand.

The ever-present breeze across the gulf played with the scarf tying her bonnet under her chin, while a stronger gust rustled her skirts. The peninsula of Bolivar Point held the distinction of bearing a constant wind from the ocean; it never ceased. Sand lightly pelted against her face, and she turned to avoid its sting.

"Would you rather walk back to the house?" he suggested. "I don't enjoy the prospect of the wind tossing you into the water."

Jule laughed. "No, this breeze is a part of me."

She faced the water and closed her eyes. Breathing in the salty air, she allowed it to rest upon her tongue while the sun warmed her face. Seagulls glided and circled above them, calling out to each other and dipping into the sea for a fresh fish. Jule longed for a few stale biscuits from the house to toss into the air so she could watch the birds swoop down to grasp one in their beaks. The rhythmic sound of billowing waves tumbling against the shore momentarily eased the unpleasant news of Mason's departure.

"You love the sea as much as I do," he said, slipping his hand around her waist.

"Aye, Captain," she replied, and they both laughed at her attempt to sound like his first mate. "But I am content to admire its many moods, not submerge myself in it."

A fishing boat crossed in the distance. The sails dipped up and down as though it rocked aimlessly without cause or reason. A part of her envied the sea's sway and pull. There were no choices to be made; life simply moved on.

"As a little boy," Mason began, "I remember watching my mother gaze out over the sea. She spent the early mornings and twilight look-ing for signs of my father's ship. The sadness in her face always made me angry with him. Once I actually told him how I felt about his being gone for months at a time."

They walked farther up the white sandy beach. "What did he say?" Jule asked, unable to picture Mason challenging his father about anything.

He chuckled and puffed up his stomach to imitate the senior Captain Channing. In a deep voice typical of the man, he said, "My boy, don't you know that what you fear most will come upon you? If I succumb to your mother's whims, then the sea has run me off. I am not afraid of it, and neither should she be."

"Sounds like him," Jule said.

"My father, the old walrus," Mason added. "But I do love and respect him, although his opinions drive me to distraction."

"You shouldn't talk about him," Jule chided, catching a mischievous sparkle in his eyes. "You owe him your respect."

"Yes, ma'am, but you take a good look at him tonight at dinner and see if he doesn't remind you of a walrus."

Silently, Jule had to agree. Thomas Channing did resemble a walrus with his wiry mustache, fleshy jaws, and bushy sideburns. The remainder of his body had grown rather portly in his land-loving days, as well.

Much too soon, their walk came to an end. They tramped up the sandy mounds in the direction of the Portier house and Bolivar Point Lighthouse.

"Have you done all of your chores?" Mason asked. "I wouldn't want your father complaining about dirty lanterns in the lighthouse."

"Today is Joshua's turn," she said with a nod. "Tomorrow is mine."

"May I help you?" he asked, patting her arm that still entwined with his. "We have three weeks, and I want to be with you every minute possible."

"What about your father? I thought he wanted you with him tomorrow?"

Mason frowned. "Surely he can't expect me to spend all of my time on the docks for the next three weeks."

Jule recognized Mason's growing resentment of his father. "Mason, are you sure you want to spend the rest of your life managing goods shipped in and out of Galveston Bay?"

He sighed deeply and avoided meeting her gaze. "No," he replied, "not in the least."

Chapter 2

Jule's heart hammered against her chest, and she shook in dread, much like discontented waves caught up in the fury of a storm. The sea. Mason loved the sea too much to give it up. . .not even for her.

"What is it you want to do?" she asked, willing her quivering voice to steady. She wanted to gaze into the depths of his blue-gray eyes, but she could not bear to see the truth.

"I would like to have my own shipbuilding company," he replied. "I have sailed the finest clippers Father could buy, and I've observed what makes them withstand the turbulent sea and sail faster than any vessel on earth. I am particularly fond of the square-riggers—windjammers. Oh, Jule, to build such seaworthy ships would give me great pleasure."

Relief flowed through her body. "What a splendid idea," Jule managed to say, and she meant it.

He met her smile, and like a boy, his dreams gushed from within. "I realize I've probably told you this before, but I've been sailing with my father since I was twelve years old. Later at eighteen, I took over one of his ships. While on board or docked at various ports, I often spend my time studying clippers and the proper way to build them. The construction of these vessels intrigues me. There's a renowned Boston builder who owns a shipyard, and whenever I'm there, I like to see his latest designs. It's always been a dream of mine, but now, I want to embark upon it before it is too late. Eventually the steamships will power the oceans."

"Then you should do it now," she stated.

"My father would be furious," Mason added. "In his mind, he will be the captain till the day he dies—barking orders and expecting everyone

287

around him to cower and obey." He paused before beginning again. "I have the money. . ."

"Oh, Mason, you would be perfect," she said, feeling giddy with the excitement of him sharing his dreams.

He kissed the tip of her nose and laughed. "You believe I can do anything."

"Absolutely." She laughed with him. "It's part of my role as your future wife."

His handsome features suddenly grew grave. "If I fail at this venture, we will be penniless," he warned. "You understand Father would gloat over my foolishness, and I would be forced to return to the sea."

"I refuse to think about such a thing. You are clever and a hard worker. I firmly believe God does not give us dreams unless He intends for us to follow through with them. But no matter the outcome, we will journey though life together and make the best of whatever God wills."

The tiny lines around his eyes deepened as he appeared to contemplate her words. "Your faith is stronger than mine, Jule, and perhaps you are right in your notion. I will pray about the matter before informing my father. Of course, the conversation with him needs to occur before I set sail."

Mason stopped to shield his eyes from the sun while Jule followed his gaze to the lighthouse. The mounting heat of mid-June glistening against the black-and-white painted structure gave it a regal glow. "Just like your lighthouse is strong and built to withstand the worst of storms, so is my father. He may refuse to complete our home. I can provide well for you, very well, in fact, but our home would not be as grand." He peered at her, waiting for an answer.

"Mason, I have never enjoyed the wealth you have. It matters less to me whether we live in a mansion or a shack near the bay. What is important is for you to follow your dreams and for me to be beside you."

A broad smile spread across his face. "Then I will proceed with talking to Father—after I have consulted God."

Jule felt his elation, and his experiences at sea certainly qualified him to own a shipbuilding company. At the age of seventeen, Mason had secured his mate papers, and by the age of twenty he'd received his master's certificate. Now at age thirty-two, Mason had captured the respect of men and the hearts of women. Young and old admired his chivalry and daring deeds on the high seas. Despite all this, Mason generally allowed his father to have his own way. And yet, she did sense a need for him to separate himself from his father's influence.

Few saw the control the elder Channing possessed over his son, but Jule had noted it on more than one occasion. It saddened her, and she wanted to talk to Mason about it. . .but she believed God should direct his life.

"I guess we ought to be leaving soon," Mason said. "Mother will be expecting us. Do you have your things ready?"

Jule nodded. The distance between Bolivar Point and Galveston Bay laid claim to nearly three miles, and Mason requested that she stay at his parents' home until the morning rather than have him row her home in the dark. Twice before she had spent the night at the three-story Victorian mansion. The home's elegant furnishings and original art disquieted her, especially with her lack of appropriate attire. Even the servants dressed better than she did.

As she thought of her light blue, faded Sunday frock, humiliation crept over her like a winter chill. She had worn it the other two occasions when she had been a guest for dinner, simply because she had no other. Regretfully, Esther Channing had a distinct way of raising her chin and regarding her rather disdainfully down the tip of a long, pointed nose. Jule dare not think what might be said tonight when she stepped into the formal dining room with her three-year-old dress. She shouldn't care. God didn't measure her worth by the clothes she wore, but to look pleasing in Esther Channing's eyes meant Jule might someday be accepted as a member of the family. Even now, the voice of Mrs. Channing echoed around Jule, making sure she heard the stories about the many young women who had paraded in front of Mason and vied for his attention.

Jules shook off such thoughts as she and Mason climbed the steps of the porch to the clapboard house she called home. Her mother greeted Mason warmly and ushered them inside. The tall, large-boned woman took giant strides across the small parlor to a rounded-back sofa and two chairs in various shades of deep brown with frayed coverings.

"Jule's papa and brother are out with the fishing boat," she explained, positioning herself on the edge of a chair.

Mason and Jule sat on the sofa, sinking deep into the worn cushions.

"Mrs. Portier, it is not necessary for your husband to be present when I come calling on Jule, although I would have enjoyed talking with him," Mason replied.

Jule's mother patted her silver spun hair pulled back tightly into a netted bun at the nape of her neck. "You are so considerate, Mr. Channing."

"Mason, please call me Mason. After all, we will be family soon."

A smile spread across her mother's tanned face, and she turned her attention to Jule. "Mind you, daughter, this is a fine man here, and I expect you to be a dutiful wife."

Jule suppressed her inward glee out of respect for her mother. "Yes, ma'am. I will do my best."

Her mother seemed nervous and resorted to smoothing the wrinkles in her dress rather than fussing with her hair. Jule felt compassion for her, knowing how much love and sacrifice she devoted to their family and how she desired the best for them all. No matter how many times Jule and Mason insisted that they would be happy to have a small wedding with simply the minister present, her mother fretted that it would not satisfy the Channings' ideas of what was necessary for their only son.

"Mother, we should be going. Do you mind?" Jule asked.

"No, of course not. And you will be home before noon tomorrow?" Her mother sighed. "I fret with you spending the night."

"It is quite all right," Mason interceded gently. "This is my mother's invitation, and I believe she has a surprise for my future bride."

Jule's eyes widened. "What kind of a surprise?"

Her mother wagged a finger. "Look at you, like a little girl wanting to know secrets." She stood and addressed Jule. "Gather your things and go on across the bay before the afternoon sun sets."

Jule entered the kitchen where the steps led to her bedroom. She hesitated before facing her mother. "Give Papa my love," she said. "And please remind him I want to tend the lighthouse tomorrow night. He needs a good night's rest."

Mason frowned, but Jule ignored him. He didn't think she should be keeping the candles lit and the wicks trimmed while other ladies slept. But Papa had developed a deep cough, and with fishing every day and minding the lighthouse, it hadn't gotten any better. She'd helped him with the duties since she was a young girl. As she hurried up the stairs, she resolved to tell Mason why she must help her family for as long as possible. The life of a lighthouse keeper involved the entire family, a commitment to the ships and their safety. She knew he would understand.

Shortly thereafter, Jule and Mason boarded the rowboat he had borrowed from his father and set across Galveston Bay. She loved the blue water, and with the wind blowing in a southerly direction, it took very little time or effort to reach the mainland. The harbor bustled with activity, from the small fishing boats to the shouts and laughter along the docks where goods were loaded and unloaded from the ships' hulls.

Once they set foot upon dry land, an open-air carriage transported them to his parents' home on Broadway. The horses' rhythmic clop along the street lured her into a future time when she would live among these same people. How strange she felt, not certain about her role as Mason Channing's wife.

Suddenly she sensed his gaze upon her and gave him the attention he deserved.

"I remember the first time I saw you," he said, slipping his arm across her shoulders.

Jule smiled. "I could never forget." How well she recalled the warm day last November when he'd knocked on her door to request a viewing of the lighthouse. "I stumbled over my words the entire time I explained the procedures of keeping the lens clean and insuring the proper amount of oil in the lamps. And I didn't wear any shoes."

"You were delightful," Mason replied. "And I didn't hear a word of the tour. I was too captivated with the beautiful, intelligent young woman before me. Remember the long walk along the beach?"

Jule nodded. "And you returned the following morning to talk to Papa."

Mason chuckled. "Asking to come calling on you proved more difficult than weathering any storm. He questioned me for an hour about my intentions. I still recall the perspiration dripping down the side of my face—for fear he'd deny me the pleasure of seeing you again."

"I had no idea what you two were discussing, so I watched from inside the house. When I saw you two shake hands, I thought you had struck a deal of some sort."

"We did." Mason laughed.

She had been in complete awe of Mason's attention, and he'd easily captured her heart with his wit, charm, and honesty.

"Do you know what attracted me the most about you?" he asked, his eyes twinkling.

"My bare feet?"

"No, my silly Jule. For the first time in my life, a woman didn't act like she needed to impress me. You were genuine, and I loved it."

"Thank you," she whispered. Her eyes caught sight of two boys playing tag. A part of her never wanted to grow up. "What is your mother's surprise for me?" she asked, attempting to convey her eagerness.

He grinned and lightly squeezed her shoulder. "If I told you, it wouldn't be a surprise, but I believe you will be pleased."

"With your mother's excellent taste, it must be wonderful."

"Oh, my darling," he said with a sigh. "You are most diplomatic, for I know Mother can be trying at times."

How well Jule knew his mother's tenacity for securing her own way. However, Esther Channing loved Mason and his father. "Whatever she has for me, I will be gracious."

His mustache curled upward. "Where were you all those years Father and Mother urged me to take a bride?"

Jule tried but failed to keep from smiling. "Growing up," she replied, nodding her head for emphasis.

The carriage stopped and Mason assisted her down. "Please wait for our return," Mason instructed the driver. "I would like to take Miss Portier for a short ride."

Carrying her threadbare bag in one hand and unlatching the gate with the other, Mason offered her his arm, and they sauntered up the walkway.

Squared by a white wrought-iron fence, the huge edifice looked formidable, even ominous, to Jule. The sight of it always took her breath away. Glancing upward to the angled bay windows, she caught sight of the ornate spindle-type white trim from the front verandah extending to the second-story balcony. Trepidation crept over her while she contemplated the evening ahead.

Once inside, Mason removed his derby hat and held on to Jule firmly. "I'm right here," he whispered. "There is no need for you to tremble."

A servant took her bag while another led the way to where Mrs.

Channing awaited them in the music room. This particular area had been painted in cream and accented in peach and gold. A black grand piano rested in one corner near two cream and gold chairs, which held a violin and flute respectively. Mrs. Channing sat perfectly erect on a gold spun sofa beside a floor-to-ceiling window, facing the piano.

"Good afternoon, Mason, Jule," the tastefully dressed woman said in greeting. She directed her attention to Jule. "And how are you, dear?"

"Very well, thank you," Jule replied, hoping she sounded the slightest bit sophisticated. "You look quite lovely this afternoon, Mrs. Channing."

The older woman, dressed in a gown of variegated shades of lavender, nodded pleasantly and lifted a cheek for Mason to kiss.

"I would like to show Jule the progress on our home before dinner," he said, escorting her to the same sofa with his mother.

"I am so excited for you, Mason. Your home will be grand," his mother replied, clasping her hands primly in her lap. "I have such plans for the interior design, and I can only imagine the gala events."

Jule inwardly shuddered. She knew nothing of arranging such things. Why, she had never been to a social affair—of course Mrs. Channing must know how inept she felt.

"Jule, dear," Mrs. Channing began, "perhaps you would like to freshen up before departing. Change clothes, perhaps?"

Cringing, Jule swallowed hard. She had no desire to be rude in response to Mrs. Channing's question, but she had nothing else suitable to wear. "I will be fine," she answered with a smile. "But I would like to freshen up."

"Go ahead, darling," Mason said with an encouraging smile. "I will be waiting."

Mrs. Channing summoned a servant, who proceeded to escort Jule to the second floor. There, in the same pale blue and rose room where she had slept the previous times, atop a bed adorned in a white coverlet, lay a lovely silk gown of misty green. Jule gasped at the yards of ruffles and deeper green lace trim. Stunned, she moved toward the bed, admiring the dress's design. She bent to touch the fabric between her fingers.

"Are you pleased?" Mrs. Channing asked.

Jule whirled around to see Mason and his mother observing her from the doorway. "It is very beautiful," she replied.

"Good," his mother said with only a faint smile. "If it fits properly, I will have my seamstress fit you for an entire wardrobe."

Jule held her breath. "Oh, you must not. I don't know what I would do with such lovely gowns."

"Wear them as my wife. With your black hair, violet eyes, and tall slender figure—anything and everything will look perfect," Mason declared.

Jule blushed at his compliment, not sure how to respond.

"Mother originally had the idea, but I picked the color of the gown."

Although he had never said or done anything to indicate how he felt, Jule was positive her clothes must humiliate him, especially when he normally viewed young women dressed exquisitely in the most elegant gowns.

"I guessed about your size," Mrs. Channing said, her petite figure standing perfectly poised. "And in the dressing room, I have selected other things for you as well."

Determined to retain her pride, Jule searched for the proper words. "Thank you," she managed. "I am honored to have you present me with such lavish gifts."

"Nonsense," his mother replied, her chin reaching rather high proportions. "I couldn't have you embarrassing our family any longer in those rags."

Chapter 3

Mother!" Mason shouted. "I will not have you speak to Jule this way."

"Son, calm down. Jule is quite aware she is marrying considerably above her station in life." His mother responded as though she and Mason were the only people in the room.

Mason's stormy eyes blazed. "You will—"

Jule lifted her skirts and positioned herself between Mason and his mother. "Mrs. Channing, I am fully aware of who I am and the social status of your family. I did not accept your son's proposal based on his wealth or name but solely because I love him. If my being here is a source of embarrassment to you, fret no more, for I shall leave." With her gaze firmly fixed on Esther Channing, she added, "Thank you for your generous gift, but I won't be needing the dress."

His mother glared at her angrily, saying nothing, but her facial expressions spoke volumes. A moment later, a look of victory calmed her strained features.

"I need transportation back to Bolivar Point," Jule said, still directing a cold stare at Mason's mother.

Suddenly Jule realized her haughty pride and outburst did not come from God. She moistened her lips and summoned the courage to address the woman once more. "Please accept my apologies for my impertinent behavior. As a Christian woman, I am chagrined at my rash words; nevertheless, it does not change how I feel."

"You are not the one to apologize," Mason said. "Come along, Jule, I will not have you stay in this house one moment longer."

Jule turned and exited the room. Her heart fluttered and she quaked from the tension of the confrontation, but she refused to allow any tears to fall. Mama had warned her Mrs. Channing might not accept her. The Portiers and the Channings had nothing in common. It didn't matter that Mason's mother had spoken shamefully. Jule's angry retort did not right the matter.

Mason's mother called for him to return, but his steps did not falter. "I shall surely faint," she cried. The front door of the three-story mansion slammed with his mother's hysteria ringing behind them.

"I'm so sorry," Jule breathed once they stood on the verandah.

"Nonsense," Mason said, his jaw anchored solidly. "Neither you nor I will ever return to this house."

He helped her into the carriage and requested the driver to take them to the docks.

"I lost my temper," she began.

Mason failed to acknowledge her statement. His body seethed with anger. "Mother would try the patience of a minister."

"You shouldn't have to choose between me and your family," Jule said slowly. Guilt settled upon her like a slowly creeping fog. "This is my fault."

"The Bible says a man should leave his father and mother and cleave to his wife," he responded. "I should have done this years ago."

"But we're not married yet, and until then they deserve your respect and obedience," she gently reminded him.

"At my age? Nonsense."

Jule picked up his hand, and he grasped hers firmly. She could think of nothing to say. How could she live with herself, knowing she had been the cause of Mason severing ties with his parents?

The longer they rode in silence, the more regret gnawed at her. She envisioned the years ahead of them— with children and without the Channings as grandparents. All involved would suffer the loss.

Mason needed the companionship of others. His personality demanded it, and surely his life vocation required it. He enjoyed his wide circle of friends, and those people were in the same social realm as his parents. Jule sensed this afternoon marked the beginning of a wedge driven between her and Mason. Someday, he would regret his decision. First, he promised to give up the sea for her, and now he had chosen her over his parents. No love should demand such a sacrifice. Her selfishness, her desires, her needs, and her inability to befriend Mason's mother led to one conclusion. She loved Mason with all her heart, and she ached with what must be done.

"Mason," Jule began, withdrawing her hand from his. "If you don't mind, I'd rather someone else took me home."

"Why?" His eyes narrowed.

"I'm breaking our engagement. I no longer want to marry you."

"Tell me you don't love me," he said quietly. "Look at me, Jule."

She slowly turned to him, defiantly holding herself aloof, but he saw the desperation in her striking violet eyes. He heard the emotion in her voice and realized she'd do anything to stop a flow of tears.

Jule's chest rose slightly as she inhaled. "I do not love you. Your mother spoke correctly. I wanted to marry you for your wealth, nothing more, but I can't follow through with it. At least, I have some decency left."

Mason met her resolve with the same determination as when he sailed into unsettled waters—stouthearted and bold.

"I remember when the captain used to catch me in a lie," Mason said impassively. "He'd warm my backside with a leather strap."

Jule's eyes widened, and her fists tightened into a ball on her lap.

"So, do I need to resort to Father's method?"

The color drained from her face. She stiffened. "Mason Channing, I am not a child. I have spoken the truth, and you must accept our broken engagement."

"Indeed not."

"Why? Have you taken leave of your senses?"

"No, Jule," he replied gently. "You love me as much as I love you. This little ruckus—"

"Little?" she asked, glancing about to make certain no one had heard.

"Little," Mason repeated. "Mother is always on a tirade about something. And she's not accustomed to people standing up to her, which we both did."

"But you said you were never going back," Jule stated, obviously bewildered.

"And I shall not," Mason declared. "It is not your fault or doing. This afternoon merely displayed an accumulation of pent-up feelings. We will find a home together, and I plan to go ahead with my idea of building ships."

"They are your parents," Jule pointed out.

"True. I love them dearly, but unless they can accept you as my wife, we have nothing in common."

"I loathe this contention," she said with a sigh. "You should marry a woman of whom your mother approves."

"Ridiculous," he countered. "God gave you to me as an exquisite treasure." He reached across the carriage and took her hand. "I will not let you go. Tell me now you don't love me, Jule."

He studied her delicate features. Her thick black tresses framed her heart-shaped face, and he fought the urge to slide the bonnet back so he could see the bluish cast of her hair against the sun. She possessed a natural pink glow to her cheeks, unlike so many women who used other means to make them appear healthy. He loved her smooth creamy skin and her pert little mouth that reminded him of a perfectly shaped bow. Did she have an inkling of what she did to him?

Mason wanted to draw her into his arms and convince her of his love, but sweet words of endearment could not heal the hurt inside her. The afternoon had been a nightmare, and he knew Jule blamed herself for the tempers flaring between the three of them. He recognized her intelligence and respected her individuality and profound faith in God. They needed to discuss the problems dividing them.

Frankly, he looked forward to securing his own quarters. He could picture a better rapport with his parents by not seeing them daily. A few days ago, he'd seen a home for sale on Sealy Street, a beautiful Victorian with many roof extensions and a tower corner. If Jule approved, he could easily purchase it and have it redecorated during his stay at sea.

He waited for her reply; his gaze firmly locked with hers. Time suspended.

"I do love you," she finally admitted. "But Mason, I simply cannot bear to be the cause of dissension with your mother. Once your father hears about your shipbuilding, he will blame me, too."

Mason understood her doubts. "Then I will take you back to Bolivar Point and make amends with Mother. Tomorrow, I will initiate a conversation with the captain and explain my plans."

Her face brightened, and a faint smile tugged at her lips. "I will pray for all of you," she whispered. Glancing down at the hand wrapped securely around hers, she continued, "I want to learn those things that will enable me to step into the role as your wife, but I need someone who can teach me without reproach."

"I know," he murmured. "If Mother cannot bring herself to have a solid relationship with you, I will find someone to help you—not for my sake, but for yours. Society's rules and latest fashions matter not for me. I am content with you as my wife. Nothing else matters."

She sighed and tilted her head. "I only want you as my husband. Even so, a shipbuilder's wife needs to know how to entertain and dress properly."

Mason enjoyed a chuckle and drew her close beside him. Life with Jule promised to be full of surprises and no doubt a little riff or two. He had wanted to have a gown designed for her before, but she'd refused, stating that she would save to purchase fabric and sew it on her own. Maybe he should not have succumbed to his mother's whim, but he thought the gesture might bring the two women closer together.

He loved Jule's spunk and her devotion to him. Most of all, he cherished her belief in him as a man.

With evening's dark blanket settling across Galveston, Mason entered his parents' home. Odd, he had not referred to the brick mansion as his own since a boy. Depending on the outcome of his conversation with his mother, he would know whether he needed to seek a hotel room for the night. He really didn't care…or did he? If Mason dealt honestly with himself, he must agree with Jule. The differences between him and his mother needed to be resolved and an understanding reached with Father about his life vocation.

Mason walked toward the lamp-lit parlor. His mother sat alone reading *Harper's Bazaar* so intently that she did not see him enter the room.

Clearing his throat, he secured her attention. "Mother, do you have a moment to speak with me?"

Her eyes were red and swollen, and he surmised she had wept all afternoon over their argument.

"Yes, I do. Are you here to collect your belongings?" she asked, her lips quivering.

He strode over to her side and knelt by her chair. "Perhaps I am, but

I believe we need to settle things between us first."

His mother burst into tears, but he elected not to comfort her. She usually resorted to such means to make sure she obtained sympathy.

"When you are in control of your emotions, we will talk," he said.

A moment later she looked at him through watery eyes and nodded.

"In order for you and I to maintain a civil relationship, you must apologize to Jule and refrain from ever insulting her again."

"But—"

"You are a good Christian woman and know how to treat others accordingly. Nothing you can say or do will stop me from marrying Jule, and if you would only try to be friends with her, you would love her as I do. I am sorry for upsetting you today, but the quarrel has brought about a long overdue stand on my part. Jule will be my wife with or without your blessing, but I prefer your blessing. I know she has not grown up in our social group, and I believe you are against our marriage for those reasons and because of your love for me."

Silence filled the room. The grandfather clock struck nine times.

"What will it be, Mother? I can remain here in this house until my ship sails, or I can leave."

"I wanted a woman from our kind." His mother sobbed.

"God chose for me the best," Mason stated, with no intention of wavering. "Jule wants to learn about fashion, design, and those other things important to you. Mother, you can be her instructor or her enemy. It is up to you."

"And you will not relinquish your pledge to marry her?" his mother asked with one last desperate breath.

"Absolutely not. If all of this centered around Jule's character or that she did not follow sound Christian principles, then I would have to abide by your wishes. But this is not the case."

She sighed deeply and dabbed her eyes with a lace handkerchief. "Very well. I give my word I will treat her as my own daughter."

"Good," Mason replied. "Then I will expect you to accompany me tomorrow afternoon to Bolivar Point, where you can formally offer your apologies."

His mother stiffened, yet she did not protest.

Mason touched her arm. "These are my terms," he stated. "It is about time you met her parents. Fine people, I may add."

She quietly acquiesced to her son's requests.

"There you are," his father called from the archway separating the library from the parlor. "Have you two settled your differences?"

Mason wondered how long the captain had been listening. "Yes, Father, we have."

"Wonderful. Now, I have news for you. Plans have changed for your voyage to Liverpool. You will set sail day after tomorrow."

Chapter 4

"What is the urgency?" Mason asked. The painful issues of the day did not need one more intrusion. He'd rather have battled gale winds amidst a thunderstorm than his father.

"The buyer wired me and needs the goods," the captain replied simply. "Didn't think you would mind. In fact, you could get back quicker and possibly advance your wedding plans."

Mason raised a brow. "Is this a bribe?"

"Possibly," his father said, resting his arm across the fireplace mantel.

Mason swallowed his irritation, sensing a real need to talk to his father about his future. He might as well get it over and done with.

"Can we step into your study? I'd like to discuss a matter with you."

The captain nodded, and they made their way to the mahogany-paneled room encased with bookshelves. The anchor and ship's wheel from the captain's last sailing vessel stood polished and noble in front of a solitary window.

His father lit a kerosene lamp and settled back in his stuffed leather chair. Mason settled into an armchair across from the desk.

"So what is on your mind?" his father asked.

Mason stared straight into the captain's blue-gray eyes. "Father, you know I have always appreciated what you've done for me. You allowed me to sail with you from the moment I could nearly reach your shoulders. You taught me everything I know about the sea—sailing, how to command the respect of the crew, and business sense. Without your wise counsel, I'm sure I would have sunk many a ship into the ocean depths." He paused and contemplated his next words.

"Thank you. It's a good feeling to know I have done well with you," his father answered.

Mason noticed his fingers were digging against the palms of his hands. Releasing them, he attempted to relax. "Your insistence that I challenge the world and learn from my mistakes has led me to an important decision." He moistened his dry lips. "For many years now, I have dreamed of building seaworthy ships. I'm particularly fond of windjammers—how they are constructed. . .the type of wood used and the craftsmanship involve. I have found a location where I could build them, and I have the financial assets necessary to venture into this endeavor."

His father rested his head on his forefinger and thumb and studied him. "What about the family business?"

Mason's stomach did a little flip. "Let me first say how much I value the hard work you have done and the fact that you desire me to step into a major role in your business, but at this time I want to proceed with my shipbuilding plans."

The captain took a deep breath and stared at Mason—a sign that he was absorbed in thought.

"Are you going to do this with or without my blessing, but you prefer my approval?" his father asked after several long moments.

Mason sighed. So he had been listening at the door. "Yes sir."

"Well, I guess I'm the one at fault here. I'm the one who taught you the value of claiming a chunk of the world for yourself. I demanded you learn the sea and tame it. You wouldn't be a Channing if you didn't seek out uncharted waters." He stood and reached to shake Mason's hand. "Congratulations, son. Far be it from me to try to stop you. I will not interfere, but I will always be available if you need me. A married man needs to consider his family, and I regret I spent too many years sailing the high seas rather than here on land so I could be with you."

Mason felt relief drench him. "Thank you sir, for the support and encouragement."

A smile crested on the captain's weathered face. "When the time comes for making a decision about import/export trade, we can sit down and talk again."

"Fair enough." Mason met his father's steady gaze with a genuine smile. For the first time, he felt his father's equal, and the warm sensation stirring through him had long been coming.

"Now, about your upcoming voyage—your last one. Here are the details. . ."

⤬

Hours later, Mason still lay awake. His head swam with all the events of the day, and he worked hard to put each one into proper perspective. Never had he expected his father's approval of his dreams, and the thought of it pleased him immensely. They'd talked for several hours about the sea, ships, the import/export business, and Jule. The captain liked her and welcomed her into the family. He said wealth or station in life did not measure a person's importance; rather, they should be judged by who they were on the inside. Mason smiled when he heard those words. In time, Mother might share the same views of his future bride. Perhaps the captain was not such a tyrant after all.

The prospect of leaving Jule in two days' time did not rest well with Mason, but the sooner he left, the sooner he would return to claim his wife. First thing in the morning, he needed to visit Bolivar Point and break the news. Hopefully, he could comfort Jule by moving up the wedding date. They had planned so many things for the next few weeks, but they had a lifetime to take picnics and walk along the beach. This trip simply brought their lives together much sooner.

A bit of excitement raced through Mason's blood. The prospect of sailing up the East Coast to New York and on to England thrilled him. Granted, hurricane season had just begun, but he chose to take his chances and deliver the goods to the various ports, collect the handsome fees for his father, and sail home. After this, the only voyage he ever intended to take again would be with his lovely bride to some secluded, beautiful island in the Caribbean.

Mason decided life offered many appealing roads, and at times he wondered if he needed God. Immediately guilt struck him. But the ideas lingered. As of late, doubts about God had assaulted him like a driving rain.

⤬

Mason allowed the warm breeze to cool his face. He tasted the salty air and noted the cloudless, azure sky. A perfect day. He cast his sights on the lighthouse at Bolivar Point and pictured Jule staring out across the blue waters. Oh, how he treasured those rare moments when she removed her bonnet and allowed the wind to blow her radiant black tresses back from her face. Sometimes she closed her eyes as though drinking in the intoxicating effect of sand and sea. He understood the reeling emotions caused by the power of nature. In one breath it offered freedom to dance atop the white crested waves, and in another, its power frightened the bravest of men.

Jule, his jewel. Nearly two months without her seemed unbearable, yet he possessed enough dreams and memories to last a lifetime.

"Thank You, God," he murmured. Strange, his thoughts turned toward the Lord again. For some time he had wrestled with questions and confusion about the God of his youth. With all the modern thinking and the changes occurring around him, he had begun to wonder if God really existed or if He had become a myth for those who feared the future.

Shaking his head to dispel such misgivings, he busied his mind with final preparations for the voyage. He dare not stay long on Bolivar Point, although the thought tempted him. With Jule, he knew no time, only the present.

From the kitchen window, Jule watched Mason row toward shore. He must have risen at the crack of dawn to arrive so early. No matter—he could share a cup of coffee with her, and there were biscuits, grits, and bacon left from breakfast. Papa ate little again this morning. Lately, he didn't desire much food and chose to sleep rather than partake of meals with the rest of the family. The debilitating cough had grown worse, leaving him pale and weak.

Joshua admitted to Jule he had taken over the fishing duties because Papa couldn't manage the weight of the nets. Jule kept telling herself that God held Papa in the palm of His hand, but she worried about his prolonged illness.

"Jule, I believe I see Mason rowing across the bay," her mother said, interrupting Jule's pondering.

"Yes, Mama. Though it seems strange to see him this early."

Her mother laughed. "It must be love, and he's thinking about those weeks ahead without you."

Jule blushed. After the uncomfortable scene at his parents' home the day before, she had wondered how he would be feeling. Last night she had prayed for him and his mother to lovingly resolve their differences.

"You run along to meet him," her mother insisted. "I will finish the dishes."

Jule smiled into her mother's lined face. "Thank you. I won't let him take up most of my day. I have to tend to the lighthouse."

Her mother nodded, and Jule impulsively planted a kiss on her cheek before rushing out the door. Barefoot and forgetting her bonnet, Jule stepped lightly from the front porch to the sand-covered pathway leading to the shore. She met Mason as he waded with the boat to land. The sight of him in a loose-fitting white shirt bulging from his broad shoulders took her breath away. Feeling herself grow warm, she glanced at the small boat dancing on the lapping waves.

"She may take flight without you," Jule said.

Mason cast a quick glance back toward the water. "She may try, but I pulled her tight."

Jule saw a rare show of apprehension on his tanned face. His handsome features were etched with concern.

"What is wrong?" she asked, momentarily alarmed as a thousand fears raced through her mind.

"You can tell," he replied with a forced grin. He grasped her waist and pulled her to him. "I love you, Jule Portier," he said softly and then kissed her soundly.

She held her breath, recognizing the tone of his voice from an encounter months ago. "You're leaving, aren't you?" she asked, speaking barely above a whisper.

He released his hold and met her gaze. At that moment, she knew the truth.

"When?" she asked, taking a deep breath and willing her fluttering heart to calm.

He urged her back into his arms and held her so close she could hear his heartbeat. "Tomorrow morning, at the crack of dawn."

She battled her tears while relishing his embrace. "This can be good," she said with a feigned smile.

"My sweet optimist," he said gently. "Can we move up our wedding date—for as soon as I return?"

"Yes," she breathed, basking in his nearness—the scent of the sea and the taste of salt upon his lips. "I will simply busy myself in sewing my wedding dress."

"That reminds me," he began, releasing her to pull out an envelope inside his shirt. "Mother had planned to accompany me in order to mend yesterday's misunderstanding, but due to the circumstance of my early departure, she wrote a letter instead." He handed her the missive, written on his mother's elegant stationery.

Jule held the letter gingerly in her hands as though it were a precious gem. "This is very thoughtful of her. Can you thank her for me and apologize for my rudeness again? I'll read it later. . .after you are gone." She hesitated. "Mason, you must have a score of things to do."

He nodded and raked his fingers through sun-bleached hair. "I can't stay but an hour." Not giving her a chance to comment, he turned to secure a wrapped package from the boat. "Mother wanted you to have this," he said.

"The green gown?"

"Yes."

"Would you like for me to keep it?"

"I would, very much."

She clutched the bundle to her heart. "Then I will wear it with pride."

"Will you allow me to purchase whatever you need for your wedding gown?" he asked, crossing his arms across his massive chest.

She grinned and tilted her head. "If it makes you happy, so be it."

"Wonderful, and I do—today and tomorrow." He hesitated then kissed the tip of her nose. "This is mid-June. We can marry the first week of September. Is that acceptable? I'd like to have the ceremony the same day I dock, but I suppose your parents will want a few weeks to finalize plans."

"I agree." She tucked her hair behind her ear and suddenly remembered how she had neglected to put on her bonnet and shoes. "Oh, Mason, I look so badly. I am sorry, and here I will not see you for two months."

He chuckled. "I want to remember you this way—like the seagulls, graceful and free."

This time tears hinted at her eyes, but she hastily blinked them away.

He must have sensed her wavering emotions for he quickly grabbed her hand. "Come, I need to tell your family a proper good-bye."

"Joshua and Papa are out fishing, but Mama is inside the house." She wanted to tell him about Papa's illness but thought better of it. What good would it do? "We will be praying for you," she added.

"No need to bother God, Jule. This will be a simple voyage; I feel it in my bones."

Chapter 5

Alarm shook the core of Jule's spirit, and her knees weakened. "Oh, Mason," she said, "we all need prayers. Who knows what could happen?"

He squeezed her waist. "Of course darling, how mindless of me. Yes, please pray for all the crew aboard the *Flying Fish.*"

She momentarily forgot his slip of the tongue and savored the precious moments she had left with him.

A short while later, Mason informed her mother of his change of plans and his desire to marry Jule sooner than originally planned. He hugged Mama good-bye and left a proper message for Papa and Joshua. Jule and Mason strolled hand in hand to the shore's edge, each one avoiding the inevitable farewell. When they finally reached the water, neither said a word.

"I must go," he said softly, "but I don't want to." Both faced the sea. His arms encircled her waist and his cheek rested on the top of her head.

He gently turned her to face him. Lifting her chin with his forefinger, he bent to taste her lips. He drew her so tightly against him that it nearly took her breath away. Mason's kiss deepened; never had his passion reached such intensity. A part of her urged him on, and another knew he should stop.

When he finally released the kiss, he continued to hold her close. "I love you," he murmured. "I will think of nothing else but you until the day I see you again."

Jule felt herself trembling; her pulse quickened and her heart pounded furiously against her chest. "Oh, do be careful, Mason. Please, don't take any chances; I've heard enough stories about your daring on the high seas to last a lifetime. Promise me, my love."

"I promise," he breathed. "And when I first reach New York, I will post you a letter."

She nodded and pulled away from him. They both realized the grief of parting, and he needed to go. "I love you with all my heart," she said, and her eyes welled with the tears she swore he would not see.

"When you whisper across the blue, I will hear it," he said, "and I will send my love from wherever I am."

Mason brushed the dampness from her cheek and kissed her a final time. He stepped away and hurried to the boat. A moment later he raised his hand and waved good-bye.

Jule's unabashed tears sprinkled her cheeks while she waved until her arm ached. "God be with you," she said, even though he could not hear. "May His angels watch over you and keep you safe."

She stood in the warm, ankle-deep water and watched the speck of the boat disappear on the horizon. Shielding her eyes from the sun's glare, she strained for one last glimpse, but he had truly gone. The time away from him sounded like forever, especially with the dangers at sea. She shivered in recalling the hurricane that had struck Galveston the previous September and killed six people.

"Please bring him home to me," Jule prayed. Then, as if God chose to remind her of Mason's earlier words, she remembered his remark of not needing to pray for him. "Touch his heart, Lord. Make him see how much he truly needs You."

❧

Mason stared at Jule's lone figure until she faded from view. Already he missed her. Already his arms longed to hold her. He had sealed her lovely face to memory—the natural pink of her cheeks and the depth of her hazel gaze. Closing his eyes, he could almost feel her silky black tresses woven between his fingers and hear the sweet sound of her voice saying she loved him. Given the opportunity, he would have brought her with him. But a woman did not belong at sea—and neither did some men.

In the weeks ahead, he'd keep busy, but he well knew the restlessness after days of riding ocean waves. Those were his thinking times, when he contemplated the future and dreamed of Jule—his jewel.

In the past, he had studied his Bible during idle moments on board ship. Mason shook his head, burdened with guilt over his doubts of the Lord. He needed to renew his dedication and commitment to the Creator. Where had those questions come from? And why had he allowed them to consume his mind?

Searching his soul deeply, Mason realized his daring escapades had much to do with his misgivings. Time and again, he had battled the odds through the worst of storms and won. Admittedly, he had come to believe in his own skill rather than in God's grace.

Jule cast a worried frown at the shadows of twilight ushering in the sunset. The hours had passed slowly since Mason's departure, but new fears filled her senses. From her post at the top of the lighthouse, she could see all around, and there were no signs of Papa and Joshua. They should have been back before now. Rarely did they stay out fishing much beyond late afternoon. The lighthouse duties ranked more important than anything else in their lives, except for serving God.

She picked up the small metal box containing matches and lit the lamps. Once they burned brightly against the reflectors, she stepped out on the catwalk to look again for signs of Papa and Joshua. The darker it grew, the more concerned she became.

Four hours later, right after Jule had trimmed the wicks, Joshua bounded up the spiral staircase of the high tower, calling her name in an anxious tone. Alarmed, she met him at the top of the iron steps.

"Is everything all right?" she asked, searching his face. "Where have you and Papa been so long?"

Her brother, a long-legged boy of fifteen, stepped into the lantern room. In the light, she could see the day had taken its toll on him.

"What's wrong?" she asked, feeling agitation wind through her body.

"Give me a moment to breathe," Joshua replied with a scowl. "I'm bone-tired, and I'm taking over the lighthouse tonight."

"No, you're not," she said firmly. "You need your rest. Please, tell me what happened today. I know something is wrong."

His face instantly softened. "Papa has pneumonia."

"How do you know?" she demanded. "Oh, I'm sorry. I'll be quiet and listen. It's just I have been so worried."

He nodded and offered a grim smile. "Papa got real sick on the boat—couldn't breathe and had an awful fever. Against his wishes, I went on to Galveston and forced him to see a doctor."

Jule knew very well the problem her brother must have had urging Papa to seek medical help. But Joshua had one strong advantage: he resembled their mother—large-boned, strong, and determined.

"He argued with me, even threatened to thrash me, but he was too weak to put up much of a fight. A friend of Mason's recognized Papa and offered to drive us to the doctor in his wagon—or I don't know what I would have done."

"Praise God. What happened at the doctor's?"

"He told Papa to get to bed and stay there." Joshua swallowed hard and took a deep breath. A lock of black hair fell across his forehead. "He's real sick, Jule. I'm afraid for him."

She reached for her brother, and he allowed her to hold him. "I saw him cough up blood, and his breathing sounds like a foghorn." Joshua paused as if stifling any urge to cry. He pulled away and towered almost a foot taller. "Go to Papa. Mama most likely needs help in keeping cool cloths on him."

Jule nodded, but as much as she wanted to help Mama, Joshua looked exhausted and was most likely hungry. Mama and Jule didn't need both of their men sick. "I want to do what I can," she began, "but I will return shortly. You tended the light for two nights in a row then lit out at sunrise with the fishing boat. You can't go on day and night sleeping a few hours here and there, Joshua, and we can't have you laid up, too."

He stiffened. "I'm the man of the house while Papa is sick."

"I know, and I appreciate all the things you do, but the lighthouse responsibilities are mine. Believe me, you will have plenty to keep you busy with fishing."

Joshua failed to respond, no doubt deep in thought about what lay ahead. Jule stood on her tiptoes and placed a kiss on his cheek.

"I've been praying," he finally said.

She smiled into his boyish face. "Good. As soon as I get back, we can pray together."

"All right, Jule." He shifted and took a deep breath. "I'm not ready for Papa to die."

Joshua's words nearly caused her to weep. "Neither am I. We will pray for healing and trust in God's peace."

※

A short while later, Jule hurried down the stairs. All the while she prayed for God to spare her father. They all knew Papa's condition had grown worse over the past weeks, but they had been afraid to talk about it. Part of the problem stemmed from the fact they lived an isolated life on the Bolivar Peninsula and relied heavily upon each other. Papa, Mama, Joshua, and Jule were more than family; they were close friends.

Once in the house, the sight of Papa lying in bed with his eyes closed devastated Jule. She expected to see him frail and weak, but she wasn't prepared to see his skin a ghastly shade of white. It looked like the bleached sand piled along the shoreline, and she didn't like it at all.

"What can I do?" she asked her mother.

Mama did not take her gaze from Papa. She dipped a cloth in a basin of water and gently patted his face. "I cannot leave him," she said. "Next to the Lord, your papa comes first."

Jule wrapped her arms around her mother's shoulders. "I understand. I will clean up from dinner, make sure Joshua has eaten, then tend the lighthouse."

"Thank you," her mother whispered, reaching up to pat Jule's hand, but still keeping her eyes on her husband of twenty-one years.

"Joshua said he has pneumonia," Jule said softly.

Her mother nodded and went about cooling his face.

"Did the doctor give him any medicine?" Jule pressed her lips together to keep from crying.

Mama nodded again, then her shoulders raised and lowered as heavy sobs racked her body.

"Oh, Mama, we must pray for God to heal him." Jule hugged her mother's shoulders in an effort to comfort her. For a brief moment, Mama allowed herself to cry.

"Yes," her mother managed, gaining control. "We all will pray. . . because the next twenty-four hours are the most critical."

Jule silently agreed. Early in the day, she had eagerly anticipated the future. But now that night had fallen, her life and the lives of those she loved looked bleak and frightening.

Chapter 6

Jule toiled during the night, keeping the wicks trimmed and wiping soot from the tower windows. Normally she slept a few hours between the lighthouse responsibilities, but not this night. While the wicks burned, she repeatedly hastened down the spiral steps to check on her father. She couldn't sleep. She dare not for fear Mama would need her to help with him. None of the family members found any rest, and all expected an even longer day ahead. By daybreak Papa's condition had not changed; if anything, he had grown worse.

To Jule, every breath became a prayer. Papa's fever had to subside; she could think of nothing but his recovery. She felt pity for her brother, who had suddenly assumed the weight of their father's illness and the financial burdens of the family. Mama, seeing Joshua's dilemma, sent him out with the fishing boat to keep him busy while they waited. Toward sunset, after Joshua returned with a good catch, Papa broke into a sweat and the fever subsided. Even as tired as they all felt, their exuberance rang from the rooftops.

In the days following, Mama refused to leave Papa's side for longer than a few minutes. She prepared meals and kept the house tidy, but little else. Joshua left each morning at sunrise with the fishing boat and helped supply the family with the extra income desperately needed for Papa's medicine. Jule minded the lighthouse at night and kept the brass polished and the Fresnel lens clean by day. She hauled buckets of kerosene from the fuel house up the one hundred twenty-five stairs, but not once did she regret the hard work. It kept her mind from Papa's illness and Mason's absence. Fortunately, Galveston Bay stayed relatively calm, a blessing for the hurricane season.

After four weeks, Papa, with Joshua's aid, emerged from his bed and sat on the front porch to watch the sea. Outwardly he joked about his family taking care of him and the easy life they were letting him live. But sometimes when he gazed out over the water, Jule saw his eyes moisten, and he never ceased to thank them for their love and care.

⨾⨾

"Tell us another one, Captain," one of the crewmen called out. "What about the time you sailed around the cape and ended up dumping your cargo to save the ship?"

Mason gave the toothless man a wry smile. How well he remembered his first voyage around Cape Horn. For five days, he and his crew had battled ferocious storms with high-speed gales and nearly lost the clipper and the men, along with his father's goods.

He glanced up into the starless night. "No more stories tonight; I need to get some sleep." After giving a few instructions to the crewmen who would be on duty during the hours before sunrise, he moved to the helm and allowed his sights to drink in the rhythm of the sea.

This voyage had already taken longer than he anticipated. Initially, he had made good time, arriving in New York in four days and then reaching Liverpool, England, in two and a half weeks. However, delays in England had kept them docked for five more days, which gave some of his men plenty of time to indulge in drinking, fighting, and the like. He seized the opportunity to purchase Jule a set of English bone china and several yards of fine lace for his mother.

Two and a half weeks later the *Flying Fish* sailed back into New York harbor and unloaded the tea and several pieces of furniture. He sent a wire to his father informing him of the ship's schedule, but the load of coal arrived two days later with an additional request to deliver a portion of it to South Carolina. The seller offered a handsome price—one not to be rejected. Mason felt certain he could make up some of the extra days with a good wind. He'd told Jule the voyage would take two months, so he could surprise her by arriving home early. If the trip continued as planned, he'd be docking into Galveston Bay more than four days ahead of schedule.

Mason watched the waves lap up against the sides—higher with each one that slapped against his vessel. He could smell the storm, too.

315

Uneasiness sped through him, an all-too-familiar surging of blood racing through his veins. His crew called it an extra sense, but Mason referred to the ominous feeling as a foreshadowing of things to come. Every sea captain yearned for high winds to carry his sails, but no one wanted to face a storm's fury. The intensity of these gusty winds alarmed him, and the sooner they reached the South Carolina harbor and unloaded, the sooner he'd return to Jule.

"You smell it, don't ya?" his first mate said.

Mason heaved a sigh. He hadn't heard the broad-shouldered man approach. "Yes, Pete, I do. It's more than the waves picking up and blowing us along."

Neither man said a word. They had been together through bad weather many times, but sharing danger didn't make an impending storm any easier.

"Order more men aloft to the rigging; replace the sails with the storm canvas," Mason said quietly. "The wind is increasing, and don't hesitate to pull in the topmast sails if it reaches forty knots."

"Aye, sir."

Mason studied the barometer and saw it had dropped. He believed in being ready for bad weather. "Make sure the rigging is repaired and the lifelines strung, too. Have a couple of crewmen check on the load of coal. We can't have it shifting during a storm."

Mason peered again at the waves. Through the lantern light, he could see the whitecaps churning. "I'm going to lie down for a few hours while you take the wheel. Wake me if the wind reaches twenty-five knots." With a wry smile, he added, "I'll most likely be awake anyway."

Descending the steps to his quarters, Mason realized sleep would not come. He wanted to be at the wheel—to steer his ship across the water and into the wind. And with a storm, he needed the navigation tools at his fingertips.

He remembered spending almost thirty hours at the wheel during gale winds at Cape Horn. Mason didn't care to repeat that feat on his last voyage.

He lit a lantern on his mahogany desk and pushed aside his chair, too restless to sit. A map of the voyage from Galveston Bay up along the East Coast to New York harbor and across the Atlantic to England lay sprawled out before him. They were off the coast of Maryland, but not close to shore. Daily, he'd been marking their journey and counting the days until he could return to Jule. What he wouldn't give for a lighthouse this night.

Opening his log atop the map, he scanned the details of his five-day delay in Liverpool and then the extra day in New York. He'd carefully added the additional port in South Carolina before sailing into Galveston, but now a storm threatened to detain them once more. This all endangered his reputation for speed.

From the corner of his eye, holding the map in place, he detected his Bible. A marker was all he'd used it for since boarding ship. Not once had he opened the Scriptures, and his prayer life amounted to rounding up the crewmen after sunrise to ask God's blessing upon the day. Regret riddled him. He reached for the leather binding, but as his fingers touched upon its grainy cover, the *Flying Fish* lunged sideways. In the next instant, Mason climbed the steps to take his position at the weather rail, all thoughts centered on the safety of his ship and crew.

Shortly after midnight, strong gales picked up more momentum and whipped the vessel about. Waves, almost as high as the ship, began to crash against the deck. Crewmen standing in knee-deep water and dressed in oil slickers tied themselves to their posts to keep from being washed overboard as the ship bucked with the storm's violence. Three sailors manned the bilge pump to remove water from the lower decks, while more men balanced on footropes to take in additional sails. Mason saw no choice but to change course. He had to turn the ship away from the wind in a complete circle.

Just before sunrise, gales approaching eighty knots dumped tons of green-gray water on the ship and its crew. The ocean roared like a devouring dragon bent on consuming them. A fourth man scrambled to help with the bilge pump while Mason, Pete, and another crewman at the wheel fought the waves' pressure against the rudder.

Only the lowest staysail and the lower topsails remained to drive the *Flying Fish*.

Oh, Lord, remember my men, Mason prayed. Realization gripped its icy fingers around him. When had he last prayed, truly prayed from his heart? Amid the storm's fury, Mason remembered an old Bible story. The Old Testament account stated how Jonah ran from God to keep from preaching to the pagan city of Nineveh. Jonah thought he could live his life apart from God. During a violent storm on the high seas, Jonah sensed the high winds were because of his disobedience to God and asked the ship's captain to throw him overboard to save the lives of those on board. God had a fish swallow Jonah and kept him inside its belly for three days—plenty of time for him to consider his sins and his rebellion.

Heavenly Father, Mason's mind shouted, *I am guilty of running from You. I have left You behind while I pursued my own glory. Time and again, You have rescued me from the jaws of death, and I have given You nothing in return but empty phrases of gratitude. Oh, please do not destroy these men when I am the one to blame. Lord Jesus, only You can command the winds to cease. Only You.*

Tormented with guilt and remorse, Mason winced from the vivid memories of the disrespect he'd shown his parents. The times he'd mocked the captain and ignored his mother. Everything they did had been for Mason's benefit. Their hard work in building the Channing empire resulted from the love they held for their son. All they had belonged to him. How selfish of him to not appreciate them more fully. And Jule...so often he took her for granted. She should have been escorted to plays and elegant dinners—the things she had never enjoyed.

Father, forgive me, for I am a sinful man.

If God so graciously spared his life and his crew, he would never again ignore his blessings.

The winds raged, shredding the thick canvas sails until they looked like helpless kite strings. The ocean belched with rage, dipping the vessel into a downward spiral then tossing it into the path of one wave after another. The wet and cold settled in his bones as he gripped the wheel to keep the *Flying Fish* afloat.

The ship creaked like a brittle matchstick.

"She's going down!" Pete shouted frantically.

"God, no!" Mason shouted. "I beg of You, spare us!"

Jule awoke with a start. She'd been sleeping during the four-hour period before trimming the wicks. She glanced about. The lamps were in order. What had startled her?

With a gasp, she remembered the nightmare. Once again, Mason battled a storm. She could see him at the wheel while the battered ship dove in and out of giant waves like a drowning man gulping for air. In one swoop, the ocean swallowed him beneath its depths.

Oh, Lord, take care of my Mason, she prayed. *Bring him back home to me.*

Chapter 7

July slipped into the torrid days of August. Jule thanked God daily for the constantly blowing breezes off the ocean that helped cool the air. Papa improved at a much slower pace than the family desired, but the doctor warned his recovery could take several weeks. The family once more resumed their high spirits, especially Joshua, who thrived in his position with the fishing boat. His joking and teasing kept them amused, and when he delivered his daily catch to Galveston, he habitually brought home a tasty treat or newspaper for Papa.

One morning, Joshua gave up a few hours of fishing to transport Jule to Galveston for a shopping trip with Esther Channing. Before Mason had left, he'd given Jule money to purchase whatever she needed to fashion her wedding gown, and Jule felt it only proper to consult his mother. Mrs. Channing assisted her in selecting a beautiful white silk fabric, yards of imported lace, and hundreds of tiny pearl-like beads.

Jule marveled at how her relationship with Mason's mother deepened. She found Mrs. Channing warm and friendly, quite different from the way she had first treated Jule. Later, Esther invited her to spend a few days in Galveston and take in the opera, partake in elegant dining, be fitted for new gowns, and enjoy a host of other niceties available to those who could afford them. Jule declined the invitation and those that followed with a meticulously written regret. Until Papa fully regained his health, she must fulfill her responsibilities at the lighthouse.

Jule stole moments from each day to sew her wedding dress while counting the days until Mason returned. This particular morning, while stitching the tiny white beadwork into place on the bodice of her wedding gown, Jule hummed a little song Mama had sung to her as a child. She couldn't remember the words, only the tune. With a heavy swoosh of the fabric, she grasped it close to her body and envisioned the admiring look on Mason's face when she wore it. The wrists and hem needed beadwork as well, and then the dress would be ready.

She expected Mason home any day. She'd hoped he would have arrived by now with the advantage of good winds, yet the uncertainty of the weather and the additional cargo taken on in New York could have easily detained him.

A rap at the door aroused her attention. Her family seldom had visitors unless a ship's crew sought refuge during a storm or a curious government official desired a tour of the lighthouse. Neither was the case today. She listened as Papa greeted the caller. Delighted to hear the deep booming voice of Mr. Channing, she hurried to the door.

"Mr. Channing, how nice to see you," she said to the distinguished-looking gentleman. "What a pleasant surprise." She loved his kindly mannerisms. In fact, she'd never seen him as a tyrant like Mason claimed. Over the weeks of his absence, she had begun to wonder if Mason had misjudged his father.

The elderly man removed his captain's hat and extended his hand to grasp hers. "It is good to see you, too, dear. I apologize for not checking on you or your father before now, and I am glad to see he is recovering." He nodded at Papa. "Mr. Portier, if you need anything, please let me know. I'd like to help in any way I can."

Papa smiled. "Thank you. I have a good family, and they're taking excellent care of me. Soon I'll be climbing those lighthouse steps again and casting a fishing net alongside Joshua."

Mr. Channing turned his attention to Jule. "May we talk? I need to discuss something with you."

She saw the lines etched around his eyes—tired, reddened eyes, the familiar sign of worry often seen in Mason. Instantly dread seized her. "What about?" she asked.

He toyed with the bill of his cap. "I'd rather we talk about the matter inside."

"Mason?" she whispered, fear rising like a change of tide.

"Yes. . .it's about Mason," he replied, meeting her gaze. "Please, I'd like for us to sit."

Papa grasped the sides of his chair to stand, but Jule touched his shoulder and attempted a faint smile. "No need, Papa. I will show Mr. Channing into the parlor."

Jule's heart sounded as though it might burst from her chest. She willed it to stop, silently screamed for it to slow down. *It might not be bad news,* she told herself. Nevertheless, she shook uncontrollably.

"Good morning, Mr. Channing," Mama said, crossing the parlor from the kitchen. She smiled then looked back and forth between the captain and Jule. "What is wrong?"

Jule took a deep breath. "Mr. Channing needs to talk to me about Mason."

Her mother wrung her hands and moistened her lips. "I see. Would you care for some coffee?"

"No, thank you, Mrs. Portier."

"Well. . .I will join Papa on the front porch."

Somehow Jule managed to usher Mr. Channing to the sofa and seat herself in a chair near him. She perched on the edge, as all proper ladies should, but so did the captain. She felt dazed. Numb. She had to learn the news about her beloved Mason.

"Please, sir. What do you know about Mason?"

He tugged on his silver beard and pulled a folded piece of paper from his jacket pocket. "Last evening I received a wire from a business associate in South Carolina." He paused and slowly unfolded the paper. Without glancing at it, he captured her anxious gaze. "Mason and his crew left New York on schedule. He should have been back before now, but a storm off the coast of Virginia must have overtaken them." He offered the wire to her.

Bile rose in her throat. The paper slipped through her fingers, and Mr. Channing retrieved it from the faded rug.

"Would you like for me to read it to you?" he inquired.

Jule shook her head. "No, sir. This. . .this has to be as difficult for you as it is for me." She took it from him and began to read:

To Thomas Channing:
    Captain Mason Channing and crew of the Flying Fish *feared*

lost during storm off Virginia coast. No trace of ship found. All presumed dead. Please advise.

Jule blinked back the stinging tears and held the missive to her heart. It could not be true. There must have been a mistake. She crumpled the paper in her hands then smoothed it out and reread it.

"They haven't found any of the ship's remains," she managed. "There's hope. Possibly an unexpected delay or Mason went ashore to make repairs."

"I pray to God you are right," he quietly replied.

She shuddered. Tears splashed against her cheeks, and she buried her face in her hands. "I pray for him every day. I can't believe God would take him from us. Oh, Lord," she sobbed, "Mason and his whole crew."

The captain stood and pulled her to him. He spoke in a tone of comfort and hope, but in her sorrow, Jule only heard the soft timbre of his voice. Unfathomable grief overwhelmed her. Uncharacteristically, she openly shed an ocean of tears for the man she loved.

"I, too, refuse to believe he is gone," Mr. Channing finally said. "My son is the best clipper captain around. He understands the ways of the sea, and he vowed not to take any chances."

Mason had made Jule the same promise.

With great effort, she lifted her head from his chest. "I will never give up hope—never."

"Neither will I. We must pray and trust in God's provision." He brushed aside a single tear from his weathered cheek.

Nodding, she bit down hard on her lower lip and reached for his hand still clasped firmly around her shoulder. "Until he returns, I will keep my nightly post in the lighthouse. No ship will ever lose its way because of me. Someday. . .someday Mason will see the light as he enters the bay, and I will be waiting."

❧

Jule stumbled through the following days. By night she tended the light, rarely sleeping between her duties. By day, she busied herself in helping Mama and Papa. When idleness approached, she walked the beach— always searching for signs of a boat heading to Bolivar Point. Mama and Joshua offered to take over the lighthouse responsibilities, but Jule could not relinquish the job for even one night.

Mama finished Jule's wedding dress and tucked it away in a trunk. Jule could not bear to look at it or talk about the probability of Mason lost at sea. The once-open relationship she had shared with her mother vanished as Jule retreated into her own quiet world.

Papa voiced his growing concern about her listlessness and lack of appetite. "Mason would not want you to pine away for him," her father said. "We all love you too much to see you this way. Please, eat and keep up your strength. If God wills for Mason to return, he will not want to see you pale and thin, but healthy and beautiful. He remembered you as lovely as a crystal blue sea; that is how he would want to see you again."

Papa made sense, and she considered his wise words. Jule saw how hard her family worked to ease her grief, saying and doing special things to let her know of their concern. Joshua made it a point to bring her favorite lemon drops from Galveston. Mama added her favorite breads and vegetables to their meals, but Jule found it difficult to abide by their wishes. Her stomach seemed to churn constantly, ready to revolt at a moment's notice.

Her solace became prayer and meditation upon God's Word. One night at her post in the lighthouse, she turned to Psalm 121 and felt God's loving arms around her:

> *I will lift up mine eyes unto the hills, from whence cometh my help. My help cometh from the Lord, which made heaven and earth. He will not suffer thy foot to be moved; he that keepeth thee will not slumber. Behold, he that keepeth Israel shall neither slumber nor sleep. The Lord is thy keeper: the Lord is thy shade upon thy right hand. The sun shall not smite thee by day, nor the moon by night. The Lord shall preserve thee from all evil: he shall preserve thy soul. The Lord shall preserve thy going out and thy coming in from the time forth, and even for evermore.*

"Thank You, Lord," she whispered, clutching the treasured Bible to her heart. "No matter what happens or how long it takes for Mason to return, I will rest in Your shadow and trust in Your care."

Chapter 8

Mason struggled to open his eyes, but each time he made the
attempt, pain seared through his head. He craved water, but he
couldn't voice his thirst. He heard voices, but he couldn't
respond. Frustrated and desperately seeking answers to the fate of his men
and the *Flying Fish*, he tried again to contact those around him. Useless.
His world spun like a whirlpool, and he reeled in the center of confusion
and pain. He struggled in the maze to lift his hands, lost the battle, and
slipped into unconsciousness.

When Mason finally emerged from the fog and his eyes fluttered
open, he focused on his surroundings. His immediate world looked small,
and as the cloud slowly lifted from his vision, he studied the scant items
in the room. He lay on a bed covered in clean, threadbare linens. Over
him, a faded quilt in pink and blue was tucked beneath his chin, which
he detested. Mason loathed coverlets around his face, but he could not
loosen them. Fear gripped him. Paralyzed. From below his chest, his body
seemed numb, devoid of any feeling. Is this what his disobedience to God
had cost? Death would be a blessing compared to living his life maimed
by his own folly. Losing his desire to scrutinize the room, he closed his
eyes and floated with the rest of his body into blissful sleep.

Sometime later he awoke again. Glancing about, Mason saw the sun
streaming through a solitary window, and from its angle, he estimated
the time as midday. Again he allowed his head to clear and determined
not to sink into the unconscious state that provided no answers to those
questions plaguing his mind.

I'm alive. The sudden thought startled him. *God spared my wretched soul. But for what and why? Where am I, and what about my crew. . .and the ship?*

The details of the violent storm and his plea for God to save them flashed vividly through his mind. How had he gotten to this place? Some of his crew must have survived. The last thing he remembered were his desperate cries to God and the realization of his sinful pride.

Mason's gaze trailed to the lone Bible near his bed. He turned his head to view it, but a fierce pounding left huge beads of sweat dripping down the sides of his face. Slowly, he pulled his hand from beneath the quilt and coaxed the coverlet from his chin. He gently examined his brow with his fingers and found a bandage wrapped around his forehead so snugly that he couldn't budge it. Tracing his fingers back across the top of his head, he felt his hair matted together, most likely with dried blood.

A recurring nightmare of him paralyzed crossed his mind and sickened him. Swallowing hard, he fought the pain to examine each arm and leg to make sure his limbs were intact. Mason had seen enough good seamen crippled and looked upon with pity. He deserved no less; God knew his unfaithfulness. He felt a thick bandage around his chest, most likely signifying broken ribs, which accounted for his painful breathing. With praises of thanks on his lips, Mason closed his eyes and tried one more time to recall what happened on board the *Flying Fish*. Nothing. The not knowing disturbed him. He, Captain Mason Channing, clipper master of the seas, had no inkling how he had reached land and who might have survived.

Releasing a heavy breath, he once more marveled at how God had seen fit to save him.

A few moments later, when he'd gained enough strength to open his eyes again, he looked about the room. A straight, ladder-back chair rested against the wall by the window, its cane seat in sore need of repair. Beside the bed stood a table with a Bible. He'd noted this before. Indeed, this haven of repose was small. If he stretched, he could touch the opposite wall with his toes.

Again the welfare of his crewmen ranked utmost in his mind.

The door creaked open, and a matronly woman entered. Clad in a gray, homespun dress, she smiled. Despite her homeliness, in Mason's eyes only Jule or his mother would have looked lovelier.

"Good afternoon, Captain Channing," she said. "I see you have decided to join us."

He braved a faint grin. "God has brought me back from the dead, ma'am." His first attempts at speaking sounded foreign, strained.

"For certain He has." She brightened. "My name is Nelly Shatterman, and I've been takin' care of you since your crew landed and brought you to my home."

"My crew?" Mason wet his lips and started to lift his head, but the excruciating pain forced him back to the pillow. He groaned and closed his eyes while he waited for the throbbing to ease.

"Ma'am. . .do you know what happened? I don't remember anything except the storm."

She placed a large hand on his forehead, and Mason was surprised to discover that the action felt comforting. "Good, no fever," she murmured. "Captain, you have laid in this bed for ten days, and before then you were lost at sea with a broken ship for nigh on to a week. That's all I know. Your first mate has been here twice a day checkin' on you, and he'll be back this evening."

Mason swallowed hard. The energy spent since he opened his eyes had taken its toll. Gratefully though, some of his crew had reached safety, and Pete had looked in on him every day. A tear slipped from his eye. He didn't deserve kindness with the way he had dishonored God.

"Drink a little water," Nelly urged. He hadn't noticed the mug in her hand. "I know it will hurt, but I will support your head a little to help."

Mason tried to oblige, but he nearly passed out. It took several long moments for the water to trickle down his throat. Vaguely he remembered the same procedure.

"Now rest," Nelly said. "It's a miracle you are alive."

Mason didn't need any persuasion. He easily succumbed to the wave of blackness sweeping over him. Much later, he opened his eyes to flickering candlelight on the table beside him. He'd been dreaming about the captain reading the Bible. As gruff as the man ofttimes appeared, Thomas Channing loved the Lord. Mason hoped he might soon be able to tell his father how much he loved him.

Blinking, he felt determined to find out if Pete had been there since he last awoke. There were so many things he needed to know.

"Cap'n?" a voice whispered.

Mason sensed a new surge of energy. "Pete?" he asked.

The lone chair scraped across the wood floor, and he saw his old friend smiling. "You old rascal," Mason said, with a faint grin. "You sure look good. What happened? What about the crew? Where are we?"

Pete chuckled. "Slow down, and I'll tell you everything. Otherwise, you'll wear yourself out and won't hear a thing until morning."

Mason started to nod, but the pain in his head stopped him. "All right," he whispered. "The storm is all I remember."

"The mainmast snapped in two and fell on you," Pete began. "You were knocked out cold, but I couldn't tend to you for the wind and water. You were lucky to have been tied to a strong mast, or you'd have been washed away."

"The men on the footropes?" Mason uttered.

Pete paused. "Cap'n, they're gone; nothing I could do to save 'em."

"How many?"

"Four crewmen and one unaccounted for," Pete replied, shaking his head. "But the rest of us survived. I thought the wind would tear her in two, but God answered our prayers."

Mason arched a brow. "Prayer? In all the years we've been sailing together, I've never been able to interest you in God or prayer."

Pete removed his cap and laid it beside the Bible. "Didn't have to," he said. "Always had you to do the prayin', and I reaped the benefits. But you were unconscious and maybe dead, and with me bein' first mate and all, well, I had to do the askin'. Cap'n, I ain't ashamed to say I cried out to the Lord and told Him I'd rather He have my soul and live with Him than die and pay the devil his due. I told Him most of the crew didn't know Him either and needed another chance."

Mason wanted to laugh, but it hurt to move. "It's worth this pain to know you're a believer."

"That ain't all, Cap'n. No sooner than I prayed, the wind began to slowly die down—not all at once, just nice and easy. I laughed and cried at the same time. The men acted like I had taken leave of my senses." Pete smacked his leg. "And I gave up drinkin' and cursin', too. I should have listened to you a long time ago."

"I'm real glad for you, Pete. You know, I wouldn't be much of a man if I didn't tell you the truth." Mason closed his eyes and paused; the pain in his head seemed to overpower him.

"Maybe I should leave you," Pete suggested. "You need to sleep."

"No, I want to tell you this. Lately, I'd been thinking I didn't need God. Got to believing all those hero tales you fellows tell about me. But during the storm, I asked God to forgive me for not putting Him first."

"Well, you and me got a real reason to live now, don't we?" Pete laughed out loud. "I've been tellin' the men about the Lord. Some are payin' attention and some aren't, but no matter to me. I'm just glad to be alive."

"You're a saint, Pete, a better man than me." Mason paused to catch his breath. "Tell me about the other men and the condition of the *Flying Fish*."

Pete scratched a whiskery chin. "Once the wind died down and the sun rose, we saw how much damage was done to the ship. I figured out where we were, but the sails were in threads. We all got busy and tried mending them the best we could and somehow got to land."

"And where are we?"

"Along the coast of Georgia. Ain't much around here but gators and Mrs. Shatterman. No way to send word to your father or Miss Portier. We're over three weeks late, and the ship still needs more repairs before she's seaworthy. Plus, Cap'n Channing has some repairin' of his own to do."

"You boys get the ship ready, and I'll be well enough to sail home."

Pete smiled. "Aye, Cap'n. I knew you'd say that. Is there anything I can do fer ya?"

Mason knew what he wanted, desperately. "Pete, would you read to me from the Bible?"

Pete picked up the Book as though it were made of gold. "Thanks to you, I can read. What do you want to hear?"

Mason closed his eyes. "Just open it and read whatever the Lord gives you."

Pete let his fingers flip through the pages. "Here it is, Captain, Psalm 121." He cleared his throat, and his voice sounded like thunder in the distance. "I will lift up mine eyes unto the hills, from whence cometh my help. My help cometh from the Lord, which made heaven and earth.

He will not suffer thy foot to be moved; he that keepeth thee will not slumber. Behold, he that keepeth Israel shall neither slumber nor sleep. The Lord is thy keeper: the Lord is thy shade upon thy right hand. The sun shall not smite thee by day, nor the moon by night. The Lord shall preserve thee from all evil: he shall preserve thy soul. The Lord shall preserve thy going out and thy coming in from the time forth, and even for evermore."

Mason relished the words. He sensed a personal message from the Lord—a confirmation of His faithfulness, even though Mason had strayed. With His almighty hand, He had protected Mason's body and soul, not simply through the eye of the storm, but through eternity.

"Thank you," Mason managed, feeling weary and noting he needed to sleep. "Until I can gain enough strength, would you read me this psalm when you visit?"

"Aye, I'd be honored." Pete set the Bible back on the table and picked up his hat. "I best be goin' now. You tend to getting well."

Mason smiled and closed his eyes. A picture of his Jule danced across his mind. His precious jewel became the last thing he remembered before allowing sleep to engulf him.

Jule climbed the spiral staircase of the brick-and-iron lighthouse. The sound of her shoes clacking against the metal steps magnified around her. It had become an accustomed sound, yet a lonesome one—matching the solitary beat of her heart. She refused to believe Mason had been lost at sea. He had been through many a storm, and God had brought him safely into harbor. Hope. Trust. The only things allowing her to put one foot in front of the other. On she ascended the circling stairs, listening to the single tap of her footsteps.

Once the lamps were lit, she heard Joshua calling her name, as was his custom, and heard him hurrying up to see her.

"Won't you have dinner with us?" he asked, once he reached the lantern room. His face was flushed from running up the stairs.

Jule shook her head. "No, thank you. I'm not really hungry tonight."

"What if I brought a plate for both of us, and we could eat together?"

Guilt gnawed at her, knowing Joshua fretted over her health, as did Mama and Papa. She offered a smile. "Of course."

He grinned back, his brown eyes sparkling. "Thanks, Jule." He turned to leave then hesitated. "I'm worried about you."

She couldn't look at him. "I know you are, and I appreciate the concern, but everything will be fine when Mason comes home."

Silence.

"He isn't coming home. It has been more than four weeks since his ship disappeared."

Jule shook her head and gazed out at the gathering darkness. She'd overheard the rumors Joshua had reported to Mama—an angel now tended the light at Bolivar Point, a young woman who had lost her sea captain.

Pretending to ignore her brother's words, she carefully chose her reply. "I think it would be perfectly lovely to share dinner up here with you."

Standing on the catwalk, Jule watched the sun rise. The day of her wedding would come in one week, but Mason still hadn't returned. The family didn't talk about it; they omitted any mention of his name. She tried harder each day to smile and feign gladness for the things God had given her, but deep inside she ached. At times she wanted to beg God to take away her pain and restore her joy, but she would not give up on Mason's return.

As the colors of pink and purple spread to blue, she watched Joshua's fishing boat bob on the waves. She knew Papa studied him, too, so anxious to resume the life he had known before his illness. Twice he had climbed the lighthouse steps and assisted her during the watch. Soon he would want to claim it again, but she could not bear to leave her post.

Melancholia blanketed her this morning. Her eyes were dry, yet she felt her very lifeblood had been drained away. She closed her eyes and recited Psalm 121.

With a heavy heart, she turned to step inside the lantern room, but a second boat caught her eye. She studied it closely, curiously, even willing it to be her Mason.

Instead of rowing past the end of the peninsula, it neared the shore. The boat stopped, and a man waded onto dry land. With her heart thumping wildly, she let out a cry.

Jule lifted her skirts and rushed down the stairs. Unable to get to the bottom fast enough, she attempted to contain her racing heart and think clearly. But she had seen him. She recognized his gait and the way he carried himself.

Flinging open the lighthouse door, she saw the man approach the house running. She saw the tousle of sandy hair.

"Mason!" The mere utterance of his name sent chills up her arms. Her legs felt weak, yet somehow she hurried to meet him.

Mason waved, and her elation gave way to tears. Moments later, his arms circled her, and he was caressing her, kissing her. She quivered at his touch, hoping against hope this was not a dream.

"It is you," she breathed, brushing her fingers across his face. "I knew you would come back; I knew you were not lost at sea."

He pulled her close. "Nearly, my darling. If not for God, I would have surely perished."

Jule gazed into his deep, blue-gray eyes, no longer stormy but calm and peaceful. "He has brought you back to me," she said. "Thank You, Lord."

"He has done more than brought back the man," Mason said, gazing into her eyes. "He has taken away my proud spirit. Oh, my sweet, precious Jule, can you ever forgive me?"

"Of course, my love. How could I not? I prayed God would speak to you," she replied, marveling in the difference in his calm features.

He pulled her tightly against him. "I spoke with Father, too. The dear man has been at the docks every morning since he received the wire about my disappearance."

"Your parents love you, Mason, as do I."

She nestled against his chest, and her fingers entwined firmly into his. The verses that had given her strength to endure each day without him went through her mind. "God gave me a special psalm to see me through these horrible weeks," she said.

"Hmm," he replied, kissing the tip of her nose, "He gave me one, too."

"Mine is Psalm 121."

Mason smiled and lightly caressed her lips. "Jule, He gave us the same scripture. Oh, my love, we will have such a wonderful, blessed life together."

A TIME
TO LOVE

by Sally Laity

Dedication

To Jessica Leigh. . .a bright and shining light
to all who know and love her.

Special thanks to Becky Ryder, office manager, Bullards Beach State Park, for supplying a wealth of brochures and information about Coquille River Light and the surrounding area. And thank you to Bill Powell, Bandon Historical Society, for answering questions regarding some pertinent historical details. Their help was much appreciated, as was the tireless slashing of critique partner extraordinaire, Dianna Crawford. God's richest blessings to them all.

AUTHOR'S NOTE

Although a few West Coast lighthouses actually have had women keepers over the years, Coquille River Light was not among them. My thanks to the people of Bandon, Oregon, for the use of their incredibly neat lighthouse in this story. I only hope my characters performed the complicated duties required to provide safe passage to vessels as satisfactorily as did the principal keeper of that time period, James Barker, and his assistant, James Cowan. They and their families have earned my utmost respect.

Chapter 1

Oregon, Summer, 1898

Perhaps it's good news," Birdie Hastings panted. Her face, typically pink beneath her salt-and-pepper topknot, glowed even rosier after bustling across the long, wooden walkway from the mainland to the lighthouse and up its steep stairs. She held out the missive.

Eden Miles wished she could be so hopeful. She laid aside the smudged polishing rag she'd been using on the brass and copper fixtures in the lantern room and, with a nod of thanks, took the official-looking mail from the housekeeper. The older woman had been such a gift since arriving on the doorstep to help out after Eden had lost her husband. She forced a thin smile to mask the trepidation turning her insides to mush. "I suppose we can always hope, can't we, Birdie?"

"Long as there's life and breath."

Just the answer one might expect from one of the world's great optimists, Eden thought. But then, neither of them mentioned how a negative response from the secretary of the treasury could have a devastating effect on both their futures. All three of their futures, in fact. She checked out the window for four-year-old Christian while she tore the envelope's flap open.

Her towhead son was on the rocky jetty below, collecting shells left behind by the tide. As he paused to watch frolicking sandpipers and oystercatchers, the slanting rays of the setting sun gilded his hair like a halo. She returned her attention to the mail.

My dear Madam:
In answer to your request for the position of assistant keeper at
the Coquille River Light, I regret to inform you that we have not yet

reached a decision. However, the board is agreeable to an additional trial period of six months, during which you may continue the duties you have undertaken since your late husband's untimely demise. After such time, we will review your case again. If the results of your efforts prove satisfactory, and upon recommendation of Principal Keeper Rutherford, we will make our final ruling in the matter.

Yours truly,
Bradley DeVille
Fifth Auditor and Acting
Commissioner of the Revenue

"What? What?" Birdie Hastings stood wringing her hands like just-washed clothes. "Are they going to let us stay, or do we pack up?"

"To go where?" Eden asked on a desperate note. She handed over the written reply to her housekeeper and stepped out onto the parapet overlooking the broad expanse of the Pacific and the mouth of the Coquille River, with the town of Bandon on its south side. The soothing shush of ocean waves and the salt-laden breeze always helped calm her spirit.

A recommendation from Sherman Rutherford. What hope was there of that? The old bachelor made no secret of the fact that he coveted the position of assistant keeper for one of his close and qualified friends. She winced. Why, the man had been almost elated when Winslow's body had washed ashore two months ago after a failed attempt to aid the crew of a grounded schooner during a gale. But Eden was not about to give in so easily. Clinging to the knowledge that to everything there was a season, she had spent her tears and resigned herself to her loss, sure in her heart that God would neither leave nor forsake her.

Eden raised her chin with determination. She'd give the principal keeper no grounds for dismissal. She had assisted her husband often enough during the past eighteen months to know she could do the job adequately. She'd get the position. She had to. There was no alternative.

"Oh, I almost forgot," Birdie said, coming to join her. With some hesitance she took a second item from her apron pocket, obviously none too pleased to be the bearer of bad tidings. "I'm afraid another letter's come back unopened. Hard to fathom, that's for sure. Something should be done about it. Well, I'd best be starting supper." With that, the housekeeper turned and crossed to the steps, her every descending footfall creating a hollow echo in the tower's stillness.

Staring with a heavy heart at the letter she'd posted to her parents mere weeks ago, Eden sighed then tucked the envelope inside her vest and gazed down at her son. It wasn't fair, that unforgiving spirit. The child was entirely blameless in all of this, and certainly he had a right to know what limited family he possessed—especially now, in view of Winslow's accidental drowning.

As if sensing her thoughts, Christian glanced up and grinned, holding a round object aloft. "Look, Mama, a new sand dollar—a good one."

"That's wonderful, sweetheart. Time to go in and wash up. You can bring the sand dollar to show me when Mrs. Hastings brings my supper tray."

"Yes, Mama." Setting his latest treasure carefully in the tin pail with the rest of his day's collection, he brushed his hands down his suspendered trousers and grabbed the bucket's handle, then skipped after the housekeeper.

Well, no sense wasting regret on things that couldn't be changed, Eden asserted. A person here on a trial basis had better work twice as hard at keeping up her responsibilities. One never knew when inspectors would pay a surprise visit, looking for any infractions or neglect.

The smallest and last lighthouse built on the Oregon coast, Coquille River Light occupied the island of Rackleff Rock, just to the north of the port of Bandon, an important center for shipping lumber from Oregon's rich forests. Constructed of white stucco over brick with a black roof, the octagonal fog-signal building had an attached black-domed, forty-foot tower housing a lantern. Its fourth order Fresnel lens served to guide ships across the treacherous bar at the river's entrance. A one hundred fifty-foot wooden footbridge connected the light to the mainland, where a double dwelling shared by the keepers occupied the sand dunes.

Eden had loved the river light the moment she first glimpsed the Italianate Victorian design and multi-paned windows. Its small size only added to its charm. Still, the duties required to tend it were far from easy, but she did her level best to see to them all.

She lifted her gaze to the Pacific, where the cool, salty breeze stirred across the waters, cresting the tops of the choppy waves with white foam.

The fierce winter weather was just a memory, as was much of spring. But even in summer the winds could be chilly on the sunniest days, and low-hanging fog often blanketed the coastal belt in the mornings and evenings. Already, traces of mist tiptoed tentatively above the glistening surface as if testing the waters before settling down for the night. Soon long wisps of white would braid around the contours of the land, masking the shoals and sandbar where the Coquille joined the ocean.

Nearly time to light the wicks, she reminded herself. She took up the rag and dabbed it into the abrasive Tripoli powder, then resumed rubbing again.

In the light morning mist, the aged stern-wheeler *Solitude* chugged up the Pacific toward the Coquille River. Owner and captain Dane Bradbury focused intently on reading currents and surface ripples ahead as he piloted his weathered vessel over the hidden shoals that easily earned the river's mouth its reputation as one of the most dangerous along the coast.

Thick fog had forestalled an earlier arrival at Bandon. Dane had lined the ship up last night with the Coquille River Light, whose faint beam somehow pierced the murk. Its familiar signature, twenty-eight seconds of light, followed by a two-second occlusion, had kept him company through the stillness of a watch broken only by the regular pattern of blasts from the fog trumpet.

Used to sailing the north coast in all sorts of weather, Dane disliked fog the most. A ship could fight strong currents and with luck stay somewhat near course, though stern-wheelers were notorious for breaking up in gales. But locked within a veil of damp whiteness, a person could lose all perspective and doubt both instincts and instruments.

The *Solitude's* shape was reminiscent of a wedding cake, with a main deck below and a hurricane deck above. A small wheelhouse perched atop the structure, and a paddle wheel nearly as wide as the vessel itself powered it from behind. Discounting the riverboat's limitations in heavy wind, Dane knew she had many notable qualities. With her spoon-shaped bow and flat bottom, she had light draft and could proceed safely with as little as twenty inches of river beneath her when her holds were empty. Even when weighted down by three hundred tons of cargo, waist-deep water would suffice.

But as the vessel neared the river entrance, the roustabouts and other crew stood at the ready with their "grasshoppers." The long sturdy wooden spars could be lowered into mud and used like giant crutches to walk the boat over sandbars that couldn't be steered around, slid over, or smashed through.

Thankfully, none of those extremes were called for on this trip, and the stern-wheeler glided smoothly into the Coquille. Dane removed his cap and wiped a sleeve across his forehead as he eased the vessel between the inbound buoys, red ones to the right and black to his left. He calculated the hours it would take for the *Solitude* to be loaded to the guards with prime Oregon lumber before he could shove off for Seattle.

Just beyond the light, he glanced back toward the paddle wheel's wake.

His eyes fell upon a vision.

She stood on the parapet, hands resting lightly on the railing as she watched his boat pass by. A rare treat for Dane's eyes, she was slender, bewitching, her tawny hair ablaze in sunlight. . .like a princess surveying her kingdom.

He smiled to himself. The indigo vest she wore over a white shirtwaist and dark skirt appeared styled after the regulation uniforms he'd seen on other lighthouse keepers—except men wore double-breasted jackets with gold buttons. But she couldn't be the tender, or surely he'd have seen her before. Nevertheless, she did appear to belong there. His arm raised unbidden in a salute as the *Solitude* chugged on toward the port at the bend of the river.

She lifted a hand in answering wave then turned and retreated into the lantern room, where she extinguished the flame and drew the curtain.

"Whew!" Riley Baker whistled under his breath as he sauntered up the steps of the wheelhouse. "Some looker, eh? Wonder where she's been all this time."

Dane gave an unconcerned shrug to his first mate and friend, whose slack-jawed expression added a gleam to deep-set hazel eyes. The guy could pick out the prettiest gal in a crowd at a hundred paces.

"A definite improvement over Rutherford, that's for sure. Go ready the deckhands for docking, huh? We're coming up on Bandon."

The redhead snapped to. "Aye, aye, sir." But partway down the steps, he turned back and looked over his shoulder with a smirk. "That's the problem with you, man. You ain't never been the curious type."

Ignoring the remark, Dane tightened his lips. Oh, he was curious, all right. He just wasn't sure why.

On previous trips past Coquille Light, he'd glimpsed men tending the flame. Thin, balding Rutherford, with a hook nose and bony frame, and the assistant, a wiry, muscular chap with dark hair and a mustache. Wiles, Miles—something like that. He'd make a few inquiries at port, see what he could find out. After all, one liked to keep up on the lighthouse keepers who provided valuable service to men of the sea.

Steering his thoughts to a different course, he let out a long, slow breath, wondering how many more years he'd fall into that category. The *Solitude* was nigh unto seven years old and living proof of her workhorse existence. All the gimcrackery around the cabins and pilothouse, which originally had made her a delight to behold, stood diminished now that it was surrounded by peeling paint, a cracked roof, and warped decks. She'd been patched so often with materials salvaged from other ill-fated vessels, she was practically chugging along on borrowed time.

Part of him wondered if his late brother would be satisfied that he'd kept her running all this time, an attempt to fulfill the dream that had perished with him that stormy night. Then, noting an outbound steamer making its way toward the ocean, he gave a greeting blast on the five-note horn and waved.

Bandon, one of the most beautiful towns in western Oregon, sported long cypress hedges, gleaming white lily beds, and gnarled pines. The port bustled constantly with typical river traffic. Along its wharves, at least a dozen ships of assorted sizes and makes were in the various phases of loading or unloading passengers and cargo, and the familiar cacophony such activity created grew louder as the *Solitude's* engines cut off. The crew tossed heavy docking ropes to workers on the wharves, who looped them around the stout posts.

Dane left the first mate in charge of overseeing the loading of their lumber shipment while most of the crew got off to stretch their legs and partake of a meal ashore. Then he went to take care of the required permits and bills of lading. Once the official business had been concluded, he headed straight for the gangplank to relieve his friend Riley.

"Ho! Bradbury!" came a booming voice from behind him.

Turning, Dane spied the friendly, lantern-jawed face of one of the men who kept things running smoothly at the wharves. "Jeffries. How're things?"

"Not too bad." The beefy fellow approached, a calloused hand held out in welcome, and the two men greeted each other warmly. "Things have been hopping here, but I s'pose that's normal for this time of year."

Dane nodded. "I noticed there were more tubs around than usual. And the new warehouse is up and running already."

"Yep. Town's growin', all right. New folks movin' into Bandon right and left, wantin' to get in on the boom in the lumber and coal trade."

"It's like that up and down the coast," Dane said. "All the settlements are filling up, spreading out. Speaking of filling up, guess I should see to my load. Always good to see you, pal."

"Same here."

But before either of them had taken more than a few steps, Dane turned back. "Say, Jeffries."

The man halted. "What can I do for ya?"

"Did I see a new keeper at the light? Rutherford retire or something?" Dane asked, assuming a nonchalant stance.

An offhanded grin widened the man's whiskered cheeks. "Oh, I reckon you mean Mrs. Miles. Nope, she's been here all along, only she's a widow now. Her husband drowned couple o' months ago."

The news stunned Dane.

"Matter of fact," Jeffries went on, "there's a load of supplies for the lighthouse that just came in. Rutherford's away on family business this week, or he'd be pickin' them up."

Dane checked the progress of the lumber being loaded and knew he'd be sitting around for a good spell before pulling out of port. "I, uh... reckon I could row 'em out there." He kneaded his jaw, assuring himself he was merely helping out. "Unless somebody else is planning to get them to her, that is."

Jeffries smirked. "Heaven knows, there's a passel of guys here who'd like nothin' better than to go out just to gawk at that pretty lady, but I don't trust none of 'em enough to go there alone. Her husband kept a pretty tight rein on her, never lettin' her get friendly with the townsfolk."

"All the more reason," Dane said, clapping a hand on the stout shoulder, "to make sure she doesn't run out of something. I'll get that stuff to her, for her dead husband's sake."

But as he followed the townsman up the rise, he wondered if that was his whole reason.

Chapter 2

Eden stifled a yawn as she saw to the morning routine of trimming the wicks for night and polishing the hundreds of glass prisms on the Fresnel lens. Then she checked and reset the clockwork mechanism which revolved around the lamp before sweeping her way down the stairs of the lighthouse. She'd washed the walls and floors two days ago, plus scrubbed the windows and their recesses, so today's chores would be fewer. She opened the log and recorded the current weather conditions and duties she'd performed since her last posting. Usually she didn't have sole responsibility for the light for two entire weeks in one stretch, so the principal keeper's expected return in a few days would come as a welcome relief.

Upon reaching the landing, she heard a knock at the door. She untied her linen work apron and hung it on its hook on her way to answer the summons.

A stranger stood there, tall and dark, with a trim muscular frame. He might have seemed imposing if his weathered face had not crinkled into an amiable smile... one somehow familiar, though she couldn't quite place him.

His grin broadened, lending a friendly twinkle to eyes gray as dusk. He removed his cap. "Mrs. Miles? Haydon Jeffries at the docks asked me to bring you some supplies. With Rutherford being away, we didn't want you to run low on anything. Dane Bradbury's the name."

"Y–yes," Eden stammered, suddenly finding her voice. "That's good of you, Mr. Bradbury. You can bring them right in here."

With a nod, the man plunked the hat atop his thick sable hair. He jogged down the outside steps and returned to the small boat he'd beached on the jetty. Moments later he came back with an armful of cartons, then made another two trips for the crates. Well-honed muscles in his back rippled as he set everything along one wall of the fog trumpet room. One crate bore the markings of the rotating library.

"Oh, splendid! New books!" Eden exclaimed, already prying open the lid to peruse the titles.

He chuckled. "A reader, are you?"

"Oh, yes. When we have a lot of empty hours to fill, books help us stay awake and alert to sudden changes in the weather. Every six months the Lighthouse Board sends out a new set of histories, novels, biographies, and magazines—sometimes even a few religious works. I read them all cover to cover." Realizing she was babbling to the poor man, Eden diverted her attention momentarily to the spines of the various volumes. When he didn't respond, she glanced up at him.

His sun-bronzed face bore a peculiar expression, but it vanished so quickly, she almost thought she'd imagined it. His dark brows raised and he grinned. "I'd imagine you want the kerosene in one of the sheds."

"Oh. Of course. I'll show you the way."

For no reason she could fathom, Eden felt keenly aware of the man following her down the steps and over several yards of the jetty's uneven rock surface. Even as she led him up the ramp to the kerosene building nearby, she tossed off her curiosity, figuring that sooner or later she'd remember where she'd seen him. "You can leave it in here," she said, opening the door of the shed.

"Will do. I'll tote it up from the boat."

But before he'd taken more than three steps, the sound of pattering feet on the footbridge from the mainland brought Christian scampering up to them. "Mama! Come see!"

Eden smiled. "What is it, sweetheart?"

"A baby bird fell out of its nest. Mrs. Hastings wrapped it up in a cloth and climbed on a chair to put it back. You have ta come see."

"Oh, how exciting. I'll be there soon, honey. I'm busy just now."

As if only now becoming aware of another person's presence, her son nibbled his lip and tilted his head back to look up at the stranger.

"Ahoy there, young man," the man said, lowering himself to one knee.

The skin at the corners of his eyes pleated with his smile, as if he'd spent years squinting against the sun's glare. "You must be the assistant keeper here."

A slow grin widened the spaces between the boy's freckles. "Naw, that's my mom. I'm Chris."

"Well, I can tell a fine lad like you must be a help when a lady needs a hand, right?"

"Mm-hmm."

"Good. Good. It's a lot of work tending a lighthouse. Your mom's real lucky to have you around."

Christian didn't answer, but a subtle puffing out of his chest revealed his four-year-old heart was taking it all in.

Eden's heart swelled just watching the exchange.

"I was pleased to meet you, buddy," the man said, standing and tousling the flaxen hair with a big roughened hand. "You be sure and look after your mama. She has a very important job here. She helped me sail into harbor this very morning."

Of course! Eden thought, feeling like a dunce. That's why he looked familiar. Dane Bradbury had sailed right past her nose a little while ago.

Christian merely stared at the newcomer for a few seconds before glancing at his mother. Then he skipped happily off in the direction of the house.

"Fine-looking boy you have there, Mrs. Miles."

"Thank you. He's a lot of company."

"Undoubtedly." He switched his attention back to her as Christian disappeared around the side of the brown-roofed duplex in the distance. "Well, I'd best leave the kerosene and be off."

She studied him as he spoke. "It was you, this morning, wasn't it? The stern-wheeler."

"Yep. The *Solitude's* my gal. Faithful, hardworking. . ."

"But why would you, a ship's captain, go to the trouble of delivering our supplies?"

He shrugged a shoulder. "Just being neighborly. Of course, it wouldn't be too handy for me or my pals to run aground on the bar or pile up on the jetty because you ran out of fuel."

She had to smile. "Well, I do appreciate that. And so will Mr. Rutherford."

"Anytime." He touched a finger to the beak of his cap. "Take care, ma'am."

"Captain."

Restraining herself from watching him make the trip to the supply boat and back, Eden returned to the lighthouse and went inside to finish up. It had been decent of the man to take time out of his own responsibilities in order to bring those things to her. And nice of him to talk to Chris that way, making him feel important. The boy missed his father and rarely had occasion to be around a man other than Sherman Rutherford.

And the principal keeper purposely kept his distance—from her child, anyway. Eden wrinkled her nose. Time to get back to work.

After hauling the last of the kerosene kegs to the shed, Dane closed the door and headed back to the boat. This was the first time he'd had the occasion to set foot inside a lighthouse—even if it did happen to be only the lower portion of this particular structure. He always blew the whistle or nodded to one keeper or the other in passing, though. He realized he was looking forward to waving to this fetching one again on his way out of Bandon.

Recollections of Eden Miles played over his mind while he left the island and rowed upriver toward his stern-wheeler. For someone recently widowed, she didn't appear to be one of those weepy, helpless sorts he encountered at times. Nor was she especially unfriendly. In fact, she'd been just the opposite. Not only did she exhibit strength of character and complete acceptance of her fate, but she appeared to fit right in at the light and exuded competency and assurance in her ability to perform well.

She was more than just pleasing to the eye, too, with those soft feminine curves and her silky hair. Allowing himself the luxury of dwelling on those alluring features for a few seconds, he smiled, then directed his course to a safer channel. He had more than enough concerns of his own to occupy him for some time.

Interesting, though, was her fondness for books. . .so unlike other women he'd met. An avid reader himself, Dane often purchased fine works for his own personal library. He devoured them in quiet moments at sea, reflecting upon the treasured thoughts and ideas that enriched his often mundane existence. Perhaps one day he'd see about getting involved once more in his real dream—shipbuilding. He'd apprenticed for a few years with one of Seattle's finest shipbuilders and sailed at length on a variety of ocean craft. Those experiences had provided him with a few ideas of his own he hoped to develop one day.

But right now, he had obligations to his older brother's memory, including paying off Paul's debts and supporting his widow and her four youngsters. That responsibility excluded the luxury of more personal desires.

Mentally switching from thoughts of his late brother to a cheerier subject, Dane focused on the young boy he'd just met. Christian. What a keen lad he appeared to be, with his mother's huge, inquisitive eyes and expressive face, perhaps her pleasant nature as well. A shame he'd be growing up without a father's guidance. "Ah, soon enough some man will come along and snatch those two up, no doubt of that."

Surprised that he'd spoken aloud, Dane shook his head. "Great. Now I'm talking to myself." Filling his lungs with a great quaff of air, he chuckled, then concentrated on the activities ahead.

ᘐ

"You've hardly touched your supper," the motherly housekeeper chided. Birdie's good-natured tone revealed true concern as she filled a china teapot with steaming water, then removed cups and saucers from the cupboard. "Lost your appetite while you slept?"

"Hmm?" In the cozy surroundings of the duplex's dining room, Eden glanced at the older woman. "Oh, sorry. It's delicious. I guess I was thinking about the new books that arrived today." Returning her attention to the roast chicken, mashed potatoes, and spiced applesauce, the delicious smells of which had grown increasingly tantalizing on her way over from the lighthouse, she sampled another portion with relish. Birdie Hastings had proved to be as wonderful a cook as she had a friend in the short time she'd been with them.

Beside Eden at the table, Chris swallowed a gulp of milk and set down the glass. "I liked that big man. He was nice."

"Yes, wasn't he?"

"What man is that?" Birdie brought over the tea and joined them. Claiming a vacant chair, she poured the hot liquid into two fragile cups, passing one across the crisp damask tablecloth to Eden before stirring sugar and cream into her own. With her index finger she tucked a loose wisp of salt-and-pepper hair into her topknot.

"Actually it was the captain of one of the vessels that sailed in earlier," Eden said, meeting the housekeeper's gaze. "Mr. Jeffries imposed on him to bring over some supplies, since Sherman's not around to collect them."

"A ship's captain, now. How odd." A frown etched a tiny V into Birdie's forehead as her round hazel eyes clouded over.

"Yes, I thought so myself."

"He was real nice," Christian added.

Eden felt a subtle warmth beneath the collar of her shirtwaist and gazed off to one of Birdie's floral needlepoint wall hangings while sipping the tea—homey touches which did much to soften the otherwise stark interior Winslow had preferred. They looked especially dainty against the newly-painted walls, another of Birdie's accomplishments. There was no reason on earth to feel unease over something so inconsequential as a stranger who'd performed a kindness out of the goodness of his heart. And even though Eden couldn't explain why, she sensed somehow that Dane Bradbury possessed a good heart.

A strange sensation fluttered through her at the recollection of the twinkle in those dusky eyes. The last time she'd felt anything of a similar nature she had been a young girl. . .one susceptible to the charms of a dashing young man of whom her parents had not approved. But that had been a lifetime ago. She was older now, and wiser. So much wiser.

She pushed out her chair and stood. "I suppose I should be getting back to my duties. Thank you for the lovely supper, Birdie."

"I'll bring you some dessert in a little while."

"Fine." Eden tipped her head in her son's direction. "I'll see you later, sweetheart. Be good for Mrs. Hastings."

Schooling herself to get back to the routine once she was in the lighthouse again, Eden opened the log and dipped the pen into the inkwell. *Supplies delivered this morning, including—* She hadn't actually noted how much kerosene Captain Bradbury had brought. Dropping the pen, she went outside and down the steps, taking the wooden ramp to the shed.

A multitoned ship's whistle blew just then, and Eden glanced over her shoulder as the *Solitude* chugged by. Obviously loaded now, the vessel rode a bit lower in the water. Her owner gave a jaunty wave from behind the wheel.

Eden smiled and returned Captain Bradbury's wave, wondering where he was sailing this time and when he might return, if ever. She'd never actually met a ship's captain before, and it seemed. . .well, different.

Suddenly aware that a whole lot of other men aboard the vessel were waving back at her, she all but choked in mortification and hurried into the kerosene shed, her face as rosy as the approaching sunset.

Chapter 3

The DaBoll fog trumpet bellowed an ear-numbing blast into the murky darkness, then stilled again until its next regulated blast not half a minute away.

"That was a good story," Chris said, oblivious to the noise. "I liked how brave those men were at the fiery furnace." He snuggled closer to Eden on the wooden bench occupying one side of the square worktable in the fog room. The flickering flames of the blaze she'd built in the hearth to stave off the evening chill and power the fog signal danced over unadorned walls and reflected against the windowpanes of the small octagonal space. How she relished the sweet times she and her son enjoyed together—so few now with Winslow gone and Sherman Rutherford away. She closed the book about Bible heroes and placed it atop the biography she'd started reading earlier. "Let me go and check the light, sweetheart, and then I'll walk you over to the house."

"Can I come, too?"

"If you're careful on the steps."

He bolted across the braided rug to the stairs, where he stopped just as abruptly to move aside. "A gentleman always lets the lady go first," he said, the inflection in his voice proving how often he'd practiced reciting the maxim.

Eden swallowed her smile. "Why thank you, kind sir." Navigating around her son, she started up, with him tripping along on her heels.

She found the oil reserves still quite full, the wicks burning brightly, casting a visible beam out into the pea-soup fog as the trumpet let loose with another five-second blast. *Not a fit night for man nor ship,* she concluded. At least the *Solitude* had sailed out of harbor hours earlier. But the relief brought by that conviction dimmed a little at having made a spectacle of herself to that vessel's entire crew. Even yet the memory filled her with chagrin. Had the captain been equally embarrassed? Suffered annoying taunts from his men?

"Is it all right, Mama?"

Christian's voice brought her back to the present. He stretched up on tiptoe to peer at the lantern.

Ignoring the flames burning in her cheeks as she checked those in the lamp, Eden nodded. "Everything's fine for the moment. We can leave now, but don't forget to keep hold of the railing on the footbridge. We won't be able to see where we're going."

Outside, the heavy mist was every bit as thick as she'd surmised. She gripped Christian's fingers in one hand and the railing in the other, and he followed suit.

"I hate this creepy stuff," he said, his voice sounding ever so small in the fading glow of the lighthouse behind them as the moist fog swallowed them up. "Nobody can see us out here."

"But God knows where we are. He'll keep watching over us."

"I forgot."

Despite her brave words, Eden couldn't dismiss her relief upon sighting the dim patches of light from within the house. She hurried the rest of the way and ushered Chris inside.

Birdie glanced up from the rocker then stood, relief apparent on her grandmotherly features. "I was wondering when our little man would be coming home to bed. There's fresh coffee, if you'd like to take some back with you."

Eden didn't need persuading. "Thanks so much. You always know just what I need."

"I just wish you could stay here where it's safe and dry," Birdie countered while Eden went to help herself. "It's a beastly night."

"Well, not much point in that wish, is there? It's up to me to keep things running smoothly right now."

"Just the same, Sherman owes you plenty for filling in for him all this time. Perhaps we can go out in the country on a picnic. The rhododendrons should be at their peak now."

"That sounds lovely. I'm sure he'll approve an outing for us." The very possibility lessened the oppressive, claustrophobic feeling always brought on by the fog.

∾

Two days later, while cleaning the lens of the soot which always managed to accumulate overnight, Eden heard someone enter the lighthouse. Then Rutherford's familiar clomping up the tower steps reverberated through the hollowness.

"Oh, Sherman. You're back," she said, not taking her attention from her work. Her peripheral vision detected his movement when he ran fingers along an edge of the lantern—as usual, checking the quality of her cleaning. "How's your father?"

He elevated his chin, making that pronounced nose all the more prominent. Even his tone had a nasal quality when he spoke. "Not well, but more or less stable. I could be summoned to his side again at any moment." Moving to peer out the window at the river traffic, he slid a hand into the pocket of his uniform slacks. A curious tension permeated the limited confines of the lantern room.

Eden kept right on polishing the glass reflectors. "We'll keep on praying for him, then."

He gave a nod. "Anything exciting happen in my absence?"

A ridiculous giddiness surged through Eden, but she managed to squelch it. "We had some supplies delivered. Books, too. I entered everything in the log. Other than a few foggy nights, it's all been normal."

"I forgot to pack up the old library before I left. I'll see to shipping those books back tomorrow. Meanwhile, I can take over here if you'd like a break."

"Why, thank you, Sherman. I do have some things to do at the house. We can talk later about my taking a day or two off."

His thin lips tightened at one corner, adding another crease next to his mouth. "As you wish. Er. . .I. . .appreciate your filling in for me while I saw to Father."

Knowing that was as much a complimentary statement as she'd ever get from the principal keeper, Eden nodded. "And I will again, should the occasion arise."

He gave a perfunctory nod. "Tomorrow we'll revert to our usual duty schedules."

"Fine. Good afternoon, then." All but tripping down the steps, she flew to the house, lighter by a gross with the great weight of responsibility removed from her shoulders for a time.

&

The countryside along the placid Coquille River was verdant with new growth as Eden and Birdie took a river packet from Bandon to a popular wooded grove several miles beyond the town, Christian and a huge basket lunch in tow. Yellow Irish furze, so prevalent in early spring, was little more than a fading memory now that a riot of wild rhododendron came to the fore, their bright colors intermingled with stunted huckleberry bushes. Here and there, pitcher plants poked their grotesque, cobra-like heads against the greenery of mossy riverbanks and rolling hills thick with gnarled oak and cedar trees.

"Ah, now, this is the life," Birdie breathed. Reclining in the shade of a maple tree a fair distance from other picnickers, she gazed up at the ever-changing cloud puffs outlined against a sky of clearest blue.

"Yes, isn't it?" Eden smoothed the other side of the blanket they'd spread out on the ground after enjoying their lunch. It had been ages since she'd taken a boat upriver to drink in the dazzling scenery. A virtual rainbow of flowers speckled the fields all around them, turning their bright faces to the sun, while katydids hummed their summer songs on the soaring temperature. She relaxed, determined to enjoy this time away from the river light.

Nearby, Chris was having a grand time chasing butterflies with his net. Eden lay down beside the housekeeper. "You're what Christian and I were missing, Birdie. If you hadn't come to our door in those first bleak days after Win drowned. . ." She paused, then went on. "Well, I would've wasted this respite by staying home and catching up on everything under the sun, just like always."

"Can't see much need for that, now that you have me."

Eden reached over to squeeze the older woman's hand. "And well we know it. You happen to be the first friend I've had since I married." She paused, debating whether a few questions would seem intrusive. "What brought you to us?" she finally ventured.

A pensive expression connected some of the lines on the careworn face, then eased into acceptance. "Oh, I expect I needed somebody, just as I figured you might. Until my Amos took sick and passed on, my life was as predictable as anyone else's. But that last spell hung on so long it depleted our savings—what we hadn't invested in a get-rich-quick scheme, that is. We'd expected the interest to see us through our old age." She exhaled a wistful sigh. "One never knows what's coming down the road. . .and I expect that's a blessing. We'd always kept to ourselves, mostly. So after my poor Amos left this world, I had no place to go."

"And with no children. . . ," Eden added, her own sympathy for the dear woman deepening.

"We had a son once," Birdie admitted, a strange little smile on her face. "Dearest angel to walk the earth, he was. But he caught a fever and died when he was almost the same age as your Chris."

Eden's breath caught. "Oh, how sad."

"All but killed Amos when it happened. But somehow we muddled through the loss. We had the Lord, we had each other, and Amos had his good job at the shipyard. At least, up till last year when he got hurt, then took sick."

"Perhaps that's why God brought you to us, then, to give you some-place to lavish all that love you have."

Birdie's smile brightened, erasing several years of lines from her face. "Could be. I sure did appreciate your taking me in."

"I only wish I could pay you better for all your hard work." Eden gave the older woman's hand a pat.

"Pshaw. What more does a person need than a good home and a rea-son to keep on living?" A few silent moments passed before Birdie spoke again. "Mind if I ask you something?"

"Not at all."

"What's between you and your folks? Doesn't seem right, them refusing the letters you send week after week."

Eden turned with a rueful smile. "That's been going on for years now. Ever since I married Winslow. I met him at a church picnic when he visited relatives in our congregation. He was so dashing, so gallant. . .at least in the beginning."

"They didn't take to him?"

"That's an understatement. But they never got to know him, really.

And the fact that he was a bit older than I. . .that didn't sit well with them either. They had a more advantageous match in mind for their only daughter. They forbade me to see him."

"Hmm. Might I guess? You ran off with him anyway?"

Eden nodded in resignation. "I thought they'd come around eventually. I thought wrong. And later I understood their reservations, only by then it was too late. I could only make the best of it. We didn't have a horrid marriage, exactly, but we really had little in common. And he put his foot down about my making other friends. I had more than a few regrets— especially when he'd lapse into one of his black moods where I couldn't reach him no matter how I tried."

"But you'd think—I mean, now that he's out of the picture. . ." Birdie's face reddening, she gave a huff.

Of the same mind herself, Eden could only agree. "I'll just keep trying. Maybe in time they'll find it in their hearts to forgive me for going against their wishes. After all, I'm the one who must live with having squandered my opportunity for love, not waiting for the Lord to guide me to the one of His choosing." Noting a peculiar look on Birdie's face, she plunged on. "But how could they not adore Christian? After all, he is a part of them, too."

As if on cue, the child darted out from behind a blooming rhododendron. "Peekaboo!" The moment of camaraderie came to an end.

❧

Eden watched a bead of perspiration trickle down Sherman's temple.

"Hold it steady, would you?" He grunted, struggling to replace the last part of the clock mechanism which controlled the workings of the lantern. "No doubt they'll dock our pay for this," he groused, "even though we were not at fault."

Refusing to encourage the man's negative opinions, Eden offered quiet assistance. The chore couldn't take much longer anyway, and once she tidied up the discarded pieces of the works, her duties for the day would be over.

"There," he said. Gingerly dusting his hands and the front of his jacket of any minute shards of debris, he gave a wry grin and came to his feet. "Good as new." He gave the long chain a tug to set the clocklike mechanism into motion. "Better, in fact."

The man had no end of pride.

"You know," he continued, "the two of us make a pretty good team, if I do say so myself. There hasn't been one complaint by an inspector since the light was commissioned—though heaven knows they've poked their snoots in here often enough with their magnifying glasses, looking for the slightest infraction."

Not certain how to reply, Eden made no comment. Lately she'd noticed him staring at her in a way that made her uncomfortable. He'd been distracted, as well, as if something were pressing on his mind. She figured he'd come out with it if she waited long enough.

"You, uh, must be. . .lonely these days," he finally blurted in typically tactless fashion. "I mean, no husband coming home at night anymore."

"We get by, Chris and me. We have Mrs. Hastings."

"Still. . ." His dull eyes darkened beneath hooded lids. "A young woman such as yourself—a handsome one, I might add—must tire of the solitude of that big bedroom." Almost imperceptibly he inched closer.

Solitude. The very word brought an entirely different picture to Eden's mind than the one Sherman Rutherford was implying. Would the stern-wheeler ever come into Bandon again? Not that she expected future visits from Dane Bradbury, but he was the first ship's captain she'd met personally. Surely that would account for her curiosity.

"So you see, I thought perhaps you might look kindly on the advantages of such a possibility," the keeper was saying. He rocked back on his heels, as if relieved to have finally spit it out.

Not having heard the bulk of the words that had droned on while her thoughts were elsewhere, Eden stared blankly at the thin face before her. "I beg your pardon?"

His expression flattened, like a sail suddenly devoid of wind. "I said, perhaps the two of us might—" He gestured significantly. "You know. Keep company of an evening. Get to know each other. A little give-and-take. More or less work toward a permanent arrangement. I would marry you, eventually, of course."

To Eden's utter horror, she snorted. Then sputtered into a giggle. "You can't be serious."

Flustered, Rutherford straightened to his full, insignificant height, his mouth a touch white around the edges. "Of course I'm serious," he affirmed, his expression hardening like granite. "After all, you seem to enjoy tending the light here, and we do function reasonably well as a team. But you know as fully as I that the position as assistant should rightly be filled by a man."

This time it was she who took offense. "Oh, I understand now. I may be allowed to stay on here if you deign to grant your approval—which you will, provided I. . .how did you put it? Keep company with you?" Her voice, normally controlled, rose to a near squeak. "Well, let me tell you, Mr. Rutherford. I will give you no reason to find fault with the quality of my work. I intend to make every possible effort to perform satisfactorily all tasks required in the regulations—in the future as I have in the past. Humph! Man, my foot." Crossing her arms over her chest, she hiked her chin.

He regarded her evenly. "Well, well. I presume we shall see, won't we? It is, after all, the opinion and recommendation of a principal keeper that carries the weight with the board."

Eden sniffed. Then taking the broom, she began sweeping the gallery floor clean. The man was as opinionated and prissy as an old-maid schoolmarm. She could understand why he sported few friends. In fact, now she could understand a whole lot of things.

Well, so would he. So would he. No matter how hard she had to work from now on, she would keep her position here. Or die trying.

Chapter 4

In his personal quarters, Dane peeled out of his soggy clothes and reached for some dry things. The driving rain would make short work of these, too, but even a few minutes' warmth would be worth it after hours of being chilled to the bone. He shoved his legs into some fresh trousers from the closet and crammed his shirttails into the waistband, fumbling with numb fingers to fasten them closed. He didn't want to leave Riley at the wheel any longer than necessary.

The stern-wheeler lurched, sending a newly acquired book toppling off the built-in bureau. Dane bent to pick it up, sliding his hand along its smooth binding. He'd never purchased a collection of poetry before, but when he'd spotted the work by Tennyson at the bookseller's shop in Seattle, the rich maroon leather and gold lettering caught his eye. He didn't plan to keep it. What he did plan—if he had the occasion to cross Eden Miles's path again—was to see that she got it. Anyone who delighted in good reading as much as she did would likely appreciate this appealing little volume. There hadn't been anything of this nature among the rotating library selection shipped to the lighthouse. Somehow, he sensed she'd like it.

He set the book on his cot beside his other purchase, a miniature wooden stern-wheeler he'd picked up for Christian, then grabbed his slicker and exited his cabin.

The entire crew appeared to be scurrying about, tying down anything that had worked loose with the vessel's rocking in the raging storm. The old wood creaked and groaned against the force of the waves sloshing over her decks.

Pellets of cold rain quickly found their way into the crevices of Dane's rain gear, trickling down his neck and onto his shirt as he made his way along the hurricane deck. Thankfully, he managed the stairs to the wheel-house, where Riley wrestled the wheel, his knuckles white from the force of his grip. "How's it going?" Dane bellowed, taking over.

"She's holding her own," the first mate shouted, cupping a hand along-side his mouth, "even in this wind." But as he spoke, an errant gust whipped the seaman's cap from his head and sent it end over end across the deck below. He bolted down the stairs in pursuit, snatching it just before it jumped ship.

Watching after him, Dane had to chuckle. Considering his friend wasn't exactly a young buck anymore, that little spurt proved he had some spry movements left in that lanky frame of his.

Hopefully the gale would blow itself out soon. Dane had a handful of passengers this trip, all landlubbers, and all sequestered below in misery. It had been awhile since any of the grim, green-faced individuals dared venture as far as the rail to hang over the side. They'd be glad to set foot on land when this was all over.

And when this was all over, they'd be at Bandon.

His thoughts drifted to Eden Miles again. . .as they'd done with surprising ease and frequency, considering. He still had to come up with a logical reason for having bought the book for her. He wasn't entirely sure himself. All he knew was he couldn't seem to banish that comely young widow from his mind—her or that little boy of hers with those huge sad eyes. A kid his age should have a pa to teach him things. . .how to fish, how to tie knots, how to sense changes in the weather. Man things.

Almost from the first moment he'd met that enchanting pair, he'd begun praying for them, asking the Lord to direct some good Christian man their way. One who would look after them, perhaps provide a home so Mrs. Miles wouldn't have to work. Surely she deserved that blessing.

She reminded him a bit of Louisa, his brother's widow, in the stalwart attitude she exuded. Dane would never forget the awful day he'd had to bear the sad news of Paul's being washed overboard in a storm like this one and lost at sea forever. The seafaring life generated far too many widows and fatherless children, which only reinforced Dane's conviction never to marry—as if he could afford to entertain such a notion in the first place, strapped as he was.

If only I hadn't left him alone at the wheel. Maybe none of that would have happened. Swallowing against a tide of regrets, Dane gulped in a lungful of air and concentrated on keeping control of the ship. The *Solitude* had been his brother's first ship—Paul's lifelong dream—and Dane would sail it as long as she could still float. He had to keep an income flowing into his sister-in-law's hands. It wouldn't undo the past, and it wouldn't assuage his guilt for being the cause of his brother's death. . .but it was the least he could do.

❧

With the ocean at her back, Eden scrubbed the salt spray from one of the windows around the lantern until it positively sparkled. She needed some way to spend her pent-up irritation, and this thankless chore fit the bill perfectly. Dipping her rag into the bucket of soapy water, she wrung it out and slapped it against the next pane.

Besides the havoc last night's storm had wrought on the lighthouse, the tempestuous forces had left the rocky island strewn with driftwood, seaweed, and other debris. Her gaze fell upon Sherman Rutherford below, clearing away the worst of it while she saw to the morning routine, and she ground her teeth.

She'd barely spoken to him since his—his *proposition,* which in her estimation was the only appropriate term for it. The man's audacity galled her. To think that she'd grant him favors, most especially the kind he had in mind, when his primary motivation was to oust her from her position just so he could fill it with some man of his choosing.

And marriage, yet—however far off in the future he'd deign to bestow that legitimacy! Bah! Eden had no desire to repeat a mistake like the one she'd made the first time, thank you very much. She and Christian would make out just fine without having to kowtow to another man. Why, there wasn't a single male on this green earth whom she considered worth his salt anyway. Not one!

A multitoned blast from a passing vessel forged into her musings.

With a start, Eden jumped. A smile came unbidden to her lips as she turned and recognized the *Solitude.*

She easily made out the ship's owner at the wheel, along with a rawboned sailor she'd noticed before. Captain Bradbury grinned and waved in passing. She smiled and waved back, suddenly unconcerned about such mundane matters as his crew or Sherman Rutherford or decisions made by the Lighthouse Board. After all, it was a really lovely day. . . .

❧

Guiding the stern-wheeler from the choppy waters of the Pacific and over the ever-changing bar at the mouth of the Coquille, Dane had spotted the activity around the river light immediately: Rutherford stacking driftwood, Mrs. Miles shining windows up on the parapet. His gaze lingered on the charming picture she made, the sleeves of her shirtwaist rolled up above her elbows, tawny hair in slight disarray. It wasn't in a prim bun this time, but long and glorious, tied at her neck with a ribbon and hanging in golden splendor down her back. He waited until she bent over to wet the rag again, then blew the horn.

"Prit' near scared the pretty little gal right off the catwalk," Riley snickered.

"Just a friendly greeting." He barely kept a lid on his own mirth at her reaction as he grinned and waved. The smile she offered in return made the sunshine pale by comparison and made the one on his face much harder to squelch.

Maybe he'd ask if there was something else he could deliver out there.

As it turned out, there wasn't. But driven by a force he wasn't about to analyze, Dane made certain that Riley and the crew were occupied with the loading of a new shipment of lumber, then he borrowed a rowboat from Haydon Jeffries. He headed for the lighthouse, the book and the toy ship in a sack at his feet. In all likelihood she'd be on duty and unavailable, so he wouldn't stay long; just give her the things and leave. He really should be taking care of his own business anyway, not starting something he couldn't possibly finish.

Nearing the island, he caught movement ashore by the duplex, and it buoyed his spirit. Eden was out and about. That should make things easier. He beached the rowboat and strode toward her, the small tokens in his hand.

Clipping roses from the lattice beside the wide front porch, she turned on his approach, and her fingers flew to the lace ruffle at the throat of her summery gown. "Captain Bradbury."

361

"Mrs. Miles." He swallowed. "I, uh, wondered how you fared in last night's storm." *Great start, idiot,* he thought, cringing.

"Probably a little better than you must have out at sea," she countered.

Dane had to laugh. "I must admit, we had a few rough moments here and there." He held out the bag. "I. . .brought you a little something. You and the boy, I mean. It's nothing, really. Just a thanks for keeping the light burning."

"Why, I don't know what to say." Surprise widened her marvelous eyes as she set down the cut flowers and took the bag. She lowered her lashes to peer inside, drawing out the book. "Oh! How thoughtful! Thank you, Captain. I shall read it later tonight, while I'm on watch."

"I hoped it might fill a few hours."

"I'm sure it will. I. . .might I offer you a cup of tea or something? I've just brewed a fresh pot."

"I should be getting back to the ship," he hedged.

"Oh, but Chris should be back any moment. He's picking berries with Mrs. Hastings. I'm sure he wouldn't want to miss seeing you. You made quite an impression on him, actually."

Her look of disappointment was his undoing. Dane rocked his head back and forth. "Well, I suppose a few more minutes won't hurt anything. Sure, I'd enjoy some tea."

"And huckleberry pie, I hope. Mrs. Hastings is an excellent cook."

"Now there's something I never refuse."

As she bent to gather the roses again, a laugh of glee announced the return of her son. "Captain!" Christian trotted up to them, a panting Birdie Hastings lagging behind by several paces, an abundance of straggly hairs proof of the effort it took to keep up with the lively youngster.

"Hello, buddy." A lump formed in his throat when the child smiled up at him, guileless eyes shining.

"The captain brought you this," Eden announced, handing over the sack.

He peeked inside. "Oh! Oh!" he cried, taking out the tiny sternwheeler. "It's just like yours! Look, Mama! Oh, thank you. Thank you." Flinging his arms around Dane, he all but stopped the circulation from Dane's waist down.

Watching Eden and her housekeeper witnessing the lad's delight in his new toy, Dane derived nearly as much pleasure as that which pooled in their eyes.

It made him pray even harder that God would send someone to love and care for Eden Miles and young Chris. *Someone truly worthy of her...of them,* he quickly corrected. He couldn't allow his thoughts to go beyond that.

Chapter 5

"Now, that was one fine, fine man," Birdie exclaimed, shortly after Captain Bradbury had left and Christian was sailing his toy boat in a washtub of water on the porch. "Not a bad one to look at, either."

Agreeing inwardly, but not about to broadcast the fact, Eden noticed she'd dropped a stitch in the crocheted dresser scarf she'd started the previous day. She unraveled the thread to redo the row.

"Yes, sir, a fine, upstanding man," the housekeeper went on. "A lady'd do lots worse than reel in a catch like him."

"Why, Birdie, I had no idea you were in the market," she teased.

"Me! Pshaw! I meant for you, Eden-girl, and you know it."

Setting down her handwork, Eden met her friend's shrewd gaze. "As I told you the other day, I wasted my chance at love. It's too late for me to wish otherwise now." She shook her head. "Besides, the man was merely being kind."

"Well, now, there's kind, and then there's *kind*," Birdie insisted. "And methinks I can tell one from the other well enough."

"And *I* think you've gone over the edge," Eden said evenly but without rancor. "Just because a ship's captain happened to come by a time or two, that hardly constitutes more than simple friendship—and that's as much as I'm entitled to, I assure you."

Birdie just smiled knowingly.

"And besides, I'm perfectly content with my life as it stands. I have no right to try kindling any sort of flame other than the one in the light-house—particularly with a man of the sea whose bills of lading may never again bring him in my direction. I do, however, enjoy the blessings of our new friendship."

The maddening smile only widened.

Miffed, Eden put her work away and rose. "Furthermore, I must change for my duty hours." Without another word, she hurried to her room.

But later, when she was all alone in the stillness of the lighthouse, no amount of busywork could keep the housekeeper's words from echoing in her mind. Especially when she tried to distract herself with a certain volume of poetry and discovered the captain had written a personal note on the flyleaf: *To keep you company in the quiet hours. Kindest regards, D.B.*

"There's kindest, and then there's *kindest*," Eden mumbled facetiously, imagining the suppositions Birdie Hastings might draw from the inscription. Setting the book aside, she started for the stairs to check the oil supply once more.

The door of the fog room creaked on its hinges.

Fine hairs on Eden's neck prickled, and she tensed then exhaled with no little relief when Rutherford came in. "Oh, it's you."

"You were expecting someone else?" he said, a sneer hinting at baser thoughts as his gaze roamed over her in blatant crudeness.

"No, actually I wasn't expecting anyone," Eden said. "My shift isn't over for a few more hours."

"Yes, I know." He sauntered to the pulley and toyed with one end of it. "I couldn't sleep. I noticed you had company earlier. A new beau, perhaps?"

"Don't be ridiculous." She stepped on the first rise.

With surprising speed, he crossed the fog trumpet room, and his hand covered hers on the handrail, halting her progress. "Because that wouldn't be. . .wise, you understand."

Eden tamped down a surge of alarm. "Are you threatening me?"

"Threatening you?" He smirked. "I'd prefer the term 'warning,' myself. An indiscretion on your part might be most. . .detrimental to your case."

"And what about one on *your* part, Sherman?" she hissed, snatching her fingers from beneath his. Without waiting for his reply, she practically flew the rest of the way to the lantern room. There she paused to catch her breath, a feat that became easier only after she heard the structure's door open and close below.

Hot tears flooded her eyes, and she sagged against the curved wall encircling the platform, feeling miserable and vulnerable and even soiled. She rubbed any remnants of his touch from her skin as best she could on her navy skirt. What if he hadn't left when he did? What if he'd forced himself on her? What then? Could she continue to insist she stay on here if this incident was a foretaste of what she might face in days ahead?

Yet, what else could she do? Where could she go?

Straightening, Eden turned to stare dejectedly out the windows at the ocean, ever constant, its waves dancing in the beam from the lamp. Not a ship was in sight. Idly she wondered if Dane Bradbury had made his next port safely. His surprise visit had been an unexpected treat. . .one she'd not soon forget. He would never know how very precious his friendship was to her. As for right now, she could only pour out her heartache to her Friend of friends, hoping His peace would come and fill her soul.

ॐ

Dane closed his Bible and lay back on the cot, propping his head in his open palms. For some reason, he felt an urge to pray. For Eden Miles. The night was calm, the ocean like silk, nevertheless, he turned over and slid to the floor on his knees.

Dear Lord, I don't know if Eden is having a problem or in some kind of trouble, but I ask that Your angels surround her even as I pray. Keep watch over her, Father, and keep her from harm. She needs someone to take care of her so she can stay home with that nice lad of hers. Bring that person into her life soon, Father. And, until then, help me to be a true friend to her. One she can trust. I ask these things in the name of Your Son, Amen.

Climbing back onto the bunk, he stared up at the wood slats on the ceiling once more. He had no reason to continue dwelling on the very enjoyable time he'd had with Mrs. Miles and her son. But since his obligations to Louisa and the *Solitude* prevented his having any real designs on the widow, what harm could it do to reflect on that heart-stopping face of hers or let the memory of her voice sing across his heart like a soft Pacific breeze? A man could get used to reveling in those things. . .especially since it was all he'd ever have. And what could it hurt? He drew a ragged breath then slowly exhaled.

Better watch it, buddy, his conscience warned. *She needs a husband, not a daydreaming sot who should leave well enough alone. You can't afford to*

consider marrying her or anyone else, now or ever. And you've prayed for her.
Just let God work out the situation.

A knock reverberated on his door. "Captain? We're picking up lights from a ship in distress," one of the men announced.

"Be right there." Actually relieved at something to otherwise occupy his overactive mind, Dane quickly dressed and went to see if they could provide aid.

❧

"You're pretty quiet this morning," Birdie commented when Eden finally got home. "Something happen during the night?"

"Oh, nothing much," Eden fudged, not wanting to alarm the sweet woman unnecessarily. She sank into one of the kitchen chairs, resting her arms on the tabletop as the housekeeper scrambled some eggs and poured orange juice into a glass for her. "I had a small problem, but once I prayed about it, the Lord filled me with peace. I trust He'll keep the matter under control."

"Well, I hate to drop this on you, weary as you look," the housekeeper said over her shoulder while she kept on cooking, "but Mr. Rutherford got called away about an hour ago. His father's taken another bad turn. He sends his apologies for causing you extra work."

Eden didn't know whether to laugh or cry, but sent silent thanks to the Lord. Weariness swamped her, but she knew a few hours' sleep would cure that. She'd already seen to extinguishing the light, filling the oil reservoirs, and replacing the wicks. Nothing else pressed at the moment except the never-ending battle against tarnished fixtures. She smiled at Birdie. "That's fine. I can deal with it."

"Good." The housekeeper dished up the meal and brought the plate to the table, setting it before Eden. "Well, have a bite of breakfast, then you can get some sleep. Chris and me will keep an eye on things."

In no position to argue, Eden did her bidding.

❧

Another two weeks hinted at the end of summer, and autumn's first kiss began tinting the rolling coastal hills. The principal keeper had yet to return from settling his now-deceased father's affairs, but Eden was in no hurry to set eyes upon that sly face again, even though his absence made double work for her.

She did wonder about the *Solitude's* whereabouts, and whether Dane Bradbury would ever happen along again. Even as she chided herself for such wayward thoughts, the vessel's familiar shape chugged into view. Eden ran a hand over her chignon and smoothed her vest, then stepped out onto the catwalk.

The boat's whistle sent a raft of butterflies to flight in her stomach, as did the welcome sight of the captain's smiling face. This time she waved even before he did. He answered with another five-note blast.

"Mama! Look! It's our captain!" Christian called from the jetty below, where he'd been sailing his miniature stern-wheeler in a shallow tide pool. He jumped up and down, waving with all his might.

"Yes, I see. But he may be too busy to visit us, dear. Don't get your hopes up." But a large part of her ignored her own admonition. She crossed her fingers, willing him to come. . .and was on tenterhooks for the better part of the next hour while she scrubbed brass fixtures with Tripoli powder.

The jaunty sound of someone taking the outside steps two at a time made her heart race. Inhaling a calming breath, she went to the door. "Good day, Captain," she said breezily. "Lovely to see you."

"Even empty-handed?" he asked just as lightly.

"Of course. A friend is always welcome here." She stepped aside, allowing him entrance. After all, the regulations did specify visitors were permissible when a keeper was present, with the exception of some duty hours. "Won't you sit down?"

His large frame dwarfed the small fog trumpet room until he took a seat on the wooden side chair she indicated, propping an ankle on his opposite knee while she took a second seat not far away.

"How have you been?" they asked simultaneously then laughed. He tipped his head in deference to her.

"Just fine. There hasn't been much fog lately. Soon enough, the winter storms will start, then we'll be kept hopping." *Stop babbling, for pity's sake,* she thought frantically. "And you?"

"Not bad." He tapped an index finger idly against his knee. "Rutherford dumped everything on you again, I hear."

"Yes." Beginning to warm under the intensity of his gaze, Eden placed her hands in her lap to keep them from trembling. She couldn't allow him to see the effect he had on her. It quite astounded Eden herself! "I don't really mind, though. He can be—well, never mind." She flushed.

"Has he ever—" As if unwilling to finish the question, Dane cleared his throat. "So, how's Christian these days?"

"Growing like a weed, as usual. He saw your ship come in and will probably come running the second he notices the rowboat."

Dane nodded. "Finish Tennyson yet?"

Unbidden, a smile crept forth. "Only a few dozen times. Let's see. . . *Sunset and evening star, and one clear call for me. . .*"

"And may there be no moaning of the bar," he finished, *"when I put out to sea."*

"You. . .enjoy his work, too?" she whispered.

"Very much. In fact, I—"

Just then the door burst open, and Chris thundered inside. He made a beeline to the visitor. "Ahoy, Captain. Would you like to see me sail my boat?"

"Sure thing, buddy. Lead the way." With a droll grin at Eden, he got up and followed the towhead outside.

It gave her an opportunity to collect herself, she decided, though she couldn't help feeling abandoned. She hastened up to the lantern to recheck things before it was time to light the wicks. While there she stepped out onto the parapet to gaze at the two sailors below. . . one dark-headed and very manly, the other young and already daring. It brought back memories of when she and Chris were part of a family of three. Perhaps, someday, things could work out that way again. . . .

Almost choking on the possibility that Birdie's ludicrous imagination was getting to her, Eden drew a more rational breath and headed downstairs as the seafaring pair came in once again, hand in hand.

"Captain says I'm gonna be a good first mate when I get big," Chris boasted, his chin high with pride as he gazed up at his hero.

"I'm sure you will be, sweetheart." Slowly she raised her own lashes to meet those entrancing silver-gray eyes, and a sensation more powerful than any she had ever felt turned her knees to liquid. She melted to the chair directly behind her.

He didn't smile but knelt to take Chris by the shoulders. "Say mate, suppose you could talk that housekeeper of yours into brewing a thirsty sailor some tea?"

"Aye, aye, sir!" he said with a sharp salute. And off he ran.

Unable to trust her voice, Eden swallowed.

Dane, however, retook his chair and affected that nonchalant pose of his. "I prayed for you one night."

She blinked. "You did? I. . .pray for you often."

"Well, same here." He grew more serious. "But I mean I felt compelled to pray. A night about, say, two weeks ago? Sometime around then. Something troublesome happen?"

Calculating back, Eden realized it could have been the very night when Rutherford threatened her. The knowledge touched her deeply. "I. . .cannot talk about it, but yes. I did have a problem around that time. I thank you for praying."

"I wouldn't want any harm to come to my favorite lighthouse keeper, would I?" he teased.

"Am I? I mean. . ." Completely flustered now, Eden felt a warm flush.

But he only chuckled. "Hey, relax. You're with a friend, you know. I promised the Lord I'd look out for you until someone better comes along."

"Is that right?"

"You bet. So every time I come to port, I'm going to row out here to check on you. Make sure everything's okay."

Despite her awareness of his very masculine presence, Eden felt herself relax a few degrees, just hearing he'd be coming back. Often, perhaps. And the news brought with it an incredibly heady sensation. "Well, then, I suppose that makes you a. . .lighthouse keeper-keeper, then."

Dane threw back his head and roared with laughter, and she could only join in.

"What's all this?" Birdie Hastings asked, arriving at that moment with a tray of tea and all its accouterments.

"Nothing at all, my dear lady," Dane announced, slapping his knee. "Nothing at all."

The housekeeper's eyes looked from one to the other a few times, but Eden maintained her casual smile. "The captain's right. It's nothing."

"Well, there's some tea here and some chocolate cake for the two of you. And I'll leave the door open, if you don't mind." Directing a pointed stare Eden's way, she collected Christian and returned to the house.

When she took her leave, Eden and Dane hooted with laughter.

After that, time passed much too quickly as he related some of his amusing sea experiences, and she told a few comical incidents as lightkeeper.

"And the next thing you know," she said at the end of one such account, "the bowsprit plowed right past the tower as the clipper piled up on the jetty outside!"

"You can't be serious," he marveled.

Eden nodded. "It came so close, we could nearly step right from the catwalk onto the deck. But amazingly, the rescue crew from Bandon was able to free the vessel a day or so after the storm ended."

The captain chuckled and shook his head. Too soon, he stood to leave. "Well, I do thank you, dear friend, for the delightful visit and the refreshments. I'll be praying for you, remember, so have no fear."

"I won't. And my thanks to you." Having risen right after him, Eden walked Dane to the door, stopping in the opening while he stepped out onto the landing.

He halted after the first stride. Turning back, he brushed a knuckle softly down her cheek, his eyes lingering on her face. "When the right man comes along, Eden, my dear—and he will, I assure you—he's going to realize what a wondrous treasure the Lord has brought into his life." Then he winked and jogged down the steps on his way back to the rowboat.

Eden couldn't move.

Chapter 6

Stiff winds blew steadily throughout the long night, whipping tall waves against the base of the lighthouse and crashing around the jutting sea stacks nearby. The wind whistled around the tower in eerie tones that kept Eden's nerves on edge. Deep darkness cloaked the outside world, except for the limited span of ocean illuminated by the ever-constant beam of refracted light from the lantern's prisms.

Blackness cloaked her spirit as well. No amount of reading could banish the loneliness that clutched her in tentacles cold as those of an octopus. Where was the happy life she had envisioned for herself in so many romantic girlhood fantasies? Why had she taken fate blithely into her own hands at seventeen and chosen her own will, without so much as consulting God? She deserved the disillusionment she'd found, deserved watching those dreams turn to ashes. Now here she was at twenty-seven, disowned by her parents, widowed with a young child to raise alone, and trapped in a job she was beginning to loathe. With no way out.

Her dead husband was the lucky one.

Choking back the tears clogging her throat, Eden fell to her knees, overwhelmed by the depth of her own bitterness. "Forgive me, dear Lord, for grieving You with such a horrid thought. I know You are aware of my circumstances, whether ordained by Your holy will or chosen by my own stubbornness. And I know You've promised never to leave me or forsake me. Your Word says that all things work together for good to those who love You, those who are the called according to Your purpose. Please help me to concentrate on the blessings in my life: Your presence, my precious son, the loving housekeeper You've sent to look after us. . .and my new friendship with Dane Bradbury."

Even the mention of the captain's name flooded Eden with warmth. For a tiny moment she wondered what her life might have been like had their paths crossed before, when she was a happy, obedient daughter living at home. Before she had chosen the wrong lot. Would God have allowed something beyond the sweet friendship which now so brightened her world?

For me, it's already gone beyond friendship, her heart admitted.

Eden took no joy in the sad truth that draped over her shoulders like a burial shroud. It was too late. She'd already thrown away her love on someone who'd taken it and trampled it underfoot. If she deserved to love and be loved again, wouldn't her parents have forgiven her and taken her back into their arms? After all, they professed to be Christians, too.

As if the captain even hinted at offering you more than friendship anyway, her better sense railed. *He made it a point to let you know he's praying for someone else to come to your rescue. Do you need a more obvious clue that he isn't looking to marry anyone, least of all you, a widow with another man's child?*

Methodically, she picked up a rag and began wiping down the stair rail. This was her life now, tending a lighthouse and a little boy. The result of the choice she'd made.

Wishing was for young girls who were innocent enough to believe dreams came true.

"Please help me, Father, to stifle my improper thoughts and feelings. Help me learn to accept my life as it is now and not to expect things I have no right to dream about. May I find all I need in You."

A gentle peace wrapped around her, increasing as gradually as the rising sun now tinting the eastern sky. Spent as though she'd survived a costly battle, Eden extinguished the lantern then trimmed the wicks evenly and refilled the oil reservoirs in preparation for going home for some much-needed sleep.

Sherman Rutherford picked that afternoon to return to his duties.

Back at work, rested and refreshed after several hours' slumber, Eden heard the keeper approaching the lighthouse just as she finished mopping the floor. She gave passing thought to arming herself with the bucket of scrub water, then chided herself for such bizarre notions. After all, she could brain him with the mop handle if she needed to. Mentally she braced herself.

The door opened, followed by Rutherford. Incredibly, the man wore a sheepish half-smile. "Before you say anything," he blurted, his hands raised in front of him, "I want to beg your forgiveness for my abominable conduct when I saw you last."

Eden's grip on the mop relaxed. So did her jaw until she realized she needed to shut her mouth.

"I know I was a beast," he went on. "You have every right to file a grievance with the board. Of course, I hope you won't feel that's necessary, since I'm groveling at your feet now, willing to do anything to make up to you for such despicable conduct."

"W–why, Sherman, I. . .don't know what to say." Of all the scenarios Eden had imagined, this had to be the absolute farthest from her mind. He was actually repenting? Dare she hope he'd allow her to stay on? Without fear of future confrontations?

"I'm most sincere, I assure you. Here, let me empty that water for you. You shouldn't be getting your hands dirty." And with that, he snatched the pail unceremoniously from beside her on the floor and went out onto the landing. She heard the splash below when he heaved the contents over the rail.

"Now," he said on his return, "what else needs doing?" He shot a glance around the fog trumpet room. "Everything looks immaculate, as usual. Splendid work, Eden. Splendid work, indeed. I can take over now. You've really earned a week off, of course—maybe even longer—in repayment for filling in for me. Do give it some thought."

Something about this new Sherman Rutherford sent off alarm bells in Eden's head. She could only wonder at the unexpected change. "I. . .was sad to hear of your father's passing," she began, untying her apron and hanging it up.

"Oh, well, it wasn't something we weren't expecting, you know." Moving to the log, he looked over the current page, then idly flipped back one or two to scan the various entries. "He's gone to his eternal reward, I'm sure."

"And the rest of your family? Your mother?"

"Fine, just fine." He pursed his lips then met her gaze. "I've. . .brought her back here, actually. She'll be living with me now."

Suddenly Eden had the suspicion that he'd come by his domineering ways quite naturally. She could almost imagine what his mother would be like. In fact, she could hardly wait to meet the woman!

❧

Dane studied the clouds gathering on the horizon. Fall never failed to bring unsettled weather on its cool breezes, and all too soon winter storms would pound the coast. Limiting his ventures south. Keeping him in his home port, Seattle.

How was Eden faring? Had the Lord answered his prayers for her and sent someone to take care of her?

Trying to visualize the man worthy of the Widow Miles, Dane came up empty. She was one in a million. In fact, if he were looking to get married and settle down, he wouldn't mind proposing to her himself.

The realization jolted him down to his boots.

"Only I can't make that kind of commitment," he muttered. "Not yet, anyway."

"Huh? You say something?" Riley Baker peered up from the charts he'd spread out on the floor of the wheelhouse.

Dane grimaced. "See if you can come up with an estimate of the time it would take us to sail to Vancouver. The one in British Colombia."

"Sure thing, Cap'n." The redhead slid a section closer and buried his nose.

Marriage, Dane thought. *Could I possibly consider taking on a wife, a child? Maybe additional offspring? Louisa's accountant says Paul's debts will be paid by early next year, but she'll still need to live and eat, and so will those kids. I can't let them down. A few years ago, I had my future all planned out then was forced to give up my own dreams. Now all I can think about is a heart-stopping smile and two beautiful blue eyes, a voice like a song, all belonging to a lady who makes me want things I shouldn't even be considering. How did this happen?*

"Well," Riley said, "near as I can figure it, it'll take—"

"Never mind," Dane interrupted.

"Huh?"

"I need to go someplace else first."

Autumn's paintbrush lavished its full splendor along the coast in a glorious blend of brilliant hues made even more wondrous by pleasantly warm temperatures as the *Solitude* rounded the island of Rackleff Rock. Guiding the vessel over the Coquille River bar, Dane strained his eyes for a glimpse of Eden Miles.

But Sherman Rutherford's bony frame came into view instead, as the principal keeper washed the outer windows of the light.

Swallowing his disappointment, Dane quickly buoyed himself with the assurance that Eden was off duty. . .which suited his purposes much better. Perhaps he could convince her to have dinner with him in town or go for a buggy ride. Anything to have an opportunity to talk. Find out if she shared any of the same inclinations he was finally beginning to explore.

He knew he didn't have a lot to offer her. His home consisted of a two-room apartment over a butcher shop. His worldly goods—a couple dozen books and a few hundred dollars. All the rest of the income from his sailing enterprise, after paying the crew's salaries, had gone to Louisa. But now that Paul's debts were nearly paid in full, he could at least plan to save some money for himself. With the apprenticing he'd already done, it shouldn't be a problem to get a job building ships again, work his way up to starting his own business. Even supporting Louisa and her children, he'd be able to provide a decent living for Eden and Christian eventually. Assuming she was interested, of course.

And that he would find out soon enough.

The minute the ship docked, he borrowed a boat and rowed to the dwelling across from the island, where he beached the rowboat and strode over to her side of the duplex.

Strange. . .the windows were closed up with the curtains drawn, and he could neither see nor hear any movement about the place. Filling his lungs, he rapped at the front door. Once. Twice.

While he waited, a rather large-boned woman came around from the other side. No smile softened the stern lines on the queenly face crowned by a coronet of silver braids. "You won't find anyone there, young man. They've gone away."

"Away?" He nearly choked on the word.

"Left yesterday, bag and baggage. All three of them." Balling a handkerchief in her be-ringed fingers, she tucked it into her skirt pocket.

Just then, the principal keeper emerged from the walkway. "May I be of some assistance?"

"Not likely. I came to call on Mrs. Miles." Even as he spoke, Dane watched Rutherford elevate his nose in a kind of subtle superiority.

"What a shame. She said something about going home. Been wanting to for some time and finally decided to do it."

"Any idea when she'll be back?" Dane had to ask.

The man shrugged. "She didn't say for sure when—or if—she'd return. No point in your hanging around."

"And where, exactly, is home? If you don't mind my asking."

"Hmm." Rutherford rubbed his chin as if in thought. "Don't rightly know if she ever said."

A cloud crossed in front of the sun at that moment. . .though later, Dane wondered if it had been his imagination. All he knew was he'd hesitated a bit too long in coming back to Bandon.

Unless the Lord wanted him to forget this grand dream he'd started to build a few too many hopes on. . . .

Chapter 7

Eden clutched her gloved fingers tightly together in her lap as the hired carriage left Santa Barbara's bustling streets and turned toward her parents' sprawling estate in the scenic rolling hills outside the city. Her insides felt as if a jellyfish had taken up residence, and not even unceasing prayer brought any semblance of peace to fortify her for whatever lay ahead.

She slanted a nervous glance at Birdie. "I don't know whatever possessed me to let you talk me into this. It's probably the second most foolish thing I've ever done in my life. I wish I'd stayed at Bandon."

The housekeeper's lips curved with a placid smile. Nothing seemed to fluster her. "Sometimes people have to see important things through personally. Letters aren't always enough."

But Eden was far from convinced.

"Sometimes it takes seeing people face-to-face. Talking things out." Birdie paused. "And at least you'll know once and for all if the matter will ever be resolved. You've sent up lots of prayers about it. Give God a chance."

It sounds so simple, Eden conceded. *But Birdie doesn't know my parents.*

"Is it much farther, Mama?" Christian asked, craning his neck at the unfamiliar new sights.

"No, sweetheart. We're almost...there." She caught herself before uttering the word "home." It hadn't had that classification for years, and likely never would again.

But when the carriage reached the brick and wrought-iron gates at the entrance and the horses started up the long, curved drive lined by autumn-hued trees, Eden nearly lost her courage. What was she thinking to come here unannounced, risking humiliation at the very least, and at worst, total rejection? She should have sought God's guidance more urgently. Waited for Him to open the door. . .or close it forever.

Before she could request to be taken back to the hotel, however, the conveyance drew up before the stately columned red-brick mansion and stopped. The driver hopped out and began removing their bags, setting them just off the edge of the drive.

Eden forced her legs to step down onto the gravel. She drew a cleansing breath and rummaged in her handbag for the fare while Chris and Mrs. Hastings also disembarked.

"Thank you, madam," the mustached man said, accepting the money with a polite tip of his hat. Without further ceremony, he climbed back onto the seat and clucked the team into motion, leaving her wishing she had asked him to wait, just in case.

But it was too late.

"Well," she said, her voice wavering slightly, "I guess it's now or never." Dredging up every ounce of gumption she possessed, she left the luggage where it lay then went up the stone walk to the immaculate verandah flanked by perfectly sculpted hedges and late-blooming tropical flowers. The edge of a Belgian lace curtain stirred, but Eden ignored it and continued straight on to the rich walnut door that framed leaded-glass panes. She lifted the brass ring and rapped.

A middle-aged Mexican maid in crisp black and white answered almost immediately, her dark eyes alight with surprise as she glanced over the threesome. "Miss Eden!"

"Is Mother at home, Maria?" Eden asked, amazed at the newfound bravado that came from nowhere.

"She is resting out by the fountain, *mi hija*. Shall I. . .announce you?"

"Thank you; that won't be necessary. I'll go myself. Come, Chris." Taking her son by the hand, she nodded to Birdie, and they walked together through the massive flagstone foyer and exquisitely apportioned living room to French doors, which opened out onto a stone patio.

Her mother, still trim and elegant despite the passage of time, dozed on a wooden patio chair amid a grouping of others. A wide-brimmed straw bonnet covered her upswept hair. An open book rested face-down on the lap of her organdy dress. Off to one side, a marble fountain sent glistening water cascading softly from its wide basin to a broader pool below.

Eden relived a raft of memories, both happy and sad, as she studied the familiar aging face for a timeless moment. Then, ever so gently, she reached out to touch her shoulder. "Mother?"

"Hmm? What?" came the sleepy response as golden-lashed eyes fluttered open, then blinked and widened with recognition. A host of unreadable expressions crossed her refined features as she sat up straighter. "Why, Eden!"

"Hello, Mother. I. . .had to come. Please, don't send me away. Us, I mean."

Gathering herself, the older woman set her book on a small table next to her and came to her feet. Light blue eyes took in the three visitors then softened with moisture as they came to rest on Chris.

Eden knew her son was the very picture of her father as a lad. She raised her chin in motherly pride and moved closer to him. "I'd like you to meet your grandson, Christian."

"Whom I would have recognized anywhere," her mother breathed in amazement as he offered his best bow.

"Grandmama," he ventured.

She cupped her tapered fingers lightly over the crown of his white-blond head and met Eden's gaze, her features gentling. She tilted her head at Birdie. "I assume you must be Birdie Hastings."

How could she possibly know that? Eden thought in confusion.

"Yes, madam."

"And a true friend to my daughter, not to mention an instrument of the Lord used to open our eyes at long last."

Watching her mother take the housekeeper's hands in hers was too much. "I–I don't understand," Eden stammered.

Her mother smiled with chagrin and took Eden by the arms, speaking in all sincerity. "I do hope you will forgive me, daughter. I've been a foolish, foolish old woman. I only hope you will find it in your heart to pardon me for wasting all this time in bitterness. Your father and I have a lot to make up to you, to Christian. I just pray you will grant us that pleasure."

Eden gaped at hearing the unbelievable even as the two women exchanged smiles.

"I take it you've no knowledge of the powerful letters your house-keeper can pen," her mother supplied in explanation. "Thanks to this friend of yours, the Lord finally got through to two stubborn old people about the forgiveness He requires of His own."

"N–no, I had no inkling she'd written." So many emotions cavorted through Eden's being, but she recognized the most prevalent one as awe at God's mysterious workings. She didn't know whether to laugh or cry as tears of happiness blurred her vision. Hesitantly, she leaned closer to her mother, wanting to hug her. . . not quite sure she should.

Her fears evaporated as two slender arms opened and drew her close in a loving, warm embrace.

"Oh, Eden, my dear," came the murmur against her cheek. "What I would give to turn back the years. But all that is left to us is this precious chance to make things up to you the best we can. We do love you so."

Eden felt a stinging behind her eyes but couldn't give in to it. "I love you, too, Mother." And she tightened the hug.

At last her mother released her and eased away. "Well, let's go inside for some refreshments, shall we?" Linking an arm through Eden's, she reached for Christian and drew him against her other side. "We have so much to catch up on. Your father should be home shortly. How long can you stay, my dear ones?"

≈⅜

Dane gazed idly at the midnight sky, seeing little more than a splash of stars against the deep blue-black overhead. The sea couldn't be more calm or the gentle night wind more refreshing. Soft voices of strolling couples drifted from the main deck, and crew members moved throughout the vessel, performing their usual duties. But Dane felt completely alone in the world.

He'd come so close to moving toward a choice which until yesterday had made more sense than any decision he'd ever made before. But it all came to nothing. Eden was gone.

Where is she, Lord? His spirit asked the question for the dozenth time. He'd received no help whatsoever from that stiff, Rutherford. A gleam in the man's eye seemed to derive singular delight from crushing Dane's hopes.

As the *Solitude* made steady progress northward, he mulled over the stern-wheeler's name. In the frenzy of trying to keep up with his own and his sister-in-law's financial concerns, the peace and quiet of his quarters had provided a welcome solace. But lately he'd come to a different opinion. Solitude was just a pretty word for loneliness. Should he give up thoughts of marriage and simply concentrate his efforts on paying the remainder of Paul's debts or chance one more trip to Bandon? He knew he was running out of time. Fall's changeable weather would soon limit sailing ventures along the north coast. But if Eden Miles was going to be lost to him forever, he wanted to hear it from her own lips.

Even if it killed him.

Then again, maybe he shouldn't bother.

❧

Eden found the week in Santa Barbara filled with an endless array of delights. Christian absolutely reveled in the attentions of his new grandparents, and Maria spoiled him royally with all manner of delicious treats from the kitchen. Birdie fit right in like a long-standing family member, and the mild California days passed with incredible swiftness.

Now as Eden waited for her father to drive them back to the wharves to catch their steamer home to Bandon, a sense of bittersweet sadness crimped her heart. Life had been lonely during the long years when misunderstanding caused her parents to shut her out of their lives. But now that the relationship had been healed and restored, she would know a whole new kind of loneliness. They would not be able to watch Christian grow up.

Her mother's voice interrupted her musings. "Well, dear, I still don't understand why you feel you must leave us again. There's no reason for you to make your own way in the world when we have this huge house with so many empty rooms."

"I know, Mother," Eden assured her. "But I have a contract to see through. And I'm interested to know if they think I'm qualified to keep my position permanently."

"Ever the independent one," the older woman chided. She released a patient sigh. "Well, in the event that your lighthouse assignment doesn't work out, please remember you and Chris will always have a home with us. And Birdie, too, if she can put up with us."

"Let me tell you, it's been a long time since I've felt so welcomed," the housekeeper assured her. "I can't thank you and your husband enough for including me during this most precious of times. I'll look after your daughter and grandson to the best of my ability. I promise."

"I've no doubt of that," Eden's mother replied.

The shiny barouche drawn by matched gray geldings emerged from the carriage house in back. "Everybody ready?" Eden's white-haired father boomed, drawing the horses to a stop.

"Be right there, Grandpapa," Chris called. He turned and threw his arms around his grandmother, then Maria. "Good-bye. Good-bye."

A round of hugs circulated among the others, and the women dabbed at their eyes with handkerchiefs, laughing self-consciously at their emotional display. Then Eden, Birdie, and Chris climbed aboard. When they pulled away, they waved until the mansion disappeared from view.

"This has been a week I shall always remember," Eden's father said, reaching a big hand beside him to pat Christian's knee. "You're a fine, fine lad, son. You take good care of your mama for us, y' hear?"

"Yes, sir. I will."

"And come visit us again soon." He turned and winked at Eden.

Later that evening, settled in the tiny cabin aboard the coastal steamer as it headed northward to Bandon and ports beyond, Eden lay still until Birdie and Chris drifted off to sleep. Her heart was so full of wonder and gratitude, she wanted to pour out her praises to her heavenly Father. But once she slid down onto her knees, no words would come...only tears of joy. She rested her head on her arms and wept until there were no more.

‸‸

"Well, well," Sherman said when Eden reported for duty her first day back. "I trust you had an enjoyable vacation." He put his polishing cloth in the box of others to be laundered then straightened, sliding his hands into his trousers pockets and eyeing her in an unthreatening manner.

"Yes, we did. Very much so, thank you. How have things been here?" She glanced around, noting that everything appeared up to the principal keeper's normal high standard.

"Nothing out of the ordinary."

"Any visitors?"

He averted his gaze. "No one to speak of. Ready to go back to work?"

"Ready and willing." With a mock salute, she went to get her work apron. But her intuition sensed the keeper hadn't told her everything. As soon as he left, she crossed to the log to see what he'd left out but found nothing amiss.

Dane Bradbury had been very much in her thoughts during her absence, and she was extremely relieved to hear he hadn't come into port while she was away. Perhaps that meant the *Solitude* might be making another appearance in the near future and she'd be able to tell the captain the wonderful news about the reunion with her parents. With that hope to lift her spirits, she headed for the tower steps to make sure all was in readiness for the evening hours.

Chapter 8

When the remainder of the month passed by without sign or sight of Dane Bradbury or his stern-wheeler, Eden began to wonder if something had happened to him. She'd come to count on his visits every few weeks—whether she'd intended to or not—and this uncharacteristic absence disturbed her deeply.

But then again, her sensible side railed, the captain did have a business to run. Perhaps more important matters occupied him. She had no right to feel slighted. Thus reproached, she pressed her lips together and continued sweeping down the tower steps in preparation for the end of the morning shift.

"Almost done, Mama?" Chris called from the worktable, where he sat drawing while waiting to walk home with her.

"Yes, sweetheart. There's only—" Just then, the heel of Eden's shoe caught the edge of a rise, and she plunged headlong down the remaining five steps. Her cry of surprise turned to one of pain when her left wrist took the brunt of her weight.

"Mama!" At her side already, Christian did his best to help her up.

"I'm. . .I'm all right," she tried to assure him, rising unsteadily to her feet. She blinked back the tears already clouding her vision and clutched her throbbing wrist.

His eyes filled to brimming. "No, you're not. You hurt yourself. Come on; Mrs. Hastings'll know what to do."

"But I'll be fine. Truly."

Every bit the little man, however, her son took over. With a surprisingly strong arm around her waist, he steered her out the door and down the steps, not letting go the whole length of the footbridge, solemn whenever she'd let out an unbidden grunt of pain.

"What's happened?" Birdie's face showed alarm when she emerged from the house on their approach.

"Mama fell. She's hurt."

"It's just my wrist," Eden said, attempting a smile. "It'll be fine, I'm sure."

"Will it, now?" the housekeeper said, pursing her lips as she observed the already-swelling limb. "I'm taking you right to town, to the doctor. Chris, go tell Mr. Rutherford to get the rowboat out for us."

No amount of resistance dissuaded the older woman, and Eden realized she could only submit to all the humiliating attention caused by her misstep. Within moments, she found herself being rowed across the river by Birdie. Eden sat in silence, her teeth clenched against the maddening pain.

Dockworkers lent their assistance at the wharf, securing the boat and helping Eden to disembark, and a lantern-jawed man came forward. "There a problem here?"

"A doctor," Birdie supplied. "Mrs. Miles needs a doctor."

"Sure thing. Doc Green's place is not far from here. I'll see if I can round up a ride for ya."

"Thanks."

"Say, ain't you Birdie Hastings?" he asked suddenly, peering more closely at her, his eyes brightening. "I'm Haydon. Haydon Jeffries. Remember? You 'n Amos used to sit in front of me at church now and then."

"Oh, yes," Birdie replied, somewhat distracted. "I remember."

"I been wonderin' what happened to you since Amos passed on, rest his soul. I'll drive ya myself. My wagon's parked right over there."

"Well, thank you, Haydon. That's thoughtful of you." And the two began a lively conversation, though Birdie often checked how Eden was doing.

Eden's discomfort precluded paying the pair much mind as the wagon bumped and jolted along the street. Not long afterward, when the physician's ministrations were finished, she came back outside, her left arm in a sling. Thankfully, she found the kind man from the wharves had waited and was amusing her housekeeper and her son with a story.

"How're ya doin', young lady?" he asked, hopping down and handing her up to the seat beside Birdie.

"It's just a sprain. I'll be fine. I'll still be able to do most of my chores at the lighthouse." Despite the nagging ache, having the wrist tightly wrapped and slightly elevated did make it more bearable.

"Well, that's good news. Coulda been worse. I'm sure my friend Dane Bradbury'll be glad to hear you're still around and working out at the island."

Eden's heart tripped over itself. Her lips parted in shock.

"He was of a mind you'd left your job and gone away," Jeffries elaborated. "Leastwise, that's what Rutherford led him to believe."

"Well, I never!" Birdie exclaimed.

"Yep. Old Dane was real put out about it. Figured he'd take more contracts up north for a spell, instead of comin' all the way down here all the time."

Eden swapped a look of astonishment with her housekeeper, but neither spoke.

"Humph. What do you make of that news?" Birdie asked a few minutes later as the current aided their return by boat to their house across from Rackleff Rock.

"At the moment, I'm furious."

"Does your arm hurt bad?" Chris's childish face scrunched with worry.

"Not too bad, sweetheart. I'm sure it'll be better soon."

Birdie paused from her work at the oars and let out a snort. "Maybe Mister High-and-Mighty will put on a magnanimous show and fill in for you for the rest of today, at least."

"Maybe." Eden didn't care to see the man just yet, nor did she want to discuss the matter in front of Christian. Averting her attention to the passing riverbank, she settled back into her other misery and let irritation turn to despair. It was all over for her and Dane Bradbury. . .friendship or anything beyond. God had closed that door for sure. Still, it pleased her to know that because of her, Dane had made a special effort to secure loads to and from their port.

❧

Later that night, after Christian had gone to bed, Eden relaxed in an overstuffed chair in the parlor, her feet propped on a footstool. Birdie brought her a cup of tea then lowered herself into a padded rocking chair nearby. "So, what are you going to do about it?"

"About what?" As if she didn't know.

The housekeeper tucked her chin and stared without saying a word.

Eden sighed. "Oh, Birdie, I had no reason to expect Captain Bradbury to keep coming by."

"Oh, didn't you, now?" the older woman chided.

"And if he's decided not to bother in the future, I don't see what I can do about it."

"You could send him a message. Haydon Jeffries is sure to know other captains who get up into his part of the country. Sooner or later it would reach your captain friend."

Eden shook her head. "But why? It's not as if there's anything between us. You know how I feel about fanning a flame I've no right to encourage." Lifting her cup, she took a sip of tea.

"That's the second time you've uttered that kind of nonsense," the older woman challenged. "No right, my foot." She grimaced.

"Well, I don't."

"And why not, I'd like to know?"

Eden set her drink on the table next to her and looked directly into Birdie's eyes. "Because, I had my chance years ago, and I wasted it. I didn't wait for the Lord to bring the right man into my life."

Birdie threw her hands up in frustration. "I know being way out here we haven't been able to get to church a lot of the time, but I see you read your Bible often enough. I just wonder if you ever pay attention to what you're reading."

"What do you mean?"

"Isn't the Old Testament full of accounts of how the Lord directs the steps of His children?"

Eden could not argue with that.

"And doesn't it tell us in Ecclesiastes that there's a time for every-thing? A time to live, a time to die, a time to reap, and a time to sow—and a time to love?"

"Yes. It does say that. But I ran ahead of God, don't you see, Birdie? I didn't wait for His time. That's what I've been trying to tell you."

The housekeeper blew out a whoosh of breath and leaned forward.

"Then let me ask you this. Haven't you read stories in the Bible about people who made wrong choices, admitted their wrongdoing, and then were forgiven by God? Hasn't He worked out this situation to your good by putting you in the right place when He brought the right man across your path? Ever think about that?"

Eden hadn't considered that particular possibility. But now that it stared her in the face, it seemed as if shades fell from before her eyes. She knew for a fact that she'd grown to love Dane Bradbury. And she knew also that it was worth every risk to find out if God truly did have more than mere friendship in mind for them at some point in the future.

A slow smile broke forth. "Would you please fetch me some writing paper, Birdie?"

Chapter 9

Early November winds teased the tall pines bordering Louisa Bradbury's clapboard dwelling in Seattle as Dane exited his sister-in-law's front door to walk the three blocks' distance to his own rooms, whistling as he went. Sale of the *Solitude* to a shipping line in the city had brought in enough cash to pay off the balance of Paul's old debts.

But that in itself had not put the spring in Dane's steps.

To think Louisa had started keeping company with a well-reputed widower from her church, a relationship which had every appearance of becoming permanent! That possibility had never entered Dane's mind. Somehow he felt Paul would have been happy for her, knowing the wife he loved would be well cared for from now on, and that their children would lack for nothing.

Breathing the first really free breath he'd taken since his older brother's death two years earlier, Dane turned up his coat collar against the chill. Let the more dedicated mariners put up with capricious weather, rough seas, and the hazards of shoals and sandbars. As for him, the future held promise enough. His former employer had been more than eager to have him back in the shipbuilding business—one he was good at and thoroughly enjoyed. Dane would receive a steady income, all of which would soon be his.

Too bad all this couldn't have transpired a couple months ago, he thought. *I could have approached Eden and declared my love. Maybe she wouldn't have gone away.* But there wasn't much point in ruing what could not be changed. Life would go on, even if it would be an incredibly empty one. He'd learn to accept it, in time.

At least he had some very poignant memories of the woman who had stolen his heart. He would draw on them for comfort in the lonely years ahead.

Smiling to himself as he reached the butcher shop, he jogged up the stairs to his small apartment on the second floor.

A grinning Riley Baker leaned against the doorjamb, his pose nonchalant, his hands in his pockets. "Ahoy, mate."

Dane grabbed the redhead in a bear hug, thumping a rawboned back beneath the first mate's heavy coat. "What brings you to my neck of the woods? Thought you'd signed on with a coastal steamer."

"Yep, that I did. One of the roosters on an incoming tub gave me a letter to bring to you." He handed over an envelope.

"Thanks." Dane pocketed the missive without looking at it. "Want to come in for some coffee?"

"Can't. Have to get back to the ship. We'll be weighin' anchor within the hour."

"Maybe next time, then." Dane put his key into the lock while Riley started down the steps.

The sailor stopped partway and turned. "How's the new job? Or maybe I should say *old* job. Miss bein' a ship's captain?"

Dane tipped his head. "I don't report for a couple weeks, actually. But I admit, it does seem strange not to be rocked to sleep at night by the ocean. Otherwise..." He grinned, letting the unspoken words dangle.

Riley nodded. "Well, here's hoping everything works out for you. Let me know when the first ship you design is ready for its maiden voyage. I'll be your officer anytime." With a parting wave, he took the remaining steps two at once.

Inside, Dane stoked up the fire to dispel the cold. When he looped his coat over a hook on the hall tree, he remembered the letter and retrieved it.

The envelope bore nothing but his name.

And the Coquille Light insignia.

≈§

In the middle of her afternoon watch, Eden heard someone mount the outside steps. Another delivery, she surmised, with a new shipment of kerosene and supplies due any day. She opened the door.

Her breath caught in her throat. "Dane!" she gasped. "I–I never saw the *Solitude* sail in." Her hand reached to check her hair. She must look a sight after scrubbing windows and polishing brass. And her work apron had to be frightfully soiled. She fumbled with its ties and managed to take the thing off and dispose of it on its hook.

The captain just grinned. "I came on a coastal packet this time. As a passenger. May I come in?"

"Y–yes, of course." She moved aside, closing the door on the cool draft when he entered, then frowned in puzzlement. "But, why would you buy passage? Where's your stern-wheeler?"

"I dumped her," he said so casually he might have been talking about the weather. "The old gal was hardly seaworthy anymore—especially this time of year. She'd served her purpose."

"Oh." Not knowing whether to congratulate or console him, Eden gave a nod instead and attempted a light laugh. "I–I thought you were the deliveryman, just now, bringing supplies."

"Not this time." He sobered, his gray gaze lingering on hers, on her nose, her lips. "How've you been?" he asked at last.

The intensity of his gaze banished the usual ease she'd always felt around him, but she struggled to keep from letting it show. Hoping overt cheerfulness would help restore her composure, she tried for a breezy tone. "Fine, just fine. Oh, my position as assistant keeper here is permanent now. The board approved me. I'm official."

"That does not surprise me. You're more than competent."

"But what will you do, without a vessel to pilot?" she had to ask.

He tilted his head then shrugged. "I'll be starting a new job in Seattle, building ships. Someday I hope to design and build my own, but that'll take awhile, of course."

So their friendship would be ending after all. He'd be in Seattle. She'd never see him again. The grim reality of it encouraged Eden to be completely candid. She swallowed, unable to maintain her gaze. "It's. . .wonderful to see you. I was disappointed to have missed you last time. What brought you by?"

"Your letter."

A jolt went through her. She knew only that she'd written from her heart.

"I. . .had to come, Eden. I couldn't stay away." Dane took a step closer, his presence seeming to fill the fog trumpet room.

At his husky tone, her insides began doing crazy things. He'd come because of her! She drew a shaky breath, knowing she should step back, give herself more space. Knowing she wouldn't. She raised her lashes.

And met a most incredible smile.

And eyes that wouldn't release hers so easily this time.

"I brought you something," he said. "Something I bought quite some time ago but never had a chance to give you." Reaching inside his coat, he drew a small, wrapped package from an inner pocket.

As Eden took the gift, her fingers brushed his, sending a tingle through her being. "You don't need to buy me things," she blurted out.

"Why not?"

She had no answer. It was hard enough to keep breathing with him staring at her the way he was and her feeling so awed because he'd come all this way just to see her. She opened the outer paper, revealing a small box.

A lighthouse pendant watch glinted up at her from midnight velvet lining. In view of the talk she'd had with Birdie, the timepiece seemed almost symbolic. She would treasure it always. "It's. . .beautiful."

"Not as beautiful as the woman standing before me." Reaching out a hand, he lifted her chin with the edge of his index finger. "You know I love you, don't you, Eden?"

Inexpressible happiness at hearing those words sent warm shivers down to her toes. "I. . .hoped you did." She moistened her lips. "Maybe I always hoped it. . . because I've come to love you, too." The whispered declaration gave her boldness, and she smiled.

"Oh, my dearest," he murmured, drawing her into his arms, the beat of his heart surging against her own. "I thought you were lost to me forever. It was as if the sun itself vanished from my life. All I had was the memory of a light in the night—one that pales in the glow of those incredible eyes of yours."

No one had ever spoken that way to Eden, and her heart contracted in exquisite pain.

Dane eased away slightly and searched her soul, then his warm breath feathered her neck as he lowered his lips to hers. The tender kiss held an ocean of promises. Eden wanted to bask in it forever and raised to her tiptoes, slipping her arms about his neck to deepen the kiss.

The door opened at that moment, admitting Chris and Birdie.

"Well, well," the housekeeper said, not quite able to suppress her smile.

"Precisely," Dane said, releasing Eden but drawing her against his side with one arm. "I'd like you two to be the first to know I've just declared my undying love to the beautiful assistant keeper of this river light."

"Mama?" Chris asked.

"That's right, buddy. I'm hoping she'll consent to become my wife sometime in the near future. . .if she's agreeable to giving up the assignment she's worked so hard for, that is. And if she'll deign to come to Seattle to live."

"Will you?" the three asked as one.

She could scarcely speak. The housekeeper's spare time lately was being monopolized by her old friend, Haydon Jeffries. And the position Eden had set so many hopes upon didn't seem to matter anymore. Something far better glowed on her horizon—the light of a love she'd thought could never be, for her, for them. Some important details remained to be worked out, but she had every confidence that if God had been able to bring the unbelievable to pass already, He could easily handle the rest. . .in His time.

"Well?" three pairs of questioning eyes regarded her.

"Yes!" She finally declared. "A thousand times, yes."

Dane hugged her so hard her ribs nearly cracked. "I don't know what I'd have done if you'd said no," he admitted with no little relief.

Christian jumped up and down.

Birdie simply beamed. "I just baked a cake, Eden-girl. Let's go celebrate."

"Yes." Smiling, Eden pulled her son into their circle of love. "If ever there were a perfect time for celebrating, this has to be it."

ABOUT THE AUTHORS

ANDREA BOESHAAR

Andrea was born and raised in Milwaukee, Wisconsin. Married for twenty years, she and her husband Daniel have three adult sons. Andrea has been writing professionally since 1984, but writing exclusively for the Christian market since 1991.

As far as her writing success is concerned, Andrea gives the glory to the Lord Jesus. Her writing, she feels, is a gift from God in that He has provided an "outlet" for her imagination. Andrea wants her writing to be an evangelistic tool, but she also hopes that it edifies and encourages other Christians in their daily walk with Him.

LYNN A. COLEMAN

Raised on Martha's Vineyard, Lynn now calls the tropics of Miami, Florida, home. She is a minister's wife who writes to the Lord's glory through the various means of articles, short stories, and a web site. She has three grown children and six grandchildren. She also hosts an inspirational romance writing workshop on the Internet, manages an inspirational romance web site, edits an inspirational romance electronic newsletter, and serves as president of the American Christian Romance Writers organization.

PAIGE WINSHIP DOOLY

Paige is the author of seventeen books and novellas. She enjoys living in the Coastal Deep South with her family, after having grown up in sometimes extremely cold Midwest. She is happily married to her high school sweetheart and loves their life of adventure in a full house with their six homeschooled children.

Sally Laity

Sally has written both historical and contemporary novels, including a coauthored series for Tyndale House, nine Heartsong romances, and twelve Barbour novellas. She considers it a joy to know that the Lord can touch other hearts through her stories. Her favorite pastimes include quilting for her church's Prayer Quilt Ministry and scrapbooking. She makes her home in the beautiful Tehachapi Mountains of Southern California with her husband of over fifty years and enjoys being a grandma and a great-grandma.

If you enjoyed
The Lighthouse Brides Collection
Look for

The Immigrant Brides Collection

The Prairie Romance Collection

The Bartered Bride Collection

The Stitched with Love Collection

The Texas Brides Collection

The Farmer's Bride Collection

Available wherever books are sold.

DiAnn Mills

Award-winning author DiAnn Mills is a fiction writer who combines an adventuresome spirit with unforgettable characters to create action-packed, suspense-filled novels. DiAnn's first book was published in 1998. She currently has more than fifty books published.

Her titles have appeared on the CBA and ECPA bestseller lists and have won placements through the American Christian Fiction Writer's Carol Awards and Inspirational Reader's Choice awards. DiAnn won the Christy Award in 2010 and 2011.

DiAnn is a founding board member for American Christian Fiction Writers and a member of Inspirational Writers Alive, Romance Writers of America, and Advanced Writers and Speakers Association. She speaks to various groups and teaches writing workshops around the country. DiAnn is also the Craftsman mentor for the Jerry B. Jenkins Christian Writers Guild.

She and her husband live in sunny Houston, Texas.